GOLDWYN

A Biography of the
Man Behind the Myth

GOLDWYN

A Biography of the
Man Behind the Myth

by ARTHUR MARX

W·W·NORTON&COMPANY·INC·  NEW YORK

791.4309
MART

Library of Congress Cataloging in Publication Data

Marx, Arthur, 1921–
  Goldwyn : a biography of the man behind the myth.

  Bibliography: p.
  Includes index.
  1. Goldwyn, Samuel, 1882–1974.   I. Title.
PN1998.A3G67 1976   791.43'0232'0924 [B]   75-37906
ISBN 0-393-07497-8

This book was designed by Paula Wiener.
Typefaces used are Janson and Friz Quadrata.
Manufacturing was done by Vail-Ballou Press, Inc.

Printed in the United States of America
1 2 3 4 5 6 7 8 9 0

To Lois, Perry, and Elsie

Contents

Illustrations appear between pages 192 and 193.

"Today there are few producers. There are no Thalbergs, Sam Goldwyns, or David Selznicks who can start a film, follow it through, and know what to do after it's complete in the cutting, dubbing music, and finishing off. Producers today are mostly agents and packagers who raise money and walk away. Real producers are a dying breed."

—Robert Evans, producer of
The Godfather, *Love Story*,
and *The Great Gatsby*

Acknowledgments

The author would like to thank the following people, whose interviews were so helpful in the preparation of this book.

GOLDIE ARTHUR	SAM MARX
MRS. HARRY BEAUMONT	AL MELNECK
EDWARD CHODOROV	DAVID MILLER
JERRY CHODOROV	MILTON PICKMAN
JOSEPH J. COHN	BOB PIROSH
HOWARD DIETZ	GILBERT ROLAND
LUCINDA DIETZ	VICTOR SAVILLE
IRVING FEIN	GORDON SAWYER
MILTON FOREMAN	PETE SMITH
ERWIN GELSEY	BENJAMIN SONNENBERG
BERT GRANET	MILTON SPERLING
HELEN HAYES	GLORIA STEWART
HAROLD HECHT	BILLY WILDER
MILTON HOLMES	WILLY WYLER
NORMAN KRASNA	COLLIER YOUNG
BILL LASKY	LESTER ZIFFREN
MARTIN LEVINSON	EUGENE ZUKOR
MARION MARX	

Also, the staffs of the Library of the Academy of Motion Picture Arts and Sciences in Hollywood, and the Lincoln Center Library of Performing Arts of the New York Public Library.

GOLDWYN

A Biography of the
Man Behind the Myth

Prologue

SAM GOLDWYN never liked anything that ever appeared in print about himself, claiming he was always being depicted as an ignoramus whose only talent was for mangling the English language. This wasn't true—he had a great many other talents—but after years of listening to Goldwynisms, both real and spurious, he became paranoid about them. Consequently, he was continually resisting everyone's efforts to make him the subject of a biography.

For example, when a newspaper reporter once suggested to Goldwyn that he write his autobiography, he replied in his high-pitched voice, slightly tainted with a Polish accent, "I don't think anybody should write his autobiography until after he's dead."

When he was working for Goldwyn in 1945, playwright Jerry Chodorov (*My Sister Eileen*, *Junior Miss*) burst into the great man's office one afternoon with what he considered a sure-fire moneymaking idea for a motion picture.

"Mr. Goldwyn," began Chodorov, all a-bubble with youthful enthusiasm, "I would like to write your life for pictures."

Goldwyn shook his head negatively. "It would be too egotistical," he said.

"Not the way I'd do it," quipped Chodorov.

The producer, who had little sense of humor where it concerned himself, didn't crack a smile. "I am leaving my life to my wife, Frances," Goldwyn said. "That is my lejacy to her," he added, pronouncing the *g* in *legacy* as though it were a *j*.

His "life" was just a small part of the "lejacy" Samuel Goldwyn left behind when he finally succumbed to old age in 1974—just nine years short of attaining the century mark.

His estate, when probated, was estimated to be $20 million—not bad for an immigrant boy who came to this country from Poland with less than twenty dollars in his pocket.

Two major film studios—Paramount Pictures and Metro-Goldwyn-Mayer—are standing monuments to Goldwyn's energy, financial genius, and unshakable belief in an untried industry.

On the Goldwyn lot is a vault containing over eighty feature films personally produced by the man whom many people in the business reverentially referred to as the Celluloid Prince, because of the aristocratic way he lived, dressed, and produced pictures. Of the eighty, several have become film classics: *Dodsworth, Arrowsmith, Wuthering Heights, Dead End,* and *The Best Years of Our Lives,* which alone collected seven Oscars.

All of Goldwyn's pictures didn't win Oscars, of course—some, in fact, were downright stinkers. But most of his films had what came to be known among Sam's friends and competitors as the Goldwyn Touch. The Goldwyn Touch was not necessarily sheer brilliance or supercolossal-sized budgets or even good box office. And it was certainly not smut or sensationalism. It was an ineffable something that had to do with quality, good taste, and honest and intelligent workmanship. A Goldwyn picture could be compared to a finely tailored suit of clothes fashioned from an expensive bolt of material—it might not always sell to the public, but you could tell it hadn't been hastily thrown together just to try to capitalize on a new fad.

Last of all, Goldwyn left behind a multitude of stories and gags (a good many apocryphal but attributed to him nevertheless) of how he mangled the English language. His accomplishments in this field were legion and of such Paul Bunyanesque proportions that modern lexicographers were forced to coin a brand-new word—*Goldwynism*—to define adequately his unique and irreverent manhandling of the King's English.

A Goldwynism, according to the *Random House Dictionary of the English Language,* is "a phrase or statement involving a humorous and supposedly unintentional misuse of idiom, as 'Keep a stiff upper chin,' but especially such a statement as attributed to Samuel Goldwyn, as 'Include me out.' "

"Include me out," together with his other most widely quoted malapropism, "I can tell you in two words: im possible," ended up in Bartlett's *Familiar Quotations* as well as in the dictionary.

According to the experts, the dictionary's definition of a Goldwynism is a rather narrow one. By Hollywood standards, a true Goldwynism was not only just a funny juxtaposition of words. Very often it was a statement stemming from Goldwyn's unorthodox logic and peculiar way of living, thinking, and doing business. Frequently his way of putting things, though comic to the ear, made a lot of sense.

One day in 1956, for example, the bookkeeper for Goldwyn Studios dropped in on his boss and said, "Mr. Goldwyn, our files are bulging with paperwork we no longer need. May I have your permission to destroy all our records before 1945?"

"Certainly," replied Goldwyn. "Just be sure to keep a copy of everything."

Another loyal studio employee entered Goldwyn's office one morning, plopped a cigar on the producer's desk, and said, "Mr. Goldwyn, my wife gave birth to a baby boy last night, and in honor of you, we're naming the baby Sam."

"Why do you want to do that?" snapped Goldwyn. "Every Tom, Dick, and Harry is named Sam."

One of the most famous and oft-quoted remarks attributed to Goldwyn is: "A verbal contract isn't worth the paper it's written on." The words are wrong, but who among us who has ever made an oral contract and lived to regret it can argue with the logic of what Goldwyn was trying to say?

Since few of his competitors could deny that Goldwyn had a brilliant but unschooled mind—at least for making excellent, tasteful, and moneymaking pictures—a good deal of the producer's word trouble had to be attributed to inattention.

At the height of his career, Goldwyn's mind was usually 95 percent occupied with the picture he was currently making, or if that one wasn't in trouble, then he was concentrating on future projects. He refused to use his brain for nonessentials like learning to speak proper English or even keeping other people's names straight.

Goldwyn had absolutely no ear for sounds, and as proof of this he went to his death bed still speaking with a slight Polish accent, though at the time he had been a resident of this country for over eighty years.

Goldwyn idolized Big Name talents and would pay salaries of $5,000 a week and upwards in order to have them under contract. But the one thing he seemed incapable of paying them was the respect of remembering how to pronounce those names correctly, and also the titles of their works.

In his initial meeting with novelist Louis Bromfield, Goldwyn, while trying to impress on the author how important the name Bromfield was, actually called him "Mr. Bloomfield."

Arthur Hornblow, Jr., whose father was managing editor of *Theater Arts Monthly*, was Goldwyn's story editor and social mentor for many years. A society-oriented, fastidiously dressed young man who knew what wine to drink with what course, Hornblow was supposedly the one responsible for giving a touch of class to Goldwyn's personal image. But one thing he could never change was Goldwyn's propensity for mispronouncing proper names.

When Goldwyn was hiring Hornblow, he persisted in calling him "Hornbloom" all through their first interview. It was an affront to Hornblow to be called Hornbloom, and after several vain attempts to correct him, he finally wrote the name Hornblow out on a slip of paper for Goldwyn to see with his own two eyes. Goldwyn glanced at it, then impatiently waved the paper aside, and said, "Show me later, Mr. Hornbloom."

To Goldwyn, Ben Kahane, an executive at Columbia Pictures, was always "Mr. Cocoon"; Shirley Temple was Anne Shirley; King Vidor was Henry King; Joel McCrea was Jill McGraw; and Farley Granger was Ginger Farley.

Dance director Michael Kidd did the choreography for *Guys and Dolls*. During the entire making of the film, Goldwyn kept calling Kidd "Mike Todd." In the beginning of their relationship, Kidd would correct Goldwyn. But it never took. And finally he grew weary of correcting Goldwyn and simply let it pass whenever Goldwyn referred to him as Mike Todd.

A year after Kidd left his employ, Goldwyn walked into Lindy's one night with Mike Todd. Sitting at a front table, waving at him, was Michael Kidd. Goldwyn beamed at his favorite dance director and stopped by his table to introduce the two Mikes to each other.

Indicating Kidd, Goldwyn turned to Mike Todd and said, "Mike, I'd like you to meet Mike—"

Goldwyn stopped in midspeech as he realized for the first time that both men couldn't possibly be "Mike Todd."

With a grin, Kidd watched him squirm, then feeling sorry for the producer, helpfully interjected his last name. Goldwyn, who could never be satisfied unless he had the last word, shot back with, "What kind of a jokester are you—all these years trying to pass yourself off as Mike Todd?"

When it came to show, movie, or book titles Goldwyn could be just as confused.

For example, when he was making a film of the Broadway hit *The Little Foxes*, he would continually refer to it as "The Three Little Foxes," according to the play's author, Lillian Hellman. *Wuthering Heights* he called "Withering Heights."

His ability to handle names and titles didn't improve with age. One evening at a dinner party in his Beverly Hills home, Goldwyn was complaining to his guests about the filth in most of the new movies. "In all my years in the business," he said, "I've never seen anything like what they're putting in pictures these days. I ran a picture last night in my projection room—disgusting. I was ashamed to even have my wife see it."

"What picture was that?" asked Billy Wilder, the Oscar-winning writer-director-producer.

"*Hello, Dolly!*" said Goldwyn.

"I don't know how it could have been *Hello, Dolly!*" said Wilder, puzzled.

"I know what I saw!" insisted Sam.

"But, Sam," said Wilder, *"Hello, Dolly!* hasn't been released yet. Zanuck's still cutting it."

"Look, I'm telling you I saw *Hello, Dolly!"* insisted Goldwyn. "And it was absolutely filthy."

"Could you give us an idea what the story was about?" asked Wilder.

"It was disgusting," said Sam. "All about these three young girls in show business—and taking drugs and having affairs to get ahead, and—"

"Sam," interrupted Wilder, "if I'm not mistaken, I think the picture you're referring to is *Valley of the Dolls.*"

"Isn't that what I just said?" demanded Goldwyn. *"Valley of the Hello Dollies!"*

Despite these unintentional but ego-shattering affronts, Goldwyn had a reverential respect for writers and their product—much more so than did most other studio heads. A Harry Cohn or Jack Warner, for example, would almost prefer to gamble on making a bad picture than give a writer what he was asking.

However, Goldwyn, while he wouldn't pay any more than he had to, wouldn't blow a deal on account of price. Although it's doubtful that he'd ever had more than a nodding acquaintance with Shakespeare, Goldwyn truly believed, along with the Bard, that "the play's the thing."

In the days when a dollar was a dollar, and not closer to a quarter, Goldwyn spent $165,000 for the screen rights to *Dead End,* and $160,000 for *Dodsworth.* (David Selznick paid only $50,000 for *Gone with the Wind.*)

Goldwyn's Diamond Jim reputation for expending enormous sums in order to acquire the best properties caused many a Hollywood wise guy to discount his ability as a producer—on the theory that he bought his success.

But that wasn't exactly true. Goldwyn couldn't always define it beforehand, but he knew what he wanted *after* he saw it in a projection room. And if he didn't see the Goldwyn Touch up there on the screen, he'd scrap the whole thing and start over—or not release the picture at all—rather than sully the Goldwyn image of good taste and high-quality entertainment.

Starting life in a ghetto, Goldwyn had great respect for the buck—and how hard it was to come by. Yet according to David Selznick, Sam would think nothing of investing "another million dollars of his own money in a picture in order to make it only ten percent better."

After viewing a rough cut of the Zola classic *Nana,* Goldwyn scrapped it completely, tossing away the $411,000 he had already spent on it. It was his own money, too; not stockholders'. Once he started to produce independently, Goldwyn financed all his pictures personally. That was another Goldwyn trademark. Although he would sometimes listen to his wife,

Frances, he would brook no interference from partners, stockholders, bankers, or any other kinds of "money men." And since most outside investors seem to feel their investment automatically gives them the right to voice their own artistic opinions, no matter how unqualified they may be, Goldwyn neatly finessed that problem by risking his own money, and standing and falling by his own decisions.

But Goldwyn's spending habits, like those of many a self-made person, were ambivalent and full of inconsistencies. While he would be willing to risk millions on a picture, it killed him to lose at other forms of gambling, and he would frequently resort to cheating to prevent such an eventuality.

He loved to play croquet, backgammon, and all kinds of card games for extremely high stakes. It was his one relaxation.

But if he happened to hit a losing streak, which was often, since he wasn't particularly good at any of these games, he would fly into a rage. Often he would attribute his hard luck to the unlikely premise that the universe was rigged against him.

To get back in the black, Goldwyn would, if the opportunity presented itself, attempt to do a little rigging of his own. In a game of gin in his own house, Goldwyn once deliberately dropped the tenth card of his hand on the floor, then shouted "Gin!" and spread his cards on the table. When his opponent said he couldn't have "Gin" with only nine cards and that he was either cheating or hadn't been dealt enough cards to begin with, in which case they'd have to play the hand over, Goldwyn exclaimed indignantly, "I've never been so insulted in my life—I'm going home." Whereupon he grabbed his hat and strode to the front door, not realizing, until he had his hand on the brass knob, that he *was* in his own home.

During the first Adlai Stevenson–Dwight Eisenhower presidential campaign, Goldwyn, a devout Republican, was playing croquet in his backyard with George Kaufman, Ben Hecht, and Charlie Lederer—all close friends and respected members of the playwrighting profession. When Goldwyn thought the others weren't looking, he tried to kick his ball through a wicket. But Charlie Lederer noticed it, and said, "If you're going to cheat, I'm going home."

"Who's cheating?" asked Goldwyn innocently.

"I just saw you kick your ball through the wicket," said Lederer.

Goldwyn studied Lederer suspiciously for a moment, then said, "Vat's the matter—are you for Stevenson or something?"

To Goldwyn, anyone who questioned his ethics was automatically a Communist, and therefore had to be for Adlai Stevenson.

A strict constructionist would have to categorize that one as a "political Goldwynism."

But as any student of Goldwynisms knows, true Goldwynisms, like the chameleon, take on many different colorings. And though some might be of doubtful authenticity, and many of them have been printed before, no book about Goldwyn would be complete without listing the most famous attributed to him:

> The trouble with this business is the dearth of bad pictures.
> I have been laid up with intentional flu.
> He treats me like the dirt under my feet.
> I want to make a picture about the Russian secret police—the GOP.
> I had a monumental idea this morning, but I didn't like it.
> Our comedies are not to be laughed at.
> You've got to take the bull between your teeth.
> There is a statue of limitation.
> I never put on a pair of shoes until I've worn them at least five years.
> I read part of it all the way through.
> Let's bring it up to date with some snappy nineteenth-century dialogue.

Goldwyn once embarrassed a woman writer by saying "cohabit" when he meant "cooperate with me."

Goldwyn often denied—and with increasing rancor as the years ticked on—saying most of the malapropisms he supposedly originated.

Most Goldwyn afficionados believe he uttered his most famous line at a meeting of the Motion Picture Producers and Distributors of America, which had been called to discuss their labor difficulties with a Hollywood union head, Willie Bioff. When Goldwyn disagreed with an important policy decision, he reached for his hat and exclaimed, "Gentlemen, include me out."

Goldwyn often swore this wasn't so. His recollection was that he had told the group, "Gentlemen, I'm withdrawing from the association."

Despite Sam's protests, it's just as unlikely that he ever said in the heat of a battle over labor troubles anything so placid as, "Gentlemen, I'm withdrawing from the association." His best Goldwynisms popped out when he was under intense pressure.

Goldwyn attributed many of his famous lines to "jokesters like George Kaufman and Eddie Cantor, who used to sit around making them up when they were working for me and had nothing better to do on my time," and overzealous press agents.

Irving Fein, who before managing Jack Benny worked for a year as Goldwyn's assistant publicity director back in the forties, admits quite candidly, "Sure we used to make up Goldwynisms all the time in order to get publicity breaks. I remember one right now that I made up—'Quick as a flashlight.' "

George Oppenheimer, *Newsday*'s distinguished theater critic, also pleads guilty to similar charges of penning spurious Goldwynisms back in the days when he was a Hollywood scriptwriter. " 'It rolls off my back like a duck' was one of mine," admits Oppenheimer. "I remember springing it for the first time on Dotty Parker and Edna Ferber when we were all sitting around the writers' table in the commissary one day."

It's not surprising then that there was such a proliferation of Goldwynisms during Hollywood's golden years, when Sam was most active. No one man as busy as Goldwyn, and who didn't have a mind for joke writing, could have possibly had the time to make up, intentionally or unintentionally, so many memorable lines as were attributed to him.

Granted that many were counterfeit, an expert counterfeiter has to have an original to work from. As Norman Zierold wrote in his book *The Moguls*, "One does not become a Mr. Malaprop without the ingredients, in this case, the producer's background, a gift for garbling his acquired tongue, and the cooperation of accomplices able to help create or embellish a legend."

Even Goldwyn admitted he had all the ingredients.

A few years before his death, Goldwyn told a reporter, "Chances are that in my lifetime I have said a few things not according to Hoyle. After all, I'm not a graduate of Oxford or high school or even grammar school. . . . I've made errors in speech, but so have scholars."

Actually, it should have been a source of great personal satisfaction to Goldwyn to have a word in the dictionary derived from his name, and two of his malapropisms end up under his name in Bartlett's *Familiar Quotations*.

After all, how many people— much less a poor Jewish boy who started out life in the Warsaw ghetto—can boast of making a similar contribution to the English language?

1

A Goldfisch Is Born

SAMUEL GOLDWYN'S HORATIO ALGER rise from poor immigrant boy to multimillionaire movie mogul and immortality in the dictionary is ample proof that America during the first half of the twentieth century was indeed the land of opportunity—especially if you were willing to work eighteen hours a day, and had plenty of luck, chutzpah, and a little larceny in your soul to help get you over the rough spots.

Sam Goldwyn came into this world with all four of those attributes, though in retrospect one would have to concede that any luck attending the circumstances of his birth and early childhood was not readily discernible at the time. Bad luck, possibly, but not good luck.

The producer was born in Warsaw, Poland, on August 27, 1881. His real name was Samuel Goldfisch, and he was the second son of Abraham and Hannah Goldfisch.

Very little is known about Abraham and Hannah Goldfisch, for despite Goldwyn's mania for publicity after he became successful, he seemed loath to talk about his heritage, except in the most superficial way. And any birth records that might have been kept in his hometown were undoubtedly destroyed in the Nazi burning of the ghetto during World War II, along with any surviving relatives who might have been able to shed some light on the subject.

However, in a short piece in the *Reader's Digest* in 1956, bearing Goldwyn's by-line but ghosted by a press agent, Sam managed to recall an incident that took place in Warsaw when he was nine years old.

> My mother had been ill for a long time and it was uncertain whether she would live. I was sobbing bitterly outside our front door.
>
> Our neighbor, an old man who wore his years with dignity, put an arm around me, quieted my sobbing and said: "Remember, Samuel, a man's most

precious possession is his courage. No matter how black things seem, if you have courage, darkness can be overcome."

Those two simple sentences made a profound impression on me, young as I was. From that moment on, I was able to face my mother's illness determined that my courage would be of help to her in her struggle to live. Perhaps in some small way it *was* a help, for her health was eventually restored.

Following that, he talked of running away from Warsaw and living in Hamburg, Germany, as a homeless waif. But there was no mention at all of his father in the entire piece.

The few facts about Goldwyn's early life that have managed to clear the obfuscation are as follows:

Abraham was a tradesman of some sort—possibly a tailor or shoemaker—and he scratched out a very meager living. He and his wife were Orthodox Jews, they spoke mostly Yiddish around the house, and they were miserably poor. They had three other children—Benjamin, Sally, and Manya—and they all lived together in a crowded slum in a haggard, horrible city under the leaden skies of eastern Europe.

Warsaw, in the latter part of the nineteenth century, was under total domination of its big-bully next-door neighbor—Russia. It was a city full of mud, poverty, and anti-Semitism, which manifested itself in occasional pogroms. The periods in between the outbreaks of violence weren't much more idyllic. The police wore great leather boots, seemingly just for the purpose of kicking poor little boys, especially poor little Jewish boys, around.

Because times were bad in eastern Europe, it was difficult enough for a Gentile to make a satisfactory living in Warsaw. For a Jew, who almost daily had to go up against prejudice and oppression, it was next to impossible. Abraham, despite remaining at his workbench from fifteen to eighteen hours a day, could not earn enough by his own sweat to feed the family and pay the doctor bills when his wife fell seriously ill and almost died, when Sam was nine years old.

Because of the family's poverty, Sam was yanked from school when he was eleven and made to go to work as an office boy in a banking firm for five zlotys a week, which was the equivalent in America of about a dollar.

Although Sam had a burning desire to get ahead, he was not happy as an office boy. He worked long hours and had a boss who used to beat him if he was late for work or voiced any dissatisfaction about his job. Sam discovered, early in his career, that he did not enjoy taking orders or listening to other people's opinions—especially if they were unreasonable, meaning they disagreed with him. This was a characteristic that stayed with him for the rest of his life.

There was another aspect of Sam's early life that didn't appeal to him. Like all good sons, he was expected to turn his meager salary over to his parents every payday. This ritual was in direct conflict with Sam's desire to save enough money so he could run away from home.

He wasn't crazy about taking orders from his parents, either. There was a maverick streak in Sam that remained with him until his dying day.

Sam Goldfisch was twelve years old, skinny, and underfed when an incident took place that totally convinced him there wasn't any future for Jewish boys in Warsaw. On his way home from work one payday, Sam was stopped by one of the heavy-booted gendarmes patrolling the ghetto. He called Sam "a dirty little Jew," and when Sam objected, the policeman beat him up and ran off with his salary.

A black eye was little enough payment for an entire week's work, but the crowning blow to his sensibilities came when a tearful Sam returned home and his mother bawled him out not only for losing his money but for tearing a hole in his only good suit.

"But it wasn't my fault," cried out Sam.

"You shouldn't have talked back to an officer," kvetched his invalid mother.

Sam decided, then and there, to run away from home. Possibly, if he could manage it, he'd go all the way to that new land he'd heard about far to the west of the Rhine—America. Sam had heard, through glowing tales sent back to the homeland from other impoverished youngsters who had already emigrated there, that in the United States everybody—even Polish Jews—had a chance to become somebody. In the new land, so the legend went, it was possible to start out with nothing and wind up a millionaire.

Well, Sam Goldfisch had the first qualification: nothing. That presented a problem, but not an insurmountable one to a twelve-year-old boy with as much ambition burning in his heart as Sam Goldfisch had.

Keeping his lofty intentions to himself, Sam stuck out his job in Warsaw seven more days and collected another week's salary. Then, with five silver zlotys jangling in his pocket, and all his earthly possessions—a few tattered clothes rolled into a bundle on a stick—slung over his skinny shoulder, he set out to make his escape on foot across the Polish countryside.

Although Sam Goldfisch's most fervent desire was to reach the United States of America, his immediate destination was Birmingham, England, where a married sister of his mother's resided with her husband, Mark Lindenshat. Sam felt that his aunt would be sympathetic to his cause, since she, too, hated Poland enough not to want to live in its depressing environment.

It was not easy to get as far as Birmingham on just five zlotys, however.

Sam's wanderings led him first to the seaport city of Hamburg, Germany. Hamburg was some eight or nine hundred kilometers to the west, but somehow—traveling mostly by foot but occasionally by horse-drawn cart, if he was lucky enough to hitch a free ride—Sam managed to arrive there within a month.

By then, all of Sam's money had run out, and he was forced to sleep on the streets or huddled in doorways. He was cold, hungry, and miserable.

After a few days of this, Sam felt he had no alternative but to turn back to Warsaw and give up his dream of America. Even living at home with his interfering parents was better than starving. But then he remembered the advice given to him by his kindly old neighbor back in Warsaw when his mother had been desperately ill: "No matter how black things seem . . . darkness can be overcome."

He resolved to stick it out, no matter what happened.

The resolution did nothing for the aching void in his stomach, but it did keep him from leaving Hamburg at the onset of the first hunger pain.

The next day fortune led the youthful runaway to a glovemaker's shop with a name over the door which was the same as that of a family who knew his in Warsaw. On a wild chance they might help him, Sam went inside. The proprietor wasn't there, but his apprentice was, a friendly young man of about eighteen named Jacob Libglid.

After Sam told him of his plight, Libglid invited him into his shop, shared his noon meal with him, and offered him a place to sleep. While the grateful Sam gnawed hungrily on a piece of German sausage and a hunk of black bread, he poured out his whole pathetic story to Libglid, revealing his longing to go to America.

Libglid was in no position himself to sponsor Sam, but upon hearing that he had relatives in England he took up a collection among his friends to raise the money for a one-way boat ride across the Channel to Portsmouth.

Sam was totally without funds again by the time he arrived at Portsmouth. He also had a communication problem, there being very few people on that side of the Channel who could understand either Polish or Yiddish.

Somehow, traveling on foot again, Sam made his way through the English countryside all the way to London. There he spent the better part of a week wandering around, begging, eating out of garbage cans, and sleeping in doorways while he tried to find someone who could help him find his way to a place called Birmingham.

Finally he collapsed on the steps of a pawnbroker's establishment. As luck would have it, the pawnbroker not only could speak Yiddish, but was a Pole, which created an additional bond between them. The pawnbroker gave Sam a shilling in return for a couple of days' work, and put him aboard a horse-drawn lorry (owned by a friend) that was heading north, with a load of used furniture, in the general direction of Birmingham.

Birmingham was a smoky, grimy manufacturing town in the English Midlands. It was a city of blacksmith shops and factories pouring smoke into the heavily overcast skies.

Most of the town's male inhabitants were metalworkers of some kind. Sam's uncle, Mark Lindenshat, was a foreman in a factory that made fireplace tools. He was by no means a rich man, but he was infinitely better off than his relatives in Poland.

After two weeks on the road, Sam was tired, hungry, and bedraggled when he turned up on the doorstep of his aunt's and uncle's modest dwelling one cold and rainy night in October, and asked to be given shelter.

The Lindenshats were sympathetic to their ragged-looking nephew's plight—to the extent that they invited him in and gave him a hot meal and a place to sleep. However, they had sons of their own to support.

The next day Sam was apprenticed out to a blacksmith's shop.

Skinny and underfed, Sam didn't have quite enough muscle in his arms to be a smithy. Neither did he have the desire to spend the rest of his life bending over a hot anvil or standing up to his ankles in horse manure, shoeing frisky colts who would just as soon kick you in the teeth as look at you.

Despite his humble beginnings, Sam was, in the opinion of most people who knew him during his lifetime, "a born aristocrat." When the blacksmith discovered that his youthful apprentice's heart wasn't where his anvil was, he fired him. This didn't sit too well with the Lindenshats, and after Sam met a similar fate in several other jobs in the metalworking line, they franchised him and his appetite out to some other relatives—Dora and Isaac Salberg—who also lived in Birmingham.

Sam was about fourteen when he went to live with the Salbergs. The following is a short account of what he was like then, according to a letter written in 1974 by a surviving nephew of Dora Salberg's—British film director Victor Saville.

> When Goldwyn came to England, he spoke only a word or two of English. He had an unpronounceable name which must have been either Polish or Yiddish, which, when translated into English, became Goldfisch. He changed his name to the anglicized version of Goldfisch on the suggestion of Dora Salberg. He was so gauche and young that Dora had to teach him how to use a handkerchief and a knife and fork, and she bought him his first pair of gloves, which quite fascinated him.
>
> Dora's husband, Isaac Salberg, moved to South Africa toward the latter part of the nineteenth century, after failing in business in Birmingham, and never returned. Before he went, he guaranteed a small sum of money with a firm of

sponge dealers in Birmingham. These goods young Goldfisch was supposed to peddle for a profit, but return the original investment to the sponge-dealing firm. Isaac got Sam this opportunity on the insistence of his wife, Dora, who was very sympathetic to Sam Goldfisch and thought he was a very bright young man, despite the fact that his English wasn't improving very rapidly.

Bright he was, but interested in remaining a sponge salesman in Birmingham, he was not. Being a salesman wasn't so bad. In fact, some people felt that because of his tenacious personality, Sam Goldfisch had quite a talent for selling. But Sam wasn't happy. He found he did not really enjoy living under the Salbergs' tight supervision. Dora was always trying to teach him manners and supervise his activities.

Sam felt that the only way he could really get out from under the yoke of authority was to put the Atlantic Ocean between him and his relatives, and as quickly as he could raise, either by hook or crook, the twenty dollars necessary to pay his fare via steerage to America.

Victor Saville concludes his letter with a rather surprising account of how the ambitious Sam Goldfisch actually financed his voyage across the ocean:

> Goldfisch's one ambition was to get to America and he left as soon as he was able to. Unfortunately he left a small debt to the sponge dealers which Isaac had guaranteed, and the firm, whose son still trades in Birmingham, came to Dora for payment. Dora had very little money so they took a small French desk and a silver photograph frame—a family heirloom—in payment. Since she was now husbandless, Dora had to work very hard, and kept a rooming house to bring up her three surviving daughters.
>
> When Sam Goldwyn's name became prominent in the twenties, and Dora was very hard up, she wrote to Goldwyn but received no reply. When Goldwyn came to London, he never went to Birmingham; his sister, Sally Linden, who had since married a son of the Lindenshats', had to come to London if she wanted to see her brother. Dora also had a daughter named Daisy, a widow at a very young age, but a good businesswoman. At one time she was the manager of a very elegant flower shop next door to Claridge's Hotel in London, where Sam and Frances happened to be staying. One day Frances walked into the shop, and Daisy could not resist telling her about her mother's connection with Sam Goldwyn as a young boy and even told the details of the sponge deal, which Daisy surmised had been the means of paying Sam's steerage fare to New York. Frances replied, "Well, that's funny, because Sam always told me that he *stole* the money to get to America."

2

From Gloves to Riches

AFTER SPENDING ten miserable days in the steerage section of a third-rate ocean liner, the fourteen-year-old Sam walked down the gang-plank at Castle Garden, New York, one morning in 1896 to be processed by the New York State immigration authorities. Castle Garden, on the southern extremity of Manhattan, where the Battery is today, was the official reception center for immigrants until the United States government took over those duties near the turn of the century and moved its head-quarters to the new Federal buildings on Ellis Island, out in the harbor and within sight of the Statue of Liberty.

Sam had brought nothing with him from the old country except the worn, ill-fitting suit he was wearing, much more faith in his ability to succeed than was justified by past performance in his previous jobs, and a gargantuan talent for mixing up English, Polish, and Yiddish syllables into one barely intelligible potpourri.

Whatever vital statistics (including the pronunciation and spelling of his name) the befuddled young man thought he gave the immigration people, *Goldfisch* came out on the official documents as just plain *Goldfish*.

Fortunately for Sam and the rest of the immigrants who had made the transatlantic crossing with him in search of new opportunity, there had been a serious manpower shortage in the United States ever since the conclusion of the Civil War. Cheap farm laborers and factory workers were needed in all parts of America, and it wasn't necessary that they be skilled or that they could even speak English. Some middle western farming states—Wisconsin, for example—were so desperate for workers that they asked newly settled immigrant residents for the names and addresses of friends back in the old country so that they could be officially contacted and urged to emigrate (which might have been how Sam Goldfish originally had heard about America).

17

Industries, too, were competing for imported laborers. Some sent recruiting agents to Castle Garden and Ellis Island to sign up cheap labor from the hordes of immigrants that were beginning to pour into the United States in the late 1890s. Recruitment stands were set up only a few yards away from the exit from Castle Garden, and the moment a likely looking prospect came through, he was immediately romanced and hustled over to a recruitment table, where he would be promised all kinds of rewards if he would only sign with them.

The newly burgeoning glove industry in Gloversville, New York, was in the same need of laborers as Samuel Goldfish was of a paying job. It was inevitable that the two would get together.

The moment Sam, looking gullible, underfed, and bewildered, cleared the immigration stalls, he was buttonholed by a fast-talking Yankee, signed up for three dollars a week, and loaded along with a number of other recruits into the back of a truck bound for Gloversville.

Gloversville was in upstate New York, about forty miles northwest of Albany. It was a factory town much like Birmingham, England, and Sam found himself right at home there.

With the help of the recruiting agent, Sam found a boarding house several miles from the factory that he could afford on his princely salary, and the next day he went to work at six A.M.

Sam literally started at the bottom, sweeping floors in the basement and unloading the skins from which gloves were made. His industriousness and fantastic energy soon won him a promotion to glove cutter at a better salary. But cutting gloves from raw skins was exacting work, and the hours long. Some days Sam remained hunched over his workbench for sixteen to eighteen hours at a stretch.

There were no child labor laws in those days to prevent children from being exploited by big business. In his book *The Americans*, sociologist J. C. Furnas informs us:

> It was a *national* shame in 1900. Less than a dozen states were seriously attempting to limit the labor of children in mills, mines, factories or stores, in sweatshops or street trades. . . . Such laws as existed were chiefly unenforced . . . all lamentably meagre. In most states it was not illegal to send children as young as 10 or 8 or 7 into a mill, and keep them at work unlimited hours.

In his 1956 *Reader's Digest* piece, Goldwyn himself recalled the hardships of his early business career.

> As a 14-year-old alone in Gloversville, N.Y., I was getting up at 6 A.M. to tramp through zero weather to work at a glove making machine. The few

dollars I earned each week had not only to support me but also to provide some money for my family in Poland. In addition, I was trying to build a reserve for the time when I would leave the factory for a better job.

Sam had enormous faith in his own future. But to insure that it be a rosy one, he let his life be guided by the old credo: "The harder I work, the luckier I get."

In addition to working long hours every day, Sam took on the additional burden of attending night school. He stuck it out for a year, or until he had mastered the English language and had soaked up enough of the rudiments of American history to enable him to pass the test to become a United States citizen, which he did in 1902.

Sam not only worked hard at his work. He was also somewhat of a social climber. He firmly believed then, as he did the rest of his life, that one never got very far hanging out with losers, or other forms of social lowlife.

By the time he was fifteen Sam was beginning to move in the upper echelons of Gloversville society. He was rarely seen in public in the company of anyone who couldn't help him get ahead.

His closest friend was Abe Lehr, whose father owned the glove factory where Sam was employed. The two met when they found themselves working at the same bench in the glove-cutting department. Lehr senior wanted his son to learn the business from the ground up, so that he would be equipped to step into his shoes if anything ever happened to him.

But like many a boss's son, young Lehr wasn't imbued with the same spirited determination to get ahead as his Polish friend who worked beside him at the glove-cutting bench. What he especially objected to were the long hours his father expected him to put in every day.

One lunch hour Abe came to Sam with a deal that he felt would be beneficial to both of them. "You'll work an hour more than the regular work day, and I'll work an hour less," Lehr proposed.

"How will that help me?" asked Sam suspiciously.

Abe explained that in return for Sam's acceptance of his proposition he would use his pull to persuade the foreman of the shop to furnish Sam with the best skins. "Don't you see, Sam? You can cut gloves faster out of good skins than you can out of bad ones?"

Since Sam was being paid on a piecework basis, he immediately saw the sense of this arrangement, and the two friends shook hands on the deal.

Soon Sam was turning out twice as many gloves as the other workers and more than doubling his salary.

This didn't go unnoticed by Abe Lehr, Sr., who immediately became suspicious, especially when he coupled Goldfish's sudden prosperity with the fact that his own son was sneaking away from the factory an hour early each day. Investigating, Lehr senior quickly uncovered the scheme and fired the two of them.

Thus Sam learned, the hard way, an invaluable lesson in how to get ahead in big business. If you're going to cheat, don't get caught.

Fortunately for Sam, Lehr senior could not conquer a father's natural leaning toward nepotism, and a week later he rehired the two conniving teenagers. "But you can't work in partnership anymore," he warned them.

Although he was making fifteen and sometimes twenty dollars a week by now, Sam Goldfish had no intention of remaining at the glove-cutting bench all his life. The job was too menial. It was also confining. He had his sights set on a career that was infinitely more romantic and, of course, rewarding. He wanted to become a "drummer," as traveling salesmen were called in pre–World War I days.

Sam had been possessed by this lofty dream ever since he had walked past the Kingsborough, the town's leading hotel, one summer evening on his way home from the factory, and had seen the many traveling salesmen sitting on the front porch with big cigars in their mouths and their feet up on the railing, looking terribly worldly, important, and prosperous.

Sam, of course, couldn't afford to stay at the Kingsborough, or even to eat in its elegant dining room. Sam had heard that a meal for a single person at the Kingsborough could cost as much as one dollar.

After he became a little more worldly himself, however, Sam worked up the courage to go into the Kingsborough when he had nothing else to do, and hang around its lobby, which was also quite magnificent. The floors were of marble, the walls carved mahogany. There were potted palms, brass spittoons, and big leather chairs. Best of all were the plate glass windows, through which, on a Saturday night, you could look out on Main Street and watch the Gloversville beauties parading by.

Sam yearned for the day when he could afford such luxury, so when he was sixteen, and he heard that his company was having difficulty finding a salesman to go out on the graveyard circuit, he decided to volunteer. The graveyard circuit was the name given to a route of small New England towns that the more successful traveling salesmen preferred not to get stuck with on their road trips. Yankee general store proprietors were notorious for being stingy and unresponsive even to the drummers' most musical sales pitches.

As a result, the graveyard circuit was to be avoided like one-day-old whiskey. But not if you were young, anxious to become one of the wealthiest tycoons in America, and were secretly in love with the boss's niece, Bessie Mona Ginzberg.

Bessie, a beautiful, doe-eyed girl with long auburn curls down to her shoulders and a distractingly good figure, was the daughter of a Boston diamond merchant—another refugee from eastern Europe—but she frequently came to Gloversville to visit her uncle, Abe Lehr.

Sam met her through his close friend, Abe Lehr, Jr., and thought he had never seen such a beautiful young lady in all his life. Sam was aware that he was a little out of her social league, and while it's believed he dated her a couple of times, he didn't actively court her. However, he had enough faith in himself and his ability to get ahead to believe that a union with Bessie was not completely out of the question in the future.

As far as his own appearance was concerned, Sam was no threat to the matinee idols of that period. By the time he was sixteen, however, Sam had developed into a very presentable, nice Jewish boy that any mother in a Philip Roth novel would be proud to have as a prospective son-in-law. He had a very prominent nose, a determined chin, large, slightly pointed ears, and deep-set blue eyes that peered out at the world as if they were appraising a diamond. He was six feet tall, carried himself with a military bearing, had an ingratiating smile and a lot of charm, despite his high-pitched voice and Polish accent, and he always dressed well, as if he were either on his way to, or had just come from, a bar mitzvah.

Sam felt that Bessie Ginzberg liked him, too. But he was also aware that she had expensive tastes and probably wouldn't settle for being married to an ordinary glove cutter.

With Bessie to inspire him, Sam screwed up his courage one day, walked into the boss's office, and asked to be given a chance selling the company's gloves on the road.

"What makes you think you can sell?" asked the astonished Lehr. "That's a man's job."

"Because I know gloves inside out," replied Sam. "I've made them."

"But that doesn't mean you can sell them," pointed out Lehr.

"Just give me a chance," persisted Sam. "I don't want any money except enough to travel from town to town. I'll go on streetcars instead of trains and I'll stay at YMCA's instead of hotels. Give me the company's toughest territory, where you've never sold gloves before."

"But sleeping in YMCA's don't mean you can sell gloves," insisted Lehr. "How do you know you can sell?"

"Because," replied Sam, looking his boss squarely in the eyes, "I've already sold you on letting me try it. And if I can sell you I can sell anybody anything."

"How do you know you've sold me?"

"Because you would not turn down anybody who offered to work for nothing," pointed out Sam, with psychological insight that went far beyond his years.

"Young man," said Lehr, with a smile of defeat mixed with admiration, "if you can talk as good on the road as you can in my office, you'll soon own my factory."

As Alva Johnston wrote in The *Saturday Evening Post* some years later, "He had a sales enthusiasm bordering on frenzy. Sam argues a man into a coma or a disorder resembling 'bends.' His victim signs anything."

Lehr was just the first of a long line of people to fall victim to Sam Goldfish's super salesmanship.

By the middle of the following week, Sam Goldfish, with a suitcase bulging with glove samples at his feet, was riding the interurban trolley to Pittsfield, Massachusetts, where his first assignment was a store which had never bought a single pair of gloves from Lehr's company.

Sam got not one, but two orders from Max Ruby, the store's buyer, that day: "Get out!" and "Stay out!" Mr. Ruby wouldn't even look at his samples.

Sam persevered for three days, driven on by visions of Bessie Mona Ginzberg's gorgeously plump figure dancing around in his head. Finally he hit upon a gimmick. Figuring out that Mr. Ruby's real name was probably Rubenstein, but that he had shortened it so that it wouldn't sound so Jewish in Yankee territory, Sam decided to address the buyer in Yiddish. If Mr. Ruby could be made aware that Sam was a *landsman*, he might be more empathetic.

Again Sam's reliance on simple psychology helped him over a rough spot. Upon hearing the first few words of his mother tongue, Mr. Ruby responded exactly as Sam had hoped he would. His scowl changed into a welcoming smile, he threw his arms around the young salesman, and exclaimed in Yiddish, "My son, what can I do for you?"

When Sam walked out of Max Ruby's office late that afternoon, he had a signed order for three hundred dollars' worth of the Lehr Company's gloves in his pocket.

Since so many of the buyers along the graveyard circuit turned out to be Jewish immigrants, Sam's career as a salesman was virtually assured.

Within three years Sam Goldfish was earning between $10,000 and $15,000 annually—a sum that probably had the buying power of $100,000 today. And by the time he was twenty, his tenaciousness, his fantastic energy, and his ability to harangue a potential buyer into submission, either in English or in Yiddish, had transformed him into one of the greatest glove salesmen not only in the New England territory, but in all of the United States.

Recalling that period of his life with pride, Goldwyn once told a reporter, "I traveled from coast to coast and often worked eighteen hours a day in order to put my product over in districts where it never sold before."

Impressed with Sam Goldfish's enormous gift for selling, Lehr made him sales manager in 1909, and rewarded him further with a large chunk of stock in the company.

Sam was now in a position to ask Bessie Ginzberg to marry him. Unfortunately, he was too late.

While Sam was crisscrossing the country fattening his bank account in the summer of 1909, Bessie Ginzberg and her mother were fattening themselves at the Sagamore Hotel, a vacation resort on Long Lake in the Adirondack Mountains.

Two other guests of the hotel at the time were Jesse L. Lasky, a prominent and debonair young vaudeville producer from New York City, and his sister, Blanche. Before turning producer, Lasky had played cornet with his sister in vaudeville. And after the act broke up, the two remained uncommonly close and lived and traveled everywhere together. That is, until the manager of the resort introduced Lasky to Bessie one evening.

Lasky was immediately smitten with Bessie Ginzberg's wholesome American-as-Mom's-cherry-strudel good looks. And evidently she was equally taken with him, because before the week was over, the two were talking about marriage. And they were married in Boston the following December.

After a brief honeymoon in Atlantic City, Lasky and his bride moved into the large apartment on New York's West Side where he had formerly been living with his sister and his mother, Sarah.

Sam remained good friends with Bessie, and often used to have dinner with the Laskys whenever he came down to New York City on his selling trips, which were becoming frequent now that he was in the money and more or less his own boss.

Although Bessie enjoyed the platonic friendship of her former suitor, the dinner invitations she extended to Sam on his trips south were not entirely without purpose. Unbeknownst to Sam, Bessie was playing matchmaker. The sooner she could pair off Sam and Blanche, the sooner she could get her sister-in-law out of the apartment.

Evidently, Bessie's matchmaking potion worked, for as 1910 rolled around, Sam and Blanche were seriously contemplating marriage.

However, according to Bill Lasky, Jesse Lasky's movie-director son, who is a real expert on Lasky-Goldwyn family lore, "It wasn't much of a love match. Sam married my aunt because he wanted to get into show business, and he figured the best way he could do that was through my father."

Lasky must have had the same doubts about Goldfish's motives. For despite Blanche's loneliness, he wasn't so sure that Sam Goldfish, with his funny Polish accent, was good enough to marry his beloved sister. On a trip north, Lasky asked a friend of his who ran a junk business in a small New England town to give him his "honest opinion" of the prospective bridegroom. This friend had met Sam Goldfish once, when the latter had come through his town in the past, selling gloves to the general store.

The junk dealer's advice to Lasky was brief and to the point: "Do everything possible to keep your sister from marrying that no-good *momzer.*"

The friend's name was Louis B. Mayer, and his negative comment regarding Goldfish's marital credentials was the first in a long series of unpleasant incidents that fed fuel into a feud between them that lasted until Mayer's death. The feud, in fact, continued past Mayer's death. On that occasion, Goldwyn reportedly told a friend, "The reason so many people showed up at Mayer's funeral was because they wanted to make sure he was dead."

After that remark made the columns, Goldwyn denied ever having said such a cruel thing about his former rival. But as with a good many of his disavowed statements, he probably did say it, for the history of mutual hatred between the two producers was long and bitter, and neither of them made much of an effort to conceal their animosity for one another.

Members of Hillcrest Country Club, Los Angeles Jewry's exclusive golfing and dining oasis, still remember a locker room argument between Goldwyn and Mayer that became so violent it actually ended in fisticuffs. It happened when Mayer, dressed only in a towel around his paunchy midriff, stepped out of a shower stall just in time to hear Goldwyn, who didn't know he was in the clubhouse, calling him a dirty bastard for refusing to loan him Gary Cooper for a picture he was contemplating. Mayer, who was built like a Japanese wrestler, promptly hauled off and socked Goldwyn on the jaw, sending him sprawling backward into a dirty towel bin. Goldwyn wasn't hurt physically, but his ego was bruised, and he immediately sent for his attorney and initiated an assault and battery suit. It took the combined efforts of a number of high-priced attorneys plus the diplomatic genius of Irving Thalberg, a close friend of both Goldwyn and Mayer, to arbitrate the matter peacefully and keep it from reaching the courts and out of the newspaper headlines.

Mayer's advice to Lasky notwithstanding, Sam and Blanche were married in 1910. But if Bessie thought she could get rid of Blanche simply by arranging a union with Goldfish, she had woefully underestimated her husband's undying love for his sister, and Goldfish's love of Lasky's mother's cooking. Lasky invited his sister to move into the apartment with her bridegroom, and since Sam now operated his sales office from Manhattan and no longer had to live in Gloversville, he went right along with this *gemütlich* arrangement.

Sam's craving for the best could not be satisfied merely by becoming the world's greatest glove salesman, earning top money. He had to improve himself culturally and every other way. He began his course in self-improvement by becoming something of a fashion plate. He had his suits made to order by Earl Benham, Manhattan's top tailor, who catered to the show business trade. He bought his shirts and ties at Sulka's and imported his shoes, also custom-made, from London. Next he employed a valet to help him dress. Eventually it became such a fetish with him not to have anything destroy the line of his lean, trim, expensively clad figure that he would refuse to carry anything, even money, in his pockets. His wife, or a friend, would frequently have to bail him out when it came time to pay a restaurant tab or a cab fare and he could come up with nothing more negotiable than an apologetic smile.

To improve his mind, Sam started attending the theater, opera, concerts, and lectures. Once a year he and his wife went to Europe. There they toured the museums and cathedrals, and Sam for the first time was exposed to the world's great works of art.

On his first European trip, Sam arranged to meet his mother in Karlsbad, Germany. Hannah was an old woman now, and a widow, and Sam urged her to move to America. "I will support you like a queen," he promised her. But she was too set in the ways of European life to make the move. "Just send me the money," she told her son.

The following year she passed away.

Sam's trips to Europe weren't only for pleasure. Being the world's greatest glove salesman, he decided to supplement his income by going into the importing business on his own. European glove manufacturers made a finer product than anything that came out of Gloversville, and they could sell them at half the price because of lower labor costs. Sam was positive he could make a healthy profit on a shipment of Parisian-manufactured gloves, until a friend pointed out that most of that profit would evaporate by the time he paid the duty on it when it came through United States Customs.

Supersalesman Sam refused to let a minor problem like that stand between him and a healthy profit. After thinking the matter through, he came up with a scheme for outwitting the Customs Department that was worthy of the cleverest of smugglers.

At the Parisian glove factory where Sam made his purchase, he instructed the shipping department to separate the gloves into two crates—one containing just left-hand gloves, and the other all right-hand gloves. He then had each crate shipped to a fictitious receiver. For example, the left-hand gloves were addressed to a "Mr. Larry Robbins, New Orleans" and the right-hand gloves were to go to "Mr. Joseph Smith at the port of New York City."

The scene now shifts to the office of the New York Customs Service, two months later. When Joseph Smith doesn't show up to claim his shipment of right-hand gloves, the department decides to put them up for public auction. The department places a notice of public auction in all the newspapers. Sam Goldfish, who has been waiting for this notice to appear ever since he arrived from abroad, grabs his hat, takes a cab down to the Battery, and is in the first row of seats when the auction, in which other unclaimed items are also up for sale, begins.

Halfway through the sale, Sam's crate of right-hand gloves is hauled out onto the stage, and the auctioneer announces: "Our next item is a crate of right-hand gloves from Paris." In response to the questions from the audience regarding the mates, he says, with a smile, "No, there are no left-hand gloves in the shipment."

Since no one at the auction is crazy enough to purchase just right-hand gloves, Sam's ridiculously low bid of five dollars for twelve grosses of imported Parisian gloves easily wins the prize.

The scene shifts again—this time to the port of New Orleans, where tricky Sam picks up the mates to the gloves in the same manner.

Without having to pay any duty on the shipment, Sam, of course, reaped a huge profit when he in turn sold the French gloves to his retailers.

Is it any wonder that before he was even thirty Sam Goldfish was the most successful glove salesman in the business, with an income of at least fifty thousand dollars' worth of purchasing power in today's dollars, and $26,000 in a savings account at the Manhattan Trust?

But just as he was not satisfied being the best glove cutter in Abe Lehr's factory, Sam could not accept being a mere salesman for somebody else's company all his life, either—no matter how much income or security the job provided him with.

By 1912 Sam was looking around for a new occupation to challenge his ghetto-sharpened ingenuity.

A friend, whose name happened to be Arthur S. Friend, a New York attorney with a prophetic sense of the future of motion pictures, suggested that Sam go into the business of making feature films. Until then, the only moving pictures being made were two-reelers, known to the trade as chasers. They were called chasers because their chief purpose was not to entertain, but to *chase* customers out of vaudeville houses between shows. This was made necessary because many patrons liked to sit through several performances of the same vaudeville show, thereby depriving newly arrived customers of a seat.

Friends knew that Sam was intrigued by the motion picture business and had been ever since an afternoon in 1911, when, with nothing else to do and some time to kill between appointments, he walked into a little theater on Herald Square and became transfixed by a two-reel Western picture called *Broncho Billy's Adventure*.

But while he agreed there was probably a future in motion pictures, Sam was also astute enough to recognize the wisdom of the old saw "Shoemaker, stick to your last." He decided to start a glove business of his own, instead.

However, before Sam's preparations to form a glove company could jell, the Democrats nominated Woodrow Wilson as their presidential candidate, to run against William Taft and Theodore Roosevelt in 1912. Sam didn't like the smell of those political winds at all.

At issue in the campaign was the Payne-Aldrich Bill, a high-tariff measure passed by a Republican-dominated Congress to protect American industry from competition from cheap foreign imports. Woodrow Wilson, a liberal who believed the path to global peace was free world trade, had promised the people, if he got into office, to have the Payne-Aldrich Bill repealed. And since Teddy Roosevelt had split the Republican vote by running on the Progressive ticket, it looked more and more, as election time neared, that Wilson would be the winner.

Sam felt if Wilson became president and made good his threat to lift the high tariff on foreign products, there would be a drastic decline in the sale of United States–made gloves. Without an import tax, European glove makers would be able to undersell their American competition because they had the advantage of cheap labor.

So as far as Sam was concerned, 1912 was no time to do anything rash like opening his own glove business. He would wait out the election and make up his mind about his own future in glove manufacturing later, after he saw what Wilson did about the tariff.

Meanwhile, Sam was seriously toying with Arthur Friend's notion about going into the movie business. A couple of more visits to that little theater on Herald Square that ran Broncho Billy Westerns convinced Sam that there was money to be made in moving pictures, but not necessarily in the production end. The place was packing the customers in.

Sam's initial move toward immortality in show business was to try to buy a theater. But after pricing a few, he found that kind of real estate in Manhattan considerably out of his reach. Suddenly it seemed cheaper to make pictures than to exhibit them. After arriving at this decision, Sam decided he needed a partner. He didn't have to look outside of his own apartment to find one.

Arriving home one evening, Sam burst excitedly into the room where his brother-in-law was sitting. "Lasky, how would you like to make a fortune?" he asked.

Lasky, who had just dropped his life savings—nearly $100,000—trying to transplant the famed Folies Bergère from Paris to Broadway—replied that nothing would suit him better. "Just tell me how."

"In motion pictures," said Sam enthusiastically.

"Motion pictures!" exclaimed Lasky indignantly. "I'm not having anything to do with a business that chases people *out* of theaters."

"I'm talking about longer films," insisted Sam. "With romantic stories that have a beginning and a middle and an end—like Broadway plays. Five-reelers, maybe. Nobody's making them."

"Are you crazy?" scoffed Lasky. "You and I would be a fine pair in that business—me, a vaudeville man, and you, a lousy glove salesman! What do we know about that game?"

"I didn't know anything about the glove business until I tried it," said Sam, with characteristic optimism and self-confidence.

"How can you make money making five-reelers and only charging a dime?" asked Lasky, more conscious about production costs, after dropping his fortune, than the inexperienced Goldfish.

"We'll charge twenty-five cents admission," said Goldfish undaunted.

"People will never pay a quarter to see a movie," said Lasky. "That's highway robbery."

"They pay a buck to get into a Broadway show," answered Sam logically.

"But that's class."

"We can give 'em class, too."

"What about the Trust?" asked Lasky, interested, but still cautious.

Lasky had hit upon a slight snag. The Trust was a vital issue in the screen industry of that period. Theaters throughout the country were at the mercy of a few companies who owned the patents on motion picture cameras and projectors. These companies collected a weekly license fee of two dollars each from fifteen thousand theaters.

You couldn't shoot a picture or exhibit it without the Trust's approval. And they would not approve any deviation from the status quo, which called for one- and two-reelers only. They were making easy money with little effort on short pictures and were afraid longer films would ruin their whole racket. Longer films might drive patrons out of the theaters if not from boredom, from eyestrain. According to medical men, even two-reelers were causing movie patrons to have blinding headaches and a permanent squint.

By 1912 picture projection technology hadn't advanced any further than the kind of entertainment producers were selling. Pictures flickered distractingly on the screen, which is how they got the name "flickers" to begin with. A five-reeler might very well be a hazard to the vision of anyone sitting through it.

Worse still, went the thinking of the Trust, the public might get to *like* longer pictures and force filmmakers into having to worry about heavier financing and acquiring genuine creative talent.

But once Sam Goldfish got his tentacles into an idea he did not let go easily. "Give the public fine pictures" was his riposte. "Show them something different from Western stuff and slapstick comedies and you'll find out what will become of the Trust. I tell you, Lasky, the possibilities of the motion picture business have never been touched. We could sell good films and long films all over the world."

But no matter how long and passionately he talked—and according to Lasky, Sam hammered away incessantly at the idea at the family dinner table for months—the world's greatest glove salesman could not sell his own brother-in-law on the notion of making movies. It took Lasky's friendship with Cecil B. De Mille, a struggling playwright of the period, to make a convert out of him.

Lasky had known De Mille for several years prior to Sam's sales pitch about the movie business. He originally had met him through De Mille's mother, Mrs. H. C. De Mille, a well-known playbroker who had an office in the Hudson Theater Building. Lasky had gone to her to engage the services of someone to write a project he had conceived, an operetta about the Far West called *California*. William, who'd already written several successful Broadway plays, including *Strongheart*, *The Warrens of Virginia*, and *The Woman*.

But William wasn't interested in working for Lasky, so Mrs. De Mille suggested he hire her younger son, Cecil, who was twenty-eight years old at the time and burning with ambition.

This suggestion didn't exactly make Lasky reach for a pen to sign up the young playwright. Cecil B. De Mille's theatrical credits to that date weren't very impressive. He'd written one flop play on his own, *The Royal Mounted*, had collaborated on another with his brother, *The Genius*, which had also failed to catch on, and he'd been an actor in *The Warrens of Virginia*, in which a child actress named Mary Pickford made her debut.

Lasky was reluctant, but Mrs. De Mille's stage-motherly instinct would not permit her to let Lasky escape without meeting her younger son.

She pulled Lasky into a back room and introduced him to Cecil De Mille. "Tell him what you have in mind," she told Lasky. "Then see if you don't change your mind."

Cornered, Lasky outlined his story idea for *California* to the aspiring writer. As he listened, a glint came into De Mille's eyes, for it was the kind of thing that could easily be made into a spectacle, which he felt was right, up his alley: historical melodrama, with plenty of opportunity for beautiful scenery, a huge cast, and period costumes.

Before Lasky had finished, De Mille started ad-libbing embellishments that were so good and exciting that the older man knew he'd found the right person to write the operetta.

But De Mille had a high opinion of what he was worth even then. He demanded a hundred dollars' advance and a twenty-five-dollar-a-week royalty.

In his straitened circumstances, brought on by the demise of the Folies Bergère project, Lasky couldn't meet De Mille's asking price, and the deal almost fell through. If it had, Lasky and De Mille probably wouldn't have become friends, and Sam Goldfish might never have wound up in the movie business. Fortunately for all three, Lasky was able to borrow a hundred dollars from his mother, and the deal was finalized. *California* turned out to be a fairly good commercial hit, and Lasky and De Mille became close friends.

Following *California*, Lasky and De Mille collaborated on several vaudeville projects. But De Mille was a restless soul. There was not enough excitement around Times Square to suit him. He used to dream about exploring the South Seas, going big-game hunting in Africa, and even joining the French foreign legion.

Lasky, who was more conservative (even in his dreams)—principally because he was tied down to a wife and by now a son, Jesse Lasky, Jr.—was always having to divert De Mille from his fantasies in order to keep him within friendship range.

One diversion that usually worked was a camping trip. In the summer of 1912, when De Mille was showing more signs of restlessness than usual, Lasky took him on a month's vacation in the Maine woods. They paddled a canoe up the west branch of the Penobscot River, and then, carrying sixty-pound packs on their backs, walked another twenty-five miles to Hunt's Camp on Kidney Pond, an area seldom penetrated by man, especially two refugees from Times Square.

The two had many misadventures, including almost drowning in some rapids, a near miss with the fangs of a rattlesnake, and a close call with a bull moose, who galloped through their encampment one night, and in so doing caught his antlers in their mosquito netting. As the enraged animal pawed and snorted at their sleeping bags in order to free his antlers, Lasky and De Mille, who were unarmed, managed to sneak away and climb a tree.

That should have been enough excitement to satisfy most city dwellers, but not De Mille. After the pair returned to New York and were having lunch one day at the Claridge Grill, De Mille said he had a confession to make.

"Jesse," he began, "I'm pulling out. Broadway's all right for you—you're doing well. But I can't live on the royalties I'm getting, my debts are piling up, and I want to chuck the whole thing."

"But what are you going to do?" asked Lasky.

"Go to Mexico," said De Mille. "There's a revolution going on down there, and I want to get in it. Maybe I can write about it."

"But you could get killed in a revolution," pointed out Lasky.

"I don't care, Jesse. I need the stimulation."

Since Lasky didn't want to see his best friend stimulated right into eternity by a bullet, he had to come up—and quickly—with another diversion to slake the younger man's thirst for adventure.

But the only thing Lasky could think of was Sam Goldfish's idea to get into the movies. Lasky still wasn't so sure how practical the idea was, but at least in that venture they could only lose their shirts, not their lives.

"If you want adventure, I've got an even better idea," Lasky suddenly exclaimed. "Let's start making movies."

The same sparkle appeared in De Mille's eyes that Lasky saw the day he told him the story of *California*.

De Mille grasped Lasky's hand, shook it firmly, and said, "Let's."

Although neither man realized it at the time, a large portion of the motion picture industry was built on that one word.

3

What's a Prospectus?

SAM GOLDFISH, of course, was delighted to learn that his brother-in-law was interested in going into the moving picture business with him.

But you couldn't start a new business without capital, and Lasky and De Mille had very little of that. And Sam himself, no matter how sanguine he was on the future of motion pictures, was not anxious to risk all his life's savings either.

So he spent several months trying to raise some capital among his friends. By the age of thirty, Sam knew many influential people both in and out of show business, and with his customary optimism, he felt he'd have no trouble talking people into lending him their money.

He waylaid bankers and Broadway producers, businessmen and traveling salesmen. Relying on the same device he used for selling gloves—incessant repetition—he spoke glowingly of screen epics and twenty-five-cent admissions and worldwide grosses.

Most people he approached thought Sam Goldfish had gone mad. To them the infant motion picture industry was no place in which to sink their money. Wise Broadway showmen and traveling salesmen alike felt that the movies were just a passing fad. Those flickering headache-inducing images up there on the screen could never take the place of live actors whose voices could be heard talking and singing. One rotten piano player in the pit playing background music was no substitute for real people.

Sam was talking himself blue in the face and getting nowhere. Then, in October 1913, on Columbus Day, he got his first bit of encouragement when he was having lunch at Delmonico's with a rich playboy who said he was interested in getting into the entertainment field and price was no object.

Immediately after lunch, Sam phoned his legal pal, Arthur Friend, who had promised to put the deal together if Sam ever raised the money. "I've finally found a backer," said Sam breathlessly over the telephone. "He wants us to meet him at the Hoffman House right away—with a prospectus."

"Great!" exclaimed Friend.

"What's a prospectus?" asked Sam.

Friend rushed right over to the Hoffman House and met Sam in the lobby. After explaining to his client what a prospectus was, Friend sat down at a desk in the lobby and hastily drew up a rough draft of one on Hoffman House stationery.

Apparently the document satisfied the prospective backer when they presented it to him later in his hotel suite, and he was about to write them a check for $25,000 when he brought up the one stumbling block that they couldn't overcome. He insisted that his girlfriend, who'd never been on the stage or ever acted before, star in Sam Goldfish's first picture.

Even though he was just a neophyte in the movie business, Sam was smart enough not to get sucked into that kind of insanity. When Sam balked, the backer withdrew from the deal, and Sam found himself out on the street again, looking for other, less romantic suckers.

Despite Sam's enthusiasm for the future of the movies, the feature picture company he was contemplating might never have got off the ground if Jesse Lasky hadn't been having lunch with Cecil B. De Mille at the Lambs Club on Forty-fourth Street on the day following Sam's last turndown.

At the lunch table, De Mille announced that he was itchy to get going in the movie venture. Otherwise he wanted to activate his original plan of joining the Mexican Revolution.

Lasky advised De Mille not to be so impatient. They couldn't make a movie until they found a property, anyway, and to find the right one would take time. Lasky assured De Mille that he'd been assiduously combing the list of available properties ever since they'd returned from the north woods, but so far hadn't found anything suitable for the kind of picture he felt they ought to make.

Since they had last discussed the matter, Lasky said he had seen Sarah Bernhardt in a four-reel feature, *Queen Elizabeth*, a film imported from France by another upstart in the business, Adolph Zukor, and the success of that picture convinced him that a good story was most important.

"We have to do this in a big way," concluded Lasky, "or not at all."

Just as Lasky and De Mille were about to leave the Lambs to return to their office, they ran into Dustin Farnum, a matinee idol who had just scored a major triumph on Broadway in *The Virginian*. De Mille knew Farnum through his brother, and being no shrinking violet, he showed no hesitancy in approaching the star.

"How would you like to star in a long motion picture for us?" De Mille asked him. "We're starting a company."

Farnum wanted to know if they had a property in mind. The two confessed that they hadn't selected one yet. Did he have any ideas?

Farnum glanced across the room in the direction of Edwin Milton Royle, who was the author of *The Squaw Man*—a play about an Englishman who came to the Wild West to hunt for his villainous brother who'd wronged the family and disappeared in Indian country.

The play, which combined the best elements of two literary styles—an English drawing-room comedy of manners and a gutsy Western—had starred an actor named William Faversham and had been a huge hit in London.

Dustin Farnum had always coveted the role since losing out to Faversham in the London production. But now he saw an opportunity to do the movie version, and he told Lasky and De Mille, "You get Royle to sell you *The Squaw Man* and I might agree to join you."

Lasky sounded out Royle and found him vulnerable to an offer. But since the new company didn't have any working capital—and, in fact, wasn't even a company yet—Lasky perforce had to be vague.

"But I'll get back to you," he promised Royle, as he rushed off to phone Sam Goldfish.

Locating Sam in his office, Lasky said, "Sam, we're in business," and told him what had transpired in the Lambs dining room.

Salesman Sam was delighted and immediately convoked a meeting between the two of them and Arthur Friend in the latter's office for the purpose of setting up a company.

Sam Goldfish agreed to put up $7,500, and induced Lasky to contribute an equal amount; then on the strength of Dustin Farnum's name, they were able to borrow $11,500 from a bank, for a total of $26,500.

Friend incorporated the new company in December of 1913, and offices were set up at 485 Fifth Avenue. It was called the Jesse L. Lasky Feature Play Company, because Lasky was the only one in the group whose name had any kind of reputation in show business. Lasky was also made president because of his show business experience, while Sam, who knew nothing about the artistic end of the theater, settled for being treasurer and general manager.

The Goldwyn of later years would throw his mother into a snake pit rather than accept a subordinate position in the credits of any company he had anything to do with, but Sam was more self-effacing in those days.

It was a lucky thing for the Jesse L. Lasky Feature Play Company that they had such an able money manipulator as Sam Goldfish watching over their treasury, because before they were finished, they would need considerably more than $26,500 to complete *The Squaw Man*, and if it hadn't been for Sam's business genius, they'd never have been able to come up with it.

Based on Sam's careful calculations and projections, $26,500 should have been more than ample to see them through the entire production. An average two-reeler in those days cost less than $1,000 to make. So how much more could a five-reeler cost? Maybe $5,000 with another $5,000 thrown in to cover the costs of any mistakes they might make because they were new in the game.

But one contingency no one had figured on was the cost of acquiring *The Squaw Man*. Edwin Royle wanted $15,000 cash for the rights to his play, and even Sam couldn't argue him into being more reasonable.

Royle had them over the well-known barrel, and he knew it. If they didn't buy his play at his figure, they'd lose Farnum. Without Farnum they'd have to give back the $11,500 they'd borrowed from the bank.

So they paid the $15,000 for the property, figuring that still left them with $11,500 to work with. Which would have been ample if Farnum hadn't suddenly given them another zinger.

He wanted $5,000 cash to star in the picture. And there was no way they could complete the production on $6,500.

Sam finally came up with a solution. Instead of $5,000 cash up front, he offered Farnum 25 percent of the stock in the company. Farnum agreed, and the Jesse L. Lasky Feature Play Company was in business.

Well, almost.

In the euphoria of putting the company together, Sam forgot one important ingredient: they still had no one to make the picture. They had a property, and De Mille to write a scenario from it. But all of them were neophytes when it came to the actual physical task of getting a movie into the can. Neither Lasky nor De Mille knew the first thing about cameras or lighting.

Sam's first move was characteristic of the way he was to operate the rest of his moviemaking life. He decided to go out after the "biggest"—D. W. Griffith. This was two years before *The Birth of a Nation*, but Griffith already had a reputation for being the greatest man in the business. He was directing pictures at that time for the Biograph Company, one of the units of the feared motion picture Trust, and he'd already experimented with a four-reeler called *Judith of Bethulia*. While no *Birth of a Nation*, *Judith* was considered a landmark in film history, because in the course of making it, Griffith had invented the close-up, the fade-out, the dissolve, and very many other camera techniques still being used today.

Sam took Griffith to lunch at Delmonico's and while plying him with expensive food and champagne, enthusiastically tried to sell him the idea of leaving Biograph and joining the Jesse L. Lasky Feature Play Company.

"You say you've never made a picture before?" asked Griffith.

"Yes," confessed Sam, thinking quickly and coming up with one of his better Goldwynisms, "but that is our strongest weakpoint." As Griffith studied him curiously with his clear blue eyes, Sam immediately explained: "That way you can be in charge of everything."

Sipping his champagne, Griffith mulled over Sam's proposition for an agonizingly long time. Finally he said, "A very interesting project, Mr. Goldfish. If you can show me two hundred and fifty thousand dollars in the bank, I think we might talk business." Sam admitted that the figure was a little out of his reach, and settled for paying the lunch check.

When De Mille heard that D. W. Griffith had turned Sam down, he volunteered to direct the picture himself. But as anxious as he was to get the picture started, Sam tried to quash that idea. "What in hell do you know about shooting a movie?" he asked with typical bluntness.

De Mille, who was young, brash, and brimming over with self-confidence, refused to let a minor drawback like that discourage him. "I can learn," he exclaimed. "Just point me toward the nearest studio."

He must have sounded convincing, because Sam immediately arranged for De Mille to spend a day at the old Edison Studios up in the Bronx, where a motion picture was in the process of being shot. From the sidelines, De Mille watched the director and cameraman set up their camera and point it toward a stone wall alongside a road. The director shouted: "Action." The cameraman cranked. A pretty girl emerged from a hedge, clambered up a wall, and ran down the road, looking back in terror from time to time at some unseen pursuer. A man met her, stopped her, and they talked with much emotive gesticulation. Then the director yelled, "Cut," and started setting up another scene.

That was De Mille's entire apprenticeship to directing, but as brief as the course was, it must have been adequate. Reporting back to Lasky and Sam Goldfish, De Mille confidently boasted, "If that's all there is to making pictures, we can make the best picture ever made." De Mille's cockiness impressed them, and they hired him on the spot to direct *The Squaw Man* for a hundred dollars a week. They also gave him some stock in the company and the impressive-sounding title of director-general.

Everything was set, except selecting a site for shooting the picture. At first Sam planned to have the picture made across the Hudson River at Fort Lee, New Jersey, where a good many one-reel Westerns and slapstick comedies were being filmed. But Lasky didn't think a two-mile trip would satisfy De Mille's thirst for adventure. "How about making it out West in real Indian country?" he suggested. "That's where an Indian picture ought to be made."

De Mille seconded Lasky's suggestion. For not only would it be difficult—in fact, impossible—to make the Jersey Palisades look like Wyoming, but weather conditions (especially in December and January) were more suitable for outdoor shooting in the sunnier climes.

"Where out West?"

They kicked around the possibilities of both California and Arizona, but after an hour, finally opted for Flagstaff, Arizona, as their location. To begin with, the train fare was cheaper to Arizona than to Los Angeles, and that was an important consideration to an infant company that had to watch every penny. But Sam Goldfish had never been a penny pincher, and he wouldn't have allowed the budget to interfere with the Goldwyn Touch if Lasky hadn't remembered seeing a great number of Indians hanging around the train depot in Flagstaff when he had traveled through that town with Hermann the Great in his vaudeville performing days. "We ought to use real Indians," said Lasky. "They're better."

Shooting the picture in real Indian territory appealed to Sam, and he gave the idea his blessings, in spite of the additional expense.

Shooting in Arizona didn't appeal to Dustin Farnum, however. He said he didn't object to being paid off in stock as long as he could live at home in Manhattan and commute to Fort Lee, New Jersey. But he insisted on being given $5,000 in cash—immediately—before he would agree to pulling up his roots and going as far west as Flagstaff, where "a man could get bitten by a rattler."

Five thousand from $11,500 would leave the Jesse L. Lasky Feature Play Company without enough fluidity in its bank account to shoot even a three-reeler on location in Arizona. They decided to forget Flagstaff and return to their original plan of shooting at Fort Lee.

But by the time they made this decision, Farnum sensed failure and demanded his $5,000 up front no matter where *The Squaw Man* was filmed. It looked as if the whole project was doomed if somebody didn't think of a way of keeping their frisky star from bolting the old corral.

This time it was Jesse Lasky's turn to lasso a backer. He talked Bessie's rich uncle—Abe Lehr, the glove king—and Lehr's brother into buying Farnum's stock for $5,000. If he had hung on to his stock for eight years, Farnum could have sold it for nearly $2 million. But at the time $5,000 looked like a fortune to him, and he grabbed it.

With his star back in the fold, Sam put two more men on the company payroll. He and Lasky hired Alfred Gandolfi, a cameraman who owned a crank-handled Pathé movie camera, and Oscar Apfel, a director whose experience had been limited to filming one- and two-reelers. De Mille, of course was the director of record, but since he knew virtually nothing about the movie business, they wisely decided it couldn't hurt anything if they also hired Apfel to sit on the sidelines and guide him.

The plan was for Lasky to accompany De Mille to Arizona, while Sam Goldfish remained in New York to take care of the business end. But at the last minute Lasky backed out of the trip. He'd never had any real faith in the movies. It had only been Sam's incessant persuasion that had got him to this point. But now that he was packing to leave New York—and God only knew for how long—he realized he had too much to lose by getting on that train with De Mille. To begin with, he had to leave Bessie and Jesse junior behind because to take them would be to expose them to the many dangers and uncertainties of traveling out West. And then there was his vaudeville producing business to think of. Who'd run that while he was away? Certainly not Sam, who didn't know the faintest thing about show business except that there was money to be made in it.

So the day he was to leave, Lasky told Sam he wanted out.

"Of the whole company?" asked the surprised Sam.

"You can use my name and my money," said Lasky, "but I want to be free to run my own business."

Sam agreed, and they actually put it in writing that Lasky shouldn't be bothered with any of the details of making the movie, so he would be free to pursue his vaudeville career.

On a day in mid-December 1913, Sam and his brother-in-law went down to Grand Central Station to wave good-by to De Mille, Oscar Apfel, and the cameraman they had hired. And following that, they went their separate ways—Lasky to his office, and Sam to his, where some additional calculations with paper and pencil convinced him that the money they had left, after hiring two more employees and renting camera equipment and buying film, plus lab costs and traveling expenses for the crew, wouldn't be nearly enough to complete the production.

With all his vigor, and it was considerable, he applied himself to the business of learning motion picture distribution. In a matter of days he knew enough about how pictures were booked to start selling states' rights for *The Squaw Man*.

In those days, a movie print was sold for a flat sum to service a specified territory and could be rerun in its assigned region till it wore out. A small state got only one print, a large state two, and a block of states like New England, four or five.

Sam generated so much advance enthusiasm for *The Squaw Man*, plus eleven other unborn epics (for which he also collected in advance), that before De Mille even started shooting the picture the Jesse L. Lasky Feature Play Company had taken in about $50,000.

Sam had done this by selling the rights to New York, New England, Pennsylvania, Ohio, and the entire Pacific Coast block of states. Sam was a genius at selling, whether he was pushing a consignment of gloves or a motion picture that had not yet been made by men who had never made one.

Not only hadn't they ever made one, but two weeks after De Mille, Apfel, and Gandolfi had left for Arizona the trio couldn't even be found. Not one word had been heard from any of them, and all of Sam's attempts to trace his picture crew in Flagstaff had failed. Perhaps, like the Donner party, they were lost in the Rockies and were dining on each other.

Finally, two days after Christmas 1913, Lasky received a telegram. But it wasn't from Arizona. It said: FLAGSTAFF NO GOOD FOR OUR PURPOSE. HAVE PROCEEDED TO CALIFORNIA. WANT AUTHORITY TO RENT BARN IN PLACE CALLED HOLLYWOOD FOR $75 A MONTH. REGARDS TO SAM. CECIL.

Sam was furious when Lasky showed him the telegram and was in favor of calling the company back to civilization, where he could keep an eye on them. But Lasky was convinced there had to be a good reason for the change of locale, and he argued the volatile Sam into being more understanding.

After several hours, Sam agreed to sending De Mille the following wire:"AUTHORIZE YOU TO RENT BARN BUT ON MONTH TO MONTH BASIS. DON'T MAKE ANY LONG TERM COMMITMENT. REGARDS. JESSE AND SAM."

Despite his success at pre-selling *The Squaw Man*, Sam Goldfish was still being cautious about the future. In fact, to hedge his bet, he was even hanging on to his job with the glove company. With a fledgling director like Cecil B. De Mille, who started out for Arizona and wound up in California, in charge of things, one could never play it too safe.

4

Babes in Movieland

HOLLYWOOD LORE has it that the reason De Mille and company proceeded to California is that when they stepped off the train at Flagstaff, the town was almost hidden by a blinding snowstorm, and there wasn't an Indian in sight.

But the simple truth is, it was a beautiful, sunny Arizona day when the Santa Fe Limited ground to a jerky halt in front of the Flagstaff train station, and DeMille and his traveling companions jumped onto the platform with their baggage and camera equipment. De Mille was clutching the only copy of their shooting script, which had been written in longhand, in pencil, during the train ride west. De Mille and Apfel had collaborated on the script, with Apfel contributing his wide knowledge of film technique and De Mille furnishing everything he knew about dramatic construction. But the one thing neither of them had thought to bring along was a typewriter. They'd planned to get the script typed in Flagstaff.

The script, they hoped, embodied the best of both their talents. But what was wrong with it, they realized the instant they set foot on Arizona soil, was that the story of *The Squaw Man* was laid in the rugged back country of Wyoming. To De Mille, who'd once been to Wyoming, Flagstaff looked no more like Wyoming than the Jersey Palisades did.

During their week of collaboration on the train, De Mille and Apfel had both blithely assumed that the West was the West, and had written certain visual effects into their script that would not be realized in Flagstaff.

Had either of them been more experienced in making pictures they could have easily, with a few strokes of their pencil, switched the locale of *The Squaw Man* and sent their young hero to Arizona instead of Wyoming. But that simple solution didn't occur to De Mille when he was standing on the station platform, surrounded by a bleak vista of Arizona landscape, while the snorting iron horse on the railroad track beside him was getting up steam to take off on the last lap of its trip west.

What did flash through De Mille's mind was that Los Angeles was at the other end of the line, and from everything he'd read about the place, it was ideal for shooting motion pictures. Southern California had a wide variety of natural scenic beauty from which to choose locations—from mountains to desert to the Pacific Ocean. Its climate was as good, if not better, than Arizona's. And most important, it probably had some film processing labs because, while no one had yet made a feature picture in the West, a few companies making one- and two-reelers had already moved there from the East to take advantage of cheaper land, labor, and all-year sunlight. The latter was a potent economic factor, because artificial lighting was still not being used in the making of motion pictures.

A final consideration flashed through De Mille's mind: with Los Angeles being eight hundred miles farther away from New York than Flagstaff, it would be eight hundred miles more difficult for the strong-arm men occasionally hired by the Trust to sabotage the efforts of maverick movie makers to track them down and cause trouble.

De Mille didn't hunger for trouble or any kind of violence—despite his earlier bravado of threatening to join the Mexican Revolution. In fact, he feared the Trust's goon squads so much that before leaving for the West he had taken the precaution of packing a revolver in his suitcase, just in the event he had to protect himself and his company's camera equipment in a shoot-out in *The Squaw Man*'s corral.

As far as De Mille was concerned, putting more distance between him and the Trust's thugs was the final selling point in southern California's favor. And as a result, De Mille and the rest of the Jesse L. Lasky Feature Play Company were back aboard the train when it puffed out of the Flagstaff station in the direction of Los Angeles.

When they stepped off the train a day and a half later, they found themselves in the old Santa Fe depot—a pueblolike structure of adobe brick and roughly hewn wooden beams, in East Los Angeles.

The city itself reflected the sophistication of its train station. It had approximately 300,000 residents—mostly ranchers and citrus fruit growers and small businessmen, with a good many Mexican and Indian laborers filling out the rest of the population. There were no tall buildings, for any structure over ten stories was in danger of toppling over in an earthquake. But there were lots of Spanish-style bungalows and Mexican hacienda ranch houses and tall palm trees. And the whole thing, which didn't comprise more than a few square miles, was surrounded by snow-capped mountains (clearly seen in the distance through smogless blue skies), orange and lemon and walnut groves, picturesque ranch country, and the Pacific Ocean.

Although De Mille had been forced to hock the family silver in order to raise funds for the trip west, he showed absolutely no hesitation about checking himself and his company into the Alexandria, Los Angeles's most luxurious and expensive hotel, which was located in the downtown section of the sprawling young metropolis, on the corner of Fourth and Spring streets. Once settled, they started ordering food and drink from room service, and otherwise spending their money recklessly, which soon gave rise to the rumor that they could afford to live in such a high style.

De Mille didn't know anybody in all of Los Angeles, but somewhere around must have been the counterpart of a Walter Winchell to herald his company's arrival, because before the sun set behind the mountains, word had spread that a group of rich Easterners were holed up in the Alexandria, with bales of money, planning a moving picture.

With that kind of press, the Jesse L. Lasky Feature Play Company soon had plenty of friends. If not friends, at least people willing to help them spend the $50,000 Sam Goldfish had expended so much energy trying to raise.

Two key figures in De Mille's rapidly burgeoning moving picture operation were L. L. Burns and Harry Revier, who turned up and introduced themselves to the director the following morning. Burns and Revier said they owned a film lab about ten miles west of the Alexandria, in a funny-sounding place called Hollywood. They said they wanted the job of developing the Lasky Company's film. De Mille told them they were a little premature; he still hadn't found a place to shoot.

Burns and Revier had an answer for that, too. They informed De Mille that there was space right around the corner from their lab that could be rented for a studio. They said the place had everything—including a stage equipped with diffusers. That sounded good to De Mille, even though he didn't know what a diffuser was. He assumed they were important, however, and he was right. (Diffusers were strips of cloth that hung above an outdoor stage to control the brilliance of the California sun. Without them, most film would have been badly overexposed.)

When De Mille asked if he could see the place, Burns and Revier piled everybody into their car—an open-top, seven-passenger phaeton—and drove them to Hollywood.

Hollywood was then about an hour's drive away, over an unpaved road which wound through the straggling outskirts of Los Angeles and a long stretch of open, deserty-looking countryside.

When he came to Hollywood the following year, William De Mille,

Cecil's brother, supplied an excellent firsthand account of what the future movie capital looked like, in a letter home.

> Hollywood itself is a suburban town, with lots of tropical vegetation, tremendous palms, etc., but it all has to be nurtured very carefully, the country being really desert and supplying best those things which grow in the desert. The general effect is rather tropical luxuriance with wild desert just outside and in plain view. . . .
>
> The usual thing seems to be to rent one of the very pretty furnished bungalows with which the place is filled and camp out, as it is always summer. Folks don't take housekeeping at all seriously and you can have your own house for $50 a month, furnished, or something like that. . .
>
> Whatever else the life may be, it is absolutely healthy . . . but the social atmosphere is that of an English regiment in India—dependent on its own members.

In Hollywood Burns and Revier drove the Lasky company down a sparsely settled main thoroughfare appropriately called Hollywood Boulevard, then turned south on a broad, shady avenue intersecting it, which they said was Vine Street.

A few hundred feet down Vine Street, Burns pulled to a stop in front of a large, rambling L-shaped building that was unmistakably a barn—not only from its looks but from the pungent aroma of horse manure and other barnyard smells that seemed to be wafting from it.

"There it is," exclaimed Burns, jumping up on his seat and pointing toward the barn. "What do you think of it?"

One of the wings of the barn ran along Vine Street. The east end backed up to an orange and lemon grove. And its southern exposure was bordered by a dirt path that today is Selma Avenue. The entire complex was owned by a man named Jacob Stern, who lived down the street in a white bungalow with a red tile roof. After inspecting the premises and finding it suitable for his purpose, De Mille made a deal with Stern to rent the barn for seventy-five dollars a month. Stern, however, reserved the right to house his carriage and horses in a corner of the barn—an arrangement that caused De Mille considerable discomfort after he set up his office in the building. Whenever Stern washed down his carriage and his horses, or a horse urinated, a stream of water flowed through De Mille's office and over his shoes. The only way De Mille could deal with the run-off was to buy a bucket and stick his feet in it whenever Stern started washing.

After receiving the go-ahead telegram from his bosses in the East, De Mille set about transforming the barn into a motion picture studio.

Stalls were turned into offices, dressing rooms, and a projection room.

One end of the barn was used as a storeroom. And in a clearing among the acres of orange and lemon trees he built an open-air stage, complete with diffusers.

De Mille soon discovered that he needed someone to help him with the secretarial work and bookkeeping, so he hired a local woman named Stella Stray, for fifteen dollars a week, and set her up at a kitchen table and straight-backed wooden chair in his office, next to his own makeshift desk. Somewhere he had acquired a battered typewriter, too.

The Squaw Man officially started filming on December 31, 1913. Extra and bit players, stunt men, carpenters, and even assistant directors were culled from the ranks of the merely curious and the unemployed who used to congregate at the hitching posts in front of the barn looking for work every morning—on sunny days, that is. On cloudy and rainy days nobody showed up, for they knew there could be no shooting without the sun. If the weather was good, they'd shoot from daybreak to sundown. There were no unions, of course, to police the number of hours spent in front of the cameras.

Trips to location spots were never arranged ahead of time, as they are today, when a studio will send out a location man weeks in advance to scout sites and contract with their owners for their use. It was all done on the spur of the moment in 1913. De Mille and a few members of his company would set out on horseback in search of a location. De Mille would be in the vanguard, looking not unlike the leader of a cavalry regiment. The crew, cast, and camera equipment would be following in two cars.

If they were looking for a church, they'd stop in front of the first one they found, unload their equipment, and start cranking away. No one seemed to object to their trespassing, or wanted to charge them for the use of the property.

From the first day he started directing, De Mille dressed himself in the garb that he made famous by becoming famous—riding breeches, leather puttees, and the turned-around long-visored cap. But contrary to what his detractors believe, this garb was not an affectation but a necessity—at least in the early days of the picture business. Riding horseback or standing around in rough underbrush all day made puttees and riding breeches an absolute must. Rattlesnakes were a real and constant hazard, and puttees were the best protection against them. Protection from the semitropical sun made wearing a hat a necessity, too. But a director found he couldn't peer through the view finder on a camera to line up a shot if he was wearing a large-brimmed ten-gallon hat. Thus the cap, because the visor could be turned around out of the way when one looked through the view finder.

Another piece of equipment that De Mille fell int the habit of carrying in his belt at all times was his pistol—and not just for protection against rattle-snakes and other forms of wildlife, such as coyotes and wolves. After a few days of shooting, De Mille realized that the rattlesnakes employed by the movie Trust were equally dangerous to his health and well-being.

Entering the film lab one morning, De Mille discovered that the previous day's takes had been unwound from their reels, thrown in a heap on the floor, and scraped, pitted, and disfigured. Someone had obviously broken into the lab and stomped on the film with his feet—not being brave enough evidently to risk setting the highly inflammable celluloid on fire.

From that moment on, De Mille instructed Gandolfi to shoot two nega-tives of every scene, in spite of the extra expense. After a day's shooting, De Mille would leave one copy of the film in the lab and carry the other to his home, a small bungalow in Cahuenga Canyon which he had rented after his wife, Constance, and their six-year-old daughter, Cecilia, had moved west to be with him.

That only solved half the problem. One night after work De Mille was actually shot at when he was carting the heavy cans of film home to Ca-huenga Canyon. Miraculously, the bullets missed his head, which is proba-bly what gave him religion and the inclination to glorify God in so many of his later epics. But after he got shot at the following evening, De Mille decided God needed a little help and he started toting a gun every place he went—just like one of the characters in the Western he was shooting. After he returned the enemy's fire a couple of times, they stopped harassing him.

It took eighteen days to shoot *The Squaw Man*, and $47,000, which was just about all of the money Sam Goldfish had collected from the exhibitors in advance.

Forty-seven thousand dollars was considerably more than their first es-timated budget, but De Mille wasn't worried. He thought he had a hit, and invited Sam and Lasky to come out West for a showing of *The Squaw Man*'s first rough cut.

Sam declined to make the trip for two reasons: He was still extremely busy selling their unfinished product to exhibitors, and Blanche had just recently given birth to their first child, a girl whom they named Ruth, and the new and nervous father felt he belonged by his wife's side.

But Lasky put business before Bessie and eagerly made the long trek to the Coast. He was expecting a triumph.

Somehow he found his way to the suburb known as Hollywood. But he immediately got lost when he tried to locate the headquarters of the picture company that bore his name. He finally ended up at the Hollywood Hotel—a sedate, countryish resort hotel, where the rich citizens of Los Angeles came when they wanted to get away from it all. Inside he strode importantly up to the desk clerk and announced, "I am Jesse L. Lasky, and I am the president of the Jesse L. Lasky Feature Play Company. Could you please direct me to it?"

"Never heard of it," said the clerk.

"Then perhaps you've heard of Cecil B. De Mille, our director?" asked Lasky.

"Never heard of him, either," snapped the clerk.

Crestfallen, Lasky was about to leave through the front door, when an elderly bellhop, who resembled a grizzled mining prospector left over from the California gold rush days, buttonholed him and said, "Tell you who might be able to help you, mister. Drive down this main road till you come to a path known as Vine Street. You can't miss it. It's a dirt road with a row of pepper trees right down the middle. Follow the pepper trees till you see an old barn. There's some movie folks working there that might know where your company is." The moment the bellhop mentioned the barn, Lasky knew he was at least close to his destination.

Lasky's reception committee was waiting for him in front of the barn— six tired-looking horses and an eight-year-old boy, who offered to take him to their leader. He led Lasky through the orange grove to the stage, where De Mille was shooting the final scenes of the Western melodrama.

After greeting his president, De Mille posed Lasky in front of a two-ton Ford truck with the name Jesse L. Lasky Feature Play Company emblazoned on its side, and took a still of him. He knew this would automatically make Lasky smile, and he wanted to send Sam Goldfish, their treasurer, photographic evidence of what would appear to be the president's happy endorsement of De Mille's extravagance in buying the truck.

But they were so over-budget now that nothing would make Sam feel good except a blockbuster of a hit.

The first screening of *The Squaw Man* took place in the barn one night toward the end of January before a select audience of about fifty people. Among them were: De Mille's wife and daughter; Jesse L. Lasky; Dustin Farnum; the female lead, Winifred Kingston, whom Farnum later married; all the featured players, including Monroe Salisbury and Red Wing, an Indian woman whom De Mille had hired instead of a professional actress because he wanted authenticity; the key cameramen, Oscar Apfel, Fred Kley, Al Gandolfi, and Alvin Wyckoff; Stella Stray, the company's combination secretary and script clerk; Mamie Wagner, De Mille's film cutter; the carpenters and lighting men; and four of Jacob Stern's best stallions. It was such a proud occasion that the men wore coats, collars, and ties, and the women, their most glamorous dresses.

Sam Goldfish had been alerted that this was the big night, and as the crowd of fifty filed into the barn projection room to take their seats on hard wooden benches, Sam was at home in his comfortable Manhattan apartment, anxiously awaiting a triumphant telegram. It never occurred to Sam that he and his partners were possibly heading for their last roundup.

Meanwhile, back in the barn De Mille gave a signal to the projectionist, the lights went off, and "JESSE L. LASKY PRESENTS" flashed grandly on the screen. Then the words went into a convulsive dance and promptly skittered off at the top of the screen. It happened again when the picture's title—"THE SQUAW MAN, starring DUSTIN FARNUM"—was projected.

Then the actors appeared—but with their legs cut off at the waist, and walking in the air several feet above their heads. In the London drawing-room scene, the floor rose and the ceiling descended, crushing a gathering of sophisticates like ants beneath a giant footstep. Groups of actors rose like pigeons and whizzed off the screen. Mountains twitched nervously and skittered away. Dustin Farnum appeared simultaneously in three places in the same scene, boiled around for a while, and then pulled himself together. The effect pretty much approximated what is seen on a television screen today when the vertical and horizontal tuners are not properly adjusted—only much worse. A few in the audience whose stakes weren't quite so high as De Mille's and Lasky's started to chuckle.

De Mille stopped the running and went into a huddle with the projectionist. After about fifteen minutes, they doused the lights and tried again, but the images on the screen still wouldn't stay put, and nobody was experienced enough in film to understand why.

"We're ruined," gasped Lasky from his seat in the darkened barn.

De Mille halted the showing halfway through the second reel and sent everybody home. The atmosphere was funereal as the audience filed out, murmuring not very comforting platitudes, such as "Don't worry," and "It's probably something very small."

Left alone, De Mille and Lasky checked the projector; it was in perfect order. They checked the film; there was nothing wrong with that, either, that they could notice. And there didn't seem to be any indication of sabotage, so they couldn't even blame the Trust.

However, if it had been sabotage, it could only have happened in the lab. This precluded any possibility of returning the film to the lab for reprocessing. To do so would have exposed the print to the risk of further crippling at the hands of whoever did it in the first place.

Lasky and De Mille glumly pondered their predicament until four in the morning. The more they thought about it, the deeper the trouble they seemed to be in. For *The Squaw Man* in its hopelessly botched condition was not just a bomb film. Sam had already sold the exhibition rights to it for thousands of dollars. They had spent every cent they had raised making the picture, and even had plenty of unpaid bills left over. If they were unable to deliver the merchandise or return the money to the men who'd advanced it to them, all four partners were liable to go to jail—Lasky, De Mille, Arthur Friend, and Sam Goldfish, who, had he been there to be told of this frightening prospect, might very well have said, "Gentlemen, include me out."

5

The Squaw Man
Makes Good

DE MILLE AND LASKY spent several worrisome days and sleep-less nights wondering what, if anything, to tell Sam, who, on the strength of the enthusiastic reports he'd been getting from De Mille, had already gone ahead and resigned from the glove company. If they told Sam the truth, that *The Squaw Man* was absolutely unreleasable in its present state, he was apt to come after them with a gun.

On the other hand, if they remained mute, he would assume "disaster" and be just as angry, as evidenced by a number of frantic telegrams their treasurer had already dispatched to the barn, demanding to know the re-sults of the showing, so he could start setting up release dates. The exhibi-tors were already hounding him for dates, and he didn't know what to tell them.

Leaving De Mille to deal with Goldfish, Lasky took off for San Francisco to straighten out some trouble with one of his vaudeville acts, Lasky's Redheads, which was playing the Orpheum Theater there. With *The Squaw Man* such a fiasco, Lasky felt it more prudent than ever not to neglect his vaudeville business. If it prospered enough, it might be the means of paying off some of the debts he had incurred by taking his brother-in-law's bad ad-vice to get into the movies.

After another twenty-four hours of procrastinating, De Mille finally sent a wire to Sam. "SOMETHING TERRIBLY WRONG WITH PRINT. PLEASE ADVISE. REGARDS CECIL."

The minute Sam received De Mille's wire, he was on the long-distance telephone to California.

"Vat's this something terribly wrong?" he asked in an apoplectic tone.

"We don't know," confessed De Mille. "The print looks all right until we put it in the projection room and try to show it. Then the images jump all over the screen."

"You can't do this to me," wailed Sam. "The states' rights men are breathing down my neck. They want we should give them release dates or give them their money back and we have no money left to give back."

"Well, it can't be shown in its present state. They'll laugh us off the screen."

"You've made a *comedy?*"

"No, Sam, it just looks that way. It has to be fixed or we're sunk."

"Well, you're the director-general. You should take the bull by the teeth."

De Mille confessed his dilemma: There wasn't anyone in Los Angeles experienced enough in film to diagnose the problem, and he was afraid to entrust the negative to the same lab they had used for the original processing because of the Trust.

"I'll think of something," said Sam. "Call me up tomorrow and remind me what it is."

According to those closest to him, Sam was always at his best in disaster. If so, this particular disaster was an inspiration to him. After concentrating on the problem for about an hour, Sam remembered meeting, on one of his money-raising trips to Philadelphia, a man named Sigmund Lubin, who was supposed to know more about film than anyone in the world. Pop Lubin, as he was known to his associates, owned and ran the Lubin Manufacturing Company, which not only made its own two-reelers for distribution, but was a leader in commercial film printing.

If anyone could help them, it was Pop Lubin.

The only trouble was, Lubin Manufacturing was one of the ten companies that belonged to the Trust. Only a fool would go to a rival company for help—especially a company that was suspected of trying to sabotage them. But what choice did they have? In its present condition, the six reels of film were unusable. Lubin couldn't cripple them any more than they already were, and there was the slim chance he'd try to help. After all, the old gentleman wasn't nicknamed Pop for nothing. He was called that because he had a reputation for being kindly, genial, and charitable. Perhaps he'd extend those niceties even to the opposition.

Taking the bull by the teeth himself, Sam phoned Lubin in Philadelphia and in lugubrious tones calculated to reduce a man of stone to tears, explained the terrible blow that fate had dealt the Jesse L. Lasky Feature Play Company.

Lubin was not unaware of the Lasky Company's existence. He had read some of Sam's advertising literature which promised that the new company would revolutionize the industry. And perhaps because he was amused rather than frightened by the pathetic efforts of this glove salesman to break into his business, he gave Sam a rather surprising answer.

"I'll be glad to look at your film, Mr. Goldfish—just bring it to my lab and I'll give you an expert opinion."

After hanging up, Sam immediately phoned De Mille back in California. "Cecil," said Sam, "I couldn't wait for you to phone me tomorrow, because you won't be there."

"I won't!" exclaimed the surprised De Mille. "Where will I be?"

"On the train going to Philadelphia," shouted Sam, explaining what had transpired since the two had last talked, and instructing De Mille to hop the next Santa Fe out of L.A. and bring the film with him.

De Mille phoned Lasky in San Francisco and told him there was still an outside chance none of them would have to go to jail. The two agreed to meet in Chicago and proceed to Philadelphia together.

Though he could ill afford it, De Mille took a drawing room on the train to Chicago. He wanted to be able to keep the dozens of cans of negative of *The Squaw Man* with him at all times, even during meals, which he had the porter serve him in his drawing room. He was determined that nothing was going to happen to that film until he delivered it into Pop Lubin's hands.

And to make doubly certain, he kept his revolver within arm's length at all times during the day, and under his pillow when he was sleeping. He didn't sleep much, however, for he could foresee nothing ahead but disaster.

Lasky joined forces with De Mille in Chicago, and the two of them proceeded to Philadelphia, via the Pennsylvania Railroad, with their precious cargo.

Pop Lubin personally met the two nervous picturemakers at the door as they lugged the heavy cans of film from the taxicab into his lab. He sat them down, patiently listened to De Mille's detailed account of their première showing, and then quizzed them at length as to the kind of camera and editing equipment De Mille had been using.

"Well, that's enough talk," he finally said. "Let's take a look at the film."

Lubin turned the film over to one of his technicians and disappeared into a back room with it.

While they awaited the verdict, De Mille and Lasky paced up and down, much like expectant fathers in a hospital waiting room. Only they weren't dreaming of passing out cigars; instead they had visions of a dirty jail cell with them in it.

Pop Lubin and his technicians surveyed the wreckage of *The Squaw Man* for about thirty minutes. When he returned, there was a solemn look on his face. His opening words weren't any more comforting.

"Gentlemen," he said, "This is very grave." He seemed to be enjoying their terror as he gazed from De Mille's scared face to his partner's. Abruptly Lubin's expression of gravity was supplanted by a broad smile.

"But I think it can be fixed," he added, his eyes twinkling like Santa Claus's.

"How long will it take?" asked De Mille.

"I'll have it for you tomorrow," promised Lubin.

In reply to their incredulous looks, Lubin explained that there was nothing wrong with the negative itself. All that was wrong were the sprocket holes, which were spaced at sixty-five to the foot instead of the customary sixty-four.

This, it turned out after a few more of Lubin's probing questions, was De Mille's fault, for in an effort to save his company some money, he had made a giant-sized boo-boo.

De Mille had purchased Eastman perforated negative stock, but as an economy measure had used unperforated positive stock and a secondhand, British-made, hand-operated machine for punching the sprocket holes. De Mille, in his embarrassment, couldn't remember whether the seller had warned him about the difference in the spacing of the sprocket holes, but if he did, De Mille was too much of a tyro, and too anxious to save money, to think that a slight technicality like that mattered very much.

That slight technicality—the difference between $1/64$ and $1/65$ of a foot— was enough to account for the erratic behavior of the picture when it was projected on the screen, and turn what should have been a victory into a rout.

But at the hands of Lubin's expert technicians, the problem could easily be corrected, and was by the next day. All Lubin's men had to do was paste a thin strip of film over the edge of the negative and perforate it properly at sixty-four sprocket holes to the foot.

Lasky and De Mille were so grateful upon hearing this relatively simple solution that they could have kissed Pop Lubin. Instead, they restrained their emotions until they reached the sidewalk, at which point they threw their arms around each other and did a little dance, to the bewilderment of the citizens of the City of Brotherly Love.

Back in their hotel room, De Mille and Lasky jubilantly phoned Sam in New York and told him the good news, then ordered champagne from room service and proceeded to get drunk.

Nobody, including Sam, who didn't get drunk because he didn't drink, was ever able to figure out why Pop Lubin had put himself out so to help three schnooks who were members of the opposition. Perhaps he figured that what was good for the picture business would in the end be good for his lab. Or perhaps he was just a nice man. There are some.

Once an accurately perforated print of *The Squaw Man* was in his hands, Sam set up an invitational trade showing at the Longacre Theatre on February 17, 1914. All the states' rights men were invited—those who had already paid in advance for the exhibition rights, plus quite a few doubting Thomases who insisted on seeing *The Squaw Man* before plunking down their money. Also among the invited were sundry relatives, close friends, and motion picture critics.

Sam Goldfish was the official host at the trade show that night. As he stood at the door, greeting potential buyers, he looked more like a prosperous bookkeeper than a showman. Small pince-nez rode the bridge of his large nose. His tall, slim figure was clothed in an immaculately tailored dark suit and custom-made shirt, with a high, celluloid Herbert Hoover–type collar. And although he was just a little past thirty, he was almost completely bald, except for a fringe of black hair around his shiny pate.

Just before the lights went out, Lasky and De Mille took seats in the rear of the theater—so that they could make a hasty escape should the occasion call for it.

The occasion didn't call for it.

This time the titles and actors stayed on the screen where they belonged. More important, the picture held up six full reels. The usual signs of boredom and dislike—the shifting of bodies in their seats, coughing, and laughter in the wrong places—were nonexistent.

On the contrary, the audience was enthralled.

When the lights were turned up after the last fade-out, the applause was heavy and genuine, and quite a number of the hardhearted states' rights men were heard to shout "Bravo" and "Make more of the same."

Sam introduced De Mille and Lasky as the actual creators, but Sam was the real center of congratulations—as well he should have been. For even though he'd had absolutely nothing to do with the artistic end of the picture, it would never have been made at all had it not been for his undying conviction that movies were good for something besides chasing vaudeville customers out of their seats.

The skeptics among the states' rights men who were at the Longacre that night must have felt the same way. Two weeks later only seventeen states remained unsold. And a week after that there were only four.

One of Sam's buyers that night was the former junk dealer from up north, Louis B. Mayer, who had turned movie exhibitor. But Mayer was enough of a showman not to let his antipathy for Goldfish diminish his enthusiasm for *The Squaw Man.* He agreed to buy the exhibition rights to it for $4,000. Months later, despite the picture's success in his theater, Mayer only remitted $2,000 when Goldfish pressed him for the remuneration. This incident contributed to the bad feeling that continued to exist between the two men even after they became successful movie magnates, with more important things to do than carry on a schoolboyish feud.

The Squaw Man was released in New York City on February 28, 1914. Incredibly, it had been less than two months since De Mille had started shooting the film in Hollywood on December 31, 1913. It was an immediate hit with both the public and the nation's critics.

Lewis Reeves Harrison, writing in *Motion Picture World*, the most influential trade paper of the day, was in the vanguard of those critics heaping accolades on Sam's first theatrical venture.

> One of the best visualizations of a stage play ever shown on the screen, *The Squaw Man* was a source of surprise and delight to me. . . . Credit must be given almost entirely to the direction and interpretation, the direction in this case embracing both form and treatment of an almost flawless production.

Other critics jumped on *The Squaw Man*'s bandwagon with equal enthusiasm. The result was that *The Squaw Man*, which had cost only $47,000 to produce, eventually ended up grossing $244,700.

The profit of nearly $200,000 meant that the Lasky Feature Play Company would not only survive to become a potent force in the motion picture industry, but that its treasurer, Samuel Goldfish, had made the right decision in saying good-by to the glove business.

Although he didn't realize it, Sam would soon be saying good-by to Lasky and De Mille as well.

6

Our Comedies Are
Not to Be Laughed At

AS LONG AS YOU agreed with him, Sam wasn't a difficult man to get along with. "Otherwise he was impossible," states one long-time associate of Goldwyn's who wishes to remain anonymous. Even Sam himself recognized he wasn't easy to get along with, according to one writer he had under contract. One day this writer came to Sam and said, "Mr. Goldwyn, I'm quitting. I'm not up to finishing this assignment."

"Why not?" demanded Sam.

"My doctor says I have low blood pressure."

"Really!" exclaimed Sam. "You're the first person I ever gave low blood pressure to."

Part of Sam's difficulty was that he was headstrong, even in matters he didn't know anything about. He didn't like to take a back seat to anybody, which is the reason he ran away from Poland in the first place, the reason he skipped out on his English relatives, the reason he quit being a glove cutter, and the reason he eventually broke up with every partner he ever had in the movie business.

Perhaps he wouldn't have had trouble with his first partners if Lasky had stuck to his original condition for joining the movie venture in the first place—that he would just lend his name to the company and let his brother-in-law run the business.

But when *The Squaw Man* turned into a moneymaker, Lasky could not resist becoming more active in the company. For a couple of reasons: (1) It didn't take much vision to see that the movies had a better future than vaudeville, and, (2) Sam Goldfish, despite his business acumen, hardly had the background in the entertainment field to be depended upon to choose the artistic ingredients that went into the making of a successful film—mainly the story, but also the right combination of directing and acting.

With the exhibitors hungering for more product, Sam set a schedule for the Lasky Company to produce at least one picture a month. But that was a pretty demanding schedule. It took Sam nearly a month just to read a potential property. Besides, nobody was writing for the screen. Where would they get properties?

Lasky and De Mille decided that their best bet was to turn to the Broadway theater for plays and actors. With De Mille's mother a play agent, the Lasky Company had an inside track to all the available plays.

Their first purchase was *Brewster's Millions*, a wild farce that had been a huge hit on Broadway. They bought this directly from the author for $5,000, which was the average price being paid then for Broadway smashes that today would go for between $100,000 and $500,000.

Others they picked up for the same price were *The Only Son, The Mastermind*, and *The Warrens of Virginia*, which had been written by William De Mille, and *The Return of Peter Grimm*, which Cecil had originally written but sold outright to David Belasco, who had put his own name on it.

To Sam's consternation, Lasky and De Mille were doing most of the selecting of the properties. Sam, of course, still dominated the business end, handling all the selling, distribution, and exploitation. But Cecil as director-general oversaw all phases of their productions and selected the properties he personally wanted to direct.

De Mille didn't have time to direct every picture. He was more painstaking in his work than other directors of the period. As time went on, he found himself developing a flair for sweeping dramatic spectacles that could only be surpassed by D. W. Griffith. Soon De Mille's shooting schedules were stretching from five to six to seven and sometimes even eight weeks.

The directorial assignments he didn't feel like touching he turned over to Oscar Apfel, who'd actually done most of the directing on *The Squaw Man* while he was teaching De Mille the business. Because of his familiarity with the film medium, Apfel could grind out pictures like sausages—one every three or four weeks.

Lasky, meanwhile, kept himself occupied traveling back and forth between the East and West coasts, buying plays, engaging stars, and building up the personnel in their Hollywood studio.

Before the year was over, they had hired three more directors, George Melford, James Neill, and Fred Thompson, to help De Mille, and could boast of such stars in their stable (which truly was a stable) as Mabel Van Buren, Blanche Sweet, and H. B. Warner.

One of the earliest indications of friction within the Lasky Company hierarchy was an ad that mysteriously appeared in the *Motion Picture World* in March of 1914, announcing the production of their second picture, *Brewster's Millions*.

The ad proclaimed Jesse Lasky "America's most artistic director," Oscar

Apfel the "acknowledged peer of directors and genius of innovators," and Cecil B. De Mille "master playwright, director and author of numerous dramatic successes."

Nowhere in the ad was there any mention of Sam Goldfish. And nowhere among the company's roster of personnel could anyone be found to take the blame for the dastardly document.

One thing is certain: *Sam* wouldn't have anything to do with composing the ad. He liked personal publicity too much. He was, however, enough of a gentleman not to mention the slight to his partners, although it no doubt contributed to his irrascibility and unreasonableness over the next few weeks.

Weeks later a second ad appeared in the *Motion Picture Herald*. This one gave due credit to all the creative staff, but announced in bold and larger type than the rest:

> Samuel Goldfish
> Head of Jesse L. Lasky Feature
> Picture Company

Sam never admitted responsibility for that ad, any more than the person who perpetrated the first misdeed owned up to that one. But when Lasky confronted him with an accusation, Sam defended himself with, "I don't know who wrote it, Jesse, but it's true. I *am* the head of the company. I have it in writing that you are to keep your hands out."

An argument over which one of the brothers-in-law was the most important to the company followed, with Arthur Friend standing on the sidelines, trying to arbitrate unsuccessfully. Seeing the whole corporate structure he'd organized about to crumble before his eyes, Arthur Friend pulled Sam out of the office and took him on a drive out to the tip of Long Island to calm him down. When a bowl of steamed littlenecks and a small boiled lobster, two of Sam's favorite tranquilizers, failed to take his mind off Lasky, Friend finally said to his boss, "Sam, why do you always fight?"

Sam refused to admit that he was a born fighter. Instead he said it was an acquired characteristic. He'd gotten it from reading about Teddy Roosevelt, who was always making fighting speeches and talking about carrying a big stick. "Theodore Roosevelt taught me that a man has to fight," added Sam. "He says the only things worth having are what you fight for."

"But you fight even when people agree with you," pointed out Friend.

"I have to keep in practice," admitted Sam.

Friend managed to pilot Sam and Lasky through these ego shoals, thus preventing an immediate breakup. And the two were still on speaking terms by the time De Mille shipped *Brewster's Millions* to New York for the film's showing to potential buyers.

To be on the safe side, Sam ran the film the night before for just himself and Lasky. It had been touted to Sam as a comedy, but before it was over he felt like crying . So did Lasky. Neither had been able to laugh once through the entire picture. The film unreeled to sepulchral silence.

"We're ruined," gasped Lasky.

"The films are no place for comedy," wailed Sam.

The Goldwyn of later years would have found a way not to exhibit the picture—at least until it was "right." If it couldn't be fixed, he'd have shelved it forever.

But that wasn't feasible with *Brewster's Millions*. All their available cash was tied up in that production. And it was too late to call off the exhibitors' showing, for the states' rights men were already in New York, prepared to make deals. They'd be furious if the Lasky Company had nothing to show them and they had to go home empty-handed.

So Sam had to suffer through a sleepless night. But he refused to put himself through the torment of seeing the picture again. While *Brewster's Millions* was being shown to a large gathering of exhibitors the next morning, Sam alternated between throwing up in the men's room and taking walks around the block.

While the last reel was on, Sam pulled himself together and walked into the theater. He was astonished to hear a roar of laughter filling the room. Another roar followed the first, and then another, and another. The tough audience was eating it up.

As Sam stood there, dumbfounded, Lasky approached him and gave his hand a congratulatory shake.

"What happened?" asked the bewildered Sam.

"Sam we forgot," said Lasky, with a victorious glint in his eyes. "A comedy needs an audience."

Since he had never sat through a comedy in an empty projection room before, Sam had had no way of knowing that it's almost impossible to laugh when you are alone in a theater. It was an invaluable lesson. Never preview a comedy in an empty house.

Sam and Lasky knew they had a hit when Adolph Zukor, president of Famous Players, their stiffest competition, strode out of the viewing room, puffing on a cigar that was almost longer than he was, and offered them his congratulations.

Zukor invited Sam and Lasky to have lunch with him the next day at Delmonico's, where the executives of that era consummated most of their deals. Their friendship with the little man with the big cigar had not yet reached the stage where they could talk about anything but generalities, but Sam and Lasky were impressed with Zukor's vast knowledge of the business, and listened, almost mesmerized, as he expounded on the glorious future of the movie business while he blew heavy cigar smoke into their faces.

Following their first lunch together, Lasky said to Sam: "Zukor and all the other big fellows in the picture business smoke cigars. Maybe we better try it."

So they bought two of the most expensive stogies the cigarette vender had to offer and promptly lit up. Lasky liked the experience and became an inveterate cigar smoker for the remainder of his life. But Sam's cigar made him sick to his stomach, and after a visit to the men's room, he vowed never to smoke another—even at the expense of never becoming as important in the movies as Adolph Zukor. He stayed away from cigarettes, too, although occasionally, in an effort to be sociable, he would light one and hold it between his fingers like a fountain pen.

The Lasky Company's third production was *The Warrens of Virginia*, which was adapted from William De Mille's play of the same name. Cecil brought his brother west to write the screenplay, and they imported an Eastern actor, Raymond Hatton, to star in the film.

This was De Mille's third picture. The success of the first two gave him courage to begin experimenting with all kinds of new camera effects and fancy lighting. *The Warrens of Virginia,* for example, was the first picture to show interior night scenes without blazing sunlight streaming onto the set through all the doors and windows. De Mille used black velvet to keep out the midnight sun.

De Mille came up with another innovation. By manipulating sunlight reflectors, he became the first director to vary the light intensity when a script called for an actor to turn down a lamp or knock it over in a struggle. Until *The Warrens of Virginia,* a set was lit one way and stayed that way through an entire scene.

Finally, he started experimenting with light and shade, striving for artistic composition and pattern. Until then most movies were sold on the basis of how clear and sharp the photography was—all the lighting was perfectly flat. A scene was highly praised if the viewers could see all the wrinkles in a man's pants or the blemishes on his face. Most American directors tried to emulate Italian pictures, most of which were shot in the glaring sunlight of the Italian Riviera and showed every detail—from bloodshot eyes to dirty fingernails. Hollywood chauvinists seemed out to prove that the sunlight in southern California was every bit as strong and blinding as any that could be found in sunny Italy.

De Mille had the foresight and courage to believe he could achieve a three-dimensional effect by casting half of an actor's face in deep shadow. Instead of copying the Italian directors, he learned his lessons in lighting from some of the master painters—like Rembrandt, Rubens, and Whistler.

In one scene, he photographed Raymond Hatton almost completely hidden by shadows, with just a portion of his face peering out of the darkness. De Mille was certain that in his third picture he had achieved a dramatic new kind of photographic beauty and quality, and confidently shipped the print off to Sam Goldfish in the East, expecting to be praised.

But when Sam ran the picture in his projection room, the subtle lighting effects ignited his explosive temper. He immediately dashed off an anguished telegram to De Mille on the Coast. "CECIL, YOU HAVE RUINED US. IF YOU ARE GOING TO SHOW ONLY HALF AN ACTOR ON THE SCREEN THE EXHIBITORS WILL PAY ONLY HALF PRICE FOR THE PICTURE."

Disappointed, DeMille showed Sam's wire to Lasky, and the two of them considered how to answer it. Finally De Mille had an inspiration, and wired back: "SAM, IF YOU AND THE EXHIBITORS DON'T KNOW REMBRANDT LIGHTING WHEN YOU SEE IT, DON'T BLAME ME. CECIL."

A few hours later De Mille received the following from their hysterical treasurer: "DEAR CECIL, REMBRANDT LIGHTING WONDERFUL IDEA. FOR THAT THE EXHIBITORS WILL PAY DOUBLE. REGARDS SAM."

Whether they would have paid double or not has never been established, but *The Warrens of Virginia*, like its two predecessors, was a successful box-office entry, and the Jesse L. Lasky Company continued to prosper and burgeon. They filmed twenty-one pictures their first year in business.

With the success of *The Squaw Man* Sam, Lasky, and De Mille began drawing equal salaries from the company. Sam started them out at $250 a week, raised them to $500 after *Brewster's Millions*, and $1,000 when *The Warrens of Virginia* became a hit. By 1916, their salary had jumped to $2,500 a week apiece. At that rate, and with no income taxes, they'd all be millionaires soon.

Unfortunately, the supply of available days that could be turned into films was beginning to dwindle. This was partly due to the rapaciousness with which Sam and his partners were able to gobble them up and put them on the screen, and partly due to the bidding of their biggest and most active competitor—Adolph Zukor. Sam found himself bidding against Famous Players for almost every play or star Lasky recommended they buy.

In 1915 Sam got wind of a block of ten choice plays that were owned by David Belasco, the dean of Broadway producers. Among these hits were *The Girl of the Golden West*, *Sweet Kitty Bellaire*, and *The Darling of the Gods*, which had starred George Arliss on Broadway.

Sam was anxious to tie up all ten for his company, because he realized that owning them would put him in a more advantageous position when he was bidding against Adolph Zukor for stars, who were always searching for vehicles.

Unfortunately, Zukor had an inside track to Belasco. He was friendly with Daniel Frohman, Belasco's assistant. Sam, however, refused to let that discourage him. While others were afraid to approach the great man without going through an assistant, Sam phoned Belasco personally and asked for an interview. At first Belasco refused to see him, but after Sam placed several more calls to him—and also managed to bump into him in his favorite luncheon spot—he realized what others had already learned: You don't get rid of Goldfish by just saying no. So finally he said yes, and sent word through his secretary that he would see Sam in his office.

After being shown into Belasco's empty office, Sam waited for what seemed like an eternity for the producer to make his entrance. When he finally did make his entrance, down a long flight of winding stairs, it was as dramatic as anything Sam had ever seen in one of his plays. His majestic head, with its mop of shaggy white hair, was bent slightly forward, his right hand was inserted Napoleon-style inside his black velvet smoking jacket, and on each step he paused for just a beat to further insure the dramatic effect.

In the presence of such a living theatrical legend, it was difficult even for Sam to gather the courage to talk about Lasky, De Mille, and the wonderful things their company had already done and were contemplating in the future—provided, of course, they could acquire great properties such as the ones David Belasco had already made famous. But somehow Sam managed to get it all out.

Belasco was impressed by Sam's enthusiasm—and persuasiveness. He also seemed to like the fact that Sam and his partners were all in their thirties. But what he liked best of all was what Sam offered him for the rights: $100,000 against 50 percent of the profits. That's when Belasco showed his true artistic colors: he snapped up Sam's offer before you could say Adolph Zukor.

The next day at lunch Sam gloatingly told Zukor of the great coup he had pulled. Zukor turned so white that Sam thought he was going to have a heart attack. Weakly the older man stammered, "Congratulations, you *momzer.*"

A hundred thousand dollars against 50 percent of the profits was the first percentage deal of its kind. And it was quite a gamble on Sam's part to make it—especially since he hadn't read any of the plays and hadn't the faintest idea whether or not they would make good pictures. Fortunately, most of Belasco's stage dramas had outdoor backgrounds, which was ideal for film purposes.

Acquiring Belasco's block of plays gave the Lasky Company immediate entrée to a number of stars they might otherwise have been unable to sign. One of these was Mae Murray, one of the most important attractions of the day. She was so anxious to appear in *Sweet Kitty Bellaire* that she signed for a hundred dollars a week, plus another hundred for her clothes allowance.

De Mille had first call on all new properties, and thinking *The Darling of the Gods* was the juiciest plum, because it had been such a tremendous hit on the stage, he picked that one to direct personally.

But *Darling of the Gods* had a Japanese feudal background and a story that was much too complicated to be understood on the silent screen. In addition, the art of movie make-up had not been refined to what it is today. The strips of tape used to transform Occidental eyes into almond-shaped ones stood out so much in close-ups that all the actors looked as if they'd just stepped out of the prize ring with Jack Johnson. The heavy drama played like farce, and after seeing a few reels in rough cut, Sam wisely decided to shelve the whole project. In that respect, *Darling of the Gods* was a "first" in Sam Goldwyn's career.

By now, the competition between the Lasky Company and Zukor's Famous Players was beginning to make Sam's life absolutely miserable. Even though Sam and Adolph Zukor had become good friends since their first meeting, and they ate lunch together at Delmonico's on an average of once a week, the two were continually bidding against each other for the same properties and stars. This caused salaries and asking prices of plays to soar to astronomical heights.

For example, when Sam tried to sign Marguerite Clark, one of the major box-office attractions of the day, to star in his next picture, *The Goose Girl*, he offered her $5,000 a week to get her away from Zukor. Zukor in turn offered her $7,000 a week to get her away from Goldfish. Zukor won, and then, to show that there were no hard feelings, loaned the actress back to Sam for $8,000 a week.

The Goose Girl turned out to be one of the Lasky Company's most successful productions, but the high-salaried trend did not please Sam. Who knew where it would all end?

Zukor wasn't any happier about the way things were going, although he had a much larger company, was turning out more pictures per year, and had some assets that were of inestimable value. One of them was Mary Pickford. He was paying America's Sweetheart $20,000 a week, plus bonuses, which brought her annual intake to about $700,000.

Over lunch a couple of times, Sam, Lasky, and Zukor had discussed merging their two companies. But the deal remained just talk until the end of 1915, when the entry of a third party in the motion picture field caused the two rivals to form an alliance to prevent extinction.

Until 1915 both the Lasky and Zukor film companies had been distributing their pictures through the states' rights men. But then one of them, W. W. Hodkinson of San Francisco, called a meeting of his compatriots in New York to form a major distributing company in which they would all own stock. They called the new releasing firm Paramount Pictures, and while its announced purpose was to distribute pictures, one of its intentions was to gang up on the filmmakers and dictate to them what they would pay for their product. Since Paramount now owned most of the theaters, the picturemakers had little choice but to go along with their terms, no matter how meager.

Paramount offered the Lasky Feature Play Company only $35,000 in advance on each picture against 65 percent of the gross revenue. Neither Sam nor Zukor could live with those terms, so they decided to fight back by merging their two studios and forming a combine of their own.

Pooling the resources of the two top producing companies in the industry would enable them to obtain the kind of bank financing they would need to make more ambitious films. With stars like Mary Pickford, Marguerite Clark, and Dustin Farnum under contract, and the kind of blockbuster movies they could turn out utilizing all that talent, they'd be able to dictate their own terms to Paramount.

Although Famous Players had greater assets than the Lasky Feature Play Company, Zukor was so anxious to join forces with Sam, Lasky, and De Mille, that he agreed to split the stock fifty-fifty.

The new company was formed on June 16, 1916, and was called Famous Players–Lasky. Adolph Zukor became president; Lasky, vice president in charge of production; Sam was elected chairman of the board; De Mille retained his title of director-general; and Arthur Friend was made secretary. Several more floors were rented at 485 Fifth Avenue, and the Famous Players staff moved in.

Famous Players–Lasky soon had Paramount right where they wanted them. The merger of the two companies meant that they were the major suppliers of Paramount product. Over 80 percent of the pictures Paramount needed to keep its theaters operating now came from Famous Players–Lasky. Paramount released the pictures of several smaller production companies, among which were the Oliver Morosco Photoplay Company and Hobart Bosworth's Pallas Pictures, but their output was inconsequential. Without Famous Players–Lasky, Paramount would have to shut down. To make sure of this, Zukor pulled another coup. He persuaded the Morosco Photoplay Company and Pallas Pictures to merge with Famous Players–Lasky. Since they were in the same plight as Lasky and Zukor had been before their merger, at the complete mercy of the distributors, the two smaller companies willingly agreed to join the one large company.

As a powerful conglomerate of four studios, Famous Players–Lasky was now in a position to dictate terms to Paramount Releasing. And they did, and the birth of Hollywood's first major studio was about to happen.

Lasky was put in charge of the studios and overseeing the production of all four companies. De Mille stayed on the Coast, directing and supervising other directors. Zukor devoted his special genius to the financial end, which later included the formation of a worldwide network of film exchanges and theaters.

The additional clout that Famous Players–Lasky now had made it possible for Zukor and friends to borrow all the working capital they needed from the Irving Trust Company. Soon plans were in the works for them to go public.

Before the merger, the Lasky Feature Play Company introduced its films on the screen with the words "Jesse L. Lasky presents." Famous Players introduced its pictures with "Adolph Zukor presents." After the merger, it was decided to continue the same practice, with Adolph Zukor "presenting" all the pictures made in the East, and Lasky "presenting" all his output on the West Coast.

Nowhere in any of the screen credits did the name of Samuel Goldfish appear. How could it? He was just chairman of the board. It would have been clumsy to have all that on the screen—at least in those days.

Today, with everyone wanting to be a "presenter," a way would have been found to include Sam Goldfish in. It would probably go something like this:

> "Samuel Goldfish
> presents
> a Jesse L. Lasky production
> of an
> Adolph Zukor film
> produced by
> Cecil B. De Mille"

Obviously Sam had never thought of that. He was much too busy with his other problems, the main one being that he was dissatisfied with his position in the company. He didn't mind Zukor being made president, for his contribution of Mary Pickford to the company's roster of stars was a major one. But Sam thought he deserved the vice-presidential post and was not a good loser when the others voted Lasky into that position.

Being chairman of the board was a nebulous job, with no real duties. It was certainly not enough to satisfy an energetic man like Sam Goldfish for very long. Restless Sam was soon interfering in areas of the company's business where he had no legitimate right. What followed were monumental battles over company policy, battles that featured much shouting, door slamming, and hanging up of phones on Sam's part.

One source of friction was Adolph Zukor's attempt to keep Mary Pickford happy by signing her brother, Jack, to an acting contract at $500 a week. Jack was a nonentity in the business, not very talented, and, according to Sam, not worth signing at all.

Behind Zukor's back, Sam phoned the legal department and shouted, "Don't draw up Pickford's contract."

"But Mr. Goldfish, Mr. Zukor said—"

"I don't care what Mr. Zukor said—that bum can't act."

Zukor howled, and retreated to his estate on Long Island to calm down and consider how to handle the unmanageable Goldfish. It took two days before he could be persuaded to return to the studio.

That incident had barely blown over when Sam crossed Zukor again. In a move typical of his diplomacy, Sam burst into Lasky's office one day when he was conferring with Mary Pickford about the script of her next picture, *Less than the Dust*.

"Jesse," Sam blurted out, "don't let Zukor butt into this picture. He's okay as an executive, but we've always made better movies than Famous Players, so see that you keep the production reins in your hands!"

Sam couldn't have chosen a worse person than Mary Pickford to say something derogatory about Zukor in front of. Zukor had built Miss Pickford into the nation's number-one movie attraction. Without his backing, the face of America's Sweetheart wouldn't be plastered on every twenty-four sheet between New York and Hollywood, and neither would she be riding around in a chauffeur-driven Cadillac or taking baths in a tub with solid gold fixtures.

She owed everything to him, and she knew it, and the first thing she did after leaving Lasky's office was run straight to Zukor and report what Sam Goldfish had said about him.

A gentle, quiet man, Zukor didn't have much to say beyond a thoughtful "Hmmmmmmnnnn."

But the next day he requested a private luncheon meeting with Lasky. After the two of them had placed their orders, Zukor turned to Lasky and said, "I'm sorry to tell you this, Jesse, but Famous Players–Lasky is not large enough to hold Mr. Goldfish and myself. He was your partner, and therefore I don't want to ask him to leave. But you'll have to choose between Mr. Goldfish and me. I'm going to the country for the weekend, and I'll await your decision there."

Since De Mille was in Hollywood shooting a picture, Lasky had to make the decision alone—and in just forty-eight hours. As Lasky later recalled, it was the most difficult decision he'd ever had to make in his career. Lasky had tremendous admiration for Zukor as both a human being and a showman. He felt that with Zukor calling the shots, their company would soon be the best film-producing and -releasing unit in the world. On the other hand, Sam Goldfish was his sister's husband; and while he may not have known very much about making movies, he was a brilliant businessman. He was also the fellow responsible for getting Lasky into the movie business in the first place. It was Sam's foresight and aggressiveness that had brought Lasky to this stage of his career.

But the business had expanded to the point where Lasky felt it wouldn't be right to the stockholders to allow a personal relationship—such as existed between the two brothers-in-law—to interfere with what he felt was best for the studio. And in Lasky's opinion, Zukor was best for the studio. So, brother-in-law or not, Sam had to go. With Sam around, there could only be more dissension. Sam would not take a back seat to Lasky or Zukor, or anyone else for long. His was the kind of dynamic personality that functioned best alone, with all the power in his own hands.

By Monday morning, when he met with Zukor again, Lasky had reached his decision. "I want you to continue on being president," stated Lasky. "But we've got to soften the blow to Sam. After all, he is my brother-in-law."

"We'll take care of your brother-in-law," Zukor assured Lasky. He promptly called a meeting of his associates to estimate the value of Sam Goldfish's share of the company's stock. They had to estimate it, because their company was not yet listed on the stock exchange. The figure they arrived at was $900,000. They didn't have that much liquidity, but their credit was good at the Irving Trust Company and they were able to secure a loan.

Being a good loser was never one of Sam's strong points. Informed of the decision, he ranted, threatened, and even cried some. And when that failed to touch the hearts of his partners, he demanded a recount of the vote.

Lasky and Friend sided with Zukor, and on September 14, 1916, Sam Goldfish resigned from the company—only three months after he had helped form it.*

Going from glove salesman to near-millionaire in less than three years in the movie business softened the blow to Sam a little. But it wasn't enough to assuage his fury with Lasky for deserting his camp and going over to the side of the enemy. He felt that he more than anybody was responsible for

---

* Eventually, through Zukor's financial manipulation, Famous Players–Lasky became Paramount Pictures. Zukor, in an effort to keep the Paramount group, headed by W. W. Hodkinson, from ganging up on him and other picturemakers again, quietly had gone around buying up the stock of Paramount Releasing. Then, at a stockholders' meeting he dramatically announced the bombshell that he was now the major stockholder. Following that, he kicked out Hodkinson, combined both the releasing and production companies, and put himself into the presidency. However, because of its trademark value, he retained the name Paramount and the releasing company's slogan, "If it's a Paramount Picture, It's the Best Show in Town."

making Lasky an important name in the movie business. Where was his loyalty?

After Sam cleared out his desk at 485 Fifth Avenue, he didn't speak to Lasky for another forty years, which is a long time to hold a grudge against someone, even a brother-in-law.

But the Goldwyn Touch and sense of drama was evident even in his bitterness. In the late 1950s, Lasky, who had long been out of Paramount himself, was down in his luck and owed the government a fortune in back taxes. Because Lasky was old, ill, and no longer could earn big money, a number of his friends in the industry, including De Mille, got together and literally passed the hat for him.

De Mille asked Goldwyn if he'd care to contribute a few hundred dollars. "I'd like to think about it overnight," replied Sam. When De Mille called the next morning, Sam said, "Yes, I'll give him five thousand."

7

Sam Goldfish Is Dead

IN THE YEAR FOLLOWING Sam's forced resignation from Famous Players–Lasky, two significant events took place in his life: (1) The name Goldwyn was born, to become a permanent part of the lexicon, and (2) Blanche divorced him.

Those who didn't know the couple very well jumped to the obvious conclusion that Lasky's action in kicking his brother-in-law out of the company made Sam bitter, which in turn affected his marriage and how he felt about Blanche.

And perhaps it was the *coup de grâce* to the marriage, but it certainly wasn't the prime reason Mr. and Mrs. Goldfish split. It couldn't have been, because on December 12, 1915—nearly nine months prior to Sam's departure from Famous Players–Lasky—the following story appeared in the *New York Times:*

REFEREE RECOMMENDS DIVORCE FOR WIFE

The referee appointed to take testimony in the suit for a divorce brought about by Blanche Goldfish against Sam Goldfish has reported in favor of the plaintiff. The defendant is the General Manager of the J. L. Lasky Feature Film Corporation, and is said to have an income of $20,000 a year.

The exact nature of Blanche's complaint against her husband never made the newspapers, but her divorce suit came as no surprise to members of the Lasky family who were intimate with the couple. In the opinion of Bill Lasky, who got it directly from his mother, who was Blanche's sister, "No two people ever lived who were more incompatible than Blanche and Sam. Put that together with the fact that Sam never really loved her much, and you've got trouble."

Blanche was a quiet, mild-mannered woman who liked to listen to music and read poetry and who was so introverted she quit vaudeville rather than have to face an audience every night. Sam, on the other hand, was loud, had an explosive temper, was unreasonable, and seemed to enjoy being the center of attention even if he had to cause controversy to get it.

There was another facet to his character that does not make for a durable marriage. Under the heading of "business," he had a wandering eye for pretty girls. Only it wasn't just his eye that wandered, in the opinion of Joseph J. Cohn, general manager of MGM for many years and one of Goldwyn's first employees. "With Goldwyn, chasing girls was a vocational disease."

That he had a true appreciation of beautiful women there has never been any doubt. He first saw Mae Murray in *The Ziegfeld Follies* of 1915, and immediately made up his mind to get her for his studio. He did. He spent a million dollars of his own money vainly trying to make an actress and box-office attraction out of European-born Anna Sten because he thought her beauty was so extraordinary. And he discovered Vilma Banky in the train station in Budapest while he was waiting to catch a train. He had her signed to a motion picture contract before his train pulled out.

"And he had a real case on Mabel Normand," recalls Joe Cohn. "I don't know if he ever caught her, because she wasn't that crazy about him and spent most of her time trying to avoid Sam. But he never stopped trying. When she was working for us at Fort Lee, Sam used to send his chauffeur-driven Pierce Arrow over to her hotel in Manhattan every morning to pick her up and bring her to the studio."

The Goldwyn Girls, whom he immortalized on film in some of his early-thirties musicals, were also Sam's own invention. Of course, Ziegfeld had the idea first, but Sam saw no reason why he couldn't have a West Coast version of Ziegfeld's long-stemmed American beauties and call them by his own name. So he borrowed the idea, hand picked most of the girls personally, and labeled them the Goldwyn Girls. From their ranks were graduated such stars as Paulette Goddard, Virginia Bruce, and Betty Grable, but probably the most illustrious of all the alumnae is Lucille Ball.

In Hollywood's golden years, any beautiful actress or would-be actress who entered a producer's office alone to be interviewed for a part did so at her own risk. A girl either had to be able to run the hundred-yard dash in ten seconds, or else not seriously object to losing her virginity, or what was left of it. Sam's office was considered no safer than any other producer's.

Actress Wendy Barrie recalls an interview in Goldwyn's office in which the producer chased her around his desk for nearly thirty minutes, trying to get her to submit to his awkward advances. Sam was in good physical shape, but he evidently was no match for Wendy. Soon he was huffing and puffing, and too exhausted from the workout to be much of a threat, even if he did catch her. After one desperate lunge, he suddenly stopped in mid-track, leaned wearily on his desk, and gasped, "I've never been so insulted in my life." It was typical of Sam's unique outlook on life that *he* was the one who'd been insulted.

When Sam pulled the same gambit with Elissa Landi, the actress stood her ground with great dignity, and tried to discourage him with, "Mr. Goldwyn, don't you know I starred in my last picture?"

"You starred in your last picture?" riposted the indignant Sam. "You stank in your last picture!"

Despite these and other stories of Sam's amorous adventures that have traversed the Hollywood grapevine, the good name of Goldwyn remained remarkably untainted by public scandal over the years that he was an active producer, which is more than can be said for most of the other motion picture moguls who were his contemporaries. Either Sam had a good relationship with the press, or else nobody took him seriously as a lover.

"Of course, you don't usually have a scandal unless you've left your wife for another woman or are keeping her on the side," believes Jerry Chodorov. "With Sam, it was probably just a ten-minute stand in his office, probably with his hat on."

But if Sam was playing around with other women behind Blanche's back, it was never brought out in her divorce complaint—at least publicly. On the other hand, incompatibility wasn't grounds for a divorce in New York State in those days; only adultery was. So take that for what you will.

But whatever the grounds, several things are perfectly clear. There was a divorce. The court ordered Sam Goldfish to pay Blanche $2,600 a year alimony and child support, and another $5,200 a year for life "in consideration of the relinquishment by the plaintiff of all claims to Goldwyn's property."

Following the settlement, Blanche moved to southern California, and into her brother's home, taking her three-year-old daughter, Ruth, along with her. For many years Ruth felt the same resentment against Sam as her mother did. As soon as she was old enough to express an opinion, she discarded the name of Goldfish and refused to speak to her father for nearly thirty years.

In 1916, however, Sam was much too preoccupied playing the gay bachelor and trying to get back into the movie business to be very upset about losing a family.

After being ousted so unceremoniously from Famous Players–Lasky, Sam Goldfish, once his initial bitterness over the break subsided, didn't waste much time sitting around feeling sorry for himself. He was, in fact, almost in a position to be envied—not quite thirty-five years old and already very rich.

Still, a man of Sam's vitality and resourcefulness, and who had devoted every working hour of the past three years to building up the Lasky Company was never going to be satisfied merely clipping coupons for the rest of his life.

Sam quickly started making contacts. By October 18, he was already negotiating feverishly to go into business with that triple-threat Yankee Doodle Dandy of Broadway, George M. Cohan. Under the terms of the proposed deal, they would form a motion picture company for the purpose of converting all of Cohan's stage hits to the screen. Cohan would star in the roles he created on the stage, and Sam would produce.

It looked like a formidable combination—Cohan's writing and performing genius, Goldfish's producing and business know-how. But the deal fell apart in November, when Cohan insisted that the new company be called George M. Cohan Film Corporation.

Having been a behind-the-scenes figure in two companies, Sam was in no mood to accept another self-effacing position. When the megalomaniacal Cohan refused to share the credit with Goldfish, Sam quietly bowed out and went looking for partners elsewhere.

He still hadn't learned one lesson: when you have partners, you have trouble. And the more partners, the more trouble. Or perhaps he just didn't have the confidence in himself as a creative producer to try going it alone just yet.

By December, Sam had found four new partners to join him in another production company: two young Broadway producers named Edgar and Arch Selwyn; Edgar's writer wife, Margaret Mayo; and stage producer Arthur Hopkins, with whom Sam had been friendly since he began mingling with the Broadway crowd.

What interested Sam in the Selwyns were their assets. Not monetary assets—with nearly a million dollars in the bank, Sam didn't need partners for financial assistance—but the very large library of copyrighted hit plays over which they had control, and which Sam coveted for films.

The Selwyns were interested in joining Sam but cautious about linking up with a man who had his reputation for getting into disputes with his partners. So before agreeing to anything, Edgar Selwyn checked Sam out with Adolph Zukor.

Being somewhat of a diplomat, Selwyn skirted the issue rather gingerly at first and confined his queries to Sam's business ability. Zukor gave his ex-partner the finest of recommendations, until Edgar Selwyn finally blurted out, "Mr. Zukor, do you know any other reason why I shouldn't go into business with Sam Goldfish?"

Zukor puffed thoughtfully on his cigar, then said, "As far as his honesty and integrity are concerned, there is none. But if you do, you'll be a most unhappy boy."

"Why?" asked Selwyn.

"Because," said Zukor, "Sam is like a Jersey cow that gives the finest milk, but before you can take the bucket away, he has kicked it over."

That scared the Selwyns off, and they notified Sam that they had decided against joining him in the movie venture.

"Give me one good reason," hollered Sam.

Rather than insult the man by telling him what Zukor said about him, the Selwyns avoided the real issue and simply confessed that they had changed their minds about going into the movie business. It had nothing to do with Sam personally.

But with Sam, you needed a better reason than that. Sam kept after them for days, wheedling, arguing, pleading, and even haranguing. A week later he put the same question to the Selwyns that he had asked when they had intially rejected him. "Give me one good reason," Sam demanded.

"We told you," replied Selwyn, wearily.

"Give me another good reason," persisted Sam.

Backed against a wall, Edgar Selwyn hemmed and hawed and finally admitted, somewhat sheepishly, "We heard you're difficult."

"Is that all?"

"Some people even say you're disagreeable," added the other Selwyn.

"Listen," said Sam, "just because I disagree with people doesn't mean I'm disagreeable."

Sam made his point, their resistance caved in, and the company was formed on December 16, 1916. A few days later they opened up offices on Fifth Avenue and Fortieth Street, opposite the New York Public Library, and leased shooting space on the Universal Picture lot.

Sam's new company looked like a real winner. The Selwyns would provide the stories, while Sam would hire the stars, produce, promote, and sell the pictures.

The only thing missing from the setup was a title for the new corporation. The partners wanted to preserve their individual identities, but didn't feel the company should be called anything as mundane as "Goldfish and Selwyn" or "Selwyn and Goldfish." Either way it sounded more like a *schlock* dress business on Seventh Avenue than a class-A motion picture company. They felt the new corporation deserved something more euphonious. So they entered their Fifth Avenue think-tank one afternoon and put their corporate heads together for a few hours.

Exactly who came up with the solution has never been established, but someone at the meeting thought it might be appropriate to amalgamate the two names. Their first effort, arrived at by taking the *Sel* from Selwyn and the *fish* from Goldfish, to form Selfish, was thrown out the moment of its birth. Who in the world could take a company seriously that called itself Selfish Pictures Corporation? So they returned to the drawing board for another stab at it, and this time, by combining the two remaining syllables,

Gold and *wyn*, came up with the ideal name: Goldwyn Pictures Corporation.

This made everybody happy. Particularly Sam. He liked the name Goldwyn so much that it wasn't very long before he decided to annex it for his personal use. In recent years Sam had become disenchanted with the name Goldfish. When he had been in the glove business, the name Goldfish hadn't been a source of embarrassment to him. People in the glove business were serious people, not given to making jokes about a man's name. Some of the appellations they had brought over from the old country were almost as funny as Goldfish. But things were different when Sam stepped out into the amusement world. The name Goldfish was ideal fodder for Broadway wits. Traveling under the Goldfish label, Sam couldn't have inspired more jokes if he had worn a kilt or had a naked woman tattooed on his bald spot.

On being introduced to Goldfish, every Broadway wise guy felt he had to come up with a devastating bon mot or forfeit his reputation as a gagster. One night Sam dropped into the New Amsterdam Theater to see Ziegfeld's *Midnight Frolic*. But Sam was late arriving at the theater, the good seats were already sold out, and the one he was finally shown to was in the rear of the house behind a glass curtain which had been placed there to cut off a draft. When Sam complained that he didn't like sitting behind glass, Gene Buck, Ziegfeld's associate, quipped, "Behind glass is the place for a Goldfish."

In addition to the jokes, another thing was happening. Mail intended for the president of the new company invariably came addressed to Samuel Goldwyn—not Goldfish. The same was true of telephone callers. Only old friends or enemies called Sam by his right name. And the longer the new company was in business, the more critical the confusion over Sam's identity became.

At first Sam viewed this identity crisis with alarm. One of the prime sources of Sam's dissatisfaction in the past was that he had worked so hard building up the name of Lasky and Zukor at the expense of Sam Goldfish. Hardly anybody outside of the business knew who Sam Goldfish was. Now that he was president of his own company, nobody still knew Sam Goldfish. Was he destined to be a behind-the-scenes magnate all his life?

But as the Goldfish jokes proliferated, and the mail continued to pour in addressed to Samuel Goldwyn, Sam came up with the perfect solution. If he legally changed his name to Goldwyn, all of the new company's publicity would have to glorify Sam personally as well.

Sam considered the name change for about a year before he instructed his lawyer, Gabriel L. Hess, to take the matter up with the New York Supreme Court. After all, a man in his mid-thirties doesn't just discard the family name without careful thought.

One thing he failed to take into consideration was the Selwyns' reaction.

The Selwyns were furious when they discovered that their partner was thinking of pilfering half their name, and they tried to stop him legally. But they soon learned they were powerless to stop him. According to the law, a man can call himself anything he wants. And as Sam's attorney pointed out, they certainly didn't have a monopoly on the syllable *wyn*.

Sam was wintering in southern California when he received the following wire from Hess, notifying him of the court's approval of the name change. "SAMUEL GOLDFISH IS DEAD. LONG LIVE SAMUEL GOLDWYN."

Thousands of corporations have been named after men, but it took Sam Goldwyn to get his name from a corporation.

8

The Trouble with Mabel

DESPITE THE BOX-OFFICE success of movies prior to America's entry into World War I, most of the intelligentsia of show business of those days were still highly suspect of the new medium. They believed motion pictures were popular entertainment, but not "class" entertainment. Sam Goldwyn, on the other hand, was out to prove that motion pictures could be both. What's more, he now had the necessary power to back up his convictions.

As president and chief stockholder of Goldwyn Pictures Corporation, he no longer had to be content with being a shadowy (albeit noisy) behind-the-scenes figure. For the first time since he had entered the motion picture field, he not only had his name (well, anyway, half of it) on the company's trademark, but was in a position to put his money where his mouth was. And his mouth, as usual, was all over the place, making his decisions heard in every phase of the new company's operations—from deciding what kinds of pictures they would produce to choosing the stars, from selling the finished product to making damn certain that the name Goldwyn received its due share of hosannas from the public.

Of course, Goldwyn had some very able assistants to advise him. His partners, Edgar and Archie Selwyn, Margaret Mayo, and Arthur Hopkins were all very knowledgeable about literary properties and theatrical values in general. And in the course of 1917 two other able theatrical men came aboard the Goldwyn ship as well—producers Sam Harris and Al Woods.

To aid him in the business end, Goldwyn reached way back to his childhood and tapped Abe Lehr, Jr., to be his chief lieutenant. The two had maintained a close personal relationship since their Gloversville days. Since then, Lehr had given up malingering and proven himself to be an able business administrator. Sam bestowed on him the title of vice president and supervisor in charge of production.

Sam recognized the value of expert advice. However, he was going to make damn sure this time that nobody in the new corporate setup would ever be in a strong enough position to challenge his autonomy if he wished to enforce it.

Whether it was good for the company to have a man of Goldwyn's limited education and show business background in complete command or whether it was just an advantage to the opposition remained to be seen. His former partners, Zukor and Lasky, couldn't have been more delighted and were chortling all over 485 Fifth Avenue. In ousting Goldwyn it never occurred to them that they were creating any serious competition. In their opinions, Sam was a super salesman but a complete clown when it came to the creative end of picturemaking.

In his *Squaw Man* days that undoubtedly was true. But in the four years that had elapsed since then, Goldwyn had acquired considerable self-education—and not just in motion picture making, although his knowledge of that by now was considerable.

When he spoke, he still had a pronounced Polish accent. But despite this and his limited vocabulary, he had a certain kind of charm that some termed irresistible, when he wanted to turn it on.

It's doubtful that he ever cracked any of the "hundred great books," but he did read the newspapers—especially the parts where there might be some mention of Sam Goldwyn or one of his company's motion pictures—and occasionally he struggled through a book of light popular fiction if it had been recommended to him beforehand as a movie possibility. He also must have known something about Sigmund Freud and his works, because as early as 1924 he actually had the gall to make Freud an offer to come to Hollywood and write a movie about psychoanalysis. Freud, of course, was too dedicated to his research to be sidetracked by Hollywood gold, and curtly turned down Goldwyn's offer. But the fact that he made an offer to Freud at all is convincing enough proof that Sam was endeavoring to expand his intellectual interests. Moreover, he was light-years ahead of his competitors in believing a movie could be made on the subject. David Selznick's *Spellbound*, the first movie about psychiatry and psychoanalysis, wasn't made until 1945.

In night school in Gloversville Sam had picked up a smattering of United States history, and through the reading he was forced to do since then in connection with his business of being a producer, he had increased his knowledge of America's past. He was, for example, familiar with the philosophic, if not the actual, contents of the Declaration of Independence and the United States Constitution—enough to have once assured a friend who was waxing pessimistic about the political climate: "I give you my personal guarantee that no one will ever tamper with the United States Constitution."

By the time Sam was thirty-five, he was a devoted patron of the arts. He attended the legitimate theater regularly and saw every play that was produced, both in this country and abroad. He had a box at the Metropolitan Opera House, where he watched his favorite divas perform in operas he didn't quite understand.

He regularly attended symphonic concerts given by the New York Philharmonic, and he was seen at most of the openings of important art exhibits, mingling freely with the Rockefellers, the Mellons, the Du Ponts, and all the other wealthy patrons of the arts.

With so much exposure to the great literary and musical talents of past and present, a little learning and polish was bound to rub off on even the dullest of dullards. And Sam Goldwyn was anything but a dullard, despite the jokes it soon would be fashionable to attribute to his ignorance.

"Sam was a very complex man," avers nine-time Oscar winner Billy Wilder, who, back in the early forties, wrote one of Goldwyn's better pictures, *Ball of Fire*, starring Gary Cooper and Barbara Stanwyck. "The jokes they tell about him—they remind me of what Herman Mankiewicz used to say about Louis B. Mayer. Mankiewicz used to say, 'Mayer may be a shit, but you don't get to be Louis B. Mayer by just being a shit.' That's how I feel about Goldwyn. He didn't get to be Sam Goldwyn by just saying 'Include me out' and 'Im possible.' He had something!"

Bert Granet, another writer-producer who worked for Goldwyn during the same period, recalls, "A bunch of us writers used to sit around trying to analyze just what it was that Goldwyn did have. A writer I was collaborating with summed up Sam's talent the best. He used to say, 'Sam Goldwyn goes up the hill and teaches foxes how to be smart.' "

Goldwyn's native shrewdness alerted him to any new trends in the entertainment world. One trend he saw very clearly in 1917—and which almost proved his undoing—was that it was the *player*, not the play, that suddenly seemed to be the important thing.

When he was with Lasky and De Mille, the three of them had strongly believed that a powerful story was the cornerstone on which every successful production ought to be built. But after Mary Pickford's comet shot up into the show business firmament, it suddenly became all-important for a motion picture company to have a galaxy of big names on its payroll. Theater owners in every part of the country were demanding personalities to advertise on their marquees and in their newspaper ads. Other important values, such as good stories and skillful direction, were quickly overshadowed in the rush to sign up future Mary Pickfords, Charlie Chaplins, and Theda Baras.

As an example of the foolish extremes to which this unhealthy syndrome was being carried, Zukor and Lasky paid the great Italian tenor Enrico Caruso $250,000 to appear in one of their features. Putting an opera singer—

even Caruso—in a silent movie made about as much sense as entering swimmer Mark Spitz in the Kentucky Derby. Without the golden tones of his beautiful voice to enhance his personality, Caruso came off as just another two-hundred-pound Neapolitan who couldn't act. The picture turned out to be one of Famous Players–Lasky's most catastrophic flops.

That gave Sam something to chortle about.

He didn't profit from their mistake, however. Soon he was making worse ones in his rush to corner the world's most glittering names for Goldwyn Pictures.

It wasn't easy, however, acquiring people who were already top box-office attractions. Most of the important names—Mary Pickford, Charlie Chaplin, Theda Bara, and Mabel Normand—were already under contract to other production companies. As a result, Sam had to look to the stage and opera for talent.

His first find was Maxine Elliott, an American-born actress who had enjoyed a twenty-year reign as the most beautiful woman on the London stage. At the time she was brought to Sam's attention by Arch Selwyn, she had just come over from England and had opened to smash reviews in *The Eternal Magdalene* on Broadway, early in 1917. "You ought to sign her up right away," urged Selwyn. "I hear the Shuberts are already after her for pictures."

Sam contacted the actress and had no trouble luring her to his office for an interview. He later confessed, in the words of his ghostwriter, that he had "never seen a human being more radiantly lovely." Her outstanding looks, plus her reputation for those looks in every hamlet in America, inspired Sam to start negotiations immediately with her agent. After a spirited battle, Sam managed to secure Maxine Elliott's services for two pictures at $1,000 a week, and immediately thereafter announced to the newspapers that the actress would be the star of the Goldwyn Pictures Corporation's first epic, which would be shot in the studios they had rented in Fort Lee, New Jersey.

Maxine Elliott's first picture for Goldwyn was *The Fighting Odds*, written by Irvin S. Cobb and Roi Cooper Megrue, both well-known magazine fiction writers.

To insure its excellence, Sam assigned Arthur Hopkins to produce it, Allan Dwan, one of the industry's most celebrated movie directors, to direct and take actual charge of the production, and hired Hugo Ballin, a well-known portrait painter of the period, to design the sets.

Hiring a celebrated artist to design the sets was an innovation conceived by Arthur Hopkins, who thought it was about time movie sets had a little class and style. Until then, most movies looked as if they had been shot in front of a garage wall.

Since Sam was out to make great pictures—Goldwyn epics, so to speak—
he eagerly embraced Arthur Hopkins's idea, and the results elevated the art
of movie-set designing from that time forward.

One idea of Hopkins's that didn't turn out favorably was his suggestion
to make the film without subtitles. Hopkins felt that it slowed the picture
down to interrupt the action with subtitles explaining the dialogue. Being
an innovator, he was certain that all points necessary to understanding the
story could be gotten over in the action, if the scenes were written and
directed properly.

The idea excited the publicity-conscious Sam, and he gave Hopkins an
enthusiastic go-ahead. Sam was sure it would be a great selling point to the
nations's exhibitors if he could advertise *The Fighting Odds* as the first
"wordless picture."

Unfortunately, the effect was disastrous. When Sam screened the picture
for the first time in front of the exhibitors, the reception was cool. The
bewildered theater owners admitted that a wordless picture was a noble ex-
periment, but said they thought their customers would resent not knowing
what was taking place on the screen—just as they did.

At the last minute before release, the picture was yanked and clumsy
subtitles inserted.

Unfortunately, understanding the picture was only half the problem; the
other half was Maxine Elliott. She may have been great on the stage, but
she was definitely not the film type. The camera seemed to magnify her age
and a tendency to overact. Her acting got laughs where it should have
brought tears.

In addition to the film's basic shortcomings, just around the time when
The Fighting Odds was being released—in April 1917—America entered
World War I. With enough ballyhoo, Sam might have been able, under ordinary circumstances, to overcome the reviews and bad word-of-mouth *The
Fighting Odds* was getting among the exhibitors. But the war spelled immediate doom to the Goldwyn Corporation's first release. Until America entered the war, American-made pictures were all the rage in the neutral
countries of Europe. A picture that was considered a stinker in America
could still get back its costs—and perhaps even turn a profit—by the time it
finished its European engagements. But with America's participation in the
war came enormous transportation difficulties in this country and abroad.
Because of troop movement priorities, filmmakers were unable to procure
space on ships and trains to move their product to the distributors. *The
Fighting Odds* couldn't fight those odds. Not only was it a total failure, but it
caused some exhibitors in the United States to cancel contracts for all future
Goldwyn pictures.

Sam quickly sprang back from that disaster with an even larger disaster—

Mary Garden, Chicago's Scottish-born opera star. Sam had first heard of her at the beginning of the war and naively assumed that movie audiences would be attracted by her prestige in operatic endeavors. Meanwhile Miss Garden had gone to Scotland to help the war effort. So Sam wired his London representative to contact her to see if she would be interested in going to work for Goldwyn Pictures. Aside from evincing no interest in becoming a movie star, Miss Garden was caught up in her hospital work and wouldn't even listen to a Goldwyn offer.

Undiscouraged by the snub, Sam waited for her to come back to America, which she did in 1917 to appear at the Met. After her opening performance, Sam immediately contacted her, filled her full of compliments, and wangled an invitation to tea in her apartment at the Ritz.

After engaging her in small talk for about an hour, Sam got around to the real purpose of his call. Mary Garden admitted she was a natural for films, but didn't feel that Sam could pay her enough to make her time spent away from the opera worthwhile.

"How much would you like?" asked Sam, prepared to write a check.

"One hundred and fifty thousand dollars," she replied.

Sam wasn't prepared to write a check quite so large. At the same time he didn't turn her down and immediately after leaving her regal presence called a meeting with his partners Edgar Selwyn, Arthur Hopkins, and Margaret Mayo.

Evidently they were all fooled by her prestige in opera. The three of them heartily endorsed Sam's recommendation that Goldwyn Pictures sign her for the sum she was asking. Sam didn't even dicker.

The news that Sam had signed Mary Garden to a film contract made headlines all over the country and confirmed his belief that he had made the right move. To capitalize further on her operatic prestige, Sam decided to star Mary Garden not in an ordinary picture, but in *Thaïs*, a French opera and most widely known of her operatic roles.

To do this, Sam parted with another $10,000 for the purchase of the American rights from its celebrated author, Anatole France. Sam was such a free spender in those days that he bought the rights to *Thaïs* even though it was uncopyrighted in America, and he wasn't legally obligated to do so. However, he did figure, why make an enemy of the French? The picture would probably earn back its expenses in France alone.

Once the picture went into production, Sam and everyone else connected with it, including Fred Crane, its director, had a premonition of disaster. Mary Garden's acting was atrocious, and she would not take direction. Her idea of acting was to heave her bosom, roll her eyes, and flail the air with her arms as violently as she was used to doing on the stage of the Metropolitan Opera House. But the kind of acting that was acceptable to opera buffs, who were there to hear her sing, would never do for silent pictures. Without music the camera only magnified her bosom-heaving and eye-rolling and turned the picture into a farce.

Not only was her acting bad, but she had the wrong temperament for being a film star. She resented, for example, any tampering with the opera's libretto by the scenario writer, Margaret Mayo, whose job it was to transfer *Thaïs* to the silent screen and still retain something of what it had with music.

The death of Thaïs in the finale was almost the death of Goldwyn Pictures. Mary Garden had quarreled bitterly with Margaret Mayo over her conception of the famous scene. In the operatic version, Thaïs the saint triumphed over Thaïs the woman. In Mayo's script it was just the reverse. Mary Garden felt that this change was intolerable, and when the producer, director, and Margaret Mayo refused to go back to the Anatole France ending, she consented to do the scene as written, but she walked through it. When Mary Garden saw the scene in the dailies, she cried out in anguish, "I knew it. Oh, I knew it. Imagine me, the great Thaïs, dying like an acrobat!"

A moment later she rushed from the projection room down to Margaret Mayo's office. "Did you see it?" stormed Mary Garden. "Did you see the way you made me die? Imagine a saint dying like that!"

Margaret Mayo gave her an icy stare, and said, "Miss Garden, you would have a hard time proving to anyone that you are a saint!"

Thaïs opened at the Strand Theater in New York late in 1917. Sam took a girlfriend to the opening, and despite his own misgivings about the film, was heartened to see the tears welling up in his companion's eyes during Mary Garden's death scene. Perhaps he and his partners had been too self-critical, he thought hopefully. But his hopes were dashed as the lights went up and his girlfriend turned to him with tears still rolling down her cheeks and said apologetically, "I never cry in movies, Sam, but this one's so awful I couldn't help it, knowing how much it means to you."

The critics and exhibitors had the same reaction. Audiences did, too. In addition, some people had Mary Garden confused with Mary Gardner, a heroine of the five-cent-picture days, who wasn't any kind of a star name. That, too, kept them away in droves.

Mary Garden wound up costing the Goldwyn Corporation a fortune—not only in dollars but in ill will.

Before giving up, Sam made a second picture with Mary Garden, *The Splendid Sinner*. This was a nonoperatic vehicle and was a better picture. But because Mary Garden had bombed so at the box office in her first movie role, *The Splendid Sinner* fared little better.

Sam had finally learned his lesson about opera stars in pictures. He decided it would be safer to turn to the screen as a source of raw acting material.

As soon as their contracts were up, he enticed Madge Kennedy, a very accomplished comedienne, away from Paramount, and Mae Marsh, a star in *The Birth of a Nation*, away from D. W. Griffith. He managed this by dangling large sums of money before their greedy eyes. Nothing comparable to the $15,000 a week he paid Mary Garden, but $3,000 a week was not to be sneezed at either.

Sam's press agents had barely finished heralding these converts to Goldwyn Pictures to the public when Sam got wind of the fact that one of the nation's biggest box-office attractions, Mabel Normand, was unhappy at Mack Sennett's Studios, and that there was a chance she could be wooed away from there if he acted fast enough.

Until then, Mabel Normand had been the exclusive property of Mack Sennett. She had appeared in most of his best Keystone Kops comedies—some costarring with another newcomer to the screen, Charlie Chaplin—and was considered by Goldwyn to be "the world's greatest comedienne."

Sam had a personal yen for Miss Normand as well and had been wanting to entice the vivacious, brown-eyed actress into the Goldwyn fold ever since he and his partners had formed the new company. But until now there had seemed little chance that she would leave Mack Sennett, who was her lover as well as employer, to perform for anyone else.

A picture called *Mickey*, produced by Mack Sennett in Hollywood in the spring of 1916, changed all that. Sennett tried to keep Miss Normand out of *Mickey*, feeling she didn't fit the starring role. She, on the other hand, loved the script, coveted the role, and threatened to quit both him and the Sennett Studios if she didn't get it.

Sennett relented because he didn't want to lose his girlfriend, but his first hunch had been correct. She wasn't right for it. From the start, *Mickey* seemed to be one of those jinxed pictures. Delays caused by illness, rain, and money problems kept the picture in production for months. During its filming, three directors quit because they refused to put up with Mabel Normand's prima donna behavior.

When the picture was finally completed, Dick Jones, the fourth director to be hired, had a fight with Mack Sennett, claiming the producer owed him thousands in back salary. When Sennett refused to pay him any more, Jones stole the negative and hid it in a safe deposit vault. Sennett was compelled to hire detectives to track the negative down, and then had to go to court to force the director to give it up.

It took a year before the picture, already written off as a flop, was released. While Sennett was deciding whether or not to release *Mickey*, the personal trouble between him and Mabel Normand grew stormier. In mid-

1917, the romance between Sennett and Normand blew up—for good, many people thought.

When Goldwyn heard of this development, he immediately contacted Mabel Normand in Hollywood and secretly arranged a meeting with her in a suite in the Hotel Muehlebach in Kansas City. There he signed her to a five-year contract, which called for $1,000 a week, with increases up to $5,000 a week by the fifth year.

Though Goldwyn figured he had pulled a great coup, Sennett was actually delighted to get Mabel Normand off his hands. *Mickey* had cost him $150,000 to make—an unheard-of sum for those days. That meant it would have to gross $300,000 to break even. The way the picture looked in Sennett's projection room, he felt he would be lucky if it grossed *three* dollars.

But Sam was overjoyed. Not only had he signed one of the country's leading box-office attractions for his press agents to shout to the world about, but now was *his* chance to make it with Mabel Normand.

According to those two chroniclers of the love life of the Hollywood gods—the late Hedda Hopper and Louella Parsons—there wasn't any doubt that Sam Goldwyn was deeply in love with Mabel Normand before he married Frances. Evidently he wasn't alone in his feelings. Everyone in Hollywood was in love with Mabel at one time or another when she was an important star. In his autobiography, Charlie Chaplin admits making a pass at her in her dressing room one evening after the two had finished their stint before Mack Sennett's cameras. While Charlie was helping her into her coat, he stole a kiss. Mabel accepted the kiss graciously, but then warded him off forever by saying, "I'm sorry, Charlie. I'm not your type. Neither are you mine."

Goldwyn wasn't, either, but once he had her under contract he did everything in his power to make her warm up to him—from giving her the use of his Pierce Arrow and chauffeur to providing her with a clause in her contract that bound Goldwyn Pictures to pay for half the clothes she wore in her movies. A Barbra Streisand or Elizabeth Taylor could have broken the company by taking advantage of such a clause, but Mabel Normand didn't even send Goldwyn a bill. If she'd been anyone else, Goldwyn would have gladly overlooked this, but in her case he wanted to impress her with his generosity. So he sent for her one day and asked, "How come I do not get a bill from you for your clothes?"

"Sammy my boy," she began—she always called him "Sammy my boy"—"I have to tell you the truth. I've bought so many clothes I didn't feel right letting you pay anything at all."

An examination of her department store bills proved that she wasn't exaggerating. She had bought twelve of everything—from the most expensive dresses to small accessories. Sam gave Mabel a lecture on the evils of being too extravagant, but since it was her wish, he didn't reimburse her.

Like many of the early movie stars who suddenly found themselves earning more money than they could possibly spend in normal ways, Mabel Normand had no idea of the value of a dollar. If she happened to take a liking to one of the "little people," as she called salespeople or lunchroom workers, she'd reward her or him with a hundred-dollar bill or a correspondingly priced gift and give it no more thought than if it had cost her only fifty cents.

At one point the Goldwyn accounting office showed an overage of $70,000 in their books. Abe Lehr traced it to uncashed checks made out to Mabel Normand. Confronted with this fact, Mabel sheepishly confessed that she cashed checks only as she needed them.

A paternalistic streak suddenly surfaced in Sam, who feared that someday his favorite star of the screen might wind up penniless. He talked Mabel into letting the accounting office invest half her weekly salary in Liberty bonds. And later on, when her contract called for her to be making even bigger money, she permitted Sam and Lehr to put her excess cash into some very lucrative real estate investments in southern California.

In matters other than money, however, she was not so agreeable. Her first picture for Goldwyn Pictures was *Joan of Plattsburg*—the story of a farmgirl who came to the big city. The picture featured a trained goose that was supposed to follow his mistress everywhere she went, just like Mary's little lamb. The goose took his work seriously. He used to follow Mabel around even when the cameras weren't grinding. One day on the studio street Mabel bent over to tie her shoe, and the goose took a nip of her ungirdled rump. Her dignity wounded more than her flesh, the tomboy Mabel jumped on the startled goose and knocked it senseless. Then she seized it by the neck, dragged it into Abe Lehr's office, and dropped it at his feet. "There's your damn man-eating duck," she screamed angrily. "If he bites me on the ass again, I'll wring his damn neck."

Aside from her explosive temper, Mabel had another fault. She was always late for work on the set in the morning, inconsiderately keeping extras and other members of the cast and crew waiting for hours. The director, of course, would be fuming, for every hour of delay meant more unnecessary dollars added to the budget, for which he was personally accountable.

Eventually, the director would have to send out a search party to find her and bring her back. Usually she'd be found in her dressing room, casually writing letters or reading a book. Her excuse for not showing up on the set until she was ready would always be the same. "I'm sorry," she would say, "but I just can't be funny so early in the morning."

After frequent complaints about her tardiness reached Sam's ears, he sat her down and gave her a fatherly lecture in which he explained that the studio could not afford to hold up shooting until she was in the mood to be funny. With a flutter of her long eyelashes, Mabel focused her large brown eyes on him and promised to do better in the future. And she did—for a few days. But when she reverted to her former dilatory ways, Sam turned the matter over to his ace hatchet man, Abe Lehr. Feeling the way he did about Mabel personally, Sam feared that perhaps he could not talk sternly enough to Mabel to make her reform. But she of the winsome big brown eyes was able to wrap Lehr around her finger just as she did the big boss.

After many attempts to get her to reform, Lehr too found himself completely frustrated. One day, when she hadn't shown up on the set by noon, he marched into her dressing room, determined to threaten to tear up her contract or take her to court if she didn't cooperate. But before he could upbraid her, she held up her hand, and said, "Wait—before you say anything." And then she reached behind her back and pulled out a photograph of herself, autographed as follows:

> To Abe, my favorite—
> Roses are red,
> Violets are blue,
> When I'm late
> I think of you.
> Love and kisses,
> Mabel

"That's the reason I'm late," she said. "I was thinking up something nice to write on your photograph. I didn't want to say just 'Yours sincerely' or something stupid like that."

Lehr's face softened perceptibly, and he forgot completely about disciplining her, as he said rather meekly, "They're waiting for you on the set, dear. Come on, I'll walk you over."

Mabel Normand's behavior notwithstanding, *Joan of Plattsburg* turned out to be the Goldwyn Pictures Corporation's first real winner. Unfortunately, its success led Sam to believe that there might be something to the star system after all. Soon he was negotiating for the services of Pauline Frederick and Geraldine Farrar, two well-known but slightly over-the-hill beauties from the stage.

At the time, Pauline Frederick was under contract to Famous Players–Lasky, where she had made several successful films under Adolph Zukor's personal supervision. But on a tip from her husband, playwright Willard Mack, that her contract with Zukor was about to expire and that she was not interested in re-signing with Famous Players, Sam met with the actress one night in her dressing room at the Lyceum Theater to discuss a deal. Goldwyn and Pauline Frederick hit it off immediately, and he signed her for $3,000 a week.

The whole thing was accomplished without any publicity, so it came as a shock to Zukor when he finally learned that one of his top stars had defected to Goldwyn Pictures. In a meeting between Zukor and Goldwyn in a lobby of a hotel in Atlantic City, Zukor accused his ex-partner of stealing Pauline Frederick away from Famous Players.

"I cross my heart, I did not steal her," replied Goldwyn. "She didn't want to re-sign with you."

"Goldfish, I don't believe you," screamed the normally quiet Zukor.

"Are you calling me a liar?" asked Goldwyn.

"No, I am just saying I don't believe you," insisted Zukor.

The argument became so heated that the two of them started exchanging blows. An actress named Alice Joyce succeeded in separating the two warring moguls, but not before Sam wound up with a glorious shiner. The black eye hurt, but the pain was trivial compared with some of the headaches Sam would soon be getting from other sources.

It soon turned out that Pauline Frederick was more of a prima donna than Mabel Normand. No matter what story Sam picked out for her to star in, she'd come back with, "I don't like it."

She was always very cagey about saying exactly what it was that she didn't like, but after interrogating her over a period of weeks, during which she was drawing an enormous salary without doing anything for it, Sam gradually discovered the source of her dissatisfaction. She simply didn't like any scenario that had not been written by her husband. She wanted to keep it all in the family.

Weary of fighting with her, Sam agreed to star her in one of her husband's scenarios, *Ann of the Rockies* and assigned Hobert Henley to direct it at the old Biograph Studio in Manhattan, where they were temporarily renting space.

Sam had several pictures in production simultaneously in various widely scattered sections of the city and was running himself ragged trying to do everything himself. So he imported a young man named Joseph J. Cohn from the West Coast to assist him. Prior to then, Cohn had been employed by Triangle Productions in Culver City, California, as an all-around trouble-shooter.

"I want you to get right up to Biograph Studios in the Bronx and keep an eye on things on the Pauline Frederick set," Sam told Cohn the first morning he reported for work. "Hobert Henley, the director, is in complete charge."

Cohn took a cab to the Biograph Studios and walked on the set, just in time to hear Willard Mack announcing to the director, "This is one picture that's going to be made the way I wrote it."

Henley, who'd been taking liberties with Mack's script, insisted the author had no right to interfere.

Fearing a shutdown of production if a serious fight ensued, Cohn ran to the nearest telephone and called Sam. "Mr. Goldwyn," he said breathlessly, "you told me Hobert Henley was going to be in charge, but I was just on the set and I heard Willard Mack say that this was one picture that's going to be made the way he wrote it. Mr. Goldwyn, what should I do?"

"I've been fighting with those bastards for three weeks now," exclaimed Sam in his high-pitched voice. "You fight with them for a change!" And he hung up.

The picture eventually was completed, but Pauline Frederick never stopped giving Sam headaches of one kind or another. After Sam convinced her that every story she appeared in couldn't be written by her husband (because he wasn't that prolific), Miss Frederick started picking on the scripts submitted to her on the grounds that they weren't up to the material her rival on the lot, Geraldine Farrar, was getting.

Desperate, Sam devised a tactic to deal with the two actresses. As was her custom, Pauline Frederick strode importantly into Sam's office one day and dropped a script on his desk. "I hate this story," she told him.

Sam read the title on the cover, then looked shocked. "How'd you get this?" he screamed. "This was supposed to go to Miss Farrar." He called in Joe Cohn and bawled him out for sending Miss Frederick the wrong script. "This one's supposed to go to Geraldine Farrar," roared Sam.

"I'm sorry, Mr. Goldwyn," said Cohn, feigning surprise.

As Sam started to hand the script to Cohn, Miss Frederick grabbed it from him and clutched it to her bosom. "Oh, no, you don't," she said. "I read it first. I'm doing this one, or I'm quitting the studio."

Sam worked the same bit of psychology on Geraldine Farrar, and soon he had two pictures grinding away on the set at Fort Lee.

But that wasn't the end of Sam's problems with temperamental stars. They quickly found new ways to torture the boss. Geraldine Farrar, for example, had spent most of her life in the legitimate theater, performing in light opera, but when she started working on a movie stage, she found that the dead silence inhibited her acting. At her request, Sam hired a string quartet to underscore her scenes while they were being shot. Since these were silent movies, the picture itself did not benefit from this extra expense. But if that's what it took to make her happy, Sam had no choice but to give in to her demands.

Then Pauline Frederick walked off her set, seemingly without reason—until she insisted on a meeting with Sam.

"Geraldine Farrar has musicians on her set," she complained to Sam.

"Why haven't I? I can't do my best work without music, either. I'd like some violins to be playing."

"But, Miss Frederick," pleaded Sam, "when you were with Zukor you had no music, yet you were doing your best work for him."

"Things have changed. I need music."

"Okay, I'll give you one violin," relented Sam.

"I want three," demanded Miss Frederick. "Just like Geraldine Farrar, or I quit."

Sam wearily acquiesced and gave her three violins. Then Mabel Normand heard what the other stars were getting and, not to be outdone, asked for a seventeen-piece jazz band, claiming it helped her comedy.

An entire jazz band, of course, was an enormous extravagance, but Sam couldn't afford to offend Mabel Normand. Her pictures—*Joan of Plattsburg, Dodging a Million,* and *Peck's Bad Girl*—were the only ones making any money for him. Moreover, he was paying her less than his other stars— only $1,000 a week.

In early 1918, fate struck Sam what turned out to be the first of a number of blows that soon had Goldwyn Pictures Corporation staggering under weighty financial losses.

In 1918, Mack Sennett, fearing the worst, but having little choice if he expected to recoup any of his investment, decided to release *Mickey*, the last picture Mabel had made for him. To everyone's surprise, *Mickey* caught on at the nation's box offices and became the most successful film of its time. It grossed $18 million. Soon Mack Sennett's company was taking out huge newspaper ads, proclaiming Mack Sennett's *Mickey* the "biggest success since *The Birth of a Nation.*"

Mickey was Sennett's, but Mabel Normand wasn't, and Sennett wanted her back desperately. In London at the time *Mickey* caught on in the United States, Sennett phoned Mabel by transatlantic cable and subtly put the bug in her ear that she was worth more money than Goldwyn was paying her and that she shouldn't have to wait until the fifth year of her contract to get what she was really worth. Mabel Normand wouldn't have been a movie star if she hadn't agreed.

"Sammy my boy," Mabel told Goldwyn. "I want five thousand dollars a week now."

"We have a contract," insisted Sam. "Not one penny more."

When Sam refused to budge on his position, hotheaded Mabel announced she was through with pictures and promptly sailed away for a rendezvous with Sennett in Europe.

Unable to cope with the problem because of his emotional involvement with his favorite actress, Sam dumped the matter of resolving her contractual complaints into Abe Lehr's lap. Lehr spent the next two months on the transatlantic phone, trying to coax Mabel into returning. Finally, after threatening Mabel with a breach of contract suit, and Sennett with a separate legal action for trying to "steal her from Goldwyn Studios," Lehr persuaded the actress to accept a compromise offer of $1,500 a week.

So she returned to Goldwyn Pictures, but she resented being forced to work at those "slave wages," and purposely made things as difficult for Sam and his partners as she possibly could. In addition to sticking to her normal habits of always showing up late for work, she hit upon patriotism as a novel means of bugging her employers.

Since it seemed that every patriotic American not in the service in the spring of 1918 was either wrapping bandages, driving an ambulance, or selling Liberty bonds, Mabel decided to do her bit for the war effort by being a one-woman camp show.

Unfortunately, this was at the expense of Goldwyn Pictures. Instead of showing up for work on the set in the morning, Mabel would often drop into one of the several large training camps in the vicinity of Fort Lee and spend the day there putting on impromptu shows for the men about to go overseas. The idea was commendable, but it cost the studio a fortune. By the time Sam or Abe Lehr tracked her down, they'd have lost a day's shooting.

Mabel didn't appreciate being rebuked about her patriotic gestures either and got back at her bosses in some peculiar ways. Once, unbeknownst to Lehr, she sprayed his suit with several ounces of cheap perfume and smeared some lipstick on his trousers in the vicinity of his fly. Then, when the executive was on his way home, she phoned his wife, posing as an anonymous friend, and said she had just seen her husband entering a very well-known Manhattan whorehouse, and suggested Mrs. Lehr look into it.

Lehr nearly lost his wife on account of that one.

Since Sam was single, Mabel couldn't pull that prank on him, but when she was sufficiently miffed at Goldwyn, she used to take great delight in doing extremely funny, but cruel, imitations of him at parties. An accomplished mimic, she could ape Sam's mannerisms and malapropisms, complete with Polish accent, with extraordinary fidelity. Since the first Goldwynism has never been pinpointed, it isn't too much of a strain on credulity to pin the responsibility for spreading Goldwynisms—in the beginning at least—on Mabel Normand's puckish sense of humor. Mabel had her captive audiences at fashionable film-folk soirees rolling on the plush carpeting of living rooms from coast to coast.

Tales of Mabel's disrespect for her boss inevitably got back to Sam (probably through his best friends), but he tried to be philosophical about it. After all, her pictures were making money for the studio. It wasn't in her contract that she also had to love him.

Despite the return of Mabel Normand, box-office receipts for Goldwyn Pictures dropped drastically during the last year of the war. People weren't going to movie theaters as much—partly because so many young men had been drafted and were out of circulation, and partly because there was a flu epidemic that kept people home. The flu epidemic, in fact, caused many theaters across the land to close.

Added to this were the customary wartime shortages—transportation, fuel, electricity, and a scarcity of labor—that were responsible for inflated production costs. The labor shortage became so acute that at one point Goldwyn Pictures was forced to shoot at four different studios around New Jersey and Manhattan in order to complete one day's production of a single picture.

By spring, the company's weekly nut was somewhere in the neighborhood of $90,000, and it was becoming increasingly difficult for Sam's controller to meet the weekly payroll. It was apparent that things couldn't continue in that manner for very much longer.

It was enough to make a man rue the day a Democrat ever became president. That *momzer* in the White House was responsible for all of Sam's troubles. He had promised to keep America *out* of the war, not get us into it and ruin the picture business. Between his tariff policies and getting us involved in the war, Wilson succeeded in making a devout Republican out of Goldwyn for the rest of his life.

Sam Goldwyn had never failed to respond to a challenge, and his World War I period was no exception.

One morning shortly after the Wilson administration had handed down an edict making it mandatory for all businesses to curtail its usage of energy by 50 percent, as well as proclaiming heatless and lightless days, Sam instructed Joe Cohn to gather all the Goldwyn employees in the studio's largest projection room.

"What for?" asked Cohn.

"For a pep talk," responded Sam enigmatically.

That afternoon the beleaguered Sam strode into the projection room and faced a large gathering of his loyal employees. Sam was never more charming or eloquent.

"Ladies and gentlemen," he began, "I go into business, and we have lightless and heatless days and coalless nights. Thank you very much for taking a fifty percent cut in salary!"

And before anybody could open his mouth to object, Sam quickly ducked through a side exit and disappeared.

9

Don't Worry, Maurice, You'll Make Good Yet

THE MAJORITY OF SAM'S employees threatened to join the army rather than take a blanket 50 percent cut in salary.

After one of Sam's pictures had to be halted midway through production for lack of facilities, its director, Harry Beaumont, said to Sam that the only sure way of beating the wartime energy shortage was to start shooting his films in southern California instead of Fort Lee. In Hollywood, Beaumont pointed out, they would no longer have to be dependent on artificial light. They could take advantage of all that free sunshine, just as most of their competitors were already doing. And just as Sam, Lasky, and De Mille had done when they made their historic film, *The Squaw Man*.

Sam agreed heartily and dispatched Harry Beaumont and his crew to southern California to look for a site where they could not only finish filming the picture they had already started, but if it proved a satisfactory location, settle their camera crews there permanently. The administration offices, where Sam was quartered, would remain on Fifth Avenue and Fortieth Street.

Because the price of acreage in Hollywood and its immediate environs was already terribly inflated due to the picture boom, Lehr investigated another lead. He'd heard through a director friend, Tom Moore, that Triangle Pictures in Culver City, California, was up for sale. If not actually up for sale, it was on the verge of being put on the market, because it was in trouble.

The Triangle Company was owned jointly by three giants of the industry—Tom Ince, Mack Sennett, and D. W. Griffith. It consisted of twenty-two acres between what is now Washington and Jefferson boulevards in Culver City. Triangle had obtained the land several years earlier from Harry Culver, a real estate developer who gave it to Ince, Sennett, and Griffith absolutely free as a promotion gimmick. He figured a major film studio in the area would bring business and prosperity to the town to which he had given his name.

And he was right. The Triangle Company, featuring such stars as Charlie Root, William S. Hart, and Charlie Chaplin, prospered for a while. And because of it, Culver City grew into a thriving southern California community.

But by the time Goldwyn Pictures decided to move west, Triangle's three partners were squabbling bitterly. According to what Harry Beaumont had heard, Griffith and Sennett felt that Tom Ince was "robbing them blind," and had ordered him to "get out of our studio."

"I'll do that," replied Ince. "But first take your studio off my land."

What Griffith and Sennett weren't aware of was that when Harry Culver gave them the land, Ince had taken the deed in his own name only. He also had most of the studio's stars under personal contract to him. Evidently Griffith and Sennett were better picturemakers than businessmen and financiers.

The upshot of the whole imbroglio was that neither side had the resources to buy out the other. Which meant that if the three partners ever expected to become disentangled, they'd have to sell to an outsider.

Abe Lehr wasted little time in wrapping up a deal to buy Triangle Pictures. In a matter of days he had arranged to buy the whole setup—land, stages, administration buildings, and dressing rooms—for $325,000. On a businessman's hunch, he also picked up a neighboring twenty acres at only $2,500 an acre, which totaled just $50,000.

Goldwyn's financial wizards in the East gave their blessings to the Triangle deal, but when they heard of the purchase of the additional acreage, they were furious at Lehr and ready to fire him, and would have if Sam, out of loyalty, hadn't interfered. At the time, of course, it was an unnecessary expenditure, but in the long run it proved to be a most judicious buy. In 1970, when those twenty acres, which for years had been MGM's back lot, were sold off, they went for twenty million dollars. In the summer of 1918, however, Goldwyn Pictures Corporation was struggling to keep its head above water. Sam and his partners had to borrow a huge sum from the bank in order to purchase the property in Culver City.

In addition to the Goldwyn Corporation's somewhat shaky financial position, its president suffered an unexpected physical setback that put him on the disabled list for much of the summer of 1918, and left the running of the company—plus the details of the move west—largely in the hands of Sam's inexperienced associates. And according to a later assessment made by Sam, the decisions his partners made when he was in the hospital cost the company thousands of unwisely spent dollars and nearly ruined the Goldwyn Pictures Corporation at its inception.

It's ironic that it should have been something physical that hampered the activities of the usually dynamic Sam during that very important summer, because for all of his life prior to then he had taken exceedingly good care of his body, and in the future would gain something of a reputation for being a physical fitness nut. He rarely smoked or drank—only chocolate sodas or root beer floats—and he was an incurable walker, never riding when he could go by foot. Even when he was much older he stuck religiously to his rigorous walking regimen, and when necessary, inflicted this habit on his companions as well.

In the summer of 1918, Sam Goldwyn was only thirty-six years old and not content to get his exercise just by walking. His lawyer, Gabriel Hess, had, in fact, talked him into joining a New York athletic club and taking up handball.

"You'll meet a lot of important contacts there," promised Hess.

One of the first contacts Sam made was with another handball player. The two collided in midcourt, and Sam fell down and broke his ankle. He spent the rest of the summer in a hospital bed with his injured leg in a hammock. Even a human dynamo like Sam found it impossible to direct the operations of a motion picture company from there—especially a company whose main components had just moved three thousand miles to the west, and whose misfortunes seemed to be compounding with the passing of every day.

Between the war shortages, the ruthless competition from his bitterest rivals, Famous Players–Lasky, the colossal failure of some of the Goldwyn Corporation's highest-budget films, the necessity of buying the Culver City property, the disappointing performances of most of his high-salaried stars, and now suddenly a broken ankle, it seemed as if the gods were ganging up on Sam in a most unjust way.

But the full realization of the deep trouble Sam was in didn't really hit home until a committee of his associates, including Al Woods, Arthur Hopkins, and Edgar Selwyn, called on him in the hospital when he was still recuperating and told him that they thought bankruptcy was inevitable. According to the Goldwyn Corporation's controller, Melvin Schay, they didn't have the cash in their checking account to meet next week's payroll.

Normally an optimistic individual, Sam lay awake all night in a bed of indecision. As the company's largest single stockholder, he was personally responsible for bank loans amounting to $900,000. Bankruptcy may have been unavoidable, as his partners indicated, but he was not willing to go that humiliating route and see everything that he'd been building for the past two years go down the drain. At least not without putting up a strong fight.

His first day out of the hospital, Sam held a conference with Melvin

Schay and arrived at a strategy that would give the Goldwyn Corporation a brief reprieve. The company had branch offices in twenty-five different cities around the country. Each one of these branches kept between $2,000 and $3,000 in cash on hand—money received from current film rentals. By extracting the cash from each of the agencies, Sam figured out that they'd have enough to meet one week's payroll.

"What happens the week after?" asked Schay glumly.

Sam shrugged. "One crisis at a time," he answered. He was sure that something or someone would come to his rescue if he thought positively.

During those bleak days in the fall of 1918, when receivership was threatening, Mabel Normand walked into Sam's office one afternoon holding a long brown envelope. "Sammy my boy," she said, "I have a present for you." And she dropped the envelope on his desk.

Opening it, Sam took out about $70,000 in Liberty bonds and the deeds to some valuable property he had advised her to buy. "Vat's this about?" asked Sam.

"It's all I've got," said Mabel, "but if it'll tide you over, it's yours."

Sam was touched, but declined her offer, saying rather poetically, "I made you put your money away for *your* rainy day, not mine."

Despite Mabel's insistence, Sam would not accept her help. He had a feeling that his luck was about to change. Miraculously, it did. The war ended the following week, and with the signing of the armistice, the fortunes of the Goldwyn Pictures Corporation immediately started to improve. With no restrictions on transportation, the European picture market suddenly opened up. Production costs declined sharply with the return of cheap energy. Demobilization brought two million soldiers back to civilian life, and with it more activity at the nation's film box offices. Theaters that had been forced to close during the war were now reopening, and some new ones were being built to take advantage of what was turning out to be a real movie boom.

The first two pictures the Goldwyn Corporation filmed on its new Culver City lot—*Laughing Bill Hyde* and *Thirty a Week*—were also showing heartening signs of life at the nation's box offices when they opened in January 1919. *Laughing Bill Hyde* was a Western starring humorist Will Rogers in his first film, and *Thirty a Week* featured a talented young Southern actress named Tallulah Bankhead. Until then, Tallulah Bankhead was a complete unknown. She'd had one bit in a movie and a walk-on in a Broadway play, and it was to Sam's credit that he recognized her talent and put her in *Thirty a Week*, in which she skillfully portrayed an heiress who falls in love with the family chauffeur and runs away with him. In reviewing *Thirty a Week*, *Motion Picture* magazine said it was "an extremely entertaining and well made film—especially when compared with all the mediocrity currently being exhibited in the nation's movie theaters." And about the young actress who portrayed the chauffeur's lover, it wrote: "Tallulah Bankhead, a newcomer to filmdom, plays easily and sincerely, as well as being optically pleasing."

Will Rogers, on the other hand, was no newcomer to show business. Prior to being discovered by Sam, he had been a headliner in vaudeville and following that, a staple of *The Ziegfeld Follies* for many years, entertaining sophisticated Broadway audiences with his celebrated homespun wit and wisdom while at the same time he twirled a lariat with more dexterity than a real cowboy. However, until he was brought to Sam's attention by novelist Rex Beach, Rogers for some strange reason had been completely overlooked by picturemakers. Rogers himself used to kid about the oversight, saying, "I don't understand it. Out in Hollywood they're signing up trained dogs and trained cats and grand-opera singers and everybody in the world but me."

Sam signed him, and in a period of two years Rogers made twelve pictures for the Goldwyn Corporation. One of his biggest successes was *Jubilo*, in which he played a tramp. "They signed me," said Rogers, "because they saw me one day in my street clothes and said, 'Let's get him—he's already dressed for it.' "

But while audience and critical acceptance of Will Rogers and Tallulah Bankhead was gratifying, it did nothing to solve the Goldwyn Corporation's immediate need for cash during the first few months following the armistice. With so many large loans already outstanding at the bank, and cash from their new releases only dribbling in, it became necessary in early 1919 to begin ferreting out private money sources. It was in quest of immediate money that Sam made one of the major blunders of his professional life. He allowed one of his associates, Al Woods, to talk him into bringing his brother-in-law, Frank Joseph Godsol, into the company not only because he had some money of his own to invest, but because of contacts he had with the Du Ponts and other sources of important capital.

Godsol was a tall, handsome, athletic man, who in today's lingo would be known as a swinger or a rip-off artist, or both. He drove a custom-built, sixteen-cylinder Hispano-Suiza automobile, and when he traveled by train it was in a private railroad car accompanied by a dozen or so maids, valets, and girlfriends. He was a big spender; the pockets of his expensive clothes always bulged with impressive amounts of greenbacks. He gambled heavily. One night he actually broke the bank of Colonel Bradley's, a famous West Coast gambling emporium, when he walked away with $96,000 in cash. And he was a lavish tipper—probably because he knew that few people other than servants and lackeys had cause to like him.

Godsol's background was none too savory. During World War I he had sold mules and trucks to the French government, which later charged him with embezzlement. Before that he had operated a Paris-based firm which exported a product known as Tecla Pearls. Tecla Pearls were imitation pearls, a minor detail Godsol neglected to tell his customers, who parted with millions to wear the phony baubles around their necks.

Except for the fact that Godsol couldn't return to France without being thrown in a bastille, he walked away from those two enterprises in better shape than the French government. He had money in abundance and enough reputation as a financier to give him a great "in" with the famous Du Pont family of Wilmington, Delaware. So even though he knew nothing about picturemaking, Joe Godsol was brought into the Goldwyn organization and installed as vice president by its board of directors.

Godsol immediately began wheeling and dealing. Whatever his reputation in the past, he was no phony when it came to making good his word about having access to large financial interests. Shortly after his ascendancy to vice president, the following story appeared in the *New York Times* on December 2, 1919.

DU PONTS JOIN GOLDWYN

The Goldwyn Pictures Corporation announced yesterday that negotiations had been completed for the entrance into its organization of large financial interests, headed by H. F. Du Pont, vice president of the Du Pont Powder Company, Eugene Du Pont, W. W. Laird of Wilmington, E. V. R. Thayer, president of the Chase National Bank, G. W. Davidson, vice president of Central Union Trust Company, among others.

The expansion will mean an increase in its capital stock to an authorized 1,000,000 shares. The capital increase follows an arrangement made by Mr. Goldwyn some months ago by which F. J. Godsol became identified with it, and Lee and J. J. Shubert, with A. H. Woods, the threatrical producers, becoming officers of the organization and contracting to deliver it screen rights to their stage productions. It is rumored that a chain of picture theaters is to be established.

In terms more recognizable to the layman, the merger meant that the Goldwyn Pictures Corporation suddenly had $7 million in cash at its disposal. It also meant that Sam had a lot more partners he had to try to get along with. And if there was one thing Sam should have learned from past experience, it was that living in harmony with partners wasn't exactly his forte.

In the heady days right after the merger, however, Sam was in much too manic a frame of mind and was much too preoccupied with reorganizing and building the studio into an entertainment colossus to have any fears about a future clash with his new partners over control of the company.

With money no longer a problem, Sam went ahead with the company's dormant plans to refurbish and enlarge the already existing facilities on the Triangle lot. He hired a top architect, Stephen Merritt, to design and build a new administration building, more up-to-date shooting stages, comfortable dressing rooms, and a commissary so employees wouldn't have to leave the lot at lunchtime and straggle back for work a couple of hours late and perhaps a little tipsy.

When completed, the new administration building—a somber-looking gray stucco edifice with stately columns and a huge iron gate guarding its entrance—ran along Washington Boulevard for a half mile. A stranger to the area might have mistaken it for a mausoleum or the front of Leavenworth Prison were it not for a tremendous sign atop the building proclaiming to the world that it was the home of Goldwyn Pictures Corporation of New York.

Behind those impressive gates, however, was anything but a mausoleum. It was the best-equipped motion picture lot in the business. Sam had an office in the new building, but his main headquarters was still in Manhattan and would be for several years to come. To keep an eye on things, however, he commuted regularly to the West Coast, where he retained a permanent suite in the now famous Ambassador Hotel on Wilshire Boulevard.

As president of Hollywood's best-equipped and largest film studio, Sam was now in a position to reimplement a concept of motion picture making that he had abandoned when he formed the new company. He decided to junk the star system in favor of making the scenario writer the key person in the producing of a motion picture.

Whether Sam was truly the champion of the writer in those days or this concept was forced upon him because of his company's inability to sign names with the magical drawing power of Mary Pickford and Douglas Fairbanks is not clear. But it is clear that he had no one under contract at his studio who could even remotely compete with the likes of Pickford and Fairbanks at the box office. Maxine Elliott, Geraldine Farrar, and Mary Garden had done nothing for the Goldwyn studio except cost it money and win for it a reputation among some Hollywood wits as being "Goldwyn's Old Ladies' Home." Even Mabel Normand was a lightweight at the box office when stacked up against Pickford, Fairbanks, and Chaplin.

Whatever influenced his decision, Sam came to the conclusion shortly after the move west that the trouble with most motion pictures was that they suffered from the lack of first-rate screen stories. Undoubtedly this stemmed from the fact that most producers in those days considered the writer the least important individual in the picture-making hierarchy. (There are many writers today who still have that complaint.) That was understandable. In the days of the silents, movies were even more of a director's medium than they are today. Since no dialogue could be heard, no dialogue had to be written. All a scenario writer had to do was to make an outline of the picture's continuity, with a brief description of what each scene contained, which the director and actors could follow if they saw fit. Usually the actors ad-libbed most of what they appeared to be saying on the silent screen. Almost any hack could write for silents. And almost any hack did.

But Sam had an idea that was absolutely revolutionary. He was sure that if he could sign all of the world's greatest literary figures and bring them to Culver City, his studio would have something no other studio had—the world's best stories plus their authors, whose names he could advertise in big lights on theater marquees *above* the names of the stars.

If the movie public would buy this concept, Sam wouldn't have to lie awake nights cursing himself for not having Mary Pickford and Doug Fairbanks under contract. Moreover, he'd be able to give the public better quality motion pictures and at the same time satisfy his stockholders and partners.

To achieve this noble end, Sam formed an organization within the Goldwyn Corporation boasting the lofty title of Eminent Authors, Inc. In theory he would hire the best writers available and give them a piece of the action in addition to a salary. In return for that, they would work in close cooperation with the producer.

To Sam's credit, he knew he wasn't qualified to decide who were the world's best writers. So he assigned novelist Rex Beach, who was already under contract, to assist him in selecting the other authors.

The first carload of literary superstars to step off the train in Los Angeles consisted of Gertrude Atherton, Mary Roberts Rinehart, Rupert Hughes, Basil King, Gouverneur Morris, and Leroy Scott. All were literary heavyweights by 1919's best-seller-list standards. (Sam also wanted to lure Washington Irving to Hollywood to do the screenplay of *The Legend of Sleepy Hollow*, which he was going to produce as a Will Rogers vehicle, and was bitterly disappointed to learn from Rex Beach that he was about sixty years too late.)

Since the whole concept of Eminent Authors, Inc., was a novel and brilliant idea, Sam lost little time in letting the rest of the entertainment world know what he had up his sleeve. A giant publicity campaign followed.

Masterminding this campaign was a bright young ex-student of the Columbia School of Journalism named Howard Dietz, whom Sam had only recently hired as an assistant in the Goldwyn Corporation's publicity department in the East.

Dietz, who later turned out to be one of America's best-known lyricists, as well as a brilliant publicist, was one of Sam's better discoveries. And like most of Sam's discoveries, it took somebody else, in this case Sam's attorney, Gabriel Hess, to discover him first.

Between Columbia and America's entry into World War I, Dietz had worked briefly for the Philip Goodman Company, an advertising firm that was doing some publicity for Goldwyn Pictures Corporation. Feeling his company needed a distinctive trademark, Sam asked Goodman's firm to design one. Dietz drew the assignment, and believing that the Goldwyn trademark ought to have an animal in it to compete with Bison Pictures' bison and Pathé's rooster, he came up with the recumbent lion framed in a "porthole" bearing the Latin inscription *Ars Gratia Artis* ("Art for Art's Sake"). Dietz favored the lion because it was the symbol of Columbia University. And what could be more appropriate to represent the strength and dignity of a Goldwyn production than the lordly king of beasts?

It was a wise choice. The MGM lion, roaring majestically at movie audiences at the beginning of every picture, eventually became as famous as some of the company's superstars.

Shortly thereafter, America got into the World War, and Howard Dietz had to quit Goodman to join the navy.

At the war's conclusion, ex-gob Dietz was desperately in need of a job and went to see his friend Gabriel Hess, the lawyer for the Goldwyn company, about using his influence to get him one in Sam's publicity department.

Hess mentioned Dietz to Sam, who consented to speak with him. But after an interview was arranged, Sam kept Dietz waiting in his reception room all day. Out of sheer boredom, Dietz rolled a piece of paper into a nearby typewriter and dashed off a letter extolling Sam Goldwyn as a maker of distinguished films to the editorial section of the *Evening Mail*.

When the *Mail* published it, Dietz, on subsequent days of waiting in the outer office, wrote other letters plugging Sam Goldwyn's attributes to other newspapers, all of whom liked them well enough to publish.

Days later Sam finally got around to sending for Dietz. After making Dietz wait while he finished dictating a letter, Sam turned to the young man and snapped, "What are you doing here?"

Dietz replied that he was the one who had written those letters, and he castigated Sam for not appreciating such good publicity. Sam offered him a job on the spot for fifty dollars a week, and Dietz subsequently rose to head of the department at two hundred a week.

Not long after joining the company, Dietz tried to improve Sam's image by making him an industry spokesman. One morning, without discussing it with his boss, Dietz sat down and wrote a letter from Goldwyn to George Eastman, the head of Eastman Kodak. In it, he pointed out that Eastman could be a great benefactor to the film industry by inventing nonflammable film—film used in the making of movies in those days being so explosive that insurance rates were practically prohibitive.

Dietz then sent the letter into Goldwyn, with a brief note saying, "This is the sort of letter you ought to write for its publicity value."

Sam signed the letter, but refused to mail it right away. "He just kept it on his desk and showed it to everyone who came in to see him," recalls Dietz today. " 'Look vat I wrote,' Sam would exclaim, waving the letter under everyone's nose. 'Read it. It's a verk of art.' " The letter didn't get mailed for days but after Eastman finally received it, he agreed with its concept, and several years later did come up with a nonflammable film.

Howard Dietz was a hard worker, but he had independent work habits that did not coincide with the company policy calling for *all* employees to be at their desks by nine in the morning. Dietz wasn't lazy, but he had a theory about himself, which he felt applied to most office workers. They may be at their desks by nine, but rarely is anything accomplished before eleven except the drinking of coffee, the smoking of cigarettes, and the exchanging of gossip. Accordingly, Dietz never strolled into the Goldwyn offices until eleven, and frequently not before noon, because those were the hours he knew he could do his best work.

After watching Dietz amble in at noon five days in a row, Frank Godsol, one of Goldwyn's lieutenants, summoned Dietz to his office and said, "Mr. Dietz, do you know that you always come to work two hours late?"

"Yes," admitted Dietz, "but I always go home early!"

A lesser man would have been fired. But Dietz had something unique to contribute to the company, which Goldwyn Pictures recognized and did not care to do without.

Dietz was a genius when it came to advertising and public relations. As young as he was, it was his copy alone that set the tone of the new company for years to come: class, intelligence, and dignity.

Soon after the inception of Eminent Authors, Inc., Dietz designed a brilliant series of full-page ads in the *Saturday Evening Post*, proclaiming the arrival of the world's best and most renowned authors on the Goldwyn lot. These writers, the ad assured the *Post*'s conservative readers, would guarantee that "all Goldwyn pictures were built upon a strong foundation of intelligence and refinement."

Dietz's publicity campaign on the eminent authors was so convincing that Sam's competitors, principally Lasky and Zukor, decided to get into the famous-author act themselves. Lasky and Zukor didn't quite believe that the public would take literary figures to their hearts with quite the same enthusiasm as they did Mary Pickford and Doug Fairbanks. But at the same time they couldn't take the chance that perhaps Tricky Sam had pulled a great industry coup. So they followed Sam's example by signing up the name writers who were left. Since Sam had pretty much cornered the American market, they had to look to Europe for their eminent authors. Through persistence and the expenditure of large sums of money, they succeeded in signing Elinor Glyn, Sir Gilbert Parker, Arnold Bennett, and eventually even Somerset Maugham.

With Hollywood being invaded by such high-caliber literary figures, local screenwriters soon found themselves being weeded out of studios in order to make room for the eminent. One of the local hacks to lose his job was a neophyte in the movie business named Darryl F. Zanuck. His unemployability eventually became so critical that Mr. Zanuck had to take a job as a welder in a shipyard until the eminent authors phase blew over.

Fortunately for Zanuck and the rest of the regular Hollywood scriptwriting fraternity, the concept of hiring name novelists turned out to be a colossal failure and very short-lived.

The root of the problem lay in the endemic difference between novel writing and screen writing. The successful novelist deals in word imagery, colorful description, and much introspection to tell a story and make the characters come to life. The silent-screen writer, especially, had to make his points visually. The ancient but anonymous Chinese gentleman to whom Bartlett attributes the phrase "One picture is worth ten thousand words" must have had the movie business in mind when he penned what has since become a cliché.

The list of novelists who have failed in Hollywood down through the years—aside from Goldwyn's Eminent Authors group—is an impressive one and includes such celebrated names as F. Scott Fitzgerald, James Jones, Joseph Heller, John O'Hara, and even Ernest Hemingway.

Never having worked at a typewriter himself, Goldwyn had no way of anticipating the pitfalls that could befall a novelist. As far as he was concerned, anyone who could dash off *The Man in Lower Ten* (Mary Roberts Rinehart), *Black Oxen* (Gertrude Atherton) and *What Will People Say?* (Rupert Hughes) would have no trouble handling a screenplay.

Once the authors arrived in Culver City, Sam spent days getting them acquainted with the lot, introducing them to the stars for whom they would be writing, and being photographed with them. Then he assigned them to lavish offices and ordered them to go to work, giving them carte blanche as to subject matter.

The results were uniformly disastrous. After reading Leroy Scott's completed screenplay, Goldwyn said, "Mr. Scott, you are undoubtedly a great novelist, but I am afraid this is not good for the movies." Goldwyn made the identical speech after reading Basil King's screenplay. "Mr. King, you are undoubtedly a great novelist, but I am afraid this is not good for the movies." In fact, after having to make the same speech to all but one of his eminent authors, Sam later came to the following conclusion in his autobiography.

> The great trouble with the usual author is that he approaches the camera with some fixed literary ideal and he can not compromise with the motion picture viewpoint. He does not realize that a page of Henry James prose, leading through the finest shades of human consciousness, is absolutely lost on the screen, a medium which demands first of all tangible drama, the elementary interaction between person and person (a fist fight on the edge of a cliff) or person and circumstance (a person trapped on a window ledge eighty stories above the ground). This attitude brought many of the writers whom I had assembled into almost immediate conflict with our scenario department, and I was constantly being called upon to hear the tale of woe regarding some title that had been changed or some awfully important situation which had either been left out entirely or else altered in such a way as to ruin the literary conception.

Of the first batch of famous authors to invade the Goldwyn lot, only Rupert Hughes was facile enough to adjust to Hollywood's standards. His screenplay of *The Old Nest* was not only shootable, but the film went on to gross over a million dollars. Rupert Hughes remained in Hollywood and became one of its most successful and prolific writer-producers and a close friend of Sam Goldwyn's. It was a friendship that Goldwyn swore was absolutely "independent of the profitableness of" their business relationship. But the fact that Rupert Hughes helped put some money in Sam's pocket certainly didn't harm their relationship.

Despite his disappointment in the works of the other eminent authors, Sam clung to his impossible dream long enough to try to proselytize George Bernard Shaw into becoming a Goldwyn writer. Sam made his move one afternoon over tea at Claridge's, when he was visiting London on a sales trip. But when Sam brought up his proposal, Shaw displayed a disconcerting lack of interest in becoming a Hollywood hack. Misreading his reluctance, Sam tried to convey to the witty Irishman that he was not just another classless, money-grubbing Hollywood producer who had no aesthetic values beyond chasing the proverbial buck. To demonstrate, Sam said, "You know something, Mr. Shaw, if I had my choice, I would rather make a great artistic picture than—than eat a good meal."

His clear blue eyes sparkling, Shaw riposted with, "Then we can never get together, Mr. Goldwyn, because your ideals are those of an artist and mine those of a businessman."

Of the famous authors Sam was able to entice to Hollywood, his most spectacular literary defeat occurred at the hands of Maurice Maeterlinck, the great Belgian poet, who was enjoying worldwide acclaim in the early twenties because his *Blue Bird* was being performed at the Metropolitan Opera.

Concurrently Maeterlinck was in New York City on the first leg of a coast-to-coast lecture tour, arranged for him by his agent, J. B. Pond, and which was to keep him tied up for the better part of a year.

Unfortunately for Sam Goldwyn, Maeterlinck's lead-off lecture at Carnegie Hall ran into enormous difficulty because of the language barrier. Maeterlinck, who spoke no English, had initially put his lecture down on paper in French. An interpreter then translated the French version into English. It was then necessary, because the poet didn't know how to pronounce English words, to have each English syllable translated into a French syllable. Each English sound was to be rendered by an approximate French sound. For example, "ainded" for *ended*, "ichou" for *issue*. Theoretically it would work, but because Maeterlinck didn't actually know what he was saying, he lost all communication with his audience, who were totally mystified by this potpourri of English, French, and Belgian to which they were being subjected.

Halfway through the lecture, Maeterlinck gave up, retreated from the lecture hall, and dashed back to the Waldorf Astoria to lick his wounds.

At this point, Professor Henry Russell, a Boston concert impresario, decided to get into the act, primarily because he saw a way to make some money for himself. Calling on Maeterlinck in his hotel room, he persuaded him to try writing for movies. Specifically, for Sam Goldwyn. When the poet showed interest, the frock-coated Russell rushed over to the Goldwyn offices and urged Sam to sign Maeterlinck to a motion picture contract.

Sam was not personally a fan of Maeterlinck's—in fact, he had barely heard of him until he arrived in New York for the lecture tour—but after listening to his literary credits he could see no reason why Maeterlinck shouldn't join his eminent authors organization. Sam immediately sent for Maeterlinck and began negotiations. Because French wasn't one of his languages, Sam tried to negotiate through a translator, but under the circumstances his usually persuasive gesticulations did not quite mesh with his verbal selling points. The translator's mouth and Sam's gestures were out of sync. Maeterlinck was completely bewildered. Sam misread his expression of bewilderment for dissatisfaction with his financial terms.

"But you'll be getting the same as I'm paying the rest of my eminent authors," promised Sam.

When Maeterlinck's face remained blank, Sam ordered his chief lieutenant, Abe Lehr, to bring in the contracts of his other eminent authors.

"I'm not fooling you," said Sam through the translator as he shoved Basil King's contract under the poet's nose. "This is Basil King's contract. You know Basil King?"

"*Non*," replied Maeterlinck after the question had been translated for him.

Sam showed him the other contracts. "You know Rupert Hughes?"

"*Non.*"

"Rex Beach?"

"*Non.*"

Disgusted, Sam turned to Dietz and exclaimed, "What's the matter with this guy? Is he dumb or something?"

Maeterlinck wasn't quite so dumb when it came to understanding figures, however—especially when those figures added up to more digits per week than the other authors were receiving. For $100,000, Maeterlinck finally was persuaded to join the Goldwyn literary colony on the West Coast.

Determined to make the most of the Goldwyn affiliation with the poet, publicity-wise Dietz cooked up a scheme to combine Maeterlinck's trip to Hollywood with a publicity junket. With Goldwyn's permission, Dietz hired a private railroad car—the same one Woodrow Wilson had used when he stumped the country for the League of Nations—to transport Maeterlinck west to the Babylon on the Pacific. Dietz also planted one of his publicity men on board the car for the express purpose of issuing at every whistle stop along the way statements by Maeterlinck on his opinions of America as he was seeing it for the first time. It was a scheme that couldn't fail to reap millions of dollars' worth of publicity for the Goldwyn Corporation.

Unfortunately Henry Russell, who accompanied his master on the trip west, didn't quite see it that way. He felt that if Maeterlinck gave away his words for nothing, he wouldn't be able to sell them at a later date, when, Russell hoped, he would have learned enough English to justify starting another lecture tour. Consequently, he persuaded his client to remain silent, despite threats and entreaties by the Goldwyn publicity staff that he should be more cooperative.

"*Non*" was all he kept saying. And as a result, he (and Goldwyn Pictures) got less publicity as the private car traveled westward than the hobos who were riding the rods underneath.

Despite Maeterlinck's obvious reluctance to meet the press as he whistle-stopped his way to California, Goldwyn's representative in Dallas—a tough Texan named Lou Remy—arranged a banquet for the poet during a two-hour stopover in Dallas. All the leading bigwigs showed up in the banquet hall, including the mayor of Dallas and the governor of Texas. In fact, everyone who meant anything at all was there except Maeterlinck. Because he was determined to discourage the public appearances, Russell gave orders for the train not to stop at Dallas but to go straight through to Houston.

When Lou Remy learned of the double-cross, he wired Tom Shaw, the MGM representative in Houston to meet the train when it stopped there and to "punch Henry Russell in the jaw." Remy received a return wire which simply stated: "Did."

In Hollywood, Maeterlinck demanded that Goldwyn provide him with a hilltop home, so that he could see the sun better. Not one to pinch pennies when great artistry hung in the balance, Goldwyn rented a mansion for the poet atop a mountain overlooking the entire Los Angeles basin. From his eagle's nest Maeterlinck not only had an unparalleled view of Old Sol from dawn until dusk, but he was so high up he could almost see the canals of Mars.

For three months, he scribbled diligently away at his first movie script. When he finally announced that he was finished, his work was grabbed eagerly from his hands and turned over to a translator, whose job it would be to change it into English. This took another three months. With each passing day, the suspense built. The production department was put on the alert, to prepare themselves for a major epic.

Finally, the script was in its final form and handed to Sam, who struggled through it and then ran out of his office, hysterically screaming, "My God, the hero is a bee!"

To everyone's surprise and bewilderment, Maeterlinck had done a film adaptation of his best seller *The Life of the Bee*.

Not quite ready to ship him back to Belgium yet, Sam decided to give the poet a crash course in basic movie writing by exposing him to the best of what was currently being ground out of Hollywood's movie mills. Day after day, for two solid months, Sam had one of his flunkies escort Maeterlinck to a projection room, where he was forced to sit through millions of feet of action pictures.

When finally Sam deemed that Maeterlinck (who by now was suffering from severe eyestrain) was sufficiently saturated with Hollywood know-how, he patted him on the back and told him to try again. Maeterlinck's second attempt at scenario writing showed that he had indeed learned his lessons well. Introspection was out, and in its place was action, action, action. The opening scene of his new script showed a Paris street, with a close-up of a sewer lid being slowly opened from below. Suddenly there appeared from the sewer the bloodied face of a bedraggled female apache dancer with a dagger gripped between her teeth. The rest of the script was even more outrageously melodramatic and was immediately shelved. So was Maeterlinck, who was as eager to get out of his contract as Sam was to settle it for fifty cents on the dollar.

Typical of Sam, there were no hard feelings when the two men parted.

Sam rode with him to the station in the chauffeur-driven limousine supplied by the studio and stood with him on the platform while his bags were
lifted aboard. Just before Maeterlinck climbed up the train steps, Sam
shook his hand warmly and told him comfortingly, "Don't worry, Maurice,
you'll make good yet."

10

When You Have a Partner
You Don't Need an Enemy

GOLDWYN'S PARTING SHOT at the poet was a piece of advice he would soon have reason to apply to his own career as a movie mogul. For despite some recent successes, his ability to run Goldwyn Pictures Corporation on profitable basis was being seriously questioned by his new investors and partners.

In the vanguard of the mutineers was one Frank Joseph Godsol, whom Goldwyn, in his quest for cash fluidity for his company in 1919, had foolishly allowed to stick his foot in the corporate door. Once all the way in the ambitious and opportunistic Mr. Godsol began a campaign to unseat Goldwyn from his presidential perch and did not let up until he got Goldwyn completely out of his own company in 1922. But as early as September 3, 1920—only six months after Godsol joined the company—a story appeared on the amusement page of the *New York Times* that was certainly a harbinger of things to come.

GOLDWYN OUT AS HEAD OF GOLDWYN PICTURES

The resignation of Samuel Goldwyn as President of Goldwyn Pictures, which he has headed since its organization four years ago, was announced yesterday. Mr. Goldwyn has also resigned as a member of the Executive Committee, but will retain his stock holdings and will continue as a member of the Board of Directors.

Mr. Goldwyn's resignation is said to have followed a disagreement with the Board of Directors on a matter of "general policy." However, it was announced that the policy of the company will continue much the same as it has in the past.

People in show business weren't exactly surprised by the announcement that Sam Goldwyn was on his way out of the third company he had formed. By 1920 it was an accepted fact around Times Square that Goldwyn couldn't get along very harmoniously with anybody but himself.

In this instance, luckily for Sam, the company found it couldn't get along without a firm hand at the controls, and after a brief and unsuccessful interlude of trying to run the company by executive committee, the board of directors re-elected Goldwyn as president in charge of production.

Despite the board's reluctant vote of confidence, the infighting between President Goldwyn and Godsol, who was now chairman of the board, continued unabated. At the root of their animosity, of course, was Goldwyn's deep-seated suspicion of any partner who dared voice a dissenting opinion around him. This Godsol was wont to do at every opportunity, for the two executives did not see eye to eye on any subject except one: that each loathed the other with a passion.

Though a veritable neophyte in the business, Godsol had ambitious ideas. Two of his pet projects were to make films of *Greed* and *Ben Hur*. Sam did not see them as potential film hits and sabotaged every effort of Godsol's to get them before the cameras while he was still in charge of the studio. Ironically, when *Greed* and *Ben Hur* were eventually made under the MGM label, following Sam's final exit from the studio, both were successful. *Greed*, in fact, became a film classic.

Between 1920 and 1922, however, Sam was back in command with enough authority to prevent *Greed* and *Ben Hur* from being made. But Sam's governing hold on his company was a tenuous one, for despite Godsol's inexperience as a film producer, he had the curious ability of being able to persuade people like the Du Ponts, the Shuberts, and the Woods that he knew more about making profitable pictures than Sam Goldwyn. And judging from the company's financial reports when Goldwyn was in full command, Godsol had a very good point. On an individual accounting basis, a number of Goldwyn pictures had made money: *Jubilo*, *The Old Nest*, *The Cabinet of Dr. Caligari*, and most of the Mabel Normand comedies. But the overall operation of the studio was beginning to sink into the red, for several reasons. In the first place, Goldwyn, in his ambitions to corner the world market, had overextended his distribution outlets. After visiting England, France, Germany, and other countries, Goldwyn opened sales offices in cities and hamlets where American films had rarely been seen. It was an admirable plan, but unfortunately the production end of his company could not grind out enough pictures to keep the selling end busy. As a result, the cost of distributing Goldwyn films ran as high as 50 percent of the gross, whereas not more than 20 percent was considered a reasonable and safe margin.

In addition to overexpanding too rapidly and unwisely abroad, the Goldwyn Corporation's weekly payroll for talent at home was much too high to make good business sense. This was due principally to Goldwyn's largess when it came to signing the "best and the biggest" in order to keep them from going over to the enemy camp run by Lasky and Zukor. But how long could a company exist paying $15,000 a week to Mary Garden and an equal amount to Maurice Maeterlinck and reaping nothing in return? Even little Mabel Normand's salary had shot up to $4,000 a week by 1921.

At least Sam could point to Mabel Normand's pictures and boast to his stockholders that they were making a profit. Not so much as her earlier pictures perhaps, for her popularity at the box office was slightly on the decline by 1921, but at least they weren't losers. Until, that is, Mabel allowed her personal involvements to encroach upon her career responsibilities.

The trouble started with the resumption of Mabel's on-again-off-again romance with Mack Sennett. Because he was in bankruptcy by then and desperately in need of a star name to put his studio on top again, Sennett persuaded his girlfriend to go to Sam Goldwyn and ask to be released from her contract, which still had nearly two years to run.

Mabel was eager to oblige Sennett, not only because she loved him, but because she was becoming increasingly discontented on the Goldwyn lot. Her main complaint—probably brought on by paranoia over her slipping career—was that the Goldwyn roster contained too many other big names to whom the studio was giving preferential treatment when it came to assigning stories and directors. It only took a little prodding from Sennett to make her voice her resentment to her boss.

Sam had ambivalent feelings about letting her go, for he was still very much attached to her emotionally (though he had never quite made the grade with her physically). At the same time he didn't again want to force her to stay with the Goldwyn Corporation against her will—not at $4,000 a week.

While Sam was agonizing over her decision, Mabel Normand started another campaign to force Sam to let her out of her contract. In addition to showing up late for work, she would frequently disappear for days at a time. When she did appear she'd deliberately turn in a bad performance. All of which cost the studio more money than it could afford.

Sam finally gave in to her childish behavior and tore up her contract, which still had more than a year to go. At $4,000 a week, it was a wise thing that he did, for her last picture, *Head over Heels*, made under the duress of her trying to break her contract, turned out to be the bomb of all bombs. It was so bad that the film was kept in the can for nearly a year and a half after it was completed before the company dared release it in 1922.

They would have made more money on it by keeping it in the can and saving its distribution costs. *Head over Heels* was an absolute disaster at the box office. And not just because it was a bad film, but because by 1922 Mabel Normand's name had been splashed all over the newspaper headlines for many months in connection with the William Desmond Taylor murder case.

William Desmond Taylor was a handsome, debonair English movie director who was found shot through the head in his Hollywood home one night. Though technically Mabel Normand was still Mack Sennett's girl-friend, it was an accepted fact that she was also having a side affair with William Taylor during the months before his demise. Reputedly she was the last person to have seen him on the night of his death.

No formal charges were ever made against Mabel Normand, but the damage was done, for in the twenties this kind of scandal was enough to ruin a performer's career. Cheap newspaper innuendo, plus persistent rumors that Mabel Normand was a drug addict, caused indignation among the movie-going public, particularly women's organizations, who called for the total banning of all pictures starring the infamous Mabel Normand.

With Mabel Normand's career shattered and his company's profits at their lowest ebb since he had started Goldwyn Pictures in 1916, Sam was in deep trouble with the other members of the board of directors and his stockholders, all of whom were willing to accept newcomer Godsol's expla-nation that Sam Goldwyn didn't know the first thing about making profit-able movies.

A meeting of the board of directors was convened on March 10, 1922,—and the next morning the following story appeared in the *New York Times.*

GODSOL HEADS GOLDWYN PICTURES

Samuel Goldwyn, President of Goldwyn Pictures Corp., one of the largest photoplay producing concerns in the world, was succeeded in office yesterday by Frank Godsol, Chairman of the Board of Directors of the company. Mr. Godsol was elected at a meeting of the stockholders yesterday. At the Goldwyn offices, it was said that Mr. Goldwyn would not retire from the organization. Mr. Godsol will continue as Chairman of the Board as well as President.

In effect the vote meant that Sam was totally out of the company except for his stock holdings, which were considerable but not nearly enough to give him any say in the running of things. But Frank Godsol was not con-tent with merely taking the presidency away from Goldwyn and also con-tinuing on as chairman of the board. In order to savor every last morsel of his revenge, Godsol set out to inflict total humiliation on the now idle Goldwyn.

After giving the matter several days of concentrated thought—days spent pouring over maps of North and South America—Godsol came up with a scheme so satanic that Goldwyn would have been pleased to have thought of it himself (for someone else, of course). Summoning Goldwyn to his office, Godsol said he had a new assignment for him, which he knew he would be happy to undertake for the company now that he had "nothing else to do."

As Sam focused an apprehensive eye on his opponent, Godsol unfolded a map of Canada and pointed to a tiny town in northern British Columbia just a couple of miles south of the Yukon. "I want you to proceed to this frontier post, establish an office there, and take full charge of it," ordered Godsol.

"It snows up there," said Goldwyn, who had developed an aversion to cold weather after spending a couple of winters in southern California.

"Nearly all year around," added Godsol with a victorious grin. Since Sam was as famous for his rages as he was for the pictures he produced, Godsol girded himself for a typical Goldwyn blast of profanity.

But in this instance, the proud Sam controlled his rage with the poise of a career diplomat. "I will not stand to have you treat me like the dirt under my feet," he said quietly. And with that he turned and made a final but dignified exit from the company that bore his name.

So for the third time in his ten-year picture career Sam was out of work, having been fired from an entertainment colossus he had helped to build. But his personal finances were in better shape than ever, and instead of having to settle for that icy hell in the Yukon Godsol had picked out for his enforced retirement, Goldwyn rented an estate fronting Long Island Sound in the swanky Kings Point section of Great Neck, Long Island. Arthur Hammerstein, the Broadway producer, shared the huge establishment with Goldwyn.

In Great Neck, Sam took it easy for the remainder of 1922 and all of 1923, enjoying the good life of a country gentleman while his battery of lawyers tried to arrive at an equitable financial settlement with Goldwyn Pictures Corporation.

But Sam was too vital a man to be content with just lying around his Great Neck estate. He made frequent forays into Manhattan to check on his investments, confer with his attorneys, and seek out new picture contacts.

Because Sam still hadn't learned how to drive an automobile, he had to rely upon his chauffeur for transportation. Typical of the Goldwyn character, though Sam knew nothing about how to operate a car, he was the complete back-seat driver, criticizing every right or wrong move his chauffeur made. During this period he was perhaps bossier with his servants than he normally was, for now that he was out of Goldwyn Pictures, he had nobody else to scream orders at. The chauffeur, in particular, had to take the brunt of Sam's rages, because he spent so much time driving him to and from the city. For a number of weeks, the chauffeur suffered in silence. But finally he couldn't take Sam's tirades anymore. One night, in an impulsive move the chauffeur drove Sam to the loneliest spot on Long Island, stopped the car, and jumped out.

"Why are you stopping here?" asked Sam, looking with alarm at the deep forest surrounding him.

"I'm quitting," announced the chauffeur, walking rapidly away.

Goldwyn had to hike seven miles along a dirt road before he could find a substitute chauffeur to drive him home, for a stiff fee.

While he was marking time at Great Neck, Sam decided to take swimming lessons. Now that he had his own private beach, he did not think it should go to waste. So he hired a lifeguard from Sands Point to teach him to dog paddle. Sam didn't learn to turn around in midstream, however, and on the first day he attempted to go swimming by himself, he swam out into the sound over his head and had to be rescued by one of his servants—an upstairs chambermaid who happened to be viewing his aquatic performance from a second-floor window.

Even out of the water Sam was frequently being baffled by his lush environment. Once, while his next-door neighbor, Broadway producer Sam Harris, was showing him through his own estate, Goldwyn came upon a sundial.

"Vat's that?" asked Sam.

"A sundial," replied Harris.

"What's it for?" asked Sam.

"It tells time by the sun," explained Harris.

"My, my, what won't they think of next!" exclaimed Sam.

Sam had never seen a sundial before, just as he had never seen a copy of Webster's Unabridged Dictionary until one night when he was embroiled in a heated game of Guggenheim at a friend's house, and the dictionary had to be consulted when a questionable word came up. (There had been no dictionary in the night school he had attended in Gloversville.)

Sam was astonished at the size of the volume.

"What a big book," said Sam. "Who wrote it?"

"Webster," answered the host.

"It must have taken him a long time."

"About a century."

"My, my!" exclaimed Sam. "Fifty years to write a book."

Sam was especially fond of the outdoors, and there was nothing he enjoyed more than to be able to swim or hike, or play croquet or golf with his friends—if the weather was good. Hailing from middle Europe, Sam was especially appreciative of beautiful weather—a facet of his character that inspired him to utter a genuine Goldwynism one lovely Sunday morning when he stepped out onto his beach. Looking around him at the bright sun and sparkling blue waters of the sound, he took a deep breath of the invigorating air and exclaimed, "What a wonderful day to spend Sunday."

Unlike the synthetic variety, made up by jokesters and publicity men, his line about Sunday wasn't meant to be a joke, which is how one can spot a true Goldwynism from the spurious. It was a plain statement of fact, with a slight but unintentional twist.

In the same category was a question Goldwyn put to his caddy one afternoon at Lakeville Country Club, when he was first taking up the game of golf. After slicing five balls into the water hazard, Sam finally made a long, straight beautiful drive to the green. Turning to his caddy, Goldwyn exclaimed, "What did I do right?"

Goldwyn had been introduced to the sporting life by a new acquaintance of his—comedian Harpo Marx, who had just joined the ranks of the famous and well-heeled when the show in which he was appearing with his brothers—*I'll Say She Is*—turned into a surprise Broadway hit.

Harpo had been a golfer even as a poor vaudevillian and was quite accomplished on the links by the time he met Goldwyn. Sam, on the other hand, had avoided the sport, claiming it was "too slow and dull" for him, until Harpo pointed out that you could gamble on the links. That side of golf appealed to Sam, who enjoyed nothing better than the thrill of risking his money at games of skill or chance. He quickly became a golf convert after moving to Long Island, where Harpo had also taken up residence on Herbert Swope's estate.

If ever a game was invented to show off two of Sam's weaknesses—cheating and losing his temper—it was golf. One day in a match with Harpo, Sam teed up his ball in a sand trap and proceeded to blast it out onto the green, just a couple of inches from the hole. Harpo, whose turn it was to hit next and whose ball was also buried in the sand, started to follow Sam's example of teeing up in the trap.

"You can't do that," shouted Sam, catching him.

"But you just did it," said Harpo.

"Yes, but didn't you just hear my caddy say I shouldn't?" demanded Sam.

On another occasion, Sam missed a two-foot putt and became so furious with his putter that he hurled it down on the green, embedding its blade in the turf, and strode off, grumbling that he never wanted to see that particular putter again.

Unbeknownst to Sam, Harpo picked up Sam's putter and used it for the remainder of the round. On the final hole Harpo sank a twenty-foot putt to win the match.

"That must be a good putter," said Sam. "How much do you want for it?"

"Oh, I couldn't sell this," said Harpo. "It's my favorite putter."

"I'll give you fifty dollars for it," shouted Sam.

"Sorry," said Harpo.

"What are you, a crook or something?" said Sam. "I offered you a fair price. Now come on, sell it to me."

Sam immediately upped the ante another fifty dollars, which Harpo again turned down. By the time they reached the locker room, Sam was in such a rage over Harpo's refusals that he was now offering the comedian $250 for his own putter. At that price, Harpo had no choice but to sell.

Sam and Harpo remained close friends for the rest of their lives, despite the fact that they were two completely different types. Goldwyn was explosive; Harpo was mild-mannered and quiet. What probably attracted them to each other was that both were completely unschooled, neither could write a letter, but both were self-made millionaires.

Despite their bickering on golf courses and around card tables, Sam loved Harpo so much that every time he would run into Groucho without his brother, he would greet him with, "Hello, Groucho, how's your brother Harpo?"

After this happened repeatedly for a number of years, Groucho became annoyed with Sam's lack of interest in Groucho and made up his mind to say something the next time the producer greeted him that way. Which he did, several weeks later at one of Hillcrest Country Club's Sunday night feasts.

"Hello, Groucho, how's your brother Harpo?" inquired Sam when they met in the buffet line.

"For Christ's sake, Sam," exploded Groucho, "why do you always ask me how *Harpo* is? Why don't you ask me how *I* am sometime?"

"That's a fine idea, Groucho," said Sam. "I'll do that sometime. But right now, how's your brother Harpo?"

That was one of Sam's strongest points: he could not be sidetracked. Take, for example, his decision to write his memoirs—a tremendously ambitious undertaking for a man whose prose—written or otherwise—was barely decipherable even to his closest friends.

"Who's going to translate it for you?" asked Arthur Hammerstein after hearing his intentions.

But neither sleet nor snow, nor his friend's jibes, nor an abysmal lack of knowledge of spelling and composition could deter Sam Goldwyn from his self-appointed task once he had made up his mind to treat the world to a book on the subject of "what made Sammy run."

He hired a ghostwriter—a journalist named Corinne Lowe—and dictated his life story to her—or at least as much of his life story as he felt it was safe to divulge. It was typical of Sam's independent way of doing things that even with the help of a competent ghostwriter he was able to disregard completely the basic principles of autobiographical writing. A reader of this book, which eventually was published under the title *Behind the Screen*, could plow through all 262 pages of it without learning any important facts about Sam Goldwyn the person. For example, it contained not one mention of his mother, father, first wife, or daughter. He did, however, discuss his ex-brother-in-law Lasky, but only to establish how he made the jump from the glove business to the movies.

Mostly the book was fan magazine pap of the most blatant sort. He devoted chapter upon chapter to throwing bouquets at the various personalities he knew and worked with in Hollywood: Mary Pickford, Charlie Chaplin, Doug Fairbanks, Will Rogers, Mabel Normand, and Mack Sennett, to mention but a few. But he never even mentioned Frank Godsol, nor the group of financiers responsible for ejecting him from his own company. Here and there he showed some insight in how to deal with temperamental movie stars, including detailing some of his tribulations with Mabel Normand, though nothing about how he felt about her as a woman. But by and large he cleverly managed to conceal his inner feelings and motivations under a welter of half-truths and evasions that some of the Watergate coverup group would have been hard put to match. Nevertheless, there was apparently great interest in anything the great Goldwyn had to say—true or false—about the glamorous movie business on the West Coast, and the book and magazine rights netted him over $100,000.

Behind the Screen appeared first in serial form in *Pictorial Review*, and as a book it became an immediate best seller when it was published in 1923.

There was no mention of Corinne Lowe on the cover, but inside the book on the flyleaf was a brief author's note, alluding to her participation in the project. "I want to acknowledge the co-operation of Miss Corinne Lowe in the preparation of these articles. But for her enthusiasm, her patience, and her splendid co-operation given me in every way, this series could never have been written." Neither, for that matter could that "author's note."

By the publication day of his book, Sam's lawyers had finally arrived at a settlement with Goldwyn Pictures. The figure they arrived at for the purchase of his interest in the company was something in the neighborhood of a million dollars, which, when added to the first million, gave him a very comfortable cushion on which to repose, heal his bruised ego, and ponder how he wished to spend the rest of his life, which still had some fifty-one years to go. At the time he was only forty-two.

Two years later Goldwyn Pictures, with Frank Joseph Godsol at its head, was in such miserable financial shape that it was forced to merge with

Marcus Loew's Metro Pictures Corporation and Louis B. Mayer Productions to form Metro-Goldwyn Corporation. In 1924, after Mayer became a power in the company by bringing in Irving Thalberg, the studio was renamed Metro-Goldwyn-Mayer. Paradoxically, and though many veterans of the picture industry aren't even aware of it, Samuel Goldwyn was never actually a part of that triumvirate that bears his name today.

But there was a good side to the story. Frank Godsol was forced out of the company in the great merger that swallowed up Goldwyn Pictures, and he's never been heard of again. Which no doubt gave Sam even more satisfaction than the million dollars he received for his stock.

11

MGM's Doing a Great Job—
They Haven't Hurt Me
One Bit

HIS LONG VACATION OVER—but at pretty enviable vacation pay—Sam Goldwyn was once again itching to rejoin the fray known as the motion picture business. Only this time he was determined to go it entirely alone.

He had been of the same mind, of course, after getting extirpated from Famous Players–Lasky by his erstwhile bosom buddies, Lasky and Zukor. But the war, the flu epidemic, and a few below-the-belt jabs from Lady Luck had played havoc with his plans of never again allowing anyone in the door who would challenge his leadership.

Now all that *tsuris* with partners, associates, and stockholders was behind him. He was starting anew for the fourth time, but with a brand-new philosophy of producing movies—a philosophy that in a few years would make him the most successful independent movie producer in the business and bring him the industry's highest honors.

Nobody has ever summed up Goldwyn's philosophy of producing any better than he himself once did when he told a reporter for *Variety:*

> I was always an independent, even when I had partners. It's not that I wanted all the profits. But I simply found that it took a world of time to explain my plans to my associates. Now I can save all that time and energy, and put it into making better pictures.
>
> Basically I am a lone wolf. I am a rebel. If a picture pleases me, I feel there is a good chance it will please others. But it has to please me first. I don't think I could go through all the disappointments and aggravation connected with making a picture the way I operate if I was not interested in the subject and regarded it as a challenge worth meeting.

Determined to stay away from stockholders, even if it meant mortgaging himself to the hilt and risking his own savings, Sam formed a new company in 1923 and called it Goldwyn Productions, Inc., Ltd. But the ink was barely dry on the newspapers carrying the story of his new enterprise when he found himself once again entangled with his old partners in a bitter controversy. He was slapped with a suit brought by Metro-Goldwyn Corporation challenging his right to produce under his own name.

The bosses of the Metro-Goldwyn Corporation thought they had a valid point. They claimed they had paid a huge sum for the purchase of Goldwyn Pictures, and that included its name, which supposedly was synonymous with quality. If Goldwyn, too, now started producing under the name of Goldwyn, the public would quite understandably be confused and not know whether it was paying to see a "quality" picture turned out by Metro, or some *schlock* piece of merchandise made by Sam Goldwyn, former glove salesman, loudmouth, and all-around troublemaker.

When Sam heard that Metro was bringing suit to prevent him from using his own name, he let out a holler that could be heard from Hollywood to Fifth Avenue and Fortieth Street. What kind of a blankety-blank country was this where an honest hard-working businessman wasn't allowed to put his name on his own product? Is that what his forefathers fought for at the Battle of Bunker Hill and the Boston Tea Party? The fact that he was the first of the Goldfisch clan to set foot on American shores had nothing to do, he felt, with the justification for his rage.

Sam came out on top in this dispute when his lawyers discovered, upon re-examining the contracts that made his exit from Goldwyn Pictures official, that it was never spelled out who was to get custody of the Goldwyn name. With this ammunition, Sam was able to force an out-of-court settlement whereby he would be allowed to release pictures under the name of Goldwyn, provided he always put the name Samuel in front of it.

Despite this Solomonich arrangement, most of the movie-going public always believed that "Samuel Goldwyn Presents" and Metro-Goldwyn-Mayer were one and the same studio. This never upset Goldwyn very much. When someone once pointed out the confusion in the public's mind, Sam replied grandiosely, "MGM's doing a great job. They haven't hurt me one bit." As with many of his more oft-quoted remarks, Sam evidently saw no humor in the fact that MGM was a giant in the industry at the time, turning out forty quality features a year to his three or four.

It's not clear who coined the phrase "I don't care what they say about me as long as they spell my name right," but it's a precept that could very well have originated with Sam Goldwyn. If he didn't originate it, it certainly could be applied to his *modus operandi*. Especially in his early picture-producing days, for there was hardly anything Sam got more of a kick out of than seeing his name in print or up in lights. He was so in love with his name, in fact, that he once let it stand in the way of his accepting a very lucrative offer to return to MGM as a full partner. He said he'd rejoin the company only if they changed its name to Metro-Goldwyn-Mayer-Goldwyn. Louis B. Mayer turned him down cold, undoubtedly sensing from the outrageousness of that demand that Sam's success as an independent producer had made him even more difficult to get along with than ever. And he was right. Success had forever precluded the possibility of Sam mellowing enough to get along with others in a business relationship.

While much of the success Sam enjoyed between 1923 and his retirement in 1960 could be attributed to his precept of hiring the best talent regardless of the cost, there is little doubt that an equally large part of it can be ascribed to his belief in the power of publicity, either personal or for his productions.

It's a Hollywood legend that when Goldwyn first branched out on his own, he called in the head of his publicity department and said, "David Belasco became a famous producer by wearing a cape and his collar wrong-side around. What can I do to make myself famous?"

It may be pure coincidence, but shortly thereafter gags about Goldwyn's malapropisms began appearing in the columns. This lends credence to the fact that no matter how vehemently Goldwyn disowned spawning them after he became Hollywood's elder statesman, he certainly must have encouraged the spread of Goldwynisms in the days when he would resort to anything—anything but bad taste or revealing intimate details of his personal life—to get his name in the newspapers.

A newspaper reporter once made the mistake of beginning an interview with Goldwyn by saying, "When Willy Wyler made *Wuthering Heights* . . ." Goldwyn allowed him to go no further. "*I* made *Wuthering Heights*," he corrected him. "Wyler only *directed* it."

Many of Sam's most ardent detractors used to ascribe his love of publicity for the name of Goldwyn to sheer egotism. Once he learned what the word *ego* meant, Sam himself did not try to hide the fact that he had an ego, as evidenced by an argument he got into one time with Herman Shumlin, the Broadway producer, over the price of a play he was trying to acquire.

"But it's a Shumlin Production," pointed out Shumlin, trying to bolster his reason for asking more than Sam was willing to pay. "A Shumlin Production. Think of that."

Sam could think of nothing more cutting as a riposte than to reply, "You know something, Herman? You're a bigger egotist than I am."

Sam did not believe that you could necessarily stampede the public into seeing a bad film just by waging a powerful publicity campaign. But, as he discovered when he was still in the glove business, salesmanship had as much to do with the success or failure of a good product as the product itself. And since publicity was an integral part of salesmanship, he always went out of his way to hire the most qualified publicity minds he could find.

Over the years, Goldwyn had under his employ a long string of brilliant press agents who later went on to achieve great success on their own. A few of his distinguished alumni are Howard Dietz, who became one of America's wittiest lyric writers of popular songs ("That's Entertainment," "Dancing in the Dark," "Shine on Your Shoes"); Jock Lawrence, who today heads a giant public relations firm with offices in both New York City and Washington, D.C.; Irving Fein, who managed Jack Benny for a number of years and produced many of his TV specials; and Pete Smith, the producer of, and the voice behind, the *Pete Smith Specialties*, those hilarious one-reel comedies made by MGM during the studio's heyday.

One reason advanced for the successes of his alumni is that they couldn't stand working for so difficult and demanding a man as Goldwyn. Success in some other field was the only way out. According to Harry Reichenbach, his first press agent, Sam was never satisfied unless he had his name in the papers more than anybody else in Hollywood.

"He liked himself and anything to do with the name of Goldwyn," recalls Dietz today. "But I don't think he knew anything about making movies. He was an interesting man, though—but how he could arrive at the pinnacle of success with so little was beyond me. I liked him, though . . . a lot better than Louis B. Mayer. Mayer was evil. Sam was just demanding."

Like most important executives, Goldwyn could also be extremely unreasonable. "I remember once," recalls Irving Fein, who was his publicity director in 1940 and 1941, when he was making *Ball of Fire* and *The Pride of the Yankees*, "we managed to get him the lead story, plus the headlines in the two most important columns in the Hollywood papers at the time—Louella Parsons's and Harrison Carroll's. That amounted to sixteen columns of headline coverage. But the day after that appeared we got Goldwyn nothing in any of the papers. Would you believe he called me into his office and screamed, 'God damn it, what am I paying you guys for?'"

Another press agent of Goldwyn's once resigned because his boss telephoned him from Palm Springs to complain that he wasn't getting enough newspaper publicity for his first Danny Kaye picture, *Up in Arms*. The publicity man couldn't understand Goldwyn's attitude. In his estimation he'd gotten the picture a great deal of newspaper publicity.

"I haven't seen it," snapped Goldwyn.

"Well, what newspapers have you been reading, Mr. Goldwyn?" the press agent finally asked.

"What do you mean, what newspapers have I been reading?" came the wrathful reply. "Don't you know I'm in Palm Springs for a rest?"

To Goldwyn, his mania for publicity wasn't a mania at all. It was perfectly rational, because pictures were his whole life, and it therefore followed that they should also be the rest of mankind's only legitimate interest. Goldwyn pictures, that is. "When people thought of anything else, they were getting off the subject," wrote Alva Johnston, in his 1937 profile of the great Goldwyn. "The mission of his press department was to keep their attention from wandering. Sam's publicity men were expected to crack down on anyone they caught not thinking pure Goldwyn. If Sam saw a newspaper full of wars, floods and crimes around the time he was releasing a new film, he'd be furious with his publicity department for letting digressions and irrelevances sneak in."

"When you worked for Goldwyn," said Harry Reichenbach, "you didn't get praise for what you got in the papers. You got blamed for what was in the papers that had nothing to do with Sam. The editorials, for example."

Pete Smith's record for satisfying Sam's unquenchable thirst for publicity was as good as anybody's. It might even be said that Pete Smith was the greatest publicity man of them all. After he left Goldwyn to beat the drums for MGM, he scored many remarkable publicity coups. But the one he'll be most remembered for is what he did for Greta Garbo. When the young Swedish actress first signed with MGM, she was so shy and unsure of her ability to speak English that she avoided interviews with more cunning than a Marlon Brando or Frank Sinatra. This could have meant instant death to her budding career, and it wasn't doing much to get Pete in solid with the studio bosses either. Then, deciding that a possible way out of his predicament was to capitalize on Garbo's shyness, Smith persuaded her to parry all newsmen's questions with five simple words: "I vant to be alone," and then close the door in their faces. That appealed to her. "I vant to be alone" became a catch phrase and helped make Garbo famous.

Smith went to work for Goldwyn in 1923, shortly after the formation of the new company. Already in production were the first two films to be released under the banner "Samuel Goldwyn Presents": *The Eternal City* and *Potash and Perlmutter*.

The Eternal City was a remake of the 1915 Famous Players–Lasky film of the same name based on the Hall Caine novel, which Goldwyn had somehow acquired. It starred Lionel Barrymore in one of his first film roles, Bert Lytell, and Montagu Love. Also in the cast was a young British actor whose part was so small he wasn't even billed: Ronald Colman.

Potash and Perlmutter, featuring Alexander Carr and Barney Bernard, was the first of three highly successful films Goldwyn made based on the Montague Glass magazine stories of two partners in the clothing business in

Manhattan's Lower East Side, and the plays made therefrom. It had a screenplay by Frances Marion, who became a staple in Goldwyn's writing factory.

Considering Goldwyn himself was on the rebound from terrific conflict with his last partners, it's probably more than a coincidence that *Potash and Perlmutter* appealed to him as basic subject matter. It's a tribute to his picture-making objectivity, however, that he could see the humor in the bickering of two partners.

At the time he formed the new company, Goldwyn invited Howard Dietz to come with him to handle his publicity. Dietz, of course, turned him down, preferring the security and comparative tranquillity of working for a major studio. In a small way Dietz's refusal proved a blessing in disguise for Goldwyn. Following Goldwyn's departure, everyone at MGM was under the threat of being fired if they had anything to do with their former boss or even talked to him. He was a pariah and was to be treated as such. But Dietz, who remained a close personal friend of Goldwyn's over the years, refused to be intimidated by Godsol's edict and was always available to talk when Sam phoned his office. At times, in fact, he operated as a spy for Sam by supplying him (on request) with vital information concerning MGM's operations that Sam couldn't obtain elsewhere.

On first inclination, Pete Smith was also tempted to reply negatively to Sam's telegram asking him to take over the new company's publicity. Smith, who was operating a thriving P.R. firm of his own, had heard from others of Sam's ferocity as a boss and how difficult he was to get along with, and he did not feel his blood pressure needed the stimulation of taking on this kind of client.

Smith's standard fee in those days was $100 a week per client. With twenty clients in his stable, he was already earning more money per week than he could possibly spend. He certainly didn't need Goldwyn, and to discourage him he wired back that he wouldn't accept the assignment for less than $200 a week. He felt that Goldwyn knew what the others were paying and was bound to feel discriminated against and resent Smith enough not to want him. But Goldwyn's reactions were always unpredictable when money was involved. "You are on," came his acceptance by return wire.

Through the rose-colored windows of nostalgia, Pete Smith today remembers his association with Goldwyn as "stormy, but challenging and fun." For most of the first year that Pete Smith worked for Goldwyn, Sam commuted back and forth between Rome, where he was overseeing the shooting of *The Eternal City*, and Hollywood, where *Potash and Perlmutter* was in production at the United Artists Studios on Santa Monica Boulevard and Formosa Avenue, where Goldwyn was renting stage space.

When he was in Hollywood, Sam lived in a luxurious suite in the Ambassador Hotel. So that not a minute of his working day was wasted, Sam would have Pete Smith meet him for breakfast at the Ambassador at seven A.M. Following that, Sam would insist that Smith walk with him to the studio, a distance of about five miles.

"He had very long legs and walked very fast," recalls Smith, one of Hollywood's better-known hypochondriacs. "I could hardly keep up with him."

Sam was always thinking "publicity" whether he was having breakfast or walking. On their way to the studio one morning Sam saw a banner advertising a rival studio's latest picture stretched overhead across Beverly Boulevard. "That's good advertising," said Sam. "That's what I want for the première of *The Eternal City*. Only instead of one banner, I want hundreds—one on every important corner in this town."

What Goldwyn didn't realize, but of which Smith was immediately aware, was that the banner was stretched between two pieces of property that were owned by the studio whose product it was advertising. Smith envisioned nothing but trouble ahead in Goldwyn's quest for "hundreds of banners." Hundreds of banners obviously meant hundreds of sticky negotiations—all taking a great deal of valuable time—with property owners. And Smith, who had other important clients to service in addition to Goldwyn, was not about to shortchange them in order to make Goldwyn's impossible task come true. He was acutely aware, however, that to oppose Sam's brainchild was to incur the man's wrath. He would have to rely on psychology to shoot the idea down.

"That's a marvelous idea," exclaimed Smith, swiftly calculating in his own mind the probable expense involved. "And it won't cost very much to get the clearances, either."

"How much do you figure for the whole thing?" asked Sam, already wary after hearing the word *clearances*.

"Well, the banner itself shouldn't run you more than fifteen bucks a piece, and about a hundred fifty dollars more per banner for the clearances from the property owners. Altogether I think we can do it for as little as thirty thousand dollars."

"Thirty thousand dollars is a little?" exclaimed Sam, beginning to rage like a wounded lion. "How could you think of such a lousy idea to get publicity?"

An idea Sam found more to his liking was one proposed by Smith one morning as a solution to Sam's regular complaints, after skimming through the trade papers, that he wasn't seeing his name in print enough. Smith suggested that Sam call in the press and formally announce that he thought there were only thirteen real actors in all of Hollywood, and then name them. At first, Sam balked, claiming he would make enemies of those actors he didn't name, but the temptation of getting so much good publicity inspired him to salvage the idea by giving it a slight twist.

"I'll only name twelve and say the thirteenth is a mystery," he said. "That way every actor or actress I don't name will think he's the thirteenth."

They tried the scheme, and Goldwyn reaped bales of publicity from it for weeks to come. Every press agent in town tried to get into the act, claiming his client to be the "mystery thirteenth." And two prominent leading men, each claiming the honor for himself, got into a fistfight over it in a restaurant, and that battle, too, made the headlines.

All of which proves that Goldwyn himself had a small genius for self-aggrandizement.

Coming back to the studio from one of his trips to Rome, Sam swept into Smith's office one day and spread out some 11" x 14" glossy photographs of himself on the publicity man's desk.

"What do you think of them?" asked Sam.

"All right," said Smith, not impressed.

"Only all right? I think they're sensational."

"They look like you, if that's what you mean," said Smith laconically.

"Pete, I'm disappointed in you," said Goldwyn. "Don't you see they're eleven by fourteen inches?"

"So?"

"So they're too big for the newspapers to put in one column. Don't you see? From now on they'll have to print my picture in two columns."

Sam almost died of a broken heart when Pete explained to him that newspapers were equipped to take a photograph as large as a billboard and reduce it to a one-column cut if they desired.

Smith had to spend almost as much time outwitting his boss as he did dreaming up outrageous publicity schemes. When Sam was traveling, for example, he was never completely happy unless he was met at each end of the journey by an impressive turnout of newspaper reporters and photographers. But unless he had a big picture in the works, Sam's arrival wasn't of itself enough of a news event to attract many members of the press. Smith, however, wasn't eloquent enough to make Sam see this. Sam kept on complaining, and making life so unbearable for Smith that he was finally forced to resort to trickery to satisfy Sam's incredible ego.

To fill out the ranks of the press corps, Smith would often hire personal friends and, if they weren't available, movie extras to show up at the train station or boat dock with cameras and notebooks. Smith would then introduce them to his boss as Mr. Wolgast of the *Chicago Tribune*, Mr. Balenbach of the *New York Times*, and Mr. Greb of the *London Daily News*. Under instructions they would then start firing questions at Goldwyn until he finally had to wave his hand impatiently and exclaim, "Please, fellas, that's enough. No more questions. I have to get home to my wife."

An interesting facet of the Pete Smith–Sam Goldwyn relationship is that Smith never once heard Goldwyn utter a Goldwynism in his presence. Nor did Smith ever resort to making them up to plant in the columns.

"I do remember one thing, though. He could never pronounce my name," recalls Smith. "He used to call me Pete Smit. Imagine anyone not being able to pronounce the name Smith."

Whether it was due to Smith's wizardry as a press agent or the fact that Sam had finally found the magical Goldwyn Touch by 1924, the year *The Eternal City* and *Potash and Perlmutter* were released, both those films were received warmly by the public and also the critic on the *New York Times*. "Samuel Goldwyn (who desires to have it known that he is "not now connected with Goldwyn Pictures") presents this new topical version of the famous Hall Caine novel *The Eternal City*." The review, dated January 24, 1924, went on to say that it was not quite as good as the original version "because what was originally designed as a love story primarily has been turned into a rough and tumble movie exploiting Mussolini and the new fascistic regime in Rome.

"Despite that, *The Eternal City* opened last Sunday night at The Strand, with a turnaway crowd. At 9:40, the start of the last show, the lobby was filled with waiting people and there was a line from the box office down nearly to 46th Street."

About *Potash and Perlmutter*, the *Times* wrote: "*Potash and Perlmutter*, be it known, are as funny on the screen as they were on the stage. This Samuel Goldwyn picture has as many laughs as a Chaplin comedy." Comparing Sam's picture with those of the great Charlie Chaplin was the ultimate in praise. Sam had achieved success once again, and this time he did it without any partners.

12

Can I Control the Press?

SOON SAM WÁS TO HAVE another partner—but this time the kind he couldn't get away from by a simple vote of the board of directors.

In 1925, it had been ten years since Sam had divorced Blanche, to whom he was still paying alimony and child support, and since he had last seen his only child, Ruth. But judging from the wide swath Sam was cutting through show business society in the Roaring Twenties, he was evidently quite content with his life as a fast-stepping bachelor.

Contentment, however, often has little to do with a bachelor's sudden decision to take a wife, or to be taken, as the case may be.

With two million in the bank, more money pouring in from *The Eternal City* and the *Potash and Perlmutter* pictures, and his status as a movie producer once again secure, Sam had to be considered one of New York's and Hollywood's most eligible bachelors by 1925—that is, if a woman didn't mind that Sam, with his bald head and jug-handle, pointed ears, didn't exactly resemble a Ronald Colman, Douglas Fairbanks, or Rudolph Valentino.

One woman who definitely didn't seem to mind was Frances Howard McLaughlin, a beautiful, dark-haired native of Nebraska, who'd come to New York early in the twenties to conquer Broadway. Her stage name was Frances Howard, and she was just twenty-one when Sam met her for the first time in 1925 at a glamorous housewarming party for three hundred people given by Condé Nast, the publisher of *Vogue*, and his wife in their Park Avenue apartment.

Though they'd never actually met before, it wasn't the first time Goldwyn had seen the lovely Miss Howard. Several years prior to the Condé Nast party, while the actress was still in her teens, she had appeared in a Broadway play called *The Intimate Stranger*, which starred Alfred Lunt and Billie Burke, wife of Florenz Ziegfeld. Miss Howard played the part of a young flapper and played it so well that Billie Burke became her biggest booster. She took the young actress to the Goldwyn office in New York City and persuaded the head of the talent department to make a screen test of her. Goldwyn, who was in Hollywood at the time, was unaware the test had been made until his talent scout ran it for him in his projection room several weeks later. At that point Sam lost his cool and started bellowing, "Why do you waste your time and my money this way?"

Despite Goldwyn's rejection of her, Frances Howard went on to make a bigger name for herself in her next Broadway play, *The Best People*. Portraying a Roaring Twenties flapper for the second time, she drew hit reviews and was hailed as one of the great beauties of the period. And indeed she was, with a slender, well-proportioned figure, large dark eyes, exquisitely chiseled features, a creamlike complexion, and raven-colored hair bobbed short in the style of a twenties flapper.

Sam saw the play, as did a number of other movie producers on the lookout for new talent. But if Sam had any interest in Frances—either professional or otherwise—he did not show it. He allowed Paramount to jump in and sign Miss Howard to a five-year contract.

Frances Howard's first starring role for Paramount was in a movie called *The Swan*, which was released in 1925. The movie was a success but Frances Howard's reviews as an actress were only fair. However, her looks drew attention, and she was soon the toast of Broadway and Hollywood.

With stardom came invitations to elegant parties such as the one given by the Condé Nasts in their Park Avenue apartment. It was there, while Frances was whirling about on the dance floor in a $300 gown bought especially for the occasion, that eagle-eyed Sam spotted her and decided to make his move. With no hesitation, Sam cut in on the couple and, after a few turns around the floor with her, danced Frances out to a secluded spot on the terrace. There, in complete privacy, he hoped to cement their relationship further by asking the glamorous ingenue for a date. His opening words, however, could have ended it. Studying Frances, he wrinkled his nose in distaste and said, "You know something, Miss Howard? You used to be fairly good looking. But now that you've gone and bobbed your hair, you look terrible."

It wasn't the usual way to start a romance, but Sam's approach to everything in life had always been, and always would be, highly unorthodox. At the time, Sam was waging a one-man war against short hair. He felt so strongly on the subject that he once instructed his press department to cable the Vatican and invite the pope to join him in his crusade against the bob.

In addition to his disapproval of short hair, Sam had a number of other decidedly male chauvinistic views on the female image. He expected members of the opposite sex to act like ladies at all times. To him, that meant no cursing, no mannish attire, no opinions that conflicted with his, and the use of only enough make-up, hair-styling, and jewelry to be effective.

Goldwyn had a passion for simplicity. Young actresses who worked for him were forever getting personal beauty hints from the boss on how to use make-up, style their hair, and dress glamorously but in an understated way.

But most girls who showed up looking for work at a typical "chorus call" on the Goldwyn lot were unaware of how Goldwyn felt, and many would arrive dressed to the teeth and made up like Sadie Thompson, thinking that was how to make an impression. It was, but not a good one.

Facing the lineup of pulchritude, Sam would address them in a friendly but blunt fashion. "All I'm looking for is fresh faces," he'd say. "So will you please wipe off your make-up so I can see you?"

Appraising them individually as he strode up and down in front of the lineup of chorines, Sam would suddenly stop in front of one of the hopefuls and say, "Hello, young lady. Would you mind removing your hat and earrings?" To another young lady, who'd obviously spent the morning sweeping her hair up, he might say, "How tall are you with your hair down?"

"Five-four, Mr. Goldwyn."

"Well, would you mind undoing that beehive so I can tell?" Or, "Has anyone ever told you that too much mascara makes you look like you could use a good night's sleep?"

One of Sam's pet peeves in the opposite sex was to hear vile language flowing from otherwise lovely lips. If Mabel Normand had accepted him, he'd have married her in spite of this fault, but the one thing he couldn't stand about her was her constant reliance on what he considered longshoremen's language whenever she didn't get her way. According to the writer Frances Marion, little Mabel once unleashed such a barrage of four- and ten-letter words at Sam one afternoon when he came down to the set to give her some advice that he actually fled his own studio for the rest of the day. It had to be awfully rough language to offend a man like Sam, who was known to have an extensive vocabulary of obscenities himself. But from Sam's viewpoint, it was perfectly all right for a man to curse. He just shouldn't do it in mixed company.

Another quality in women that repelled Sam was aggressiveness. Any young woman who didn't recognize the fact that she was a member of the "weaker sex" would never get an invitation to Sam's apartment or to the little dressing room on the Goldwyn lot, where in later years Sam regularly disappeared every day after lunch to "take a nap," supposedly by himself.

He didn't even like to employ aggressive females, though he made an exception in Lillian Hellman's case because she was such an able writer, and "besides, I need her." But during the years of their working relationship, when Lillian Hellman was writing such fine films for Goldwyn as *The Little*

Foxes and *These Three* (her adaptation of *The Children's Hour*), they quarreled incessantly, and sometimes violently. Although Miss Hellman didn't label herself as such in those days, she was one of the earliest known women's liberationists. As a result, she was not afraid to tell a man like Goldwyn that he didn't know what he was talking about, or even "to go fuck himself."

But except for Frances Howard's short hair, Sam saw nothing in her appearance or behavior the night he met her at the Nasts' that portended that she would ever be anything but the most helpless and submissive of females.

In fact, Frances's reaction was so ladylike that she didn't even seem to take umbrage at Sam's ungentlemanly remark about her unbecoming hair style. Her exact words in reply have never been documented, but the results—nearly fifty years of happy marriage—indicate that she could take criticism very well. At least from a fellow she thought could do her career some good. As Frances confessed many years later, she was aware when Sam cut in that he was an important Hollywood producer. So instead of telling him off, she played it cool and accepted his invitation to go out to dinner with him later in the week at the Russian Eagle Restaurant, one of Manhattan's "in" bistros in the mid-twenties.

But Frances was not prepared for the suddenness of Sam's matrimonial attack. They had barely finished their first course at the Russian Eagle Restaurant when Sam asked Frances to marry him. Frances was flattered, but she would not commit herself that night. A date with a man twice her age was one thing, but marriage was something that had to be given more than a few minutes of consideration, even if he was reputedly a millionaire and rapidly becoming a power in the movie business. She stalled her suitor for several days—not the wisest of tactics when dealing with anyone as impatient as Goldwyn.

When no answer was forthcoming, Goldwyn took things into his own able hands. Four days after their date at the Russian Eagle Restaurant, the following headline, complete with story, mysteriously appeared in one of the New York papers: "SAM GOLDWYN TO WED FLAPPER." The story announcing the couple's intention to wed had, of course, been released by Goldwyn's publicity department on Goldwyn's instructions.

Ignoring the newspaper story, Frances continued to date Sam, but she still hadn't given him any conclusive answer by the second week of their courtship. The suspense was driving Sam right up the wall of his office. It was even beginning to give him second thoughts about the wisdom of marrying such a stubborn, though beautiful, creature.

Their romance reached the crisis stage when Dr. A. P. Giannini, founder of the Bank of America, and his wife invited Sam and Frances to dinner and to a performance of *Tannhäuser* at the Metropolitan Opera House one night in mid-April.

After his experience with divas in the movies, Sam had grown to hate grand opera. But Frances gave Sam no opportunity to turn the invitation down. "Oh, I'd love to see *Tannhäuser*," she gushingly replied. "Wouldn't you, Sam?"

"Of course," lied Sam, immediately adding (obviously for Frances's benefit) that he could think of no more enjoyable way of spending an evening.

That Sam was lying quickly became evident as soon as the curtain rose on the first act of *Tannhäuser*. Sam immediately began to squirm and yawn in his chair in the Gianninis' box and kept this up for most of the performance. The times he wasn't squirming he was dozing off.

After the opera Frances expected Sam to take her and the Gianninis out to supper at Lüchow's, but instead he hurriedly thanked his hosts, then hustled Frances into a taxi and ordered the driver to take them to her apartment, where she lived with her widowed mother.

"How'd you like the opera?" asked Sam as they pulled away from the curb.

"I liked it fine," replied Frances.

"You mean it?" He wrinkled up his nose in distaste in the same way he had when he criticized her short haircut.

When Frances assured him that she had indeed "adored" the performance, Sam's incredulous expression turned into a scowl. He suddenly saw the rest of his life filled with hundreds of excruciating evenings of grand opera.

Clearing his throat, he announced hurriedly, "You know, Frances—I've been thinking this whole marriage project may be a mistake. Here you are, just getting a good start on your career; and here I am—I've had a pretty good time so far in my life and—well—what do you say we forget I ever—"

"Are you trying to take back your proposal?" asked Frances.

"Yes," answered Sam. "We're not going to get married."

"Oh, yes we are," snapped Frances. "You can't call it off now."

"It's never been on," protested Sam. "You vouldn't say yes, and you vouldn't say no."

"I must have said yes, because I saw a story in the paper that said I did."

"I put it there," confessed Sam.

"I know," said Frances, "and now you're going to have to go through with it."

"But we've got nothing in common," said Sam. I hate the opera. And our backgrounds are different. I'm Jewish—you're Catholic. What would our children be?"

"Catholic," shouted Frances. "And no nonsense about it!"

The argument was going full blast when the cab pulled up in front of

Frances's door. As the driver turned around to stare at the two quarreling lovers, Frances leaped out of the cab and ran into her apartment.

Frances barely had time to take off her coat and hang it in the front closet when the telephone rang. It was Sam on the other end of the wire.

"Frances," said Sam, in a meek tone, "I'm sorry I lost my temper."

"Is that all you've got to say? You should be sorry for a lot more than that."

"Oh, I am," said Sam. "I'm also sorry you have such a bad temper."

At that, Frances hung up, then left the receiver off the hook so that Sam couldn't ring her phone any more that night. But she forgot to tell her mother she didn't want to talk to Sam. Early the next morning, Frances's mother knocked on her door and said, "Mr. Goldwyn's on the wire. Who does he think he is, calling you before eight?"

Frances groped her way to the telephone, where for twenty minutes she listened to an anguished and apologetic Sam ask for her forgiveness. He told her he didn't mean any of those things he said. He loved Frances. He loved opera. They had lots of things in common, including their short tempers. In fact, they had so much in common he could hardly wait to see her again, so they could begin discussing them.

Frances listened unemotionally as Sam pressed her for a date that night.

"No, I'm busy tonight," replied Frances.

"Then this afternoon? I'll take you to tea at the Plaza."

"I'm busy then, too," she said icily.

"What about this morning? Surely you're not doing anything this morning."

"It just so happens I am," replied Frances. "I have to go downtown and have some photographs taken at eleven o'clock."

"I will go with you," persisted Sam. "Just drive down Park Avenue past the Ambassador. I will be standing on the sidewalk at ten forty-five."

Frances told him that the photographer was on the west side of town in the theater district. It would be out of her way to drive past the Ambassador.

"You'll be doing yourself a favor," pleaded Sam.

"I'm late already—I won't have time," said Frances, slamming down the receiver.

But some instinct—it must have been love—impelled Frances at the last minute to change her mind and instruct her cab driver to go past the Ambassador on the way downtown.

It was a cold, windy day in April, but good old reliable "never-say-anything's-impossible" Sam was standing in front of the Ambassador when Frances drove by in the cab, even though he had not known for sure she'd meet him.

Sam was a comic figure as he stood on the sidewalk, with his unbuttoned suit coat flapping in the breeze, and clutching a corsage of wilted gardenias in one hand while he tried to hold his Homburg on his head with the other.

The Ambassador was on the opposite side of Park Avenue from where Frances told her driver to stop. In order to reach the cab, Sam had to zigzag his way through the speeding traffic like a football player dodging tacklers. The corsage in his hand only added to the allusion that he was a ball carrier.

Hopping into the cab beside Frances, Sam handed her the corsage. "They're kind of brown at the edges," he apologized, "but I didn't have time to find a florist. I had to buy them used from some lady who was walking by with them pinned to her lapel."

"Oh, they're beautiful!" exclaimed Frances, as they kissed and made up.

Later in the afternoon, Sam sneaked out and bought Frances a twelve-carat diamond engagement ring, which she also didn't refuse.

Ten days later, on April 23, 1925, Sam and Frances made plans to drive over to the city hall in Jersey City to get married. In those days, one could marry in Jersey without a three-day wait, and evidently Sam, once he got Frances this close to the altar, was anxious to finalize the marriage contract before any further lovers' quarrels could erupt and throw a monkey wrench in his plans to take the beautiful actress to bed. However, it was a cliff-hanger right up to the moment he said, "I do."

Just as Sam, in a dark, double-breasted suit complete with carnation in his buttonhole, was leaving his apartment to pick up Frances in his long black Pierce Arrow, he received a phone call from the bride-to-be.

"Sam, there's a new magazine just out called the *New Yorker*. I hear it's very clever. I wish you'd stop and get me a copy on the way over."

Evidently Sam saw nothing in her request that indicated she planned to spend their wedding night reading, and on the way to Frances's apartment he had his chauffeur stop the car at a newsstand while he jumped out and picked up a copy of the magazine, which had only been in existence since February 21 of that same year.

Sam had never seen the magazine prior to his wedding day, and while his chauffeur was driving him the rest of the way to Miss Howard's apartment, he started leafing through it. To Sam's great surprise, the first thing he saw in the magazine was a "profile" of Sam Goldwyn titled "The Celluloid Prince," along with a Fagin-like caricature of him, which emphasized his worst features—a long, somewhat crooked nose, pointed ears, suspicious eyes under heavy arched brows, and a pate that showed as much bare skin as stripper Fanne Foxe's rear end.

The text of the piece, which covered two full pages and which was unsigned (although Sam later found out it had been written by Carl Brandt, his own press agent), was more deflating than his caricature. Every good thing it said about him was counterbalanced with something equally bad. It described Sam as a man without a background, without education, and with a mind and temperament that suffered from lack of discipline. Notwithstanding those shortcomings, the article went on, Sam was able, by sheer urge of some "divine spark within him," to build up that colossal enterprise at Culver City known as Metro-Goldwyn-Mayer.

It said Sam looked and dressed like a gentleman, but to hear him speak was a shock. It said he shouted a great deal and that he had a vocabulary of only ten words—"words used by a prize fighter who had gone into the cloak and suit business." At the same time, the article pointed out that Sam had an "instinctive love of beauty" that was his greatest trait next to his "acquisitiveness."

Delving into his early life in the Polish ghetto, Brandt wrote: "Somewhere he must have discovered that the rule of life in order to live, is not to let live. This philosophy, humanized by a democracy like ours, means outstripping the other fellow by any means possible that does not land one in jail."

Nevertheless, the article admitted that Sam Goldwyn was probably the greatest, most colorful filmmaker in Hollywood, a Gulliver among Lilliputians. It said he was close to being a genius

> because his insensitiveness to the feelings of others was a trait often found in genius. To be under his command even temporarily is a living hell, but to meet him as an equal is refreshing after the surfeit of over-educated, clever young men with nothing to say who seem to fill the world at present. It is almost painful to see him groping, struggling, bludgeoning his way to clarity, agonizing over ideas he feels but cannot express, a man struggling with his own greatness, a man whose night school education is inferior to his destiny. There are so many stupid people in the movies who cannot see beyond their noses, narrowminded and timid little men, that Mr. Goldwyn stands out from among them a dramatic figure—an inspired buccaneer.

"That profile of me in the *New Yorker*—it was the worst thing I'd ever read of anybody," he was to recall later. "I was afraid if Frances read it before the ceremony that she would break our engagement."

As the car stopped to pick up his bride, Sam hid the magazine under his topcoat. But halfway to Jersey she asked him if he had remembered to pick up the *New Yorker*.

"No, I forgot," lied Sam, and when he thought Frances was looking the other way, he opened the window and started to slip the magazine out of the car.

But Frances caught Sam in the act and demanded to see it. Trapped,

Sam sheepishly handed her the *New Yorker* and said, "Okay, here it is. Read it and make up your own mind."

After three weeks of knowing Sam personally, there was evidently nothing Frances could read that would scare her off, and the marriage proceeded as scheduled.

Edgar Selwyn, Sam's former partner, but still his friend, was to be best man at the wedding. When Sam had asked Selwyn to stand up with him, he had sworn Selwyn to secrecy about the coming nuptials.

"Why?" asked Selwyn.

"I don't want any publicity," said Sam.

"*You* don't want any publicity!" exclaimed Selwyn in an incredulous tone.

"No," repeated Sam. "I do not want any publicity."

It was a strange twist in Sam's character, which Selwyn was at a loss to figure out. Never before had Sam shunned publicity. Attributing the switch to the possible good influence of the bride-to-be, Selwyn respected Sam's request and kept mum about the wedding.

It therefore came as quite a surprise to Selwyn when he stepped out of his own car in front of the Jersey city hall and saw a mob of newspapermen ganged around the bride and groom. The newspapermen stayed right through the wedding, following which Sam graciously posed for myriad pictures and tirelessly answered all their questions.

As the newlyweds were about to step into their car to return to the city, Selwyn tugged at Sam's coat sleeve. "Hey, Sam," he said, "I thought you didn't want any publicity."

"Can I control the press?" exclaimed Goldwyn.

13

Sam Goes Hollywood

ALTHOUGH SAM COULD WELL AFFORD IT, there was no honeymoon in the south of France or aboard a luxury liner. Sam and Frances spent their first night together as man and wife in a cramped drawing room on board the Twentieth Century Limited, but not in the same berth. According to an account of their wedding night given by Frances to a friend in Hollywood years later, Sam took the lower berth for himself and gave his bride the upper.

"I could see then what my life as Sam Goldwyn's wife was going to be like," recalled Frances with a wry smile.

The reason there was no time for a real honeymoon was given in an account of the Goldwyn marriage in the *Jersey Journal* dated April 24, 1925. "The producer and his bride went straight from the ceremony at the city hall to the New York Central Railroad Station, where they boarded a train for Hollywood. Mr. Goldwyn is going to Hollywood to make one or two pictures."

The last line of the story was easily one of the biggest understatements of the century. Before Sam hung up his producer's gloves in 1960 he had produced eighty-eight more films under the banner of his independent company, Samuel Goldwyn Presents.

While Sam was an independent in every sense of the word, unencumbered by partners of any sort all those years, making pictures "only to please myself," as he said many times, and disdaining the advice of others, it has long been known in film circles that his wife Frances wielded considerable influence over many of his business decisions. It was Frances, in fact, who first saw and called to Sam's attention the article in *Time* magazine about the problems of returning World War II servicemen that was the genesis of Goldwyn's most successful, Oscar-winning film—*The Best Years of Our Lives*.

Even Sam, who was loath to give credit, even where it was due, to anyone beside himself, was willing at times to concede that Frances was a power in his movie company. "Frances is the only boss I ever had," he once told a reporter from *Variety*, then quickly added with a broad grin, "but I don't always listen to her."

Frances's involvement in the business didn't happen overnight, although she once confided to a friend that even during their three-week whirlwind courtship, Sam was always talking over his business problems with her and asking for her advice, which she freely gave. But her more active role was an evolutionary process that grew naturally out of the proximity of being husband and wife, with easy access to each other's ideas on a subject mutually dear to them—the picture business and how to make a barrel of money in it.

Certainly Frances Howard didn't start out with any overt ambition to be the power behind the movie kingpin's throne. In fact, in the beginning Frances had so little ambition to be anything but a good housewife to Sam that after only a week of marriage on the West Coast she succumbed to his chauvinistic entreaties to give up her own acting career to devote all of her time to being Mrs. Samuel Goldwyn.

"I wasn't much of an actress, anyway," she later admitted. Although her first and only motion picture, *The Swan*, in which she costarred with Adolphe Menjou, was successful, the critics were in accord with Frances's assessment of her acting. "She was delightful on the stage, but doesn't come off in the movies," wrote Louella Parsons, one of the Goldwyns' best friends even after that.

Louella's review, plus a spate of other lukewarm notices of her acting debut, may have been the reason Paramount Studios was so willing to oblige Frances when she asked them to tear up her contract. But if Frances thought retirement from acting meant she would be able to spend the rest of her life basking in the California sun at the edge of a swimming pool, she badly underestimated what it was like to be the wife of one of the most important moguls in the business. Being Mrs. Sam Goldwyn turned out to be a full-time job for the retired young actress, inexperienced as she was in running a large household, or even a small one. Because she had been on the stage since she was sixteen and had lived with her mother, who did all of the cooking and cleaning, she was relatively helpless around a kitchen. But necessity quickly changed all that.

Shortly after moving to southern California, Sam and Frances bought their first house—a two-story white stucco dwelling with a green tile roof, set in the middle of a neatly manicured lawn on the corner of Hollywood Boulevard and Fuller Avenue. Although its boxy architecture gave it the appearance of a small-town public library, their new home had everything necessary to make an important movie executive and his wife comfortable: plenty of large rooms downstairs suitable for entertaining, including a dining hall that could seat twenty-four; several guest bedrooms upstairs in addition to the master suite; an Olympic-sized swimming pool replete with cabana; and beautifully landscaped grounds planted with palm and citrus trees and other semitropical foliage.

Today Hollywood Boulevard and Fuller Avenue isn't a very desired neighborhood among the status seekers and wealthy, being less than half a mile from Grauman's Chinese Theater, a Hamburger Hamlet restaurant, and a car rental lot. In fact, many of the grand old houses of silent picture days have been torn down and their lots subdivided to make room for cheap apartment buildings. But when Sam and Frances settled there, many of the greats of Hollywood lived and played in that neighborhood, in mansions similar to their own.

On the same block with them lived Constance Talmadge, one of the reigning movie queens of the day; Frances Marion, one of Hollywood's best-paid and most prolific screenwriters; and Joseph Schenck, president of United Artists Studios.

Because a movie mogul was expected to entertain on a scale commensurate with his income—and Sam was reputed to be earning $75,000 a week at one point—the Goldwyn house was staffed with an impressive array of full-time servants—Swedish cook, butler, chauffeur, upstairs and downstairs maids, laundress, gardener, and swimming pool man.

As lady of the house, Frances had to oversee the staff, plan the meals, and play hostess at the Goldwyns' regular Saturday night soirees, which were attended by many of the superstars of the twenties: Rudolph Valentino, Mary Pickford, Doug Fairbanks, Vilma Banky, Rod La Rocque, Dolores Del Rio, John Gilbert, Charlie Chaplin, Will Rogers, Harold Lloyd, Tom Mix, Florence Vidor, Norma and Constance Talmadge, and Marion Davies.

Presiding over a dinner table at which so many glittering names were gathered would have been a frightening experience for even an older, more experienced hostess. But Frances proved equal to the challenge, as she was to do in so many other areas of Sam's life.

Before many months of living in Hollywood had passed, necessity forced Frances to overcome her fears and inhibitions, and she acquired the poise and know-how necessary to develop into one of the most popular and accomplished hostesses in the movie capital. Soon—even among Hollywood's most sophisticated—it was considered a treat to be invited to dine at the Goldwyns', for the food and service were always excellent—Frances spent thousands on the proper china, silverware, and crystal; the company was stimulating; and the price was certainly right. In addition to setting a beautiful table, the hostess herself was not a bad-looking dish, which one night prompted Mary Pickford to remark to her host, "You know something, Sam, Frances has beautiful hands."

"I know," replied Sam. "Someday I'm going to have a bust made of them."

Though most people in Hollywood sought them, invitations to the Gold-wyns' formal dinner parties weren't easy to come by. Despite Sam's humble beginnings, he was a snob when it came to choosing the people he wanted to grace his dinner table. Just because you were successful in Hollywood didn't automatically guarantee you an invitation to Sam's house. If he had a choice, he much preferred the company of a Pulitzer Prize–winning author, an important publisher, or perhaps the president of United States Steel. So enamored of moneyed or society names was he that he once gave Jimmy Roosevelt, son of Franklin D., a job in his studio which literally entailed no duties, just so he could boast to his friends that the president's son was working for Sam Goldwyn. And Sam a Republican yet!

By the same token, Goldwyn hired Lady Sybil Colfax, an aging British noblewoman, to be the story editor in his London office. About the only qualification Lady Colfax had for the job was that she was a movie fan, but Goldwyn felt that having her on the payroll added the necessary touch of class to his picture-producing image. Oddly enough, Lady Colfax wouldn't have accepted the job if she hadn't erroneously believed she was working for Metro-Goldwyn-Mayer instead of just plain "Samuel Goldwyn Presents." When she discovered her error, she immediately resigned.

Another illustration of Goldwyn's innate snobbish streak occurred during a party he and Frances threw in the mid-forties which was attended by not only some of Hollywood's greatest names, but a host of society people, including Elsa Maxwell and the late Evalyn Walsh McLean, who at the time was the owner of the legendary—and some say cursed—Hope Diamond, which New York jeweler Harry Winston just recently donated to the Smithsonian Institute. One of the other guests at the party was Benjamin Sonnenberg, a highly regarded New York public relations man whom Goldwyn had recently hired at the sum of $50,000 a year just to see what he could do about changing his image from Mr. Malaprop to something more befitting a man of his wealth and prestige in the industry.

As luck would have it, Sonnenberg found himself seated at the dinner table between Elsa Maxwell and Evalyn Walsh McLean—perfectly charming conversationalists but not the glamorous actresses Sonnenberg was hoping to draw as dinner partners. But he was stuck and made the best of it until the end of the evening, when he couldn't resist saying to Goldwyn, "Hey, Sam, what's the big idea of sitting me between Elsa and Evalyn with all this sexy stuff around?"

"You don't want to sit next to actors and actresses," said Sam, completely serious. "They're a waste of time." To Sam, actors and actresses were only the window dressing at his fancy parties.

Occasionally, to fill in vacancies around his dinner table so that his honored and more important guests would have an audience, Goldwyn would issue "command performances" to employees he especially liked. One of his favorites was Collier Young, who was Goldwyn's chief assistant for about five years during the late thirties and early forties. Today Collier Young is better known as the creator of many popular TV series, including "Ironsides," "Mr. Adams and Eve," and "The Rogues."

"I think one of the main reasons Goldwyn liked having me around," recalls Young today, "was that I was kind of Ivy League—Brooks Brothers suits, button-down collars, Dartmouth, and all that. He liked that. Also, I was married to a very pretty girl at the time . . . a Powers model. And Goldwyn wasn't above admiring pretty girls. Anyway, we were dinner guests at his house at least once a week, usually at one of his 'state occasions.' "

One day just before quitting time, Goldwyn called Young into his office and said, "Collier, I want you and Valerie to come to dinner tonight at my house."

"I can't," said Young. "Valerie and I already have another date."

"You'll be sorry," said Goldwyn, highly upset. "Buddy Manchester's going to be there. We will have some very interesting talk."

Though he didn't want to admit it, Young didn't have the faintest idea who Buddy Manchester was. Reiterating his apologies, Young made his exit and dismissed Buddy Manchester from his mind until the next morning, when he was again summoned to Goldwyn's office.

"Well, you missed a wonderful evening," said Goldwyn. "We talked about politics . . . national and local. We talked about world conditions. What this man knows, he could fill a book with."

Still puzzled, Young said, "Who'd you say was the honored guest?"

"I told you," snapped Goldwyn, annoyed. "BUDDY MANCHESTER!"

Unable to contain his curiosity any longer, Young returned to his own office, dialed the Goldwyn residence, and asked to speak with Mrs. Goldwyn.

"Hello, Frances, this is Collier," he said when he got her on the phone. "Will you please tell me something? Who in hell is this Buddy Manchester Sam says you had to dinner last night?"

Frances laughed and said, "Oh, Sam means Manchester Boddy." At the time, Manchester Boddy was publisher of the *Los Angeles Daily News*.

Except for an occasional "ceremonial" glass of champagne, Goldwyn was a teetotaler, and he didn't especially enjoy watching other people get drunk either. As a result, he wasn't the most gracious host around the cocktail hour—an hour he sometimes reserved for story conferences at his home with his writers. Now if there was one thing Sam deplored even more than having to drink himself, it was to see his employees drinking—especially writers, every one of whom he felt was a potential candidate to wind up a dipso, if he or she wasn't careful. It was a axiom Sam couldn't shake: all writers were drunkards, and it was up to him to do his utmost to save them from a drunkard's grave.

Playwright Jerry Chodorov, a one-drink-before-dinner man, remembers the first time Goldwyn invited him to be at his house at five P.M. sharp for a story conference. Promptly at five, Chodorov rang Goldwyn's doorbell. Goldwyn opened the door personally and, without another word of greeting, quickly said as he ushered the writer into the front hall, "You don't want a drink, do you?"

It wasn't that Goldwyn was stingy with his alcohol (although he may have felt it foolish to waste money on something he considered harmful to the body). It was simply that he was somewhat rabid on the subject of keeping fit. He ate simply and rarely more than one helping of anything. His one weakness was ice cream sodas, and it was nothing for him to polish off two at one sitting. He believed that ice cream and dairy products were good for him. It therefore came as a blow to Sam when his doctor informed him that all that ice cream, chock full of butterfat, might be injurious to his health, which he guarded with all the zeal of a hypochondriac.

"Instead of ice cream, you should have two cocktails before dinner," recommended the doctor.

"Alcohol?" exclaimed the dismayed Goldwyn.

"Yes, Sam, it'll open the blood vessels."

Collier Young was having dinner at the Goldwyns' the first night Sam tried taking the doctor's advice. Young, in fact, fixed Goldwyn the first Old Fashioned he ever drank. Before taking it, Goldwyn looked at the glass in his hand as though it contained arsenic, then polished off the drink with a couple of fast swallows. He grimaced as he returned the empty Old Fashioned glass to Collier Young.

"Shall I fix you another one?" asked Young.

"No, thanks," answered Goldwyn.

"The doctor said you should have at least two before dinner," Young taunted him.

Goldwyn thought about it a moment, then said, "Fuck the doctor!"

One obligation incumbent on all Goldwyn's guests was the observance of strict punctuality. Because Sam didn't drink, he was impatient to get to the dinner table. People were invited for a quarter to eight, and if they still weren't there by the dinner hour of eight-thirty, Sam would instruct Frances to start the meal without them. "My husband will not wait dinner for anybody," Frances used to complain. "We're almost alone in this in Hollywood."

Other hostesses in the movie capital, who sometimes didn't serve until ten or eleven P.M., eventually became so attuned to Sam's stomach timetable that when they were inviting the Goldwyns back, they would say to Frances over the phone, "You give Sam a snack beforehand so he won't be hungry if we don't sit down until late."

In addition to running the Goldwyns' social life, Frances soon found herself picking out her husband's clothes. She believed he looked best in conservative dark suits and small checked ties, and he listened to her opinions when they visited his tailor together to choose the material for a new suit.

Since, as noted earlier, Sam was almost fanatical about not wanting to carry anything bulky in his pockets which would spoil the sleek line of his expensively crafted suits, it was now up to Frances to bring along money for dinner and the keys to the front door whenever they left the house. And if Frances was not accompanying him, it would be incumbent on her to see to it that somebody else was the keeper of the keys and his pin money.

While employed by Goldwyn, Collier Young once had to accompany his boss to New York on a business trip. Frances was staying home on that occasion, but she did drive Sam and his traveling companion to the Union depot and then walked with them down to the railroad tracks to make sure they got off all right. Just before they boarded the train, Frances slipped a roll of hundred-dollar bills to Young.

"What's this for?" he asked.

"You'll need this and more—for tips and meals," said Frances. "Sam never carries anything in his pockets. I don't want him to get stuck and have to wash dishes in some restaurant."

But it was Sam's reading habits that led to Frances's active involvement in the business as his unofficial but not-so-silent partner.

Despite his night school education, his years in the movie business, and his constant hobnobbing with literary greats, Sam still read at the snail's pace of a second grader. His lips had to silently pronounce every word on the page before its meaning could be successfully telegraphed to his brain.

As a result of Sam's cripplingly slow reading pace, scripts and other literary material he hadn't yet waded through would pile up on the night table beside his and Frances's bed. During the months immediately following their marriage, Sam had even less time for reading in bed, and the pile grew larger.

Inexperienced as she was at being a housewife, Frances was a fastidious housekeeper. She couldn't stand to see the unsightly pile of scripts beside their bed grow taller and taller—until it finally began to resemble a leaning tower of Pisa of books and scripts. So out of sheer housewifeliness she began reading the scripts in her spare time and making comments about them to Sam when they were alone.

"Delicate comments, I might add," she later recalled. "But Sam listened to me."

The more Sam listened to her "delicate" comments, the more he encouraged Frances to read them, the more stock he took in her opinions—and the smaller the unsightly pile of scripts became.

So due to his inadequate schooling Sam found a lazy man's way out of the burdensome chore of reading all the scripts, story treatments, and books that a studio head was constantly being inundated with by his story editors, directors, stars, and well-meaning friends. It was far easier, he discovered, to turn the chore over to Frances and let her tell him the story. Consequently, the acceptance or rejection of many an important writer's script hung on Frances Goldwyn's ability as a storyteller.

In that regard, Frances's role wasn't too much different from the ordinary studio reader's, that is, to read longer works and synopsize them. Of course, Frances was in a much more influential position than a studio reader, despite her frequent disclaimers to the contrary. "You might say I just cooperate in his thinking," she used to tell reporters and gossip columnists. "But when Sam says 'no' to one of my notions, it's 'NO!' and that's all there is to it. He's the boss and I'm well aware of it. Sam may like to make people think I'm a big important executive to him, but I'm more like a housekeeper around the studio."

In later years Frances actually assumed all the housekeeping responsibilities around the studio. It was up to her, for example, to see to it that the twelve "star" dressing rooms on the Goldwyn lot were properly fitted out for whatever important personage was to occupy them. And that included redecorating them to suit an individual star's tastes as to color and style. Frances had a fetish for cleanliness and was not above getting down on her hands and knees and doing a little scrubbing herself when she wasn't completely satisfied with the cleaning maids.

Frances also fell heir to the task of supervising the running of the studio commissary and the executive dining room, where Sam lunched with his close associates and special friends. Except for the MGM commissary, which was a notable exception (especially its chicken matzo ball soup, which was world famous), most studio food was barely edible (and still is). But Frances and Sam believed that their employees, be they superstars or the lowliest grips, deserved the finest, and without having to leave the lot for it. So Frances insisted on hiring first-rate chefs and ordering only top-quality groceries. As proof of this, the Goldwyn Studio commissary showed a financial loss every year after Frances took over its supervision.

By 1926, Frances had not yet assumed a major role in Sam's professional life. She was still very much the unliberated housewife whose lot it was to sleep in the upper berth when asked and who, in between her domestic chores, dutifully read the scripts Sam brought home, told him the plots, and acted as chief sounding board to his ideas.

Early in 1926 Frances found herself about to take on an additional job, one that would keep her busy for many years to come—motherhood.

Columnist Louella Parsons had gone along with Frances to her doctor's office the day she was informed that she was pregnant. Later the two women returned to the Goldwyn house and broke the news to Sam together. According to Louella, Sam was delighted at the prospect of being a father again. And he was, because except for paying for his daughter's support, he hadn't had the opportunity to play the role of a father since Ruth was two years old—the last time Blanche had allowed them to see each other. Ruth was now thirteen. Moreover, he hoped that the family's new addition would be a boy, because he had dreams of dynasty dancing around in his head; he wanted an heir to take over the studio after he retired and carry on the Goldwyn tradition.

Frances did not disappoint him. At 4:15 on the morning of September 7, 1926, as Sam Goldwyn nervously paced the corridor outside the delivery room on the maternity floor of the Los Angeles Good Samaritan Hospital, Frances, under the care of Dr. Titian Coffey, gave birth to an eight-pound son.

The proud father immediately named him Samuel Goldwyn, Jr. Evidently Sam had not yet formed the opinion he so eloquently expressed years later—"Every Tom, Dick, and Harry is named Sam."

Although a governess was immediately added to the Goldwyns' staff of servants, motherhood, with its attendant responsibilities, forced Frances, for a few years at least, to curtail her interest in the business and wedge her reading and storytelling activities in between her duties as housewife and mother.

Fatherhood, however did not curtail any of Sam's activities. In fact, if anything, it spurred him on to greater productivity at the studio.

By the end of the decade, Sam produced fifteen more pictures, made important stars of Joan and Constance Bennett, Lewis Stone, Lois Moran, Vilma Banky, Doug Fairbanks, Jr., Jean Hersholt, and Ronald Colman; let a couple of potential box-office giants slip through his acquisitive fingers because he underestimated their talent (Gary Cooper and Bette Davis); and was responsible for turning out several minor classics of the period—namely, *Stella Dallas, The Dark Angel,* and *Bulldog Drummond.*

One potential star he didn't miss out on but who almost got away was the British import Ronald Colman. Colman had had an unbilled part in *The Eternal City,* but apparently had made so little impression on Goldwyn that he forgot completely about him until he saw him in Henry King's picture *Romola,* which was filmed in Rome and starred Lillian and Dorothy Gish. Although the picture was a dog, Goldwyn immediately saw Colman's possibilities as a romantic lead and quickly signed him to a long-term contract.

Sam got his money's worth, and then some. Colman became the keystone of his next twenty-five pictures, either starring or costarring in all of them, including Goldwyn's first talking picture, *Bulldog Drummond.* Sam gave him a variety of talented leading ladies, however—Vilma Banky, Lois Moran, Belle Bennett, Lily Damita, and Helen Hayes, in what was only her second movie role, *Arrowsmith.*

Because she was a Broadway actress, used to appearing in no more than one or two plays a year and then pouring her heart and soul into every performance, Hayes could never understand how Colman could go from one picture to another without even a break and possibly do justice to the roles. One day she asked Colman how he managed it. "Oh, I just bring the body to the studio and do anything they ask me," said Colman with a cavalier smile. "You'll never last in the business if you get too emotional about it." Colman evidently had the right attitude, for his movie career lasted almost to the day he died in 1958.

Many of Goldwyn's very early pictures starring Ronald Colman have long been forgotten (as well they should be) and are barely worth mentioning: *Tarnish* (1924), a dreary soap opera adapted by Frances Marion from a Broadway play and directed by George Fitzmaurice (who had also directed *The Eternal City* and was one of Sam's favorites); *A Thief in Paradise* (1925), in which Colman played a derelict in Samoa who ends up marrying a rich San Francisco socialite—also written and directed by the Marion-Fitzmaurice team; and *His Supreme Moment* (1925), about a mining engineer who falls in love with a movie actress—another forgettable epic dished up by Frances Marion and George Fitzmaurice.

But *The Dark Angel,* released six months after Sam's marriage to Frances, is well remembered both for the quality of the film and because it introduced Vilma Banky, one of Sam's major discoveries, to American audiences. But as was the case with many of Sam's discoveries, someone else had actually discovered Vilma Banky first and starred her in several films made in her native Hungary. If it had been otherwise, Miss Banky's picture probably would never have been in the window of a photographer's shop in

Budapest late in 1924, when Sam was visiting that city with the thought of opening a sales office there.

Sam was attracted to the photo by the Rubenesque beauty of Miss Banky and stood staring at her likeness in the window for several minutes, before continuing on down the street. The thought must have occurred to him that he could make a star out of her, but he made no attempt to put the idea into action until he was standing in the train station about to leave Budapest several days later. Then a stroke of bad luck turned out to be extraordinarily good luck. While he was attempting to board his train, the authorities started to question Sam's passport—the trouble arising, no doubt, over the fact that he was a Jew. Hungary at the time was notoriously, and sometimes actively, anti-Semitic, and any Jew traveling in that country was actually taking his life in his hands. But Sam, who had locked horns with some of the toughest people in the glove and movie businesses, was not about to be scared away from opening an office in a city that was a potentially good movie market by a little outbreak of anti-Semitism. However, while he was arguing with the authorities his train pulled out of Budapest.

Sam eventually settled his difficulties in his usual way—by haranguing the officials into a complete state of confusion and then submission in his half-Polish, half-English tongue. And he was waiting for another train to come along when he noticed the girl from the photographer's window standing incarnate, just a few feet from him, looking more beautiful than in the picture.

Gallantly tipping his Homburg, Sam introduced himself as Sam Goldwyn, head of his own movie company in Hollywood. She, in turn, introduced herself to him as Countess Vilma Banky, which she pronounced in a guttural Hungarian accent. Undeterred by her title, Sam said he wanted to bring her to Hollywood for a screen test. If she passed it, he promised, he would start her at $250 a week for the first year, with increases up to $750 by the fifth year.

A great believer in the theory that money talks (and certainly better than he did), Sam whipped out his wallet and handed the surprised Miss Banky $2,000 in crisp American bills. "Then I believed he was the great Sam Goldwyn," she later admitted to the press. "Until then I thought he was a fake."

Sam missed a few more trains before the deal was finalized on paper, for it is not easy to make a deal with a Hungarian under any circumstances, much less while standing on a train platform. But when Sam finally left Budapest he had a five-year contract with Vilma Banky tucked away in his pocket.

Arriving in Hollywood at the beginning of the year 1925, Vilma passed her screen test with flying colors. Glowing with the feeling of a Meglin

Kiddy mother, Sam immediately called a press conference and announced to the world that he had just put "a real countess under contract," and that her first film for him would be *The Dark Angel*. He then whisked his find off to New York City and a round of press conferences and well-publicized social events designed to make the name of Countess Vilma Banky famous from coast to coast. Vilma Banky, in fact, was Sam's date at the Condé Nast party when he became so smitten with Frances. And it was to oversee the production of her first picture—*The Dark Angel*—that Sam had to rush back to Hollywood with Frances without taking a honeymoon.

There were problems with making a star out of Vilma Banky. For one thing, she didn't speak very fluent English, which in itself didn't matter much since talkies still hadn't arrived. But there were times when it was important for her to *understand* English.

Miss Banky had a tendency to eat all the wrong foods and put on weight. It was therefore imperative when she went to a restaurant to order foods with the least caloric content. But since she could barely speak English, it was difficult for her to order anything, and what she did order was usually fattening.

As Sam watched in horror, Vilma started to blow up like the Goodyear blimp during the preproduction period of *The Dark Angel*. Sam finally grabbed the bull between the teeth, to borrow one of his choicest Goldwynisms, and undertook to teach her enough English phrases himself to enable her to order sensibly in a restaurant. This was a little like Donald Duck trying to teach Zsa Zsa Gabor to speak Japanese. Nevertheless, Sam eventually managed, in the way one teaches a parrot to talk—by constant repetition—to get Vilma Banky to learn to say, "Lamb chops and pineapple" whenever she was ordering food. This was all he could ever teach her, and consequently that's all she subsisted on for her first two years in Hollywood. But the pounds did drop off, and her figure soon returned to the same sylphlike proportions that had originally caught Sam's eye in Budapest.

Not only that, in the fad-conscious Hollywood, "lamb chops and pineapple" soon became the "in" diet for people with weight problems—probably because the publicity-conscious Sam was able to persuade the management of the Brown Derby Restaurant to list lamb chops and pineapple on the menus as "The Vilma Banky" diet plate.

In addition to controlling her diet, there was also the problem of her hair. On Sam's instruction, the hairdressers at the studio had lightened Banky's hair to a nice honey color, but Sam was not satisfied with the hairdos they'd been able to come up with. As a last resort he had Frances invite her over to lunch one Sunday. There, while they were sitting around the pool, Sam said to Vilma, "You know, Vilma, your hair isn't right yet."

"Vat's wrong with it?" she asked.

Sam couldn't articulate what was wrong with Vilma's hair, just as he often couldn't tell one of his directors why he didn't like a scene he had just shot. He just knew "I do not like it" and would insist that it be done over—a hundred times if necessary—in order to get the effect he wanted but couldn't quite put into words.

It was the same with Vilma Banky's hairdo. When he couldn't articulate his displeasure, he sent Frances upstairs to her dressing room to fetch a comb, brush, and hairpins. Then, sitting Vilma Banky down before the mirror in the front hall, he proceeded to work out a glamorous hairstyle for the actress himself by trial and error. Frances later recalled, "Sam had a few hairpins sticking out in the wrong places, but basically the style he came up with was the one Vilma wore in *The Dark Angel* and *The Son of the Sheik*."

The Dark Angel was the story of a British army officer who was hiding from his fiancée the fact that he had been blinded in World War I. It had a fine screenplay by Goldwyn's favorite writer of the period, Frances Marion, who fashioned it from a hit play by H. B. Trevelyan, and it was directed by George Fitzmaurice.

It's important to mention here that whenever Sam found a writer he had good rapport with and on whom he could rely, such as Frances Marion, he would stick with that person until his luck ran out or the person was no longer available. Frances Marion did more than a dozen screenplays for Sam during the next few years before talkies came in. After talkies, Sam's favorite writer became playwright Sidney Howard. And following Howard's shocking death in a tractor accident on his New England farm in the late thirties, Lillian Hellman became the "one" writer Sam always called for when he had an important project—until he had a fight with her.

The Dark Angel was both a critical and box-office success and established Vilma Banky as an important star, and Colman and Banky as one of the screen's leading romantic teams. That film also considerably enhanced Sam Goldwyn's reputation as an independent producer.

In his review on October 12, 1925, the *New York Times* critic wrote, in part:

> One cannot help being charmed by the gentle charm of the love story and also by the echoes of the World War. . . . Vilma Banky, the Hungarian actress who was engaged by Samuel Goldwyn, is a young person of rare beauty who might be American or English, with soft fair hair, a slightly *retroussé* nose and lovely blue eyes which have the suggestion of a slant. Her acting is sincere and earnest and her tears seem very real. She is so exquisite that one is not in the least surprised that she is never forgotten by Hilary Trent (played by Ronald Colman) when as a blinded war hero he settles down to dictating boys' stories.

After her success in *The Dark Angel* Vilma Banky received an offer from another studio to play opposite Rudolph Valentino in *The Son of the Sheik*.

Sam surprised everyone by letting her take the part. However, he didn't do it purely because he was such a generous fellow. By bestowing on Vilma the opportunity to engage in passionate love scenes with Valentino before the cameras, Sam was hoping to cook up a real romance between the two—a romance that, ideally, would end in marriage and a big Hollywood wedding. In that, the crafty Sam foresaw millions of dollars' worth of free publicity, which would continue long into the future, just as it had with the union of Mary Pickford and Doug Fairbanks.

Sam's scheme didn't work out quite that way. After Sam loaned Valentino his hottest sex symbol, the ingrate fell in love with Pola Negri instead during the filming of *The Son of the Sheik*. He and Vilma only became good friends.

For several days after Valentino and Pola Negri announced their intention to wed, Sam was in a deep depression over his misfired publicity scheme. Vilma was doing all right, but she hadn't yet excited the public enough to suit Sam. What Sam was looking for was something that would make her front-page news.

He found it one day, with the arrival in Hollywood of Henri Letellier, a French newspaperman. Sam had become friendly with him on his numerous trips to Paris. Letellier expressed a desire to watch Rudolph Valentino and Vilma Banky shooting *The Son of the Sheik*. So Sam took him onto the *Son of the Sheik* set and the two of them looked on while Vilma and Valentino played one of those "deep-breathing," nostril-twitching love scenes for which the Latin lover was so famous. The scene was so realistic that Letellier remarked to Sam, "Valentino must really love her."

"Unfortunately, he doesn't," said Goldwyn.

"The man must be craz–zee," opined the Frenchman. "Any European I know would be daff–fee over Miss Banky."

At that, the publicity wheels of Sam's mind started spinning crazily. Suddenly Sam exclaimed, "Henri, do you know anyone in Paris you could get to send a cable to Miss Banky? Someone you could trust to keep quiet about it afterward?"

Somewhat puzzled, Letellier said he knew one man he thought he could trust. "Good," said Sam, and the next thing Letellier knew, he was sitting in Sam's office, talking to his friend over the transatlantic phone, while Sam, at his side, was telling him what to say.

The next day Vilma Banky received a cable from a Baron Lukatz, professing a love for her more ardent than Cyrano's for Roxane. At the same time, the president of Goldwyn Pictures, also known as Sam Goldwyn, received a cable from the baron, claiming he had been engaged to Vilma when she was still living in Budapest. He said he had been waiting for months for her to return to the banks of the blue Danube to marry him, and now that she insisted on remaining in Hollywood, he was holding Goldwyn Pictures and Rudolph Valentino personally responsible. By evening, Sam had seen to it that all of Hollywood knew about the love-crazed Baron Lukatz. And by the following day Baron Lukatz's passion for his long-lost countess was front-page news from coast to coast.

Banky, who had had a long string of lovers before coming to America, was quite understandably hazy as to whether or not she'd ever known, or been intimate with, a Baron Lukatz. Consequently, whenever newspapermen queried her on the subject, her replies, in her fractured English, were so garbled as to seem deliberately evasive or coy. Which just served to fire the imaginations of the gossip-hungry reporters all the more. They attacked their typewriters with renewed vengeance, which didn't seem to displease Miss Banky, who went right along with the hoax as Sam fed the flames of gossip with new fuel. To keep the drama going, Sam had Lukatz wire Rudolph Valentino that he was coming to the United States on the next ship to fight a duel with him. More cables followed that one. Lukatz was having trouble getting into the United States. Lukatz was being detained at Ellis Island. Lukatz was trying to enter via Mexico. Lukatz was forced to return to his homeland without the one love of his life. And, finally, Lukatz was threatening to do away with himself.

To Sam's great pleasure, the headlines proliferated.

While Sam was playing this drama out to its final dénouement, Vilma Banky fell in love with Rod La Rocque, one of Hollywood's several pretenders to Rudolph Valentino's throne. When this happened, Sam wisely let Baron Lukatz fade quietly away, for he knew that with a pretentious Hollywood wedding in the offing, it wouldn't be long before Vilma would be back in the headlines again—this time with Rod La Rocque.

To be sure there'd be no quiet little elopement Sam personally sponsored the wedding, which took place at the Church of the Good Shepherd in Beverly Hills, on January 27, 1927. Hollywood has rarely seen a more lavish affair. It cost Sam $25,000 of his own money, which was not even tax deductible. Practically every notable in Hollywood was in attendance: the Harold Lloyds, Mary Pickford, Doug Fairbanks, Charlie Chaplin, Cecil B. De Mille, Norma Shearer, Marion Davies, William Randolph Hearst, Will Rogers, and even Tom Mix, who arrived in a purple cowboy outfit and driving an open carriage pulled by four white horses. And like the old-time premières, there were thousands of milling spectators on the street outside the church.

Sam gave the bride away, and Louella Parsons was matron of honor, as cameras, both movie and still, ground away from scaffoldings that Sam had somehow got permission from the local diocese to rig both outside and inside the flower-bedecked church.

Despite the Hollywood hoopla, the Goldwyn Touch was very much in evidence. Those who attended the wedding remember it as being not just colossal, but one of the most elegant and dignified affairs of its kind in Hollywood history—dignified, that is, up until the guests at the reception afterward began to steal the floral decorations and the roast turkeys and baked hams.

To Sam, every cent he spent on Vilma Banky was worth it. After the grosses from *The Dark Angel* started pouring in, Sam called a press conference and announced that he was rewarding Vilma Banky by "voluntarily" tearing up her original contract and giving her a new one starting at $2,000 a week and rising to $4,000 a week on the fourth year.

Whether the gesture actually was voluntary, or he was simply coerced into such magnanimity by an actress ready to bolt if he did not come through, will never be known. But judging from Sam's usual dealings regarding money matters, it was probably the latter that was responsible for the raise. Though willing to pay top dollar for services rendered, Sam will never be remembered for many moments of purely spontaneous generosity—at least that he made good on.

For example, William Selwyn, one of Goldwyn's casting directors, was especially good at finding young actresses whom Goldwyn could sign and mold into stars. One such find was Joan Evans, whose star appeared in the show business firmament for a brief time back in the thirties and then fizzled out. But when Selwyn discovered her, Goldwyn thought he had another Helen Hayes and promised Selwyn a rich bonus if he could bring him another newcomer with equally fine prospects. Selwyn diligently combed the countryside from Hollywood High to Broadway and finally came up with Phyllis Kirk. At the moment of Selwyn's discovery, Sam was in a hospital, recovering from a prostate operation. But he was so anxious to see Selwyn's find that he asked him to bring her to his hospital room.

Sam talked with her, studied her, then sent her away so he and Selwyn could talk. "She's good," said Sam. "I like her. I'll sign her up."

Selwyn reminded Sam of the promised bonus. Sam had difficulty remembering it. Selwyn jogged Sam's memory. Sam nodded and said, "Okay, comes the time you need a prostate operation, it's on me." At the time, Selwyn was only forty—years away from the day such an operation might be necessary.

14

Sam Joins the Moguls

MANY OF SAM'S former associates shook their heads in disbelief following the success of *The Dark Angel*. They felt it must have been an accident. But when he came up with another hit—*Stella Dallas*—right on *The Dark Angel*'s heels, his worst detractors began to look at the former champion glove salesman with new respect.

Stella Dallas had a screenplay by Frances Marion, was directed by Henry King, and starred Belle Bennett in the title role. It also introduced a newcomer to the screen named Lois Moran, who, according to the critics, pulled off a stunning tour de force in her portrayal of Stella Dallas's daughter both as a child and a young woman. In addition, the cast included Ronald Colman, Douglas Fairbanks, Jr., Jean Hersholt, Alice Joyce, and Vera Lewis.

In his review of *Stella Dallas* on November 17, 1925, the *New York Times* film critic wrote:

> The slender rapier triumphs over the spiked bludgeon through the unfurling of the screen conception of Olive Higgins Prouty's novel *Stella Dallas*. It is a picture with a powerful appeal, sad and stirring, and a subject that in most respects Henry King has directed in a masterly fashion. It is a story that will wring many a tear from those who go to the Apollo Theater.

Sam Goldwyn may not have had a college graduate's reading speed, Sam may not have had a large vocabulary, Sam may not have had an even temper, but he seemed to have a visceral feeling about what the public wanted.

Stella Dallas was an out and out tear-jerker—a naughty word in most critics' lexicons—but it was done with such quality that most reviewers found themselves admiring it as much as the general public, which always can be counted upon to gobble up pictures of that genre with the same rapaciousness as they do the popcorn in their laps.

As his rivals were discovering, quality was the main secret to Sam's burgeoning string of successes. A large measure of that quality was born of Sam's undying belief in starting out with the very best property money could buy—usually a successful play or novel—and then hiring the best people available to transfer it to film. But an equally large component had to be Sam's inherent good taste. Where he had acquired it nobody could say, least of all Sam. But he had it in abundance. Sam, for example, didn't believe there was any place on the screen for obscene words, nudity, or excessive violence, and he didn't believe the public wanted that kind of fare, either. Which is why he made the prediction late in his career that "gangster films and pornography" would never last. This was one of the rare instances in his lifetime when he grossly miscalculated the public taste. Even so, he refused to give in to the trend and never made a gangster picture or one exploiting sex in his entire career. Or one that encountered *any* censorship problems. That's because he was a firm believer in film as family entertainment.

"I believe in sex," he used to say, "but a man shouldn't be embarrassed to bring his wife or children into a theater." He also used to say that he wondered what some of today's producers expected to do for an encore after they had shown everything there was to know about sex.

In addition to good taste, Sam had an instinctive eye for beauty; he could take one glimpse of an actress and know there was something wrong with her clothes, make-up, or hairdo. He exhibited the same unerring judgment in looking over a movie set. If it didn't seem right to him, he'd order it torn down—at the cost of thousands of his own dollars—and have it rebuilt to conform to his sense of aesthetics. If that meant a long delay in starting the picture, so be it.

The care he took, which most of the time led to fine quality, was, in a sense at least, born of necessity. As an independent, risking his own capital and competing on the open market with the large Hollywood film factories, Sam had to make superior pictures or quit. The majors had dozens of producers under contract, but Sam was the only producer on his payroll. There was no way he could compete with them on an output basis. During Hollywood's halcyon days, the combined output of the major studios—MGM, Paramount, Fox, RKO, Columbia, Universal—was some 600 feature films. During his most active days, Sam produced no more than three or four films a year. But this gave him an advantage in the race for quality. With a smaller producing schedule, he had the time to supervise personally his entire output. The production heads of the other studios were forced to delegate their authority and divide their energies. The results weren't always top-quality films, because there weren't that many top-quality minds that could be hired to assume the large workload. On the few occasions when Sam had more than a couple of pictures in production at once, he might delegate authority to an associate producer and let him have his name on the screen beneath his executive producer credit.

George Haight, an ex-Broadway playwright, and Merritt Hulburd, a former *Saturday Evening Post* editor, worked for him in that capacity during the mid-thirties. But they had little authority because Sam didn't trust any other producer's judgment.

Not being infallible, of course, Sam produced a few stinkers over the years without any extra producing help. Three notable examples: *Nana*, *Woman Chases Man*, and *The Adventures of Marco Polo*, in which Gary Cooper as Marco Polo was seen eating spaghetti in medieval China.

Characteristically, Sam always claimed to have been out of the country when his worst pictures were being made and put the blame on his subordinates. In the case of *Woman Chases Man*, Goldwyn blamed the fiasco on a man who wasn't around, either—playwright Eddie Chodorov, brother of Jerry and himself the author of several hit plays, among them *Kind Lady* and *Oh, Men, Oh, Women*. But he *had* been around. Goldwyn once tried to hire him to write a screenplay based on a screen treatment having the unfortunate title of *Woman Chases Man*. But Chodorov, no man to toady, gave *Woman Chases Man* one swift reading and informed Goldwyn that it was "atrocious" and that he would have nothing to do with the project. Furthermore, he stated, Goldwyn would be out of his mind if he didn't abandon it himself.

Goldwyn lost his temper and promptly had Chodorov ejected from his studio. He then went ahead and made the picture anyway and, of course, it flopped.

Years passed, and Chodorov's agent recommended his client to Goldwyn for another project.

"Chodorov . . . Chodorov!" exclaimed Sam explosively. "I won't have anything to do with that bum. He was connected with one of my worst failures."

Fortunately, *Woman Chases Man* was one of Goldwyn's few losers at the box office.

Part of the credit for Sam's success must go to the fact that, as wealthy as he became, he never forgot the lesson he learned as a glove salesman: that you could make the finest quality gloves in the business, but if you couldn't sell them to the public, what good would it do you?

Consequently he never allowed his interest in the selling end of the business to be overshadowed by his producing chores. There may have been those who believed that the Goldwyn Touch was mostly luck, but everyone

in show business venerated Sam as a supersalesman. Because of his un-
equaled ability at stirring up excitement about his forthcoming films, Sam
could always get better prices for them from the exhibitors than other independents were getting for their product. Theater owners complained that
Sam was "holding them up," but nearly all of them paid what he demanded. One who refused was Abraham Finkelstein, who owned a large
theater in Minneapolis. Learning of this by phone from his midwestern
representative, Sam exclaimed indignantly, "I'll go there myself and show
you how to sell pictures!" And he hopped the next train for Minneapolis.

When he heard that the great Sam Goldwyn was coming to visit him,
Finkelstein, a tall, elderly, stoop-shouldered, softspoken man, did Sam the
honor of meeting him at the depot with his chauffeur-driven limousine.
Back in his office, Finkelstein listened with grave courtesy to Sam's sales
pitch. He even admitted that he liked the picture very much. Obviously
Sam felt he was getting through. But the moment Sam mentioned the
price, Finkelstein pressed a buzzer on his desk. In walked two men in the
uniform of lunatic asylum attendants, carrying a large net, which they
threw around Sam as they led him out the door.

After conquering his initial rage, Sam returned to Finkelstein's office
later that afternoon and said he appreciated a good practical joke as well as
anybody. He then announced that he would build a theater in Minneapolis
and run Finkelstein out of business.

Whereupon Finkelstein reached for his hat and said, "Come with me,
Sam. I'll show you the best sites. I'll get you a good deal. I know the man
who owns all the property."

He drove Sam around Minneapolis, pointing out all the best sites for
movie theaters and quoting prices as outrageous for acreage in Minneapolis
in 1926 as he felt Sam's asking price was for his film.

"That's a good deal?" exclaimed Sam indignantly, after Finkelstein quoted
him a $100,000 figure on a piece of property that appealed to him but
which was worth, at the most, $25,000. "Tell him I offer fifty thousand
and not a penny more."

"He won't take it," said Finkelstein.

"How do you know until you ask him?" demanded the outraged Sam.

"I just know," replied Finkelstein.

"Then tell *me* his name," exploded Sam. "I'll ask him."

"His name is Finkelstein," said Finkelstein.

Perhaps because of his unhappy experience with Finkelstein—but more
likely because he felt his pictures could be even better if he were to devote
more of his time to producing and less to dickering with obdurate theater
owners over prices—Sam made a move in 1926 that once again seriously

compromised his position as a completely independent film producer. He allied his organization with United Artists—a company that had been set up in 1919 by D. W. Griffith, Charlie Chaplin, Doug Fairbanks, and Mary Pickford as an outlet for their independent pictures, which could not compete on an individual basis with the larger and stronger releasing organizations of the major studios. The theory behind the formation of United Artists was that by representing the "indies" in one united bloc, it would have more clout and thus be able to demand and get a reasonable price for its product from the theater owners.

By the time Sam decided to cast his lot with United Artists, its other member-owners were Joe Schenck, who was running the studio for the others, Charlie Chaplin, Mary Pickford, and Douglas Fairbanks. Several years later British film producer Alexander Korda also became a member-owner. But though they were all names to be contended with across a board-room table, in theory at least Sam was not taking on any troublesome partners when he allowed himself to be elected a member-owner of United Artists in 1927. As a member-owner he would share equally in the profits of the company with the others, but he would remain completely autonomous regarding his own productions. Under that arrangement, Sam felt, there could be no bitter disagreements of the kind that caused the dissolution of his past associations.

Once again Sam overestimated the ability of the rest of the human race to be able to get along with his even temper. Before long the wrangling between himself, Pickford, Chaplin, and Fairbanks was to reach such a pitch that all four partners would be sending their lawyers to represent them at stockholders' meetings, because they weren't talking to one another.

Sam had high respect for Chaplin as a comedian. In fact, he thought he was probably the funniest man who ever lived. But he had a much lesser opinion of him as a businessman and associate. After tangling with Chaplin at a couple of board meetings, Sam said of his business practices, "The only thing Charlie knows about business is that he can't afford to take less."

The main bone of contention between Goldwyn and the others in the United Artists setup was that as time went on, Sam felt there was an unfair distribution of the profits. Each partner was sharing equally, but their output wasn't equal. Between them Doug Fairbanks and Mary Pickford made only six films and Chaplin only one picture in Goldwyn's first five years as a member-owner of United Artists. Meanwhile Sam was cranking out quality films at a steady three-or-four-pictures-a-year clip.

In 1926 Goldwyn released *The Winning of Barbara Worth*, a high-quality Western in which an engineer from the East (Ronald Colman) competes with a cowpoke for the love of a woman (Vilma Banky—who else?). The cowpoke was played by a tall, lanky, "shit-kicking" young man who really came from the West—Helena, Montana—and who actually had been a cowboy. His name was Gary Cooper.

Cooper, oddly enough, had not migrated to Hollywood to be an actor. His ambition had been to become a cartoonist on a newspaper. But when no cartooning jobs were available, he sought extra work to keep from starving. Central Casting sent him over to the Goldwyn Studios one day. It was there, in his outer office, that Goldwyn noticed the diffident Westerner, dressed in an ill-fitting suit and cowboy boots, sitting nervously on a bench. Sam thought he'd be ideal for the part of the cowboy in *Barbara Worth*, and after cross-examining the young man and getting a few "yups" in reply, Sam ordered a test made of him. He liked the results and signed him for fifty dollars a week.

The picture was successful, with the young man from Montana turning in a very competent performance literally playing himself—a shy cowpoke. Despite that, Sam let him go after using him in that one picture, feeling he would be much too difficult to find parts for in the future.

Sam paid dearly for this mistake. Paramount immediately signed Cooper to a long-term contract, at $200 a week, built him into a superstar, and when Sam wanted him ten years later, he had to pay him $3,000 a week to get him.

Sam followed *The Winning of Barbara Worth* with two more Banky-Colman starrers, *The Magic Flame* and *The Night of Love*, which introduced Sally Rand to movie audiences (but with all her clothes on), and *The Devil Dancer*, starring Clive Brook, Gilda Gray, and Anna May Wong.

The Devil Dancer, released in 1927, offered something new to audiences— a musical score. It contained no spoken dialogue, for that technique hadn't been perfected yet. But it did have a soundtrack with background music on it.

Though still in its infancy, sound was about to revolutionize the picture business.

There had been sporadic experimentation with music and sound effects on film as early as 1921. But in 1927 Warner Brothers stunned the world of silent-film makers by releasing a film version of the Broadway hit *The Jazz Singer*, starring America's favorite minstrel, Al Jolson. Not only was there spoken dialogue in *The Jazz Singer*, but in one lachrymose sequence, Jolson sang "Sonny Boy" to a youngster on his lap.

The dialogue in the Jolson picture was used sparingly, and not in every sequence. Nevertheless, it was obvious to most people that the motion picture business was about to undergo a great change. This realization had many veteran producers quaking in their puttees. Not only was it an enormous expense to convert to sound, but not every silent-picture actor or actress had a good voice for talkies, or enough stage acting experience to be able to handle dialogue. For example, it was discovered in his first talkie that John Gilbert, one of the greatest of silent-day screen lovers, had a high-pitched, girlish-sounding voice that over the screen soundtrack got laughs in what were allegedly serious romantic scenes. Other sweethearts of the silent-picture era were inclined to lisp or croak, with the same disastrous consequence—audiences either hooted, whistled, or went into paroxysms of laughter the first time they heard their former screen favorites open their mouths in a love scene. Glittering careers, such as John Gilbert's, were tragically cut short.

So there was ample reason for people heretofore making thousands of dollars per week to panic at the thought of suddenly losing their cushy livelihoods.

There were others, however, Joe Schenck among them, who felt that talkies were just a passing fancy. The thing to do was just wait the novelty out.

Sam Goldwyn, himself uncertain as to what the future would bring, decided to play it safe. He continued to make silents up until 1929, but he cut his production schedule in half while he waited to see which way the winds would blow. *Two Lovers* (starring Vilma Banky and Ronald Colman); *The Awakening* (starring just Banky); and *The Rescue*, a cinematization of the Joseph Conrad novel (starring Colman and Lily Damita) were all he turned out after *The Devil Dancer*.

By the end of 1928, however, Sam was able to get a much clearer idea of what the future portended. For it was in 1928 that Warner Brothers released the first "all-talking" picture—*Lights of New York*, starring Helene Costello and Cullen Landis.

After seeing the lines around the block to get into *Lights of New York*, Sam knew there was no way he could any longer avoid making talkies if he wished to remain in the business.

Cautiously, Sam told Frances Marion to prepare a script that would contain "some sound effects" and "some dialogue." The story was titled *This Is Heaven*, and it was to star Vilma Banky and James Hall.

In a move typical of the way Sam Goldwyn operated all his life, he tried to find the best sound engineer in the business to help him hurdle the frighteningly wide crevasse between silents and talkies. He found him in the person of Gordon Sawyer, a twenty-three-year-old native Californian with a bachelor of science degree in engineering from UCLA.

Sawyer was one of Sam's most important discoveries. For this young man turned out to be a near-genius when it came to setting up studio sound systems. But like a good many of his major discoveries, Sam did not actually discover Gordon Sawyer—Joe Schenck did. However, if it had not been for a ruling made by the FCC in 1927, neither of these esteemed Columbuses could have claimed the honor, and Hollywood would have lost one of its finest sound technicians.

After getting his degree in electrical engineering, Gordon Sawyer started building broadcasting studios under contract. Commercial radio was also on the horizon and everyone was trying to become a broadcaster. But in 1927 the FCC clamped down on the practice of issuing broadcasting licenses to just anyone, which practically put Gordon Sawyer out of business. Casting about for someone who could utilize his highly specialized talents, Sawyer decided to go to Hollywood, because talkies were just then coming in.

In Hollywood, Sawyer sought and got an interview with Joe Schenck, president of United Artists. Schenck was impressed with Sawyer's background and hired him to install the first sound system at United Artists, which he did, at a cost of over $250,000.

Schenck was pleased with the work he did, and gave him a permanent job as head of United Artists' sound department. By then Sam Goldwyn was ready to start making talking pictures, so Schenck put the two of them together, and they stayed together for the next forty years, with Sawyer choosing to remain with Goldwyn Studios after Sam split with United Artists in 1939.

In one of the rare instances when a former Goldwyn employee had anything good to say about his boss, Sawyer remembered, on the occasion of his retirement from the company in 1968, that he and Goldwyn had got along beautifully from the start.

"Maybe that's because Sam and I had the same birthdate—August twenty-seventh. But actually we were quite the opposite. Mr. Goldwyn was interested in the artistic end of pictures and publicity; my interests were strictly electrical and mechanical. As a result, he never tried telling me what to do."

Whatever the chemistry between them, it worked.

During his years with Goldwyn, Sawyer won seven Academy Awards and twenty-nine nominations for best achievement in sound, on such blockbusters as *The Best Years of Our Lives, Wuthering Heights, Porgy and Bess, Hurricane, In the Heat of the Night,* and *Guys and Dolls.*

However, when Sawyer started in the business, awards were the least of his concerns. There were too many legitimate problems to worry about and try to solve. For one thing, sound equipment was heavy and clumsy. "When we went on location, we had to take along twenty tons of sound equipment, gas-driven motors to work the generators, etc.," recalls Gordon Sawyer today. "As a result, we didn't go on location very much."

Another problem: sound wasn't recorded on the film soundtrack, as it is today. It was recorded on discs, like record platters. When the movie was being shown in the theater, the projectionist would play the sound disc on a victrola at the same time as the film was going through the projector and then hoped the two would be in sync.

"But sometimes," says Sawyer, "the phonograph needle would skip a groove or two. As a result, a male voice might start coming out of female lips, and vice versa. The picture would get big laughs when it wasn't intended to."

Recording on discs posed another problem. It meant that sound couldn't be intercut. If there was a lot of dialogue and action taking place in one scene, but in different locations within the scene, there had to be separate camera and sound setups for each bit of action and dialogue. This meant that the entire set had to be lit all over at the same time and at the same light intensity. Sometimes there'd be as many as eight vignettes within the larger scene being photographed at once, with eight times as many powerful lights turned on as would be needed if the same scene were being filmed today. The result of this would be intense heat—sometimes rising as high as 125 degrees—on the sound stage. "A great many actors and actresses couldn't take the heat," remembers Sawyer, "and there'd be considerable fainting. Especially among the Goldwyn Girls, who had to do a lot of dancing."

Another problem that made shooting tedious was that the early sound equipment picked up unwanted interferences—a car honking on the street or a toilet flushing—from as far as a block away and magnified them clear out of proportion. The simple unfolding of a piece of paper or the unwrapping of a stick of chewing gum in a scene made a crackling noise as loud as machine-gun fire. A lover's panting on the screen might sound like a lion's roar. And there was that ever-present hissing or frying noise that underscored all the dialogue, sometimes obliterating it completely.

Too much action or movement in a scene caused the dialogue to grow distractingly loud or fade out completely, depending on the distance between the actor doing the talking and the microphone.

Sam dumped these and many other problems in Gordon Sawyer's lap to solve and gave him carte blanche as to what he could spend. He had but one proviso: " 'That I can amortize the cost;' " says Sawyer. "But that was the marvelous thing about working for Mr. Goldwyn. I used to have lunch with him in his private dining room, and he always used to say, 'You get what you pay for.' "

Sawyer's long years of service plus his impressive shelf full of Oscars seem proof that Sam, once again, got his money's worth. Among Sawyer's many contributions to the industry: the traveling microphone boom and the idea of planting mini-mikes in flower pots, down the front of actresses' dresses, and behind furniture in order to keep the level of the sound constant in scenes where there was a lot of movement.

Sam had one problem in connection with making his first talking picture that even a genius like Sawyer couldn't solve—Vilma Banky's Hungarian-flavored accent.

Despite Sam's exhortations at the arrival of sound that she'd better put herself into the hands of an English tutor, Vilma would not undertake the task of learning to master English or at least to shed her Hungarian accent, which, if anything, was more guttural after three years in America than it had ever been. Or perhaps it was just too late in her life to learn a new language. At any rate, in *This Is Heaven* her accent was so broad that American audiences needed an interpreter to know what she was talking about.

Today her performance could have been saved by a technique known as looping—dubbing an understandable voice into the soundtrack in synchronization with her lip movements. But looping was unheard of in 1928. Vilma Banky and the audience were stuck with the actress's own voice.

As a result, the New York opening went over with something less than a bang—in fact, it was more like a whimper. The *New York Times* reviewer labeled *This Is Heaven* a "harmless but not too original fable." He gave Miss Banky's voice, which had never been heard before, a left-handed compliment when he wrote, "She has a charming Hungarian accent, and most of what Miss Banky said could be understood." He qualified this, however, by pointing out that she spoke in only one scene in the entire picture. He concluded by saying, "During one juncture she aroused a gale of merriment by telling her *vis-à-vis*, James Hall, not to be funny."

After hearing "gales of merriment" in the wrong places in theaters from coast to coast, Sam regretfully came to the conclusion that Vilma Banky was through in pictures, and so, for that matter, was his sure-fire romantic team of Banky and Colman, who luckily had missed being in *This Is Heaven*. Unfortunately for Sam, Miss Banky's contract still had two years to run, with an obligation on his part to pay her about $250,000. Even more unfortunately, Miss Banky refused to let Sam out of his obligation and insisted upon being paid the full sum he owed her while she sat out her contract. This was in marked contrast to the ladylike behavior of Geraldine Farrar, who, when she found herself losing popularity and becoming a burden to Sam some years earlier, voluntarily tore up her contract, thus relieving Sam of the obligation of paying her a quarter of a million dollars.

Having lost the distaff side of his romantic team, Sam had no intention of risking the other half by putting Colman in a vehicle that could ruin his career as well.

Colman's stage-trained voice posed no problems such as the ones that sent John Gilbert, among others, scurrying into early retirement. His diction was good and his voice was full of manly resonance. But the eccentric behavior of the primitive sound equipment was still something to be contended with, especially in the tender romantic sequence. Heavy breathing sounded like a cow in labor, and the whispering of sweet nothings frequently came off like two snakes hissing at each other.

As a result, Sam was wary of presenting Ronald Colman as a great lover, despite his previous success with feminine audiences. As far as he was concerned, there would be no serious billing and cooing in a Goldwyn picture until the sound apparatus stopped making Romeos sound like barnyard imitators.

To avoid this problem, Sam decided to yank his number-one star out of romance and put him in melodrama, which didn't require great love stories in order to be successful.

He chose *Bulldog Drummond* as Ronald Colman's first talkie and engaged Sidney Howard, one of America's leading playwrights, to write the screenplay, which was based on the British stage hit of the same name.

Engaging Sidney Howard (author of *They Knew What They Wanted* and *The Silver Cord*, a huge hit in 1926) to help him bridge the gap between silents and talkies might very well have been the real genesis of Sam's growing love affair with "the writer."

He'd been on the same track, of course, when he'd formed Eminent Authors, Inc., nearly a decade earlier, but two factors had derailed the scheme: He had chosen authors obviously unsuited for screen writing, and he'd given them carte blanche with ideas. But when talkies started to raise their noisy head, Sam returned to his earlier thinking that the writer is supreme and therefore the keystone of every successful production. And in a talking picture, Sam felt, there could be no doubt of the writer's worth. In talkies good dialogue had to be more important than subtitles had been in silent pictures. In retrospect that seems like a rather obvious conclusion, but amazingly there were a great many producers and directors around in those days who still didn't see it that way. In fact, one old-time director once stated to the press, "We don't need anybody to write dialogue. Just put the actors into situations, and let them say what pops into their minds."

Any director who lets an actor make up his own dialogue has got to fail in the long run. Which is why that gentleman and a number of other directors with similar delusions didn't last very long after talkies came in.

A few present-day directors have experimented with letting actors ad-lib dialogue throughout an entire feature-length movie, the theory being that the spontaneity of an ad-lib line achieves a degree of realism not possible to attain with well-rehearsed, written dialogue. And a few exponents of the technique—notably John Cassavetes—have achieved some success with it, especially in the eyes of the avant-garde critics and art-film buffs. But by and large ad-lib scenes that continue for any great length of time are more soporific than entertaining, and dangerous to fool around with.

After a few early-day talkies failed, the ad-lib school of picturemaking was quickly supplanted by the method of putting every bit of dialogue and action down on paper and adhering to it religiously on the set. Once it was recognized how important good dialogue was, a new job was born within the industry—that of the dialogue director. It was the duty of the dialogue director to sit on the set with the open script on his or her lap and keep scrupulous track of any deviations from the correct dialogue and call them to the director's and cast's attention.

In converting from silents to talkies, Goldwyn was astute enough to recognize that the ear is more critical of bad dialogue than is the eye.

Such lines as generally seen in subtitles: "Unhand that woman, you knave, or I will put you in your grave" and "Have pity on me, sir. You are a strong man, and I am but a defenseless woman"—when put into actors' mouths had audiences rolling in the aisles in hysterics.

Sam properly decided that if the theater was the ideal training ground for actors and actresses, the same yardstick could be applied to the people who wrote the dialogue for stage plays. And having seen and admired Sidney Howard's work on the stage, he was quick to accept his story editor's suggestion that he hire the celebrated playwright to write the screenplay for *Bulldog Drummond.*

It was a happy marriage from the start. Howard wrote a first-rate script, of a genre that was brand-new to the screen in those days—the self-satirizing melodrama. It was about a British private eye who had a James Bondish way with women, and it was filled with not only believable, witty dialogue but also lots of action. The latter was in itself a novelty in talking pictures, because most talkies prior to *Bulldog Drummond* were *all* talk and *no* action.

In trying to imbue *Bulldog Drummond* with the kind of quality he thought it deserved, Sam borrowed another custom from the stage—rehearsing the script in its entirety, using real sets and props, before a single foot of film was shot. Most Hollywood directors frowned on that practice, believing it to be unnecessary and too time-consuming. The usual custom was to run through a scene quickly, then shoot it—over and over until it was right. It was not unusual for there to be as many as thirty takes of a single scene before a director was satisfied. Obviously a form of rehearsing in itself, but a costly practice inasmuch as the cameras were rolling and expensive film was being wasted.

Wanting no further truck with this hit-or-miss method, Sam demanded full rehearsals, "just like on the stage," from his director, F. Richard Jones. In the long run it saved time and money, not to mention that the performances were smoother because the actors knew their dialogue and the action that was to go with it. Sam was so pleased with the results that he insisted that every picture he produced from *Bulldog Drummond* on be completely rehearsed before he'd allow the cameras to roll.

Perhaps because *Bulldog Drummond* was his first all-talking picture and Sam wanted to be doubly sure that it was good, he became a greater stickler for detail during its filming than he had ever been. The opening scene of the picture, for example, takes place in a very staid British men's club peopled by a number of Colonel Blimp characters. When a waiter breaks the silence by dropping a spoon on the plush carpeting, Sidney Howard had one of the members exclaim: "What is the meaning of this infernal din?"

Sam liked the scene when he saw it in the projection room, but afterward complained to Richard Jones that he thought he heard the word *din*. Was that true?

Jones corroborated that.

"What does this word *din* mean?" asked Sam, contorting his face in puzzlement.

"It means noise," replied Jones

"Then why didn't the writer say *noise?*" demanded Sam. And he ordered Jones to reshoot the scene, substituting the word *noise*.

Since the set had to be rebuilt and the actors rehired, this involved considerable expense—approximately $20,000 more. But in the end, Sam must have felt that all the care and attention he lavished on *Bulldog Drummond* were well worth every extra penny. For both the public and critics were delighted with the final product, which starred, in addition to Ronald Colman, Joan Bennett, in her first screen role, and Lilyan Tashman, one of the great beauties of the day.

Sam, Frances, and Colman traveled to New York City to be present at the opening of *Bulldog Drummond* at the Apollo Theater on May 2, 1929. Mordaunt Hall's review in the *New York Times* the following morning was an unqualified rave.

> Those who are wont to fling flip comments against talking pictures had better spend an evening at the Apollo Theater, where Samuel Goldwyn last night presented before an appreciative gathering his audible picture translation of that clever, bright melodrama *Bulldog Drummond*. It is the happiest and most enjoyable entertainment of its kind that has so far reached the screen.

The *Times* reviewer also paid tribute to the "acting of Ronald Colman and Joan Bennett," "the flexible cross cutting," the "speedy action," "the artful camera work," and "the set design."

And he capped the whole thing off with: "In the audience last night was the bashful Mr. Colman, who escorted Mrs. Goldwyn to a box which was soon the cynosure of all eyes. He bowed before the film was screened, and he bowed afterwards."

Seeing Mrs. Goldwyn mentioned in the body of the review as the "cynosure of all eyes" must have given Sam additional satisfaction, for it obviously meant that the name of Goldwyn was beginning to mean something to the public. No longer was Sam Goldwyn just a faceless man behind the scenes who raised the money for the real creators. Sam was a star in his own right, and one well on his way to becoming a superstar among Hollywood producers for the next four decades.

15

The Ziegfeld of the Pacific

ALONG WITH EVERYTHING ELSE, the movie business was hit hard by the stock market crash in October 1929, and the long depression that followed—the worst in United States history. Large and small businesses were closing, throwing millions out of work; stockbrokers were jumping out of windows; and former bankers were hawking apples on street corners for five cents apiece.

Sam Goldwyn personally wasn't hurt too badly by the market crash. He owned a few blue chip securities that plummeted along with the others on the big board, but since he wasn't on margin and owned them outright, his losses were mostly paper losses. Even so, the bulk of his money was either in cash or invested in his picture company.

However, there was a general box-office slump across the nation, causing many an "indie" to go into bankruptcy and the others to pull in their reins. Sam did neither, preferring to meet the challenge of decreasing revenue head on—with his usual enthusiasm, imagination, and the free spending of his own money on high-budget pictures.

Sizing up the depressed state of the public, Sam decided that the best way to entice customers back into theaters was to give them something to cheer them up—music, laughter, and lots of pretty girls. To implement this noble endeavor Sam bought the film rights to Florenz Ziegfeld's hit Broadway musical *Whoopee*, which had a book by William Anthony McGuire and great songs by Gus Kahn and Walter Donaldson.

Sam also signed its star, Eddie Cantor, to re-create the role he played on Broadway—that of a hypochondriacal Easterner on the lam from the outraged parents of the girl with whom he elopes, and who gets mixed up with some Indians and "bad guys" out West.

On Broadway *Whoopee* had been a typical Ziegfeld extravaganza, featuring expensive scenery, sure-fire comedy and songs, the Ziegfeld lineup of gorgeous girls dressed as Indian maidens in very scanty (for the time) Indian costumes, and real horses for the Indian maidens to ride.

Because he wanted his movie to be as much of an extravaganza as the stage show, and he himself was unfamiliar with the making of girlie musicals, Sam hired Florenz Ziegfeld, also known as the Great Ziegfeld, to help him produce the picture and Busby Berkeley, who'd staged the dance sequences on Broadway, to do the same for the film.

Whoopee was one of the first Broadway musical comedies to be brought to the screen. One that preceded it by a few months was *The Cocoanuts*, starring the Marx Brothers in their first film. But *Whoopee* was larger in scope, and it was historic for another reason. It was the first film ever to employ Busby Berkeley's innovation of shooting the dance sequences from all angles, including virtually downward from above—a shot that has since become a cliché kidded in all movie satires of the period.

In keeping with his policy of using the author of the original work to do his own screenplay, Sam signed William Anthony McGuire to put *Whoopee* into script form. That is, he thought he had signed him, but just as McGuire was to go west, some Broadway producer claimed he had him under contract to write a stage musical. McGuire didn't care to honor that commitment, feeling the stage producer had lost his option on his services by letting the contract run out. But before McGuire could go to work on *Whoopee* lots of epithets were exchanged between Sam and the other producer. With no solution in sight, Sam's lawyer recommended that the contractual problem be arbitrated by a disinterested third party.

"All right," Sam finally agreed to that suggestion. "I'm a fair man. I'll submit anything to arbitration. But remember, no matter what is decided, McGuire goes to work for me."

With his usual perseverance, Sam won out, and McGuire went to work for him.

During the preproduction stages, Sam emerged victorious from a couple of his battles with Florenz Ziegfeld, too. Ziegfeld wasn't actually Sam's partner in the venture; technically he was an employee with the title of associate producer. But he was the closest thing to a partner Sam had had since his exodus from MGM in 1923, because part of the terms of Ziegfeld's sale of *Whoopee* to Goldwyn was that he be allowed to share in the profits. Getting that, he felt he should have a voice in how the picture was made, and where.

Because his home base was in New York, Ziegfeld suggested that Sam make the picture on Long Island. But Sam held out for the West Coast. After days of arguing with Ziegfeld over the long-distance phone, Sam finally overcame his opposition by insisting, "But, Ziggy, the facilities are so good in Hollywood. For instance, we have that Indian scene. We can get the Indians right from the reservoir."

Ziegfeld went to his grave claiming that Sam had actually said that. So did William Anthony McGuire, who swore in front of friends that he had been in Sam's office when Sam was making that phone call.

Around Broadway, Ziegfeld was called the Great Ziegfeld not only because he was considered the world's greatest showman, but because as a connoisseur of female beauty he was supposed to have no peers. Sam, however, didn't see it that way. When Ziegfeld didn't show up on the West Coast in time to help pick out the chorus, Sam, feeling he knew a pretty girl when he saw one, went ahead and made the selections on his own.

When Ziegfeld saw them for the first time, he grudgingly admitted that some of Sam's choices were attractive, but was able to find a flaw in each of the pretty maidens. "She's too short," "She's too fat," "Her tits aren't big enough," "She has a big nose," and so forth.

Sam felt Ziegfeld was carping only because he hadn't had a hand in making the selections, but being a democratic man, he gave Ziegfeld the opportunity to try to top his choices. Ziegfeld rose to the bait. He scampered back to New York, selected two dozen of his best Ziegfeld girls and, at his own expense, transported them to Hollywood. There, on the Goldwyn lot, a beauty contest was held to make the final determination.

Sam's chorus, thereafter known as the Goldwyn Girls, were judged the prettiest. As proof of even the Great Ziegfeld's acceptance of this, he took several of them back to New York after the filming of *Whoopee* and put them in his next *Follies*. Among that batch were Virginia Bruce and Paulette Goddard.

One phase of making musicals at which Sam wasn't so expert as he was at picking out girls was the musical end itself. It's been suggested by more than one composer in the Hollywood musical scoring fraternity that Sam had a tin ear. He may have had some instinctive genius for putting his famed Goldwyn Touch on every other end of the business—costumes, settings, characters, dialogue, plot construction, and publicity, but when it came to music, every composer who worked for him swore he knew nothing, and had stories to back up their claims.

When Sam was making *Whoopee*, for example, he heard Busby Berkeley refer to a certain rhythm used in a time step as "two-four time." Thereafter, whenever Sam wanted to refer to a similar beat, he would call it "two-by-four time."

He once told another composer who was scoring one of his serious dramas that his music would not do at all.

"What's the matter with it?" asked the composer.

"There's not enough sarcasm in it," replied Sam. He meant not enough "bite."

After the Cole Porter song "Night and Day" became a hit in one of the early Astaire and Rogers musicals, *The Gay Divorcee*, Sam told the Goldwyn music department: "We must have a song like 'Night and Day' in our new picture."

It was not, of course, an easy order to fill. But Sam insisted he would not be satisfied with anything less. Meanwhile, he kept raving to his friends about what a song "that 'Night and Day' is." After hearing him pay tribute to the tune for about a month, a friend whose house Sam was visiting one night played a record of "Night and Day" for his guest's enjoyment.

Sam cocked an ear toward the speaker as the first strains of the chorus filled the room, then asked, "What tune is that?"

In 1934, Sam made a picture of Tolstoy's *Resurrection* and called it *We Live Again*. In it, there was a scene that was supposed to take place in a Eastern Orthodox church during Easter services. Sam insisted to composer Al Newman, who was head of his music department, that the "service music be *authentic* Eastern Orthodox." After Newman composed the music and had it recorded on the soundtrack, Sam was so excited with the results that he rushed around the lot, calling executives away from important work to hear a playing of the Eastern Orthodox Easter service music in his projection room. Unhappily, the projectionist had forgotten to rewind the soundtrack since playing it for Sam the first time. So what Sam and the others heard was the soundtrack going through the machine backward, playing the music backward. Catching his error, the projectionist was about to call it to Sam's attention and start over, when he heard murmurs of "great," "magnificent" coming from the audience. Too scared now to mention his error to the vituperative Sam, the projectionist allowed the entire Eastern Orthodox Easter service to be played backward to its conclusion, at which point the projection room rang out with applause and assorted "bravos" for Al Newman (who, fortunately, wasn't there).

Despite Sam's lack of musical knowledge, *Whoopee* drew unqualified raves from the *New York Times* and *Variety*, the so-called bible of show business.

In the *New York Times*, October 1, 1930:

> So excellent is the fun fashioned by Eddie Cantor in the Ziegfeld-Goldwyn screen adaptation of *Whoopee* which was presented last night at the Rivoli before a smart audience that those who had been compelled to fight their way through the throng on entering the theater room forgot those annoying experiences once the picture was under way.

Sime Silverman, the founder and editor of *Variety*, wrote: "Sam Goldwyn's system seems to be working out. He doesn't make 'em often, but when he does he makes 'em good, and making 'em good, they make good. Like *Whoopee*, another Goldwyn-made, and this time a smash."

Besides being the hit of the picture, Eddie Cantor pulled one of the most talked-about practical jokes of all time in front of the Rivoli Theater opening night.

Everyone of importance—including Mayor Jimmy Walker—attended the opening. And everyone of importance arrived in expensive limousines, mostly chauffeur driven. Not Cantor. Dressed in high hat and tails, and with his wife, Ida, beside him on the front seat, he pulled up to the curb in front of the marquee in a broken-down Model T Ford that he'd rescued from a junk yard earlier that day. When the stunned doorman asked the pop-eyed star of the picture if he'd like him to park his car for him, Cantor replied, "No, thanks, just sell it and keep the change."

Whoopee was a great commercial success, too, making an instant movie star out of Eddie Cantor. This inspired Sam to encore with five more highly successful Cantor musicals over the next five years: *Palmy Days* (1931); *The Kid from Spain* (1932); *Roman Scandals* (1933); *Kid Millions* (1934); and *Strike Me Pink* (1936).

All of these featured various famous and not-so-famous leading ladies opposite Cantor—Gloria Stewart, Ruth Etting, Sally Eilers, Ann Sothern, Ethel Merman, and Charlotte Greenwood, to name a few—and the usual assortment of beautiful Goldwyn Girls. And all were produced with Sam Goldwyn's usual loving care and meticulous attention for detail.

In *Kid Millions* Eddie Cantor played a bumbling schnook—somewhat on the order of the early Jerry Lewis character—who, toward the end of a series of humorous misadventures, unexpectedly inherited $77 million. To show his gratitude, Cantor opened an ice cream plant, where poor children could come and eat their fill for nothing. It was a sequence full of imaginative invention—a skating rink made of ice cream, with real skaters skimming around on it; girls milking Dresden china dolls; people boating in scooped-out bananas on lakes of melted chocolate; and skiers sliding down mountains of whipped cream.

Sam was way ahead of Disney in this kind of whimsy, and to make it really colorful, he decided to shoot the sequence in a new process called Technicolor. (Color was so expensive in those days that all producers, including Spend-a-Million Sam, used it only in scenes that would most benefit by color, but never the whole picture.)

Shooting the ice cream factory sequence in color would add a couple of hundred thousand more to the budget, but to Sam price was no object, provided the color of the ice cream was true to the flavors it was depicting. To this end, Sam was on the telephone nearly every day with Dr. Herbert Kalmus, who was president of Technicolor and also the inventor of the process.

"Listen, Doc, remember one thing," Sam exhorted Kalmus daily. "The vanilla's got to look like vanilla, the chocolate like chocolate, and the strawberry like strawberry."

Since ice cream was Sam's favorite dish, he had to be considered one of the world's leading experts on the subtleties of its various hues and flavors.

Recognizing this, Kalmus promised Goldwyn he would get perfection, and he worked his lab technicians overtime to prepare for the moment he would have to prove it to him on a movie screen—probably the first case on record of a dish of ice cream having to take a screen test.

Finally one Friday night, just when the Goldwyn staff were preparing to leave the studio for the weekend, Sam called a meeting of everyone on the payroll of *Kid Millions*. This was attended by his production assistant, the debonair Arthur Hornblow, Jr.; the writers of the screenplay, George Oppenheimer and William Anthony McGuire; director Leo McCarey; the set designer, Richard Day; and Al Newman. At this meeting, Richard Day exhibited his mockup of the ice cream factory set; Al Newman played some of the Bert Kalmar and Harry Ruby music; and Sam, every other minute, kept reminding everyone, "But more important than everything is that the vanilla should look like vanilla, and the chocolate should look like chocolate."

For the *pièce de résistance*, Sam, wearing the victorious smile of a man with a carefully hidden surprise up his sleeve, took everyone into his private projection room to view the screen test of the dish of ice cream that Dr. Kalmus had prepared. As the room went dark, there on the screen, against a background as white as the polar cap, appeared the rich, dark brown image of a large plate of chocolate ice cream.

As the group stared at the screen in awed silence, George Oppenheimer heard Goldwyn in the seat next to him smack his lips loudly and exclaim, "Mmmmmmmmmmmm, strawberry!"

Mordaunt Hall, writing in the *New York Times*, must have been able to tell chocolate from strawberry, however, for in his review of the picture, he had the following to say about the ice cream factory sequence: "The lavish ice cream factory scene, filmed in the new Technicolor process, is the most successful example of fantasy in color that Broadway has seen outside of the Disney cartoons."

While Sam felt it was perfectly all right for him to hold up production for days while he carped, quibbled, and fretted over some minor detail that could not possibly influence the box-office take one way or the other, he would frequently show irritation when he suspected an employee of concentrating too long on nonessential trivia.

A case in point was a vitriolic exchange that took place between Sam and Leo McCarey while the latter was directing the third Cantor musical, *The Kid from Spain*, in 1932.

The story of *The Kid from Spain*, a confection whipped up by William Anthony McGuire, Harry Ruby, and Bert Kalmar, concerned a New York taxi driver (Cantor) who, while hiding from some gangsters who were out to get him because he had witnessed a crime they had committed, was forced to cloak his true identity behind the guise of Don Sebastian, the world's foremost matador (played by Sidney Franklin, the only American bullfighter of note). In the final sequence, of course, Cantor was forced to go into a bullring with a real bull in order to prove to the United States border authorities, who, too, were after him, that he really was Don Sebastian.

To give the picture authenticity, Sam decided that the bullfight sequence must be shot in a real bullfight arena. The location-scouting crew chose the closest one—the bullring at Tijuana. But the scheduling of the location trip was unfortunate. It was the rainy season, and as a result, McCarey had to postpone shooting for several weeks in a row while he waited for the sun to come out from behind menacing dark clouds.

Meanwhile back at the Goldwyn Studios, Sam, with no dailies to look at, was growing increasingly tense, fidgety, and irritable. Not only wasn't any progress being made on the picture, but his location crew and stars were eating and drinking like there was no tomorrow and running up enormous bills at the posh Agua Caliente Hotel, where they were being billeted.

Finally Sam received assurances one night from both McCarey and the weatherman on the *Examiner* that the next day would be "nothing but sunshine." The weatherman goofed, however, and the following evening around six, Sam received a call from McCarey informing him that again there had been no shooting that day, on account of rain.

Sam listened to McCarey's apologies for as long as he could, then shouted his ultimatum: "Listen, Leo, tomorrow we shoot, whether it rains, whether it snows, whether it stinks."

The last clause, McCarey believed, was an example of Sam's belief in the power of using more words than necessary to score a point—even if they didn't make sense.

Lucille Ball didn't make her appearance as a Goldwyn Girl until *Roman Scandals*. In this musical, a satire on Roman days in Nero's reign, the pop-eyed Eddie Cantor played a Roman slave trying to elude a date with some hungry lions in the Coliseum. But Lucy, like the rest of the Goldwyn Girls, didn't have much to do for her seventy-five dollars a week except stand around in a scanty Roman costume and look pretty. This wasn't difficult for Lucy in 1933, for she was an extremely attractive natural redhead by any standards, which was the only reason Freddy Kohlmar, the head of Goldwyn's talent department, had signed her in the first place.

For those not acquainted with it, Lucy's story prior to her becoming a Goldwyn Girl reads like a bad daytime soap opera. She was born in Jamestown, New York, and raised in Montana, where her father, a miner for Anaconda Copper, was killed in a mining accident. When she was still in her teens, Lucy struck out for New York City, where, among other jobs she held, she was a soda jerk, a dancer, and a photographer's model. She was on the verge of getting her first big break in a show when she was crippled in an automobile accident in Central Park and forced to spend the next five years in a wheelchair, being supported by her widowed mother. After a miraculous recovery, she was starting to make a stage comeback at the age of twenty-five, when Kohlmar spotted her comely face and trim figure in a chorus line and signed her to a Goldwyn Girl contract.

In Hollywood, Lucy shared a small rented house with her mother, her younger brother, and her grandfather, an avowed Communist, whose only contribution to the household was to sit around all day and read the *Daily Worker*, while predicting, "Tomorrow comes the Revolution."

Lucy was no revolutionary. She had set her sights on becoming a big star and having all the luxuries that went with it. But several weeks of posing as a Roman mannequin convinced her that being a Goldwyn Girl wasn't the way to achieve stardom. Besides, the inactivity of simply looking pretty bored her and frequently drove her to clowning around on the set more than Cantor was doing in the picture.

"Lucy's funny faces, pratfalls, and wisecracks had everyone in stitches," remembers actress Gloria Stewart, who played the part of Princess Sylvia in *Roman Scandals*. "She was like the campus cutup at college."

But being known as the "clown" of the Goldwyn Girls did not satisfy Lucy's restless spirit or her thirst for fame. Nobody of any importance on the Goldwyn lot seemed to think enough of her clowning to give her a speaking part. Lucy, however, tried her damnedest to get the Great Goldwyn to notice her, even if it meant making him angry. One of her favorite ways of taunting Sam was to drive her car up to the front of his office building when he was having an important story conference, slam on her brakes, and toot her horn loudly. Then when the enraged Goldwyn would storm out onto his second-floor balcony, Lucy would call up to him with wide-eyed innocence, "Can the writers come out and play with me now?"

Not only did the crusty Goldwyn frown upon this kind of behavior during the working day, but he let Lucy go when her contract as a Goldwyn Girl expired. Columbia Pictures immediately signed her to a stock contract—also at seventy-five dollars a week—but consigned her to a career of appearing in little else but "B" pictures. Slightly embittered, Lucy referred to herself at the time as "Queen of the B's." And she remained nothing more than that until Desi Arnaz rescued her in the early fifties and the two of them became America's number-one TV comedy team.

But Lucy wasn't the only major talent Sam Goldwyn failed to appreciate during the making of *Roman Scandals*. On the strength of George Kaufman's success writing musical comedies for the Marx Brothers (*The Cocoanuts* and *Animal Crackers*), Sam hired him to collaborate with Robert Sherwood, another giant of the Broadway theater, on the screenplay for *Roman Scandals*.

Sam paid Kaufman and Sherwood good money, and they in turn wrote what they considered a very funny script. But Sam didn't think it was funny enough. "Where are the jokes, boys?" he kept saying. "I want more jokes."

They insisted that they didn't write jokes per se—they wrote "character" lines that would get laughs when played in front of an audience. "Just trust us."

"I trust you, but it's not funny enough," insisted Sam, who didn't know from such highbrow terms as "character" lines.

"Tell us how you'd like us to fix it," said Kaufman.

"I can't tell you how to fix it," said Sam. "I just know what's right when I see it."

Sam's inability to express exactly what he felt was wrong with a script drove many an author to the brink of exhaustion, despair, and finally to the point of actually throwing in the towel and walking off the job. Sam's line, "I'll know it's right when I see it," was very little to go on when one had to rewrite a script. As a result, it was nothing for a writer to have to do a scene over for him fifteen or twenty times before he saw what he liked. And according to the army of secretaries and story editors who slaved for him over the years, there were at least "eight" drafts of every script he filmed piled up on his office shelves.

"He just didn't think he was getting his money's worth unless you did a number of rewrites for him," recalls Collier Young.

George Kaufman and Robert Sherwood weren't about to rewrite what they believed in, no matter how loudly Goldwyn shouted. Furthermore, they told him so and boarded the next Super Chief for New York City.

Sam immediately hired William Anthony McGuire, and Arthur Sheekman and Nat Perrin (two former Marx Brothers writers), to punch up the script of *Roman Scandals*. Whether this trio improved on the original or merely added jokes of the kind Goldwyn demanded is a moot question. At any rate, their script was the one that Goldwyn finally shot, giving Kaufman and Sherwood only "story" credit and the other three an "additional dialogue" mention. The picture was successful, with the reviewer from the *New York Times* having only one complaint: "The dialogue wasn't up to Kaufman and Sherwood's usual standard."

When Kaufman and Sherwood left for the East Coast, Sam still owed them $25,000 under the terms of their contract. But Sam refused to give it to them, claiming they hadn't completed their obligation. The two were finally forced to sue Sam, and three years later finally settled with him for $20,000. Most of this, however, had been eaten up by legal bills.

It was this experience that caused George Kaufman to resist all overtures by other producers to lure him to Hollywood, until Irving Thalberg enticed him there in 1936 to write *A Night at the Opera* for the Marx Brothers.

Tales of Kaufman's and Sherwood's unhappy experience with Goldwyn were quick to reach the ears of other Eastern playwrights, all of whom were basically a more independent breed than their West Coast brethren. This resulted in some playwrights, like the highly successful team of Ben Hecht and Charlie MacArthur (*The Front Page*, *Twentieth Century*) exercising extreme caution when dealing with Sam.

When Sam wanted Hecht and MacArthur to write the screenplay of *The Unholy Garden*, which was to star Ronald Colman and Fay Wray, the team insisted that it be spelled out in their contract that Goldwyn wasn't allowed to speak to them until they had finished the entire script. They also demanded that their salaries be paid to them "in cash" at the end of each workday.

Because Sam needed Hecht and MacArthur more than they needed him, he swallowed the indignity of being mistrusted and every afternoon at five had an envelope containing the required cash dropped off at their office. But after that experience he never could quite shake the conviction that all writers—even those with the biggest reputations—were racketeers who were out to skewer him or at least not give him his money's worth.

Walking down a corridor in his writers' building one day, Sam noticed through an open door to one of the offices a young man sitting at a desk, staring thoughtfully out the window while gnawing on a pencil. Sam purposely strode past the door three more times just so he could peek inside to spy on the room's occupant. Each time the man hadn't changed his pose— he was still staring and gnawing. On the fourth pass-by, Sam altered his course and entered the office.

"Young man," he demanded, "what are you here?"

"A writer, Mr. Goldwyn."

"Then why aren't you writing?" roared Sam, striding angrily back into the corridor.

Even Ernest Hemingway wasn't above Sam's suspicions. In 1937 Goldwyn's story editor, Sam Marx, approached his boss with what would seem like a highly tempting proposition.

"Mr. Goldwyn," said Marx, finding it hard to conceal the excitement in his voice. "I just had lunch with Ernest Hemingway. He's working on an exciting new novel that I think we can buy if we act fast. I think he can use some cash."

"Tell me the story," said Goldwyn. "Completely."

"I can't, because Hemingway hasn't finished it," said Marx.

"You're trying to make me buy a story that's not even finished?" said Goldwyn, glowering suspiciously at Marx.

"Yes, but it's by Ernest Hemingway," said Marx. "He knows what he's doing. Believe me, he can finish it."

"What is that Hemingway trying to do—rob me?" exclaimed Goldwyn.

Marx was finally forced to report back to Hemingway that Goldwyn wasn't interested in buying an unfinished novel. The novel turned out to be one of Hemingway's best—*For Whom the Bell Tolls*, the great Spanish Civil War story which Paramount made into a picture with Ingrid Bergman and Gary Cooper.

In view of the current practices of studios plunking down a half a million in cash on the basis of a one-page outline of a proposed Neil Simon comedy or an Irving Wallace sex novel, Sam's rebuff of Ernest Hemingway certainly seems an example of how penny wise and pound foolish he sometimes could be. But perhaps it wasn't so much pound foolishness as the fact that he was wise enough to recognize his own limitations. After all, if he didn't know a script was "right" until he saw it in its final polished version, how in the world could he be sure if a story was any good for pictures if it hadn't been written yet?

As he had discovered when he was dealing with the eminent authors, even *finished* novels weren't the safest bets for pictures. The scores of novels owned by studios but still unfilmed because they couldn't be successfully dramatized were proof of that. Which is probably the reason Sam still felt safest culling his raw story material from the stage, or from *finished* novels of such overwhelming popularity or exceptional social significance that he couldn't turn them down for fear someone else would get them.

Since Sam was closer to being an illiterate than an intellectual, one would assume that his views on making films of social significance would pretty much coincide with the old Hollywood cliché downgrading "message" films—"Pictures are for entertainment, messages should be delivered by Western Union."

But curiously Sam was a leader in believing that movies could both entertain and say something important, and he was one of the first Hollywood producers to risk his own capital to back up this belief. In 1931, he made two socially conscious films, *Street Scene* and *Arrowsmith,* and following their successes he never totally abandoned the concept that audiences would swallow pills of social content provided they were wrapped in enough sugar coating. Being a good businessman, however, Sam usually hedged his bets by continuing to turn out the safer product concurrently. In addition to the

Cantor vehicles that rolled off the Goldwyn assembly line at least once a year for the first six years of the depression, he also turned out a number of quality "programmers" made purely for audience entertainment: *One Heavenly Night*, starring John Boles, Leon Errol, and Lilyan Tashman; *The Devil to Pay*, with Ronald Colman and Loretta Young; *The Unholy Garden*, with Ronald Colman, Fay Wray, Estelle Taylor, and Henry Armetta; *Tonight or Never*, with Gloria Swanson; *The Greeks Had a Word for Them*, with Ina Claire, Joan Blondell, and David Manners; and *Cynara*, with Ronald Colman and Kay Francis.

But it was the important pictures—the ones that other producers said either couldn't be made or shouldn't be made—that intrigued Sam and started the adrenalin flowing in his creative processes.

"Mr. Goldwyn didn't know the meaning of the word *impossible*," recalls Goldie Arthur, who was his secretary for many years. "Once he made up his mind to do something, nothing stopped him. If need be, he'd even take his case up with the head of a government in order to get it solved."

A case in point was the time, much later in his career, when he tried to sell his library of fifty pictures to England for television. This infuriated the British Cinema Exhibitors Association, who threatened a boycott against all United States film distributors. Sam launched a counter-assault by complaining of "economic blackmail" directly to the British prime minister, Alexander Douglas-Home. He also sent a copy of his communiqué to the prime minister to the British Cinema Exhibitors Association. Alexander Douglas-Home was not anxious for a confrontation with the United States at the time and suggested the CEA compromise. As a result, they quickly capitulated and revised their stand to permit the showing of films five years or older on British TV.

If prime ministers were no obstacle to Sam, why should he be frightened by "impossible" properties?

The "impossible" properties that Sam was warned away from by well-meaning friends, associates, and rivals, but which he went ahead and made anyway, are a veritable list of Academy Award contenders and winners and box-office champions. He was told not to make *The Pride of the Yankees* because there had never been a picture about baseball that was successful. *Wuthering Heights* was too morbid. *The Little Foxes* had too many disagreeable characters. *The Children's Hour* was about lesbianism (a verboten subject, warned the Hays Office). *Street Scene* was too depressing. *Dodsworth* wouldn't have any appeal because it was about middle-aged people. And *Arrowsmith* was about a doctor and therefore had to be incredibly dull.

As was his wont, Sam went directly to the source to find the screenwriter for *Street Scene*, his first attempt at producing something of special significance. He hired Elmer Rice, who'd also written the Pulitzer Prize–winning play. Rice had never done a screenplay before, however, so Sam gave him King Vidor, one of the best directors in the business, to assist him in putting the story of murder and marital infidelity in a New York tenement into screen form. To that, Sam added a blockbuster cast consisting of Sylvia Sidney, William Collier, Jr., Estelle Taylor, and Beulah Bondi.

Because it was a Sam Goldwyn production and heralded with plenty of the kind of advance publicity a new Goldwyn offering always generated, there was a great deal of interest in the movie version of *Street Scene* among the general public. An overflow crowd attended its splashy opening in New York City on the night of August 25, 1931, and loved every minute of it, even to the point of wildly cheering Sylvia Sidney, who was in the audience, after the final fade-out.

The *New York Times* was not quite so enthusiastic the next morning, saying *Street Scene* was "slightly overproduced" and "not quite so good as the Pulitzer Prize play from which it was adapted, for the acting lacks the naturalness of the original work." However, the reviewer paid it enough compliments to make it a large grosser and concluded his critique by saying, "It is a swiftly moving version and a good picture, and those who have not seen the stage play should be more than satisfied with this Sam Goldwyn Production."

But Sam's crowning achievement of the early thirties was his screen version of the best-selling novel *Arrowsmith*, which was also Sinclair Lewis's crowning achievement, for it, along with *Main Street* and *Babbitt*, won him the Nobel Prize for literature in 1930.

Despite the fact that it was a prestige novel, *Arrowsmith* wasn't the easiest story to transfer to the screen. It wasn't a "doctor" story in the sense that "Marcus Welby, M.D." is. It contained no exciting operating-room scenes, with patients hovering between life and death, or Bob Young talking a terminally ill patient out of leaping from a sixth-floor window. It was the simple story of a midwestern doctor who had to make a choice between "fundamental research" for the good of humanity and his immediate human needs. In other words, should Dr. Arrowsmith give up his lucrative practice and high income in order to find a cure for pneumonia? On this decision also hinged the success or failure of his marriage to the New York society girl he married following the death of his first wife.

In addition to the fact that *Arrowsmith* didn't contain much action, it was extremely episodic in nature, which didn't make it a very safe bet for the screen. But Sam had confidence that a master craftsman could solve the script problems, and good acting could overcome its talkiness and sedentary scenes.

Sam hired John Ford to direct the picture and Sidney Howard from his pool of favorite New York playwrights for the script-writing chores. Howard wrote a powerful script that still reads well today. To play Dr. Arrow-smith, Sam again went with his old reliable—Ronald Colman. With his Eng-lish accent and debonair manner and looks, Colman may not have been the prototype of a middlewestern family doctor—he seemed to belong more in an English drawing room or with the Bengal Lancers in India—but who could go against his track record as a matinee idol and box-office attraction?

But no one could quarrel with Sam's choice of Helen Hayes to play Leora, the doctor's first wife, who dies of bubonic plague in the last reel.

Helen Hayes was one of the few important actresses to appear in an early Goldwyn film that Sam didn't claim to have discovered first. He couldn't. She was already a Broadway star, married to playwright Charles Mac-Arthur, and was just finishing her first film, *The Sin of Madelon Claudet*, for MGM, when she was recommended to Sam by his old friend and associate Edgar Selwyn, who had written the screenplay and directed the tear-jerker. The picture hadn't been previewed yet—it wasn't even in rough-cut form—when Selwyn showed Sam some scenes from it in which Helen Hayes ap-peared.

Impressed with her performance, Sam immediately sent for the actress and confidently offered her the part of Arrowsmith's wife at a salary in the neighborhood of $2,000 a week. Sam was not prepared for a turndown, for despite the obstacles everyone expected him to encounter, *Arrowsmith*, with a screenplay by Sidney Howard from a Nobel Prize novel, was considered a "prestige" film, and every good actress in the business was vying for the role of Leora.

But what Sam had no way of knowing was that Helen Hayes had just undergone a traumatic experience in making her first film. *The Sin of Made-lon Claudet* had been a troubled film from the start. There'd been writer trouble, director trouble, and producer trouble, with the resultant wear and tear on the actors appearing in it.

"I was shaken up terribly and unhappy with the movie business by the time Sam wanted to hire me," recalls Helen Hayes. "I don't know whether Sam knew it or not—I don't know how he couldn't have the way news goes whirling around in Hollywood—but we had a lot of trouble making *Claudet*. In the middle of shooting they threw out the whole script and hired Charlie, my husband to do a complete rewrite. Poor Charlie! He poured his life's blood into making it a good picture. He worked every night on new scenes and handed them to me as I left for work in the morn-ing. Somehow it got made that way, but it was an ordeal I never wanted to live through again. In addition, no one had much faith in the final product before it was previewed, so you can imagine how unhappy I was when Sam sent for me about *Arrowsmith*. I knew that *Arrowsmith* was considered the last word in aristocracy of the business, with a screenplay by Sidney Howard and it being a Sam Goldwyn production. But all I wanted to do was go back to New York and forget the whole picture business."

That's the frame of mind Helen Hayes was in when Sam sent for her and made his offer.

"Look, Sam," said Miss Hayes, deciding to level with the producer, "I really don't want to do any more movies. I've had my try at it, but I don't think I'm a picture actress. I want to go back to the legitimate theater. That's where I belong."

Sam was in a state of shock; he thought she was angling for more money, and he offered her more.

"It isn't the money, Sam. I just don't like the picture business."

"You'll like working for me," said Sam. "I make great pictures."

"I know you do," agreed Miss Hayes.

"You're not telling the truth," said Sam. "You don't believe I make great pictures, do you? Well, I'll prove to you I do." And he rang for his secretary. "Bring me that letter," he barked when she appeared.

"What letter?"

"The one about *Street Scene.*"

The secretary went out and returned a moment later with a typed letter which Sam proceeded to read aloud to Helen Hayes. The letter was full of superlatives about what a "monumental achievement" *Street Scene* was and singled out its individual virtues for special mention: a "great screenplay by Elmer Rice," "inspired direction by King Vidor," "Academy Award performances by Sylvia Sidney and William Collier," "and magnificent production by Samuel Goldwyn." The author summed up his thoughts by predicting that *Street Scene* would be a huge moneymaker.

After reading the letter aloud, Sam turned it over to Helen Hayes for her own inspection. The young actress could hardly suppress a guffaw when she saw Sam's name and signature at the bottom of the page. It was a letter he had written to his New York sales department to fire up their enthusiasm. It was probably the only case on record where Sam was more persuasive on paper than he was orally.

"Of course, it wasn't actually his letter that changed my mind," remembers Helen Hayes with a wistful smile. "I think I really wanted Sam to talk me into it. I think I secretly believed if I was good in *Arrowsmith*, it might wipe out the people's memory of what a failure I was certain *The Sin of Madelon Claudet* would be. And so I finally accepted the part.

"But *Arrowsmith* wasn't without trouble. Ronald Colman didn't feel the part of the doctor was right for him, and he was walking through it, giving a poor performance and stinking it up in general when Sam heard about it.

He came down to the set . . . sat Ronny down in a corner, and had a long heart-to-heart talk with him. I don't know what he said, but after that Ronny was better.

"Then we'd been shooting about a week, when MGM previewed *Madelon Claudet* in one of those funny places—some gashouse district—where they always previewed in those days. I think it was Huntington Park. At any rate, the audience was filled with people wearing leather windbreakers—the picture was so bad, they laughed it off the screen and the producer decided to shelve it—it was a real dog. But when Irving Thalberg, who was head of production for Louis B. Mayer, came back from a trip, he said, 'Whatever happened to *Madelon Claudet?*' And the producer told him it was a dog. But Thalberg insisted on seeing it. And after he did, he said it could be good, if they'd only remake the final sequence. Thalberg called Charlie in, and the two of them worked out a new final sequence together. And Charlie did the rewrite. But then the thing was, I was working on *Arrowsmith* by that time. When could I do the retakes? they asked me.

"We only got one full day off in those days—Sunday. Saturday was always a half workday. But that's all I had to give MGM, and they agreed. And so I was sneaking off and working on Saturdays and Sundays for a couple of weeks on *Claudet* and shooting *Arrowsmith* the rest of the week.

"Then the funniest thing happened. I'll never forget it, because of what it says about Sam and how perceptive he could be about little things. And unreasonable.

"Charlie and I were having dinner at the Goldwyns' one Saturday night. It was one of their usual Saturday night parties, with a lot of big names there. After dinner, I announced that I had to go home—because I had to get to bed—like a fool, my mind slipped. Anyway, Sam picked it up like Sam Spade."

"Why do you have to go to bed early?" asked Sam. "It's Saturday night. You don't have anything to do tomorrow."

Pinned down, she replied guilelessly, "I have to do some retakes on *The Sin of Madelon Claudet.*"

According to Helen Hayes, Goldwyn nearly blew the roof off in his anger. "Retakes!" he roared. "Who gave you permission to make another picture on my time?"

"Well, it's only retakes," insisted Helen Hayes, trying to talk her way out of the corner she had got herself into.

Sam wasn't interested in hearing any extenuating circumstances. In front of all his guests, he picked up the phone and called Irving Thalberg's house. A servant answered and said that Thalberg had already gone to bed. Thalberg wasn't a well man even in those days (he died in 1936 at the age of thirty-seven) and usually retired early if he could. But Goldwyn wasn't interested in his health at that moment and insisted that the servant rouse him out of bed.

"Listen, you son of a bitch," screamed Sam after he got Thalberg on the wire, "Helen Hayes is working for me. Either you stop shooting *Madelon Claudet*, or she is out of *Arrowsmith*. And I don't care if I have to start all over again with another actress."

It was a suspenseful moment for the youthful Miss Hayes. "I was really frightened that he really would fire me," she remembers today. "But fortunately for me, Irving was very nice about it. He stopped the retakes at once. And I didn't finish them until I was through with *Arrowsmith*."

It was not, of course, terribly unreasonable for Sam to insist that Thalberg call off the retakes so Miss Hayes could give her all for him and *Arrowsmith*. In identical circumstances, any producer might have acted the same way, though another producer might have handled the situation a little more delicately and not embarrassed the fearful Miss Hayes by yelling at her and Thalberg in front of a large Saturday night gathering of important people.

Beyond that, the foxy Sam might have been trying to delay purposely the release of *The Sin of Madelon Claudet*, so he could come out with a picture starring the talented Helen Hayes first. Besides, if *Madelon Claudet* was as bad as it was rumored to be, her association with a "stinker" might hurt the box office of *Arrowsmith*.

If that was Sam's tactic, it failed, for *Claudet* was released on October 30, 1931, two months before *Arrowsmith* was ready to be shown to the public.

Ironically, the earlier release of *The Sin of Madelon Claudet* only helped *Arrowsmith*. After undergoing the repairs suggested by Irving Thalberg, *The Sin of Madelon Claudet* opened to resoundingly good notices. Helen Hayes received the lion's share of them, with Mordaunt Hall of the *New York Times* writing: "This actress's performance in a difficult role leaves only the regret that the powers that be did not put her into a more cheerful study. . . . *The Sin of Madelon Claudet* is a powerful chronicle which no doubt will have a strong popular appeal."

It did have a strong popular appeal, and when *Arrowsmith* opened two months later in the same year, it was able to benefit from having its leading lady already well known to picture audiences from the Atlantic to the Pacific. Not that it needed the benefit of all that reflected publicity to succeed on its own.

Arrowsmith may have been about a "dull" doctor, but it received exciting reviews when it opened at the Gaiety Theater in New York City on December 7, 1931.

Mordaunt Hall of the *New York Times* wrote on December 8: "Samuel Goldwyn, the proven picture producer who has quite often shown a desire to lead the public rather than follow it, is responsible for the intelligent and forceful film version of Sinclair Lewis's Nobel Prize novel *Arrowsmith.*"

Edwin Schallert, the critic for the *Los Angeles Times*, called *Arrowsmith* "powerful, somber and dramatic . . . of that genre of pictures that mean something decisive for the betterment of the screen," but he singled out Helen Hayes for special praise. "Helen Hayes comes near being the topmost actress on the screen. After seeing *Arrowsmith* one can say this without much doubt or equivocation. I don't know at the moment who I would nominate as her rival. . . . In this portrayal she makes our Garbos, Dietrichs, Shearers and Swansons, clever as they be, look like amateurs."

So successful was Sam Goldwyn's production of *Arrowsmith* that it even pleased the author of the original work, Sinclair Lewis. In an "exclusive" interview with Lewis for the wire services, Norbert Lusk wrote: "Following the opening of *Arrowsmith* at the Gaiety Theater Monday night, Sinclair Lewis, the author, said that it was the first adult talking picture he had ever witnessed and that he had cried throughout."

At Academy Award time, *Arrowsmith* received nominations in four categories: best picture, best screenplay, best cinematography, and best art direction. But it did not win the gold statuette in any category. *Grand Hotel*, with an all-star cast including Greta Garbo and John and Lionel Barrymore, walked off with the best picture award. Evidently the academy was in the habit even then of giving an Oscar to the biggest although not necessarily the best picture of the year.

Curiously, Helen Hayes was not nominated for best actress for her work in *Arrowsmith* either. But she won top acting honors, anyway, for her performance in *The Sin of Madelon Claudet*. Probably, the academy didn't want to spoil her by giving her two Oscars in the same year.

Not winning the Oscar for best picture, though a disappointment to Sam, was not too bitter a pill to swallow, for a nomination is considered high praise, also. But his failure to win an Oscar established a trend that was not to be broken for many years. In the years following *Arrowsmith* thirty-four of Goldwyn's pictures were nominated by the academy in one or more (usually more) categories, and the Goldwyn sound department won eight Oscars. But Sam, personally, never received an Oscar for producing the best picture until *The Best Years of Our Lives* walked off with seven of the gold statuettes in 1947.

Helen Hayes, despite her stunning success in Hollywood, returned to her first love, Broadway, after making *Arrowsmith* and never again worked for Sam Goldwyn. "But I wish I had, darn it," she said recently in a wistful tone. "Working for Sam was the nearest I've ever felt out in Hollywood to being back in the theater. The good theater that I'd been working with in those days . . . the theater of Jed Harris, . . . Gilbert Miller, and George Abbott."

Sam should have heard those words of tribute from the first lady of the theater. It would have pleased him terribly.

16

Maker of Stars

ALTHOUGH HE TOOK A LOT of kidding on the subject from his peers and magazine profilists, Goldwyn's batting average as a star maker was as good as anybody else's in Hollywood.

He may have passed up Gary Cooper and Bette Davis, but he made stars of Belle Bennett, Lois Moran, Vilma Banky, Teresa Wright, and Dana Andrews. While he didn't, strictly speaking, discover Will Rogers and Eddie Cantor, he did gamble his own money to put them in movies for the first time.

Ronald Colman was just another leading man until Sam put him under contract; Laurence Olivier was a little-known English thespian before Sam cast him as Heathcliff in *Wuthering Heights;* David Niven had never worked as an actor at all before Sam signed him; and Danny Kaye was a minor sensation in New York nightclubs, as well as the comic in *Lady in the Dark* on Broadway, but no one was knocking down any doors to sign him for movies before Sam cast him in *Up in Arms.*

Goldwyn also took a chance on a World War II veteran named Harold Russell, who had hooks for hands and who had never acted before. He put Russell in *The Best Years of Our Lives,* and he not only won an Oscar in 1947 for best supporting actor, but also a special award "for bringing hope and courage to his fellow veterans" through his appearance in the film.

But Sam's strikeouts, like Babe Ruth's, were spectacular, too. He passed up Clark Gable because he thought his ears were too large and stuck out too far. He passed up Greta Garbo not only because he thought her feet were too large, but because he also didn't believe she had the class to become a major star. He based this judgment solely on the fact that the first time she came to the Goldwyn manse for dinner, he caught her in the kitchen enjoying a coffee klatch with the Swedish help, with whom she could converse in her native tongue and feel more at ease than with Sam's important guests. The snob in Sam surfaced and blinded him to her classic beauty; all he could see was a "peasant" girl who was not his image of a Goldwyn heroine. And, finally, he failed to sign Robert Montgomery because he and his talent department couldn't make up their minds fast enough about how photogenic he was.

Sam first saw Montgomery in a featured (but not leading) role in a Broadway play in 1928 and ordered a screen test made of him. He felt he would be perfect for the male lead opposite Vilma Banky in what turned out to be her last Goldwyn picture—*This Is Heaven*. But the first screen test of Montgomery was disappointing. On the screen Montgomery's neck seemed too long. Sam's advisers recommended that he "pass" on the New England blue blood.

To this Sam replied, "His neck isn't too long—his shirt collar is too short."

He wired his New York office to have his good friend and connoisseur of clothes, Arthur Richman, have shirts made for Montgomery that would de-emphasize the length of his patrician neck, and then shoot another test of him.

Sam's orders were carried out, and on the second try Montgomery's neck passed the test with "flying collars." But Sam had vacillated too long. By the time he got around to signing Montgomery, the actor had second thoughts about going to Hollywood and confessed to Sam, "I don't think I want to be in a silent film." (*This Is Heaven* was silent except for the final sequence, in which Vilma Banky spoke for the first time on film and caused laughs rather than heart flutters.)

So Montgomery returned to Broadway, where he became a major star in *Possession*, a play produced by Sam's former partner Edgar Selwyn. As a result, when Montgomery finally went to Hollywood, he signed with MGM, at Selwyn's instigation, and he never did work for Goldwyn.

On the other side of the coin, there were occasions when Sam, in his eagerness, signed someone too quickly and lived to regret it.

During the early thirties, friends of Sam's who were tennis enthusiasts—among them director Mervyn LeRoy—talked the producer into putting Frank Shields, America's Davis Cup star and top-ranking player, under contract. Not that Sam played tennis, nor had any desire to make a picture about tennis, but because Shields, apart from his talent on the court, was an exceptionally handsome man, six feet tall, with a perfectly proportioned body and a profile more classic than Barrymore's.

He certainly seemed like a good bet for pictures—if only he could be taught to act. In the screen test Sam made of him, his profile was everything people said it was, but his shortcomings as an actor showed up glaringly.

However, at LeRoy's urging, Sam signed Shields and put him in the hands of an acting coach. Meanwhile he thought it prudent to keep him out of pictures until his acting became less wooden.

During his training period, which went on for about six months, Shields was on full salary, but he had plenty of time for what he could do best— play tennis. Because of his skill at the game—and tennis was a popular sport in Hollywood as long ago as the early thirties—Shields was in constant demand to play in exhibitions around town, not only with other leading lights of the tennis world, such as Bill Tilden, Fred Perry, and Ellsworth Vines, but also with important picture personalities—Charlie Chaplin, Errol Flynn, Gilbert Roland, and Ginger Rogers, who were all fairly adept with a racket.

One day, Shields was in the middle of an exciting net duel at the Beverly Hills Tennis Club with Tilden, Vines, and Milton Holmes, the club's owner and famous tennis coach, when he received an urgent phone message from one of Goldwyn's minions. He was to report *at once* to Mr. Goldwyn at the studio.

Believing he was finally going to be given a part in a picture, Shields disappointed the spectators by immediately halting the play and racing back to the studio without even changing out of his tennis clothes. Bounding up the stairs to Goldwyn's office three at a time, Shields breathlessly presented himself to Goldwyn's receptionist, who promptly showed him into Goldwyn's inner sanctum.

Sam looked critically at the handsome Shields standing at attention before him with racket in hand, then snapped, "Tennis you know. Practice acting!"

Later, Frank Shields appeared in a small role in one Goldwyn picture— *Come and Get It*, starring Edward Arnold and Joel McCrea—but his acting never advanced beyond the amateur stage, and Sam eventually dropped him from his payroll.

But the cost of trying to make an actor out of a born tennis player hardly put a dent in Sam's bank account. His entire investment was just a few months' expenditure of a stock player's salary. He should only have gotten off that easily with Anna Sten, the Russian-born actress he imported to America in 1932.

Of all Sam's strikeouts, it was Anna Sten's curves that caused him to go down swinging the hardest.

Prior to being signed by Goldwyn, Anna Sten had starred in *The Yellow Passport*, *Girl with the Hatbox*, and other Soviet films. Following that she received permission from the Russian authorities to go to Berlin, where she appeared in three talking pictures: *Sturm der Leidenschaft*; *Trapez*; and *Der Mörder Dmitri Karamazov* (from *The Brothers Karamazov* by Dostoevski), in which she played the seductress, Grushenka.

Sam saw her in *Karamazov* during his annual combination business and pleasure trip to Europe in 1932, was impressed with her portrayal of Grushenka, and immediately hit upon the idea of repeating with Anna Sten his previous success with Vilma Banky. Besides, foreign stars were suddenly all the rage in Hollywood: Greta Garbo, Marlene Dietrich. Why not Anna Sten? From what Sam could see of her on the screen, Miss Sten certainly had all the requisites: a gorgeous body, a seductive face, and a beguiling if slightly enigmatic smile.

But in his crazy desire to mold Anna Sten into another Vilma Banky, Sam overlooked something he couldn't see but which his ears certainly should have been able to detect: that torrent of guttural Slavic sounds issuing forth from her sensuous lips.

Or if Sam heard them, he was so mesmerized by her dazzling beauty that he chose not to remember that Vilma Banky's success with him had been in silent films, and that her failure to learn English was the cause of her bowing out of the movies as soon as talkies came in.

Undaunted by the memory of the disastrous *This Is Heaven*, Sam, before leaving Berlin for America, went ahead and signed Anna Sten to a five-year contract at $3,000 a week. If Anna drove a hard bargain, it was probably because she had a smart man for a husband, Dr. Eugene Frenke—called "Doctor," as was the custom in Germany, because he had a doctor of law degree from the university.

Dr. Frenke, a short, aggressive, middle-aged German, who spoke English with an accent almost as impenetrable as Anna's, had a booming law practice in Berlin, but he gave it all up to accompany his young wife to Hollywood, where he let all their new friends call him "Doctor" under the misapprehension that he was a medical man. Frenke never bothered to correct their error, feeling the M.D. misnomer lent his character the dignity befitting the husband of an actress being groomed for stardom by the great Sam Goldwyn.

That Anna was receiving the full star treatment there was never any doubt. Even before Anna arrived in Hollywood, with twelve trunks full of the latest Parisian gowns, Sam had ordered Lynn Farnol, his chief publicist of the time, to bang the drums for Miss Sten long and loudly in preparation for her arrival. And by the time she had been in America only a few weeks, every newspaper and magazine from New York to Hollywood was bombarded with photographs of Goldwyn's latest foreign import in seductive poses, and with reams of copy extolling her beauty, her glamor, her mystery, and her talent ("More mysterious than Garbo," "Sexier than Marlene Dietrich," etc., etc.).

When Sam's associates first laid eyes on Anna at the studio, they were not nearly so impressed with her looks and talent as Sam had led them to believe they would be. For that matter, Sam himself (though he wouldn't admit it) was somewhat disappointed in her when he met her again on this side of the Atlantic. In the first place, her English was worse than he remembered it being (Dr. Frenke had to interpret everything she said, and it wasn't too easy to understand Dr. Frenke, either). And in the second place, her figure was now a little on the zaftig side, which should have been no surprise to anyone who'd ever watched her eat. Evidently Sam had never had that pleasure. But now that constant proximity in the studio commissary every noontime afforded him that opportunity, he noticed she had an appetite like that of heavyweight champion Primo Carnera. (Shades of Vilma Banky's early days in Hollywood; those Europeans *do* enjoy their food.)

While he was trying to decide on a property in which to launch her career properly, Sam put Anna on a diet, hired a full-time masseuse to knead off her excess poundage, and made her and her husband join the Beverly Hills Tennis Club so she could take regular exercise. When she wasn't fighting the battle of the bulge, she was taking English and dramatic lessons.

Later, Sam also showered her with singing and dancing lessons, because by then he had decided what the launching vehicle would be—*Nana*, the Zola story about a French courtesan. Why he chose *Nana* has always been a secret between Goldwyn, Arthur Hornblow, Jr., his story editor at the time, Dr. Frenke, and Frances. Possibly the thinking was that Anna, with her European accent, would come off more believably in a film with a French background. But the story of *Nana* required that whoever played the lead role be able to sing and also dance the cancan, neither of which Anna could do at the time Sam hired Willard Mack and Harry Wagstaff Gribble to write the screenplay.

Another of *Nana*'s many drawbacks was the raciness of the original material at a time in Hollywood when nudity and four-letter words were fit subjects for stag films only. The Will Hays Office, formed by the majors to police their own filth, wielded such a tremendously large censorship stick that it even dictated the maximum length screen kisses could last (fifteen seconds) so as not to arouse the audience.

Considering that, it would be impossible to make a very faithful film version of the Zola book, which, in addition to being about a whore, had one sequence in which Nana, in an effort to humiliate Count Muffat, her elderly paramour, forced him to get down on the floor completely nude, on all fours, and pretend to be a "woolly bear" and then a dog, while she, also nude, looked on in amusement. There was no way the lustiness of *Nana* could be put on the screen in 1934. Any screen adaptation would have to be completely bowdlerized before it would be acceptable to the Hays Office, not to mention Sam, who also disapproved of any kind of blue material.

Perhaps scriptwriters Willard Mack and Harry Gribble were able to convince Sam they could bring the project off with good taste, without losing the value of the classic novel. At any rate, Sam bought the idea and was not in the least bit discouraged when his army of English coaches, dramatic coaches, and singing and dancing instructors reported back to him, after he'd been paying Anna full salary for about a year, that she was not responding to treatment.

Her English coach said he could teach her to pronounce words, but her dramatic coach added that when she tried to put them into complete sentences, they were devoid of meaning. Her singing coach told Sam, "Miss Sten has a small but disagreeable voice." And she had even less aptitude for dancing than she had for singing and acting. One day during a dance rehearsal for *Nana*, Sam himself grew so frustrated watching her try to learn the cancan that he himself jumped off his chair and hopped around the rehearsal hall on his left foot and tried to wrap his right leg around his neck, in an effort to demonstrate to her that anyone, even a middle-aged man, could learn to do the cancan.

Added to the problems of trying to teach her English, singing, and dancing, and keeping her unbridled appetite bridled, Sam also had to put up with constant interference from Dr. Frenke.

After only a few months of living in Hollywood and being a member of the Beverly Hills Tennis Club, where he rubbed elbows every day with some of the finest minds in the film industry—Norman Krasna, Billy Wilder, Frank Capra, Robert Riskin, and Willy Wyler—Dr. Frenke began to act as if he knew more about making pictures than Louis B. Mayer and Goldwyn put together. With the kind of *chutzpah* often associated with a member of the Teutonic race, Dr. Frenke was soon telling everyone on the Goldwyn lot, including Goldwyn, what was best for his wife's career. As the more discerning appraisers of talent were beginning to suspect, nothing was best for his wife's career except early retirement. But Frenke didn't see it that way. He liked all that money that was rolling in every week, and he didn't want anything to louse up his high style of living. On her income he could invest heavily in the stock market in the mornings, and in the afternoons mingle with the Capras and Wylers at the tennis club and from them get fresh ideas on how to make a picture for his wife.

At one point Dr. Frenke's interference became so unbearable that Sam, in an effort to get him out of the way, gave him a job as an assistant director on another picture and sent him off on location to Catalina Island for three months. But giving him work in the industry merely compounded Dr. Frenke's belief that he knew something about filmmaking. And when he returned to the Hollywood mainland, he was more of a "take-charge" guy than ever.

Despite the obstacles, Sam the Unconquerable plowed resolutely forward in an effort to imprint the Goldwyn Touch on Anna Sten.

He gave her a supporting cast consisting of Phillips Holmes and Richard Bennett, two fine actors; a director who had come through for him many times before, George Fitzmaurice; and he hired the foremost couturier in the country to design the exquisite Second Empire costumes Nana was supposed to wear.

Before the film itself went into production, Sam ordered a trailer shot to advertise the forthcoming film epic. The script of the trailer called for Anna to appear first as Anna Sten and introduce herself to the audience with the words "Now I am Anna." As she spoke those lines, her Anna image was to dissolve into the character she was to play as she said, "Now I am Nana."

George Oppenheimer, who had just replaced Arthur Hornblow, Jr., as Goldwyn's story editor and man Friday, was chosen to direct the trailer. But as he recalled in his recent book of reminiscences, "Unhappily her accent was so thick that 'Anna' and 'Nana' sounded identical. Try as I might, I could not correct her."

That should have told Sam something, for she'd been taking English lessons for nearly a year by that time. But Sam was blind to her defects and ordered the cameras to roll.

After the first day of shooting, Sam and Fitzmaurice looked at the dailies together. What they saw reaffirmed what the director had been telling Sam for weeks, that Anna was an excellent pantomimist, but that she could not coordinate her gestures or body movements with what came out of her mouth. She'd gesture first, then deliver the words in a hurried, Slav-accented mumble. When it was possible to distinguish a sentence or two, what one heard bore no resemblance to spoken dialogue. It was too mechanical-sounding, as if, parrotlike, she'd learned her lines by rote without comprehending their meaning, which, of course, was the case.

But Sam refused to be discouraged that early in the game. As far as he was concerned, a woman as beautiful as Anna Sten would be a star no matter what came out of her mouth. And he again exhorted his director to march forward into the valley of death.

Because of the communications gap, however, shooting was slow, with some scenes requiring as many as twenty-five takes before Fitzmaurice, out of sheer exhaustion, deemed one good enough to be printed. As a result, the entire production fell behind schedule, causing costs to mount and tempers to flare. This in turn not only made nervous wrecks of Sam and Fitzmaurice (whose responsibility it was to bring the picture in on schedule), but also of Anna Sten. Under the strain of the director's constant

reminder to speak "more naturally, darling," Anna was frequently collaps-
ing on the set and having to rest on "Nana's bed"—a gorgeous piece of Empire furniture heavily carved with figures of swans and doves which the set
department had designed to be the "ultimate" in Nana's beds. While the
star swooned, her husband would shout for brandy to revive her, and the
morale of the production crew would sink one level lower.

One day while Anna was resting on her swan bed between takes, the
cameraman, who was setting up a crane shot overhead, accidentally stuck
his foot into a fuse box, got a shock, and fell ten feet to the floor, where he
lay unconscious near Nana's bed. Meanwhile, the queenlike Anna, suffering from her own exhaustion, didn't even bother to open her eyes.

The studio doctor was hurriedly summoned, and he arrived on the set
moments later with little black bag in hand. But upon seeing Anna
stretched out on her swan bed with eyes closed, he immediately assumed
she was the patient, ran straight to her side, and slipped a stethoscope down
her magnificent cleavage to see if she was still breathing.

Thinking she was being raped, Anna leaped off the bed and ran around
the set screaming in Slavic hysteria. This set off a chain reaction among the
rest of the neurotics, and pretty soon everyone was running wildly around
in an effort to still the fears of the offended actress. Peace was eventually restored, but the day's shooting had to be cancelled, and future crane shots
were outlawed on the *Nana* set by edict of Goldwyn himself.

By then Sam was beginning to have some misgivings about the prac-
ticability of continuing under the existing set of circumstances. He ordered
his film editor to put together a rough cut of what had been shot so far—
about half the film—and sat down and looked at it one afternoon in the
quiet of his own projection room.

What he saw was a picture that was definitely without the Goldwyn
Touch. In fact, it looked like a satire on itself. Sam immediately ordered
the whole thing scrapped and announced that he was starting over from
page one of the script with a new director.

Sam's bookkeepers and assorted advisers suggested that he reconsider
such a move. He'd already spent $411,000 on the production. Did he want
to throw all that down the drain? What could a new director accomplish?

Sam's reply was characteristic of his philosophy of producing pictures for
the rest of his life. "I don't care how much it costs. It is my money I am
spending—not any investor's. We will shoot until I am satisfied."

It was probably unfair of Sam to blame the entire fiasco on Fitzmaurice.
After all, the Hollywood maxim goes, a director is only as good as his
actors and the script he has to work with. Anna Sten was as much to blame
as anyone. But it wouldn't have made any sense for Sam to fire the actress
he was trying to rocket into stardom. And it would have made even less

sense to start all over again with the same director, who, no matter what his past record had been, was definitely unable to get a decent performance out of Anna Sten.

So Sam fired Fitzmaurice and surprised everyone by replacing him with Dorothy Arzner, the most prominent woman director of the thirties.

A native of Los Angeles, Dorothy Arzner was born in 1900 and grew up on the fringe of the movie business. Her father, Louis Arzner, had owned the Hoffman Café, a restaurant in downtown Los Angeles, where the elite of the silent movie days used to gather to break bread when they were dining out. Charlie Chaplin, Mack Sennett, Lew Cody, Wallace Beery, Jesse Lasky, and Cecil B. De Mille and his playwright brother, William, were just a few of a great many personalities who were Louis Arzner's steady customers. During her school and college days, Dorothy used to mingle with her father's famous clientele. These contacts gave her the desire to get into the film business, but since she didn't have the looks or the talent to be in front of the cameras, she took the only kind of job for which she was qualified following her graduation from USC in 1918. William De Mille got her a job as a secretary at Paramount. From secretary she worked her way up to script girl, and following that she became a film editor—one of the best in the business. But that didn't satisfy her ambitious nature, and, upon reaching that plateau, she asked Jesse Lasky, who was production head of the studio, if he'd let her direct a film.

Lasky's first reaction was, "Definitely not." It did not appeal to him to use a woman director in a predominantly male business. But Arzner kept after him until, by her threatening to go to another studio, Lasky agreed in 1927 to give her a shot at directing a low-budget silent they were preparing called *Fashions for Women*. Another major breakthrough for the feminist movement in Hollywood, and Dorothy Arzner had done it single-handedly.

Following *Fashions for Women*, Dorothy climbed to the top of the Hollywood ladder very rapidly. In addition to making a number of other silent films, she was probably the first woman to direct a talkie and by 1932 she was considered so good at her trade that David Selznick signed her to direct *Christopher Strong*, which was to star a brand-new picture personality he was promoting—a tall, thin, high-cheekboned society type named Katharine Hepburn.

Christopher Strong was only Hepburn's second film, but Sam was so crazy about it when he ran it in his projection room that he immediately rang for his production assistant and said, "Get me Dorothy Arzner for *Nana*."

Physically, Dorothy Arzner was just the kind of woman who turned Sam off. She wore her hair short, she dressed in mannishly tailored clothes, and she was extremely opinionated. For Sam to send for a woman like that to

Cecil B. De Mille in puttees, with actor Monroe Salisbury in ten-gallon hat. Identifiable members of the cast are Winifred Kingston, female lead, with feather boa in her hat, and Milton Sills, far right.

Dustin Farnum, far right, pointing a gun at *The Squaw Man*'s heavy in black and white chaps.

(above) Cecil B. De Mille, D. W. Griffith, and Mack Sennett at the time of Goldwyn's purchase of Triangle Studios.

Sam Goldwyn with Pauline Frederick on a movie set, 1919.

(left) Sam Goldwyn, at approximately forty years of age, the successful film mogul.

(below) Sam with one of his eminent authors, Mary Roberts Rinehart.

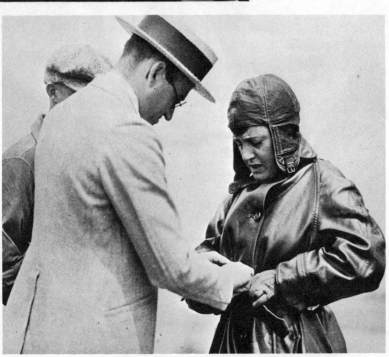

Sam Goldwyn with William Wyler, circa 1940.

Composer Hoagy Carmichael, Fredric March, and amputee Harold Russell in Goldwyn's Oscar-winning film *The Best Years of Our Lives*. The latter two won awards for best actor and best supporting actor.

A smirking Sam with his two awards—the Thalberg Award and his Oscar, circa 1947.

Vittorio De Sica, Italian film director, visiting the set of *Hans Christian Andersen* and chatting with the film's star, Danny Kaye, and Sam Goldwyn, 1952.

Samuel Goldwyn welcomes Bolshoi Ballet prima ballerinas Nina Pimofeyza and Luidmila Bogomolova to the world première of *Porgy and Bess* at the Warner Theater. It was the first event of its kind for the Russian dancers.

Mr. and Mrs. Samuel Goldwyn celebrating their thirty-sixth wedding anniversary, April 23, 1961.

The triumvirate responsible for *The Squaw Man* and most of Hollywood, some fifty years later—Jesse Lasky, Sam Goldwyn, and Cecil B. De Mille.

Sam Goldwyn, Jr., at the dedication of a new sound stage at Goldwyn Studios. Seated behind him at left are William Wyler and Merle Oberon, 1975.

extricate himself from his difficulties is some indication of how desperate he was at the time he decided to start anew with *Nana*.

But male chauvinist or not, Sam had always been a gambler—with both money and ideas. He'd already failed with a male director. Perhaps a woman's touch was what *Nana* needed. He said as much in an interview for *Silver Screen* magazine in December 1933: "There are certain things a woman has to bring to direction that perhaps a man has not, a certain understanding of feminine psychology, of the tricks, humors, emotions of a woman in love that a woman can bring out better than a man."

Sam's hunch was correct. Dorothy Arzner had great rapport with the European actress and swiftly restored order and high morale to the *Nana* set. There were no more swooning episodes or outbreaks of temperament. Dorothy Arzner banned Eugene Frenke from the set. Shooting went off smoothly, and right on schedule, and the camera work by Gregg Toland was good enough to win several European awards.

Unfortunately there was nothing Dorothy Arzner could do about a weak script. She told Sam before taking the job that she "wished the script could be stronger" (certainly the diplomatic way of phrasing it), but Sam insisted it was not the script that was troubled—only the directing and the actors, which "Dorothy Arzner can correct," he added flatteringly.

He was mistaken for one of the few times in his professional life. The script Willard Mack and Harry Gribble had concocted was so far removed from Zola's intentions when he wrote the novel that the French author could consider himself lucky to have been dead thirty years by the time Sam and his writers turned it into an Anna Sten vehicle.

Not only was Nana's character changed from prostitute to a nice girl who got into trouble, and the dialogue stilted, cumbersome, and a travesty of the original, but the writers also took liberties with the power and symbolism of Zola's ending, which saw Nana dying horribly of smallpox in a Paris hospital, where her once beautiful body, which had destroyed so many men, lay like a rotting ruin in a deserted room. In the Goldwyn version, Nana commits suicide in the final scene so that two brothers who love her will be free to fight for France in the Franco-Prussian war.

It's long been the wonder of film historians, and Goldwyn admirers specifically, that Sam, who was usually so meticulous about remaining faithful to an author's original work, should in the case of *Nana* have strayed so far afield.

But what Sam hadn't been able to accomplish in the film he more than made up for in his advance publicity campaign, which was being waged by Lynn Farnol, his publicity chief.

For weeks before *Nana* opened at the world's largest theater, the Radio City Music Hall, the Manhattan newspapers were filled with ads heralding the arrival on the screen of Sam Goldwyn's latest find. There were also a great many interviews with her in the papers, along with photos of Anna in every suggestive pose decorum would allow.

In addition, Farnol waged an extensive billboard campaign the likes of which few New Yorkers had ever seen before. Huge billboards of Anna in seductive poses were plastered all over Manhattan—on Foster and Kleiser twenty-four sheets overlooking Times Square, on the sides of buildings, in railroad stations, in men's rooms, on the sides of Fifth Avenue buses, and on all main highways leading to and from the city.

By the time *Nana* opened at the Music Hall on February 2, 1934, Anna Sten was better known to some Americans than Charles Lindbergh and the Burma Shave sign.

Such throngs attended the opening that some New Yorkers had to resort to hand-to-hand combat in order to get into the Music Hall to see the miracle that Sam Goldwyn's drum beaters said he had wrought. Sam and Frances were on hand, too. And it must have pleased Sam enormously, after all he'd been through to bring his baby to the screen, to learn that on opening day *Nana* broke all existing box-office records at the Music Hall.

Then came the reviews—not so bad as they could have been, thanks in large part to Dorothy Arzner, but definitely not what are known in the trade as "money reviews."

The critic in *Variety* wrote: "Sam Goldwyn has brilliantly launched a new star in a not so brilliant vehicle, and the satellite eclipses her setting." And Mordaunt Hall of the *New York Times* wrote the next morning:

> Anna Sten, the flaxen haired actress from the Ukraine, who attracted no little attention in her portrayals in several Soviet and German productions, makes her American debut in Samuel Goldwyn's *Nana*, which was launched yesterday before imposing throngs at the New York Music Hall. She is a flighty and vivacious Nana, if not the woman one visualizes while reading the Zola book.
>
> This Nana captures one's attention, but unfortunately the story in shadow form has not been worked out with the necessary dramatic impact. . . . Through Miss Sten's efficiency and charm, and the splendid portrayals of such players as Mr. Bennett, Mr. Owens and Mr. Grant, it offers a fair measure of entertainment, and even though it wanders far from Zola's work, sometimes catches the illusion of Paris in bygone days.

Knowing how much blood, sweat, and tears had gone into the production, the critics, perhaps, were being kinder to Goldwyn than he deserved.

The ticket-buying public took no such pity on him. Word of mouth that "Sten is a bomb" and "Goldwyn laid an egg called *Nana*" spread through Manhattan like a California brush fire. By the second day the crowds had thinned to the point where you could fire a gun through the lobby of the

Music Hall and not hit anyone except a few ushers and maybe the popcorn vender.

Sam's gamble to toss away $411,000 worth of bad film and start all over turned out to be a poor investment, for *Nana* fared poorly at the nation's box offices everywhere it played. In fact, the junked version probably couldn't have done any worse. But at least the new version wasn't totally embarrassing, and it won for Sam the reputation that was to stick with him to the end of his producing life—that he would spend any amount of money to keep from letting down the good name of Goldwyn. And if he failed, as he did with *Nana*, it was not from lack of trying.

Sam's "Anna Sten" period uncovered another facet of the Goldwyn character. If he had faith in a particular talent, he did not abandon that person just because he failed once with him or her.

Besides, maybe it was his fault for putting her in a story with a Parisian background when she was a Russian. To correct that error, he decided that her second picture should be based on Leo Tolstoy's *Resurrection*—the story of a Russian prince who seduces a Russian servant girl and impregnates her, which starts her down the path to prostitution. After the authorities send her to prison for a crime she didn't commit, the prince plunges into a Russian orgy of remorse. Sam had the story rewritten by the screenwriters Maxwell Anderson and Preston Sturges and gave it a title more appealing to American audiences, *We Live Again*. And to make sure none of the true Russian values were lost when transferring the story to the screen, Sam also hired Rouben Mamoulian, a Russian himself, to direct the film. Mamoulian had just finished directing Greta Garbo in *Queen Christina* and had good rapport with foreign actresses.

One non-Russian was Fredric March in the part of the prince. March himself must have felt the role wasn't right for him because he turned it down after a first reading of the script. He claimed the part was small and unsympathetic. But Sam spoke loud and persuasively in favor of the script's merits, pointing out that Mamoulian wouldn't have consented to direct it if it weren't a good script. He then offered March twice his usual salary, which immediately altered March's negative opinion about the script, and he accepted the role.

March was never completely happy about his part, however, and one day Goldwyn, while visiting the set, found him standing around looking awfully morose as, nearby, Anna Sten sat preening herself before her dressing-table mirror.

Deciding to bolster March's flagging spirits, Sam patted him on the back and said in a loud voice, "Freddie, you got the best part in the picture." As the words came tumbling out of his mouth loud and clear, Sam suddenly noticed Anna Sten frowning at him. "And Anna," continued Sam without missing a beat, "you got the best part, too."

To launch *We Live Again* properly, Sam decided to give it another one of his all-out publicity campaigns. But for many weeks, Lynn Farnol couldn't come up with an ad that suited Sam. "We're not telling the public anything," complained Sam. "It's too exaggerated."

Finally Farnol came up with an ad, which read: "The greatest motion picture in film history, by the world's most outstanding writer. The directorial genius of Mamoulian, the beauty of Anna Sten and the producing genius of Goldwyn have combined to make the greatest entertainment in the world."

"That," said Sam, "is the kind of ad I like. Facts, facts, facts."

In recent years—probably because of the rash of memoirs from people who knew Goldwyn or worked for him during his "Anna Sten" period—much has been written about the "bombs" and "two-ton duds" he produced trying to make a star of her following *Nana*'s failure to catch on at the box office. But either people's memories have dimmed through the years, or else they just believe it stylish or clever now to disparage and poke fun at Goldwyn's ability as a producer and picker of talent.

The fact is that *We Live Again* and Sten's third picture for Goldwyn, *The Wedding Night*, got very good notices in all important papers. So did Anna Sten's ability as an actress.

We Live Again opened at the Radio City Music Hall on November 1, 1934, and Frank Nugent, the *New York Times*'s first-string motion picture critic, wrote a review that could hardly be called a "flop" notice.

> With the blessings of Mr. Goldwyn ringing in her ears, the enchanted and golden haired Miss Sten triumphs handsomely in the latest screen edition of *Resurrection*, which had its first showing yesterday at the Music Hall.
>
> For a time Mr. Goldwyn's kindly efforts to publicize the electric Muscovite had the unhappy effect of making her look like the screen impresario's private discovery. Miss Sten, of course, is not simply a young woman of extraordinary charm and unusual talent, but an experienced actress with a distinguished background in the Russian and German cinema and the Soviet State Theater. . . . Mr. March, as the dashing and gallant Lieutenant, is so naively buoyant that it is sometimes difficult to believe in his conversion to the side of the people. But this is just a minor complaint. All in all, this is one of the best screen transcriptions of the Tolstoy novel ever to be done.

Despite many other good reviews, *We Live Again* did not attract a large audience and so was a disappointment to Sam financially.

Still he persevered in his belief that Anna Sten was a major star. On his third outing with her, he decided to abandon the classics, feeling they were a wee bit too heavy and melodramatic for American audiences. On George Oppenheimer's recommendation, Sam bought an original story of Edwin

Knopf's that had a background of tobacco farming in Connecticut and hired Edith Fitzgerald to write the screenplay.

In this vehicle, called *The Wedding Night*, Anna, the daughter of a Polish-American farm couple, falls in love with a handsome novelist who is doing research in Connecticut for a new book. The novelist is unhappily married to a sophisticated city girl who has chosen not to accompany him on this trip, which gives him and the farm girl an opportunity to fall in love. Anna's father, who has old-world standards, disapproves of the romance and forces her to marry the loutish son of a neighboring family, who are also Polish-Americans. On her wedding night Anna refuses to respond sexually to her husband, who becomes upset and runs off to kill the novelist. In the ensuing fight, Anna is killed instead.

Sam cast English actress Helen Vinson as the novelist's wife and decided to go after Gary Cooper to play the novelist. But this presented obstacles, for Cooper, after starring in *Lives of a Bengal Lancer*, *A Farewell to Arms*, and *Design for Living*, was now one of Paramount Studio's biggest stars, making $100,000 a year.

Money of course, was no object to Sam (though he would have preferred to get Cooper for the fifty bucks a week he was paying him when he let him go), but persuading Zukor to loan him out would take all the resourcefulness Goldwyn could muster. And even that might not work. But finally he hit upon what he thought was the right approach and phoned Zukor.

"Hello, Adolph," he said, after getting him on the phone. "You and I are in big trouble."

"What trouble?" asked the puzzled head of Paramount.

"You've got Gary Cooper and I need him."

Sam was still in trouble after the phone call. For Zukor summarily rejected his request by hanging up on him.

Sam was still brooding about this rejection when one of his spies informed him that Gary Cooper's contract with Paramount was about to run out and that the gentleman from Montana was open to offers from other studios.

"You mean Zukor isn't re-signing him?" exclaimed Goldwyn.

"They're negotiating," said the informant, "but they're not getting anywhere."

As it turned out, Gary Cooper was not only open to offers, but he was especially amenable to one from Goldwyn because Sam was the one who had given him his first break by putting him in *The Winning of Barbara Worth*, and he had always wanted to work for him again someday.

Armed with this news, Sam invited Cooper and his wife to dinner, discovered what Zukor was offering him, and buttered that deal by quite a few thousand dollars. The exact figure agreed upon was $150,000 per year.

Since Sam and Rouben Mamoulian had not hit it off terribly well during the making of *We Live Again*, Sam dumped him in favor of King Vidor for this third crusade into the valley of disaster with the Russian actress. Besides having done *Street Scene*, Vidor had also directed *Cynara* for Sam back in 1932. Since *Cynara* was also about marital infidelity, Vidor seemed the right man to direct *The Wedding Night*.

Judging from the reviews, Sam had made a wise choice. Frank Nugent, in the *New York Times*, wrote in part:

> With the assistance of King Vidor, Hollywood steps out of its emotional swaddling clothes in *The Wedding Night*. In uncommonly adult style, Mr. Goldwyn's new production describes the progress of a thwarted romance between a gin-soaked novelist and a Polish farm girl in Connecticut tobacco country. *The Wedding Night* displays an unusual regard for the truth, and it is courageous enough to allow an affair which is obviously doomed to end logically in tragedy. . . . Helen Vinson is excellently right as the wife, playing the part with such intelligence and sympathy that she contributes definitely to the power of the climax.

Variety said:

> It's the sort of production which will bring splendid and deserved notices, but which may not react at the box office to the same extent. Miss Sten gives a finely sensitive performance. Her hands supplement her face in conveying her emotion, and she lives the role of a simple Polish girl who sees only the glamour of the dashing stranger.

Variety could see the handwriting on the wall. So could Sam. If the talented and beautiful Miss Sten could get those kinds of reviews in important publications and still not pull anyone into the box office, which again proved to be the case with *The Wedding Night*, then he might as well forget about her.

If he couldn't make a star of Miss Sten after lavishing millions of his own money on her, then nobody could. Which turned out to be the case.

After Sam dropped her contract, Anna and her husband went to England, where in 1937 she starred in a picture called *Two Who Dared*. This was produced and directed by Dr. Frenke, who was now posing not only as a doctor, but also as a producer and director.

The *New York Times* said of her first picture without Goldwyn:

> *Two Who Dared*, produced in England by Eugene Frenke, is a routine little number, aggressively uninspired in plot, pallid in performance and given to some of the worst directional clichés. . . . Henry Wilcoxon, late of Mr. De

Mille's *Crusade*, and Anna Sten, one of the darkest moments in Mr. Goldwyn's career, have the doubtful honor of playing the dashing Captain and the peasant maid.

Without the Goldwyn Touch, Anna Sten was nothing. After appearing in five more films for various shoestring producers, Anna moved to New York City with her husband and quickly faded from the limelight. In the 1960s Anna made a brief try at a comeback, appearing in a few bit parts in motion pictures and TV, but has since dropped out of sight again, being listed in the Screen Actors Guild files as "inactive."

Sam's acquisition of Gary Cooper had an aftermath that was not entirely unexpected. One evening in the summer of 1936, a process server posing, to the Goldwyns' butler, as a member of the United Artists board of directors talked his way into the house, where he attempted to slap Sam with a subpoena from Adolph Zukor summoning him to court to answer charges of luring Gary Cooper from Paramount and to show why he should not pay some $5 million in damages for so doing.

Sam had already gone to bed and refused to come downstairs. Instead he suggested that the caller be put in telephonic communication with Abe Lehr, his boyhood friend from Gloversville and now his personal executive assistant.

This was done, and Lehr, from his own home in Beverly Hills, convinced the young man he could deliver the papers to him instead of to Mr. Goldwyn. After receiving authorization to do this from the federal court clerk, the process server retrieved his hat from the extended hand of the butler and left the Goldwyn home.

Zukor's complaint charged Sam with "a breach of morals and ethics," and alleged that Paramount and Mr. Cooper had already agreed on the terms of a new four-year contract, which Cooper had been quite willing to sign until "interference by Goldwyn and the Goldwyn company thwarted and prevented such a move."

"In the 25 years I have been in motion pictures," Zukor's claim went on, "I have never permitted our executives to interfere with the negotiations between a star of another company and that company for the continued services of the star. That has always been and always will be a matter of principle without organization.

"Our attorneys have advised us that such conduct as that alleged is not only a breach of good morals and ethics, but is a violation of law and gives us a legal right of action against Goldwyn."

Sam might have been "unprincipled," but he must have been within his legal rights, for according to Eugene Frank, a vice president of Paramount Pictures Corporation today and head of its West Coast legal department, "the lawsuit was settled amicably, and as part of the settlement, Goldwyn made Gary Cooper's services available to Paramount for a picture."

But his experience with Zukor failed to teach Sam to be any more charitable in his dealings with his fellow producers. If anything, his successful acquisition of Gary Cooper gave him the courage to pull more of the same.

In 1935, for example, David Niven, fresh from England, but with no acting experience, could get a job in Hollywood only as an extra. He had made several tests, but nothing had come of them. Socially, however, he was more successful. Being handsome, debonair, English, and also quite expert at polo, a popular game among the upper crust in Hollywood in the thirties, Niven was invited to a lot of parties. At one of them was Irving Thalberg, then in the throes of casting *Mutiny on the Bounty*. As a publicity stunt, Thalberg decided to cast Niven as a member of the *Bounty*'s crew, in a nonspeaking role.

The moment Thalberg's announcement hit the trades, Sam contacted Niven's agent, asked to see one of the previously turned-down tests of him, and after viewing it in his living room with Frances one night, signed him to a seven-year contract. And Thalberg was one of Sam's best friends.

If you happened to be just a friendly enemy, as Jack Warner was, Sam showed even fewer scruples when dealing with you.

During the late thirites, Eddie Chodorov wrote a moderately successful play called *Those Endearing Young Charms* which Jack Warner liked and offered to buy for a picture for $35,000.

Except for the signing of the contracts, the deal was closed when Jerry Chodorov, knowing Goldwyn was also looking for a property, mentioned his brother's play to Don Hartman, Goldwyn's story editor at the time. Hartman read the play and recommended to Goldwyn that he buy it immediately.

Sam sent for Eddie Chodorov, sat him down in his office, and worked out a deal for him to get $75,000 for the property. In the midst of this session the phone rang, and the caller turned out to be Jack Warner, demanding to speak to Sam. "Sam," said the outraged Warner, "what about this Chodorov play? I hear you're trying to steal it from me."

"What play?" asked Sam.

"*Those Endearing Young Charms*," snapped Warner.

"I never heard of it," lied Goldwyn. "I don't know what you are talking about, Jack." And he hung up.

Eddie Chodorov, who was not anxious to make an enemy of a man as powerful as Jack Warner for the sake of a few extra thousand dollars, said to Sam, "Mr. Goldwyn. You can't pretend you're not doing this. Mr. Warner's going to read about it tomorrow in the trades."

"Fuck Warner," said Goldwyn, with the gleam of victory in his eyes. "Fuck Warner!"

In the forties, Sam tried to steal Alfred Hitchcock away from David Selznick, even though it was generally known around Hollywood that his contract with the director of the highly successful *Rebecca* had two more years to run.

When Selznick heard what Sam was up to, he was furious and sent a three-page, single-spaced letter to Sam excoriating him for his unethical conduct. After reminding Sam of some recent favors he'd done for him, Selznick concluded his letter with:

> I regret that I have to write you in this vein, and I do so not because I have any reluctance about rebuking you orally, for you know from our past relationship that I have never been hesitant about such matters when I felt you to be in the wrong. I write you now, first, because I want it a matter of record, in connection with my future dealings with you; and second, because I have learned from experience that it is impossible to get you to listen to this many words unless they are in writing.
>
> With best wishes for a fine and reformed New Year,
>
> Sincerely yours,
> David Selznick

Sam couldn't reform because he never believed himself to be in the wrong in any matter. Anyone who's ever worked for him can tell a story to illustrate this point.

Long before the Hitchcock incident, Sam once phoned Selznick and invited him to bring his company to the Goldwyn lot and make pictures there. As Sam saw it, the two of them could save money by using the same offices, sound stages, and other studio facilities. Selznick wasn't keen on the idea, and said no to the offer. Within fifteen minutes, according to Selznick, Sam turned up in his office.

"You're afraid of me, aren't you?" said Sam.

"Yes, I am, Sam," replied Selznick. "Why should I think I'm the only man in Hollywood who can live with you?"

"I'll tell you what I'll do," said Sam. "If you or any of your people ever think you're not getting a fair deal from me, you can come direct to me and I will prove how wrong you are."

"That's just what I'm afraid of," said Selznick.

Darryl Zanuck heard another variation on the same theme, when Sam phoned him during the Zukor litigation over Gary Cooper to complain, "How do you like that dirty bastard, Zukor—saying I stole Gary Cooper?"

"Well, didn't you?"

"No, I just offered him more money to come with me. A man has a right to make more money, doesn't he? This is America, isn't it?"

"I hate to agree with Zukor, but in this case, Sam, I can't go along with you," said Zanuck. "They were already in negotiations. Zukor's right."

"That's the trouble with this business," shouted Sam. "Nobody ever sticks together!" And he hung up on Zanuck.

If, on the other hand, another producer tried to raid the Goldwyn talent camp, Sam would rage like a lioness protecting her young.

A producer at another studio once borrowed a Goldwyn writer for two hours one afternoon in order to get some free advice from him on how to fix up a script that was in trouble. Since the writer, a friend of the producer's, had no assignment at the time, he gladly donated his services.

But when Sam found out about this treachery, he immediately phoned the other producer and called him every four-letter word he could think of.

"Sam, be reasonable," pleaded the producer. "It's not like I was taking him away from something he was doing for you."

"That's not the point," said Sam. "If you wanted to borrow him, you should have asked me first."

"What would you have said?" asked the producer.

"No!" replied Sam without any hesitation.

17

Since When Are We Making Pictures for Kids?

SAM'S "ANNA STEN" PERIOD, usually referred to as his "darkest hour," was followed by one of the brighter periods in his producing career. Between 1935 and 1937 he produced *These Three*, based on Lillian Hellman's *The Children's Hour*; *Dodsworth*; and *Dead End*. He also produced four other films that, while not exactly classics, were all solid moneymakers bearing public seal of approval: *The Dark Angel*, a remake using Fredric March and Merle Oberon in the Colman and Banky roles; *Barbary Coast*, starring Edward G. Robinson, Miriam Hopkins, and Joel McCrea; *Strike Me Pink*, the last of the Eddie Cantor musicals; and *Come and Get It*, based on the Edna Ferber novel about lumberjacks in the Wisconsin woodlands.

But except for *Barbary Coast*, which was just a costume melodrama that served well as the featured attraction on a double bill, all were milestones of one sort or another.

Strike Me Pink proved that no matter how popular the star or how powerful the producer, you can only get a certain amount of mileage out of the same formula before the critics start complaining and the public stops coming.

Writing in the *New York Times*, Frank Nugent said: "*Strike Me Pink*, the latest gift from the Ziegfeld of the Pacific, appears to lack some of his customary expansiveness and much of the comic invention that has made the well known father of five one of the screen's most likeable funny men."

Strike Me Pink did all right at the box office, but there was enough public and critical resistance to convince Sam that Cantor had run his race, at least in this kind of vehicle, and he called finis to their professional relationship.

The Dark Angel was the first of many successful and famous films in which Merle Oberon would star for Sam Goldwyn. But contrary to Hollywood legend and what many magazine and newspaper feature writers have fed the public, Sam did not discover Merle Oberon. At the time Sam hired her, Miss Oberon had appeared in half a dozen films both in America and Great Britain, and in one that shot her to stardom, Alexander Korda's *The Private Life of Henry VIII*, in which she played Anne Boleyn to Charles Laughton's Henry. Moreover, she was also married to Alexander Korda, who by the time Sam made *The Dark Angel* was one of the member-owners of United Artists.

Come and Get It, along with *These Three* and *Dodsworth*, all released in the same year, 1936, saw the beginning of the long, successful, and sometimes stormy relationship between Sam and director Willy Wyler, which culminated with the two of them picking up Oscars for *The Best Years of Our Lives* in 1947.

These Three was also the beginning of the Goldwyn–Lillian Hellman relationship that saw Hellman eventually supplanting Sidney Howard as Goldwyn's number-one writer.

And *Dead End*, in addition to being a fine film, made stars of Humphrey Bogart, Marjorie Main, and the Dead End Kids (Leo Gorcey, Huntz Hall, Bobby Jordan, and Billy Halop).

For Sam to bounce back with three smash hits after his defeat at the hands of the Ukranian sorceress was probably due to his reversion once again to his earlier producing theory that "the play's the thing." As was the case with Mary Garden, Pauline Frederick, and some of his other vintage mistakes, he had temporarily let the glitter of a star blind him to the wisdom of Shakespeare's advice.

But sometime during that period when he was sinking with Anna Sten, it must have dawned on him that he was going about the business of making films backward: first you buy a good story, *then* you find someone to put in it. Basic picturemaking for Sam Goldwyn, and therein lay the real secret behind his biggest successes. There are those who found fault with that *modus operandi*, claiming it takes no talent to be able to buy the best and that, at most, it is an eclectic one.

That, of course, is lint picking at its pickiest, for that is all a producer is supposed to do—choose a property that will make a first-class film, sweeten the package with the right director, writer, and actors, and guide everyone in the proper direction. For every producer who can write and direct as well as put the package together, there are fifty who can't. And of those who do all three, they generally do one, two, or all three of the crafts badly. The writer-director-producer usually flops because he is badly in need of someone on a higher level to look objectively at his work and tell him what is wrong with it.

Being the man who can guide a production in the right direction is just as important as the sum of all its parts. But before there can be something to guide, there must be a property on which to go to work—and the right one, at that. Sam was always on the lookout for the right property, and it kept him in a constant state of restlessness.

Whether he was on a holiday or in the hospital recuperating from an operation, he always looked at everything—book, play, or magazine story— with the same thought in mind: Will it make a successful film, and one that I can be proud of?

His associates were expected to be in the same state of watchfulness at all times. And God help the story editor who let a story get away, or who steered Sam in the direction of one he should have skipped.

Following the release of the last Anna Sten picture, Sam called George Oppenheimer into his office and said, "George, I want you to look for a story for me that will have everything—comedy, color, songs, suspense, spectacle, and vast appeal for children and adults alike."

It was a herculean assignment and ordinarily Oppenheimer would have told him he was asking the impossible. But Oppenheimer was in no position to talk back to Sam. In fact, he had been on shaky ground with Goldwyn ever since he had got him to buy *The Wedding Night*. And while it hadn't exactly been Oppenheimer's fault that the picture had died at the box office, Sam nevertheless associated him with "one of my worst failures."

Which was why, in the words of Sam Marx, who followed Oppenheimer as Goldwyn's story editor, "Paradise turned into hell for almost everyone who worked for Goldwyn after a few months."

Oppenheimer, however, had not quite reached the point of believing he was in purgatory when Sam gave him this assignment. In fact, he rather liked the money Sam was paying him, not to mention the weather in southern California, and he was hoping he'd be able to come up with some worthwhile property to suggest to Sam to help secure his job another few months.

Inspiration struck as Oppenheimer was leaving Goldwyn's office. Why not *The Wizard of Oz?* Unless his memory failed him, the L. Frank Baum book seemed to fit every one of Sam's specifications. Oppenheimer immediately dispatched a messenger to Pickwick Books on Hollywood Boulevard to buy a copy of *The Wizard of Oz*, and that night at home he read it. He was right. The book had everything but songs, and those could easily be put in.

The next morning Oppenheimer wrote a synopsis of the *Oz* book, together with his ideas on how to turn it into a major film, and showed it to Sam.

Sam had never heard of, let alone read, any of the *Oz* series. But according to Oppenheimer's recollection of that day, "he seemed not uninterested, which was the best I could hope for in the present climate of disfavor."

A thin smile on Sam's lips gave Oppenheimer the courage to add that *The Wizard of Oz* was one of the two or three greatest-selling children's books in the history of American literature. That sold Sam, and before the day was over he was on the phone issuing orders to Abe Lehr to get in touch with the L. Frank Baum estate to find out how much it wanted for the motion picture rights.

Goldwyn paid $15,000 for the book, and only after it became his property did he decide to read it, the same short volume with large print and many illustrations that Oppenheimer had picked up at Pickwick Books. An average reader could probably get through that edition of *The Wizard of Oz* in a couple of hours. But late that afternoon—he had started reading before lunch—Sam dropped into Oppenheimer's office, his face wreathed in smiles.

"George," he said, "that book. I can't put it down. I'm where the house falls on the witch." (This episode occurred on page 17 of the edition he was reading.)

The second day Oppenheimer entered Sam's office. He was sitting behind his desk, smiling and reading.

"George," he said, looking up from the *Oz* book, "all I do is read, read, and read. I don't even listen when Frances talks to me."

A week later Sam finished reading the book. But suddenly the smiles disappeared, and his opinion of Oppenheimer's story judgment was even lower than it had been after he had seen the first week's grosses of *The Wedding Night*. Sam not only didn't like *The Wizard of Oz*, but now that he had read it in its entirety he hated it. And he bawled Oppenheimer out for making him waste $15,000 on something he couldn't use. "It's a fantasy," raged Sam. "Fantasies don't make good pictures."

A few hours later Oppenheimer was in his own office, brooding about having to work for Goldwyn when Leland Hayward, who was then a literary agent, wandered through the door, looking for someone's phone to use.

After Oppenheimer told him his latest troubles with Sam, Hayward's face lit up with inspiration, and he grabbed the phone and called Jock Whitney. Hayward and Whitney held a brief conversation, following which Hayward said to Oppenheimer that Whitney and his sister, Joan Payson, would buy *The Wizard of Oz* from Sam at a considerable profit. It seems the pair had a financial interest in Technicolor and were looking for a property that would lend itself to the new color process.

Feeling sure this would redeem himself in Sam's eyes, Oppenheimer brought the news to his boss. But instead of being happy, Sam growled, "Don't believe everything you hear."

"But it's true," said Oppenheimer. "If you don't believe me, call Leland in here."

Sam glared at Oppenheimer, then said, "Mind your own business, will you, George?"

Sam's dog-in-the-manger attitude was either sheer perversity because he didn't like Oppenheimer anymore, or else a brilliant example of his business acumen. He held on to the property long after he did Oppenheimer, and then finally sold it to MGM at a price far higher than what Leland Hayward had offered.

It's obvious Sam never thought *The Wizard of Oz* could be the hit it was, but perhaps if he had had Judy Garland under contract to play Dorothy, and Harold Arlen and Yip Harburg to write "Over the Rainbow" for her, he might have looked at the whole project through different eyes. Hindsight is easy. There were plenty of other producers in Hollywood, including Disney, who never thought there was a movie in *The Wizard of Oz*, either.

But nobody ever said being Goldwyn's story editor was easy. Nobody ever said being Goldwyn's "anything" was easy. He was always full of surprises. It was never possible to know from one day to the next just what kind of story material interested him at the moment. And he always kept you off balance by laying down rules and then breaking them.

No one found that out more quickly than the man who followed Oppenheimer as Goldwyn's story editor, Sam Marx—a tall, heavy-set, lugubrious-looking man with a newspaper background and several years' experience as the head of Metro's story department. Shortly after going to work for Goldwyn, Marx came to him one day and suggested he buy a story by E. M. Hardwood, an English playwright.

Marx started to tell Goldwyn the story, which was about a mythical kingdom, when Sam held up his hand to stop him. "Wait a minute," said Sam. "I don't like mythical kingdom stories. I make a rule for you. As long as you work for me, don't bother me with any mythical kingdom stories, or stories where they write with a quill pen."

Months passed and David Selznick previewed *The Prisoner of Zenda*, which got rave reviews in the trade papers the next morning.

The moment Sam finished reading the reviews, he called Marx into his office and said, "Do you know a book called *Graustark?*"

"Yes, Mr. Goldwyn."

"Do you think you could buy the rights for me?" asked Sam.

Marx said he would try, tracked down who owned them—Joe Schenck—and after considerable haggling, set a deal to buy them.

As soon as the deal was finalized, Marx walked into Goldwyn's office and said, "Mr. Goldwyn, you are now the proud owner of *Graustark.*"

Instead of being happy, Sam glowered at him. "Sit down," he ordered. Marx sat.

"Are you my story editor?" asked Goldwyn.

"Yes, sir," replied Marx.

"Who suggested *Graustark?*"

"You did, Mr. Goldwyn."

"But you're my story editor. Why should *I* have to suggest *Graustark?*"

"I'll tell you why, Mr. Goldwyn. Right after I came to work for you, you made a rule. No mythical kingdoms, you told me. Now, in case you don't know it, *Graustark* is a mythical kingdom."

Goldwyn thought it over a moment, then retorted, "Yes, I remember—but I didn't mean classics."

After reading a synopsis of *The Citadel*, a best-selling novel about a doctor by A. J. Cronin, Goldwyn decided it would make a good vehicle for Merle Oberon and told Sam Marx to buy it for him.

Marx phoned Cronin's agent in New York and made a verbal commitment for Goldwyn to buy *The Citadel* for $15,000—a bargain for a best seller by A. J. Cronin, even in those pre-inflation days.

That night Goldwyn previewed the much-maligned *Woman Chases Man*, a screwball comedy with Miriam Hopkins and Joel McCrea, and discovered it was practically unreleasable. He drove back from the preview in the same car with George Haight. Haight was the associate producer of *Woman Chases Man*, and Sam never let him forget it during the ride back to Beverly Hills from the preview theater.

In fear of losing his job, Haight tried to distract Sam by telling him he never should have bought the "Cronin book" because the medical theme was too "introspective" to make good screen material.

The red-herring tactic worked. Sam temporarily forgot about *Woman Chases Man* and even thanked Haight for pointing out the weaknesses of the Cronin book. The next morning Sam called Marx into his office and stunned him with the announcement that he had changed his mind about buying *The Citadel*.

"Why?" asked Marx.

"Because it's about a doctor. All doctor stories lose money."

"What about *Arrowsmith?*"

"That lost money, too." Sam would lie to back up a point.

"Well, we can't back out now," said Marx. "I closed the deal yesterday. It would be embarrassing to say we changed our mind."

"Tell him I changed it," said Goldwyn.

"That would be embarrassing to you," said Marx. "Your word would never mean anything again."

"Okay," said Goldwyn, reaching for the phone, "then I do it. That way *you* don't have to be embarrassed."

Whereupon he phoned Cronin's agent and said, "This is Sam Goldwyn. I am not interested in the Cronin book."

"But your story editor already made a deal with us," said the agent.

"Well, he had no right to," said Goldwyn. "He doesn't have the authority to make deals." And he hung up.

"That was Sam's idea of not embarrassing me," recalls Marx. "Telling the agent I didn't have authority. I still cringe thinking about it."

The Citadel was another case where Sam dropped a valuable property too soon. After he let it go, MGM bought the rights for $30,000 and made it into a successful film starring Robert Donat and Rosalind Russell.

It's difficult to conceive how a man who tossed away $411,000, some say foolishly, to salvage *Nana*, and who would, in the near future, spend twice that to reshoot some of *Come and Get It*, could be so cautious when it came to acquiring a novel by A. J. Cronin. But Sam was full of those ambivalences in his spending habits.

In acquiring the rights to *Dodsworth*, for example, Sam exercised such caution that it wound up costing him $140,000 more than he needed to have paid. Sam first heard of the Sinclair Lewis novel in 1932 through his good friend Sidney Howard, who had written the screenplay for *Arrowsmith*. Howard, in fact, was just winding up his work on *Arrowsmith* when he informed Sam that he had just finished reading *Dodsworth*, that he thought it would make an excellent motion picture, and that he knew from Lewis's agent that it could be bought for $20,000.

But Sam was not interested, even when told that the book had sold some 85,000 hardback copies in two months—tremendous for those depression-racked days. To Sam it did not seem like movie material, and he was not completely wrong in his assessment.

Like *Arrowsmith* in construction, the novel *Dodsworth* was a loosely strung together series of episodes about a retired auto manufacturer who goes off to Europe with his wife to enjoy his sunset years, and there in the old-world milieu finds retirement not so enjoyable and his wife of many years practically a stranger to him.

Though a best seller, it was not one of Lewis's better novels. And as movie material, it lacked action and its scenes were quiet, talky, and sedentary—of the drawing-room comedy-of-manners variety.

"I'll pass," Sam told Howard after reading the novel.

"Well, if you don't want it for a movie, then I think I'll get the rights to it and dramatize it for the stage," replied Howard. "I just wanted to give you first crack at it."

Master craftsman that he was, Howard went ahead and fashioned *Dodsworth* into a hit play containing fourteen scenes. It starred Walter Huston and Fay Bainter. After it opened at New York's Shubert Theater in February 1934, to smash notices, Sam bought the screen rights for $160,000—an astronomical figure for those years—and hired Sidney Howard to do the screen adaptation.

"I don't understand you, Sam," said Howard. "Two years ago you could have had it for twenty thousand."

"I don't care," replied Sam. "This way I buy a successful play, something already in dramatic form. With this, I have more assurance of success and it's worth the extra money I pay."

While there are some who find fault with that approach, and quibble that it's not creative producing, no less a director than Academy Award–winner Willy Wyler finds it "very bright, very intelligent."

In a way, Sam's kind of producing could be likened to going to the track and putting your money on a good horse that pays short odds rather than a long shot. In the long run you'll win more money betting on the best horses, for what good are big odds if the horses you pick keep losing?

But occasionally Sam was willing to put his money on the horse with long odds, provided the jockey was somebody he respected and who had a winning record. His production of Lillian Hellman's *The Children's Hour* is an excellent example of Goldwyn's willingness to gamble both in his selection of story material and its method of execution.

It also shows a great deal of wisdom—more wisdom than is credited to him by the following Goldwynism which was making the rounds at about the time *The Children's Hour* opened to smash reviews on Broadway and became one of the long-run plays of pre–World War II days.

After reading the smash notices, Sam told Merritt Hulburd, "Maybe we ought to buy it."

"Forget it, Mr. Goldwyn," said Hulburd. "It's about lesbians."

"Don't worry about that," replied Sam. "We'll make them Americans."

An apocryphal Goldwynism if ever there was one. To begin with, Sam was much too aware—and, yes, even sophisticated in his way—ever to have said a simple-minded thing like that. And secondly, he had Lillian Hellman under contract at the studio long before he ever thought about making *The Children's Hour* into a film, and since they had lunch together in his private dining room nearly every day, it's impossible to believe that at some time during their conversations the subject matter of her hit play, which was still running on Broadway, did not come up.

Actually, Sam's acquisition of *The Children's Hour* and his decision to film it was an outgrowth of a relationship between him and Lillian Hellman that sprouted when he put her under contract as a screenwriter for $2,000 a week in 1935. As the author of America's newest hit, Lillian Hellman, at the age of thirty, was suddenly up there in the theatrical limelight alongside such giants as Kaufman, Sherwood, and Moss Hart.

Sam's deal with her had nothing to do with *The Children's Hour* except in the sense that it brought her to Sam's attention as a writer. Signing America's leading female dramatist to an exclusive contract was a large coup for Sam, who reveled in not only employing star names but also entertaining them in his new home—a two-story Georgian Colonial of some 6,000 square feet and fourteen rooms that sat astride a hilltop high above Sunset Boulevard and the rest of Beverly Hills.

Sam and Frances had built their new residence in 1933, after it became evident that their first home on Hollywood Boulevard was in a passé section of town. Hollywood was no longer an orange-blossom-scented suburb, but a very commercial-looking extension of greater Los Angeles. Everyone who could afford to either had already moved, or was moving west to Beverly Hills, Brentwood, and even the beach.

The Goldwyns could certainly afford to, so with this in mind, Sam sneaked away from the studio one afternoon in 1932, found a real estate broker in Beverly Hills, and announced he was in the market for a lot on which to build.

The broker obliged the famous Mr. Goldwyn by putting him in his car and driving him up into the as-yet-undeveloped hills north of Sunset Boulevard. After winding his way through some narrow, circuitous mountain roads, the broker parked the car in a dead end in front of five brush-covered acres on the rim of Coldwater Canyon. The lot had a magnificent view of the city and was large enough for a house, swimming pool, tennis court, and all the other accouterments required to make an important movie mogul and his family happy.

Sam paid the asking price of $5,000 without quibbling and another $5,000 for the lot next door, just to make certain no neighbors could encroach on his privacy.

Returning home after closing the deal, Sam said to Frances, "Get in the car. I have a surprise for you."

"What kind of surprise?"

"I bought a lot. Come drive me there. I show it to you."

So with Frances at the wheel of her roadster and Sam directing her, they spent four hours driving up and down hillside roads looking for their lot. But since most of the hills were undeveloped, every lot, street, and dead end looked the same.

Finally Sam had to admit that he was completely lost and had to enlist the aid of the real estate broker in order to show Frances the site of their new home.

Frances loved the lot but regretted the day she ever became involved in a house-building project with a husband as impatient and volatile as Sam.

When the house was in the blueprint stage, Sam and Frances argued about every little detail and never could agree on anything in spite of the fact that they had a first-class architect to guide them. All Sam cared about was that he have a place "to show my pictures."

He favored using the living room to show films, in case they had a large group over, but Frances was not for disfiguring the living room walls with unsightly movie projector peepholes. She wanted wall space for paintings and other objects of art she and Sam had collected over the years—a couple of Renoirs, a Picasso, a Matisse.

Their disagreements finally erupted into such bitter quarreling that if it had grown any worse they would not have needed one house, but two—in separate sections of the city. Rather than get a divorce, Sam finally agreed to turn the whole project over to Frances. He couldn't be bothered anymore. He had a studio to run and enough trouble on his hands with that damn husband of Anna Sten's.

Nothing could have made Frances happier than seeing Sam step aside. She knew what their requirements were and she could articulate them to the builder. And so she supervised the whole project, from drawing-board stage to furnishing and decorating the completed structure. The house cost $28,000 to build, plus another $5,000 for the tennis court, which had to be cantilevered.

If Frances's account can be believed, Sam never saw the lot or house again until the day they moved in eight months later.

On moving day, Frances picked Sam up at the studio after work and drove him to the new house, which, in her estimation, had everything to make her husband happy: A huge entrance foyer, with a broad, winding staircase and a mahogany-banistered railing that ran up to the second-floor landing. A large living room filled with English antiques. A formal dining room that could comfortably seat twenty-four guests, with a sparkling crystal chandelier overhead. A wood-paneled den that was a combination den and projection room. Two large connecting his-and-hers suites upstairs. Several guest rooms for visiting dignitaries. And a large bedroom for Sam junior, who was then seven years old and a day student at Black-Foxe Military Institute.

Once at the house, Frances let Sam roam through its interior by himself, silently inspecting the miracle she believed she had wrought. But it was a worry; Sam could be awfully fussy at times.

Sam went through the first floor without a word of complaint, and most of the second. Frances breathed easier as she waited in the foyer down below for Sam to finish his inspection tour and make his final, official judgment.

Suddenly, Frances heard a roar from the upstairs landing.

"Frances!" Sam yelled down, leaning over the railing.

"Something wrong, Sam?" asked Frances with trepidation.

"Yes," replied Sam. "There's no soap in my soap dish!"

It took seven in help to run the new establishment, but you couldn't stint when you were the Great Goldwyn and were expected to entertain people like Sidney Howard, Fredric March, Eleanor Roosevelt, and Lillian Hellman.

Lillian Hellman's first assignment for Sam was to rewrite *The Dark Angel* into a talkie which would star Merle Oberon and Fredric March and be directed by Sidney Franklin. Because this was Miss Hellman's first moviewriting experience, Sam gave her a collaborator, an English playwright he also had under contract whose name was Mordaunt Shairp.

It was the custom in those days to have weeks of story conferences between the writer and the director before any words were immortalized on paper. As a result, Hellman and Shairp would meet every morning around ten at Franklin's house, discuss the story in generalities for a few hours, eat a leisurely lunch, talk some more until five, and then break up, having accomplished little. At least in the opinion of Lillian Hellman, who felt that occasionally they even lost ground. As she wrote in *Pentimento*, her recent book of memoirs, "The next day whatever we had decided would be altered and sometimes be scrapped because Franklin had consulted a friend the night before or discussed our discussions with his bridge partners."

Hellman, a well-organized, disciplined writer who was used to turning out a certain amount of pages daily when left to her own devices, eventually became so bored with the routine at Franklin's house that she would flop down on one of the couches, turn her back to her collaborators, and take a nap.

When Franklin complained one afternoon that it was rude of her to fall asleep on him, Miss Hellman left, packed her bags, and took the next plane for New York, where she shut herself in her apartment and refused to answer the phone or doorbell for days.

When she finally did answer the phone, she found herself locked in verbal combat with Sam Goldwyn, who, upon learning what her complaint was, promised that, if only she'd return to the studio, she could go to "a room by yourself and start writing." He also said he would give her a raise.

Still smarting from Franklin's unkind words, Miss Hellman told Sam that she'd think about it, hung up, packed her bags again, and took the next ship for Paris. When Sam located her in a small Left Bank hotel a week later he offered her a new long-term contract, with clauses specifying that she had to work only on stories she liked, and when and where she pleased.

Unwittingly Lillian Hellman discovered that the secret to survival under

Goldwyn's rule was to be independent to the point of being unattainable. Well, one of the secrets. The other was to be able to "deliver" when called upon to do so. In that respect, she never failed him.

Returning to Hollywood, Miss Hellman completed her first film-writing assignment for Goldwyn, and rather successfully, if the following *New York Times* review of September 6, 1935, is to be believed: "Even if there is just a hint of overstatement in Mr. Goldwyn's belief that *The Dark Angel* is destined to achieve screen immortality, the impresario's first photoplay of the season is a happy adventure in sentimental romance. Lillian Hellman and Mordaunt Shairp have written a highly literate screen adaptation of Guy Bolton's play."

While Merle Oberon's first picture for Goldwyn was successful, Miss Hellman apparently did not feel it worthy enough of her own talents to want her name connected with it today. When she was writing about her first experience as a Goldwyn writer in *Pentimento* she didn't mention *The Dark Angel* by its title at all. She merely referred to it as an "old silly."

But that association gave Miss Hellman the opportunity to sell Sam the idea of making a film of *The Children's Hour*, which, though it was enjoying one of Broadway's longest runs, was considered unsuitable for pictures because of its homosexual taint and therefore was still begging for its first offer from Hollywood.

Always interested in acquiring a hit of such stature, and having a good track record of accomplishing the "impossible," Sam was definitely interested in *The Children's Hour* and made a personal appeal to the Hays Office (the organization set up by the industry for self-censorship) to lift its ban of the play as movie material, provided it was done tastefully. But the censorship office remained unalterably opposed. Lesbianism on the screen! Who ever heard of such a thing? And how could it possibly be done tastefully?

The Hays Office was so adamant in its refusal that it wouldn't give its stamp of approval to any film even bearing the title *The Children's Hour*, no matter how watered down, because of the connotation already associated with it from its Broadway run.

So obviously Sam never told Will Hays, or anybody else, "We'll make them Americans," but he did become interested in the project when Lillian Hellman came up with an idea on how to fool the Hays Office. Sam would not make *The Children's Hour*. Instead, he would pay her to write an original script based on her play, which would have a brand-new title, *These Three*, and a slightly altered story.

Originally *The Children's Hour* took place in a boarding school for young girls and was the story of two of its teachers—Martha Dobie and Karen Wright—who have "an unnatural affection" for each other, and a tangle of lies spread about them by Mary, an evil little girl, who is one of the students.

Since the dénouement of the story hinged on whether Mary had lied or told the truth about Martha's homosexual attachment to Karen, Miss Hellman suggested eliminating the homosexual relationship and making it a heterosexual romance between Martha and a boyfriend. That way, argued Miss Hellman, Sam's production could remain within the circumspect boundaries laid down by the Hays Office and still not lose any dramatic values. Furthermore, if they changed the title to *These Three*, the fact that they were filming *The Children's Hour* would be completely disguised.

The fact that Sam said yes to the idea of producing *The Children's Hour* without reaping the benefit of being able to use a title that was already presold to the public amply demonstrates that Sam frequently operated on a much higher artistic plane than did his peers in Hollywood—the ones who complained that he was successful only because he bought hits. When *they* bought hit books or plays, they frequently threw away everything else but the title, much to the anger and embarrassment of the original authors and usually to the detriment of the film.

Here Sam was going to make *The Children's Hour* but keep that fact a dark secret between himself, Lillian Hellman, and a few members of his staff, which at the time consisted of Merritt Hulburd and George Haight, assistant producers; Jock Lawrence, his chief of publicity; Richard Day, his art director; Freddy Kohlmar, in charge of casting; and Gordon Sawyer, head of the sound department.

Willy Wyler, who was to direct the picture and then go on to become the director on whom Goldwyn relied the most, was not yet under contract. Nor had he ever worked for Sam before, though he was a veteran in the business, having directed his first film, a silent called *The Crook Buster*, for Universal in 1925.

Since then Wyler had directed a long string of low-budget action films for Universal and several "A" pictures, including *Counsellor at Law* with John Barrymore and Bebe Daniels, and *The Gay Deception*, a light, romantic comedy, starring Francis Lederer and Frances Dee, which Jesse Lasky produced for Fox in 1935 after he was kicked out of Paramount.

"But I was free-lancing when Goldwyn sent for me," recalls Wyler. "At the time I was considered a young, up-and-coming director, but practically unknown. Then I got a call from my agent saying Goldwyn wanted to see me. It seems he had seen the picture I had just made for Lasky, *The Gay Deception*, and he liked the direction—liked the picture—and so he sent for me to do *The Children's Hour*."

Wyler, who'd seen *The Children's Hour* on Broadway, couldn't believe his ears. "*The Children's Hour!*" he exclaimed when he first was told of the project by his agent. "My God, he can't make that into a picture. How in hell is he going to do that?"

"Look, he's going to do it," said the agent. "So what the hell do you care? Go see him."

"Jesus, I'm sure curious how he's going to do it," mused the puzzled Wyler.

However, at his agent's urging, he agreed to a meeting with Goldwyn in the latter's office. Also there was Lillian Hellman, whom Wyler met for the first time. "During that meeting," recalls Wyler, "Lillian made me realize how her play could work. She pointed out that the main theme of *The Children's Hour* was not lesbianism, but the power of a lie, and that the lesbianism thing was just incidental and not necessary to the story. I was very impressed with that idea. Then I saw the script she'd written, which was a very fine one. Instead of the lesbian theme there was a conventional triangle, and it worked very well."

Working for a man like Goldwyn turned out to be a broadening experience for Wyler, who was used to the penny-pinching ways of the front-office executives at Universal and Fox.

By the time Wyler agreed to direct *These Three*, Sam had already assembled a superb cast—Merle Oberon and Miriam Hopkins to portray the two schoolteachers, and Joel McCrea to play the boyfriend. The only part that hadn't been filled was that of Mary, the evil little girl.

Wyler proved his ability in that department by casting an unknown named Bonita Granville in the part of Mary. The picture made a star of her at the age of eight.

Wyler's cameraman on the film was Gregg Toland, who'd been under contract to Sam since 1929, who'd done most of his important pictures, and who was considered one of the top cinematographers in the business. The other four at the time were: James Wong Howe, Leon Shamroy, Lee Garmes, and Joseph Ruttenberg, MGM's first-string cameraman.

Like all of Sam's productions, it was "top cabin" all the way. Unlike many of them, it was comparatively smooth sailing, for the script worked, the director understood what the author was after, and so did the actors.

Wyler only had a couple of problems. One was learning to get along with Gregg Toland. "I was in the habit," recalls Wyler, "of saying to other cameramen with whom I'd worked, 'Put the camera here and shoot it with a forty millimeter,' or 'Move the camera this way,' or 'Light it this way.' Suddenly Toland wanted to quit the picture. I didn't understand why. Finally he came to me and told me he wasn't a man to be told every move. After I learned you didn't tell Gregg what lens to use, you told him what mood you were after, we got along beautifully."

Problem number two, of course, was learning how to cope with Sam, who, if such a thing were possible, was even more inarticulate when telling a director what he wanted, or what was wrong, than he was with writers. "He was a man," remembers Wyler, "who made a great deal of sense, and a great deal of nonsense. The reason we were able to get along together so successfully over a period of eight years—we made eight successful pictures in a row—was because I was able to separate the sense from the nonsense."

One particular piece of nonsense Wyler will never forget occurred following a screening of the rough cut of *Dead End* in Goldwyn's home. When the lights went up, Sam complained about a scene toward the end of the picture that wasn't clear to him.

"It seemed all right to me," said Wyler. "What don't you understand about it?"

Goldwyn shrugged. "I don't know. It's just not clear."

Wyler insisted that it was perfectly clear, and as proof turned to nine-year-old Sammy junior, who was standing nearby listening, and said, "Do you understand that scene, Sammy?"

"Sure," said Sammy, and he went on to explain the scene in great detail, with all its ramifications.

Sam heard his son out in controlled rage, then wheeled on Wyler and snapped, "Since when are we making pictures for kids?"

But of all Sam's directors, Wyler was able to cope with Sam the best. "I think," recalls Wyler, "because I paid attention to the sense and disregarded the nonsense. And Goldwyn, after he had confidence in me, would usually defer to my judgment. Not in business matters, but in artistic matters.

"Our disagreements would always be from the point of view of . . . well, that we were both trying to make the best picture possible.

"When I first came to Sam, I was astounded by his willingness to spend money. I had just come from Universal, where we made cheap pictures. And the only thing the studio ever cared about was how much they cost, were we overschedule? were we overbudget? and so on. Nobody cared if it was good or not. But Goldwyn was a man who was not like that. I once had a discussion with him when we were making *These Three*. I told him I didn't like a scene I had done, and he said, 'Then why don't you shoot it over?'

"I was astounded. No producer had ever said such a thing to me before. But he insisted again, 'Well, shoot it over.' That meant a lot of money to him, because he was personally financing all his pictures. But this opened a whole new vista for me—it made me think bigger and better. Because that was how he thought and what he had always done himself. Lots of times he didn't know how to make it better, but he wanted it better, nevertheless.

He wanted things to be classy. Along with that he also wanted everything to be very beautiful. All the women had to look fine, the clothes had to be perfect—even if it didn't fit the story."

Despite Sam's and Lillian Hellman's efforts to disguise *The Children's Hour*, nobody was really fooled, including the much-feared Hays Office. But because Goldwyn, Hellman, and Wyler had handled the original subject matter so tastefully and with such skill, *These Three* received nothing but praise when it opened in New York on March 3, 1936, at the Rivoli Theater.

"*These Three*, the screen version of Herman Shumlin's stage production of *The Children's Hour*, at the Rivoli, is an honest, sensitive, beautifully acted film that deserves the admiration and respect of all moviegoers," wrote the *World Telegram*. And the *New York Times*'s Frank Nugent predicted that "*These Three* will surely end up on the list of ten best films of 1936."

These Three even got raves in Boston, where Mayor Frederick Mansfield had banned the play during its tryout tour as being "indecent and revolting."

What was especially gratifying about the spate of good reviews that *These Three* evoked throughout this country and abroad was that *The Children's Hour* was still running on Broadway, in its seventy-first week, in easy reach of film critics who might wish to refresh their memories of the original work before sitting down to their typewriters. Normally such accessibility results in unfavorable comparisons with the original work, but not this time.

Paradoxically, when Wyler, under the aegis of the Mirisch Company, made a remake of *The Children's Hour* in 1962, using the lesbianism theme and its original story and title, the film was an abysmal failure, both critically and at the box office.

Dodsworth, which Sam waited to buy until it was in dramatic form because it would be somewhat foolproof, turned out to be the stubbornest of the two properties to lick. Most of the problem was in getting a good shooting script. And this became a problem only because Sam didn't fully understand the subject matter, according to Eddie Chodorov, whom Goldwyn paid $50,000 to write the movie script after Sidney Howard turned the job down.

"Sam thought he had bought a story about the automobile business and not retirement," recalls Chodorov. "He thought that Sinclair Lewis had made a mistake in writing the novel, and that Sidney Howard had made a mistake in dramatizing it. Finally, I had to explain to him, 'Mr. Goldwyn, this isn't a story about automobiles. What Lewis did was pick out an industry as a background. As far as this story is concerned, Dodsworth could have been in the shoe business or even the hair tonic business.' But Sam kept insisting I didn't understand it. He wanted the story opened up, made exciting."

Chodorov tried to give Sam what he wanted, but quickly realized that Sidney Howard's dramatization of the novel couldn't stand any tampering with. Written in fourteen scenes, the play was close to screenplay form and needed very little else done to it. Howard had constructed it very carefully and very cleverly to conceal some of the novel's basic story flaws. But Chodorov found out it was like a house of cards. Move one card and the whole thing falls apart.

Realizing that, Chodorov finally turned in a screenplay that was not basically any different from the stage version. "I just wrote about five new minutes of introduction," says Chodorov, "and about five minutes at the end—where Dodsworth goes back to Mary Astor—that thing on the boat."

But Sam wasn't satisfied and wanted rewrite after rewrite. And when Chodorov wouldn't give him any more he hired other writers—about five of them over a two-year period. "The expenditure was enormous," recalls Chodorov. "There must have been about eight different drafts before he finally realized I was right, that you couldn't tamper with Sidney's play construction. So he wound up doing it exactly as Sidney wrote it—including stage directions and movements."

Once Sam had been won over into believing that the play was the *only* thing in *Dodsworth*'s case, he went whole hog and hired Walter Huston, the star of the play, to portray the title role, even though Huston was no draw in pictures. Huston was a fine actor, though, and according to Brooks Atkinson, the *New York Times*'s distinguished drama critic, his performance was one of the "foremost virtues of the play."

Sam surrounded Huston with two good female names, however—Ruth Chatterton in the role of Fran, his self-centered wife, and Mary Astor, who was just on the ascendancy as a film star, as Edith Cortright, the "other woman," who finally wins him in the end.

David Niven made his first appearance as a Goldwyn actor in *Dodsworth*, too, although he had played some bit roles for other studios since Sam had originally signed him. Curiously, this was something Sam had insisted upon when he signed Niven to a seven-year contract—that he *take* jobs with other studios.

"I won't put you in a Goldwyn picture until you've learned how to act," Sam had told him when they were making the deal. "But now you have a base. Go out and tell the studios you're under contract to Goldwyn, do anything they offer you, get experience, work hard, and in a year or so, if you're any good, I'll give you a role."

In the interim Niven had appeared briefly in *Bluebeard's Eighth Wife* with Gary Cooper and Claudette Colbert for Paramount and *The Charge of the Light Brigade*, an Errol Flynn starrer, for Warner Brothers.

Now he was deemed ready to act for the Great Goldwyn, and he was given the part of a dapper, sophisticated-type Englishman. However, a few reviewers evidently still didn't think he was ready. One of them wrote of Niven's performance: "In this picture we were privileged to see the great Samuel Goldwyn's latest discovery, Mr. David Niven. All we can say about this actor is that he is tall, dark and not the slightest bit handsome."

Although the story's background was Europe, most of *Dodsworth* was shot at the Goldwyn Studios on the United Artists lot at 1041 North Formosa Avenue in Hollywood. Rarely did any producer, including Sam, go to the expense of sending an entire movie company to Europe in the mid-thirties. If there had been one European location, Sam might have sprung for it. But to go wandering all over Europe in those days was simply out of the question.

"So we did all our major photography on the back lot," recalls Wyler. "But we did send a second-unit cameraman to London, Paris, Vienna, Montreux, and Naples for background shots. I gave him detailed instructions, of course, and the sets were then built so there would be similar props in the foreground to go along with the rear projection of matching locations."

Rear projection—otherwise known as process-screen photography—enabled characters to sit or stand and even perform limited action in front of a screen on a sound stage and appear to be anywhere in the world that the picture being projected in the rear depicted. Of course, it wasn't as good as the real thing, but the average picturegoer, not on the lookout for it, rarely knew the difference, especially when it was employed by a master of photography like Gregg Toland under the direction of a highly skilled director like Willy Wyler.

Dodsworth went before the cameras in the spring of 1936, and there were few problems during the shooting. Having played the part for nearly two years on Broadway, Walter Huston was as comfortable in the role as he would be in a pair of old slippers and hardly needed any direction at all. Ruth Chatterton, the consummate film star, naturally had her own interpretation of a role that another actress had made famous on the stage. "She wanted to play Fran like a heavy," says Wyler, "and we had momentous fights every day." David Niven played the role of an Englishman rather woodenly, in spite of the fact that the part should have been right up his cricket lane, but the picture didn't suffer too much on account of it because his was a relatively minor role.

The performer who did give Sam a few anxious moments was Mary

Astor—but not because of her capabilities as an actress. Halfway through the filming of *Dodsworth* a scandal involving Mary Astor and playwright George S. Kaufman, with whom the actress had been having an affair, erupted in lurid newspaper headlines that had the whole town of Hollywood worried.

The affair had begun in 1935, long before anyone had thought of using Mary Astor as the "other woman" in *Dodsworth*. At the time they met, she was under contract to Warner Brothers, and Kaufman was in Hollywood writing the script of *A Night at the Opera* for MGM and the Marx Brothers.

Both were married—she to Dr. Franklyn Thorpe, a prominent West Coast physician, and he to Beatrice Kaufman, with whom he had an arrangement whereby both led separate sex lives though they shared the same living quarters when he was in New York.

During his stay in Hollywood Kaufman and Mary Astor were introduced socially, became infatuated with each other, and soon were meeting nightly in his villa at the Garden of Allah, Hollywood's swingingest hotel of the period.

The affair went on during Kaufman's entire sojourn in Hollywood, with occasional field trips to Palm Springs, where he was collaborating on another play with Moss Hart. When his assignment in Hollywood was over, the affair ended, as all of Kaufman's affairs did, with no hard feelings, and his returning to his wife in New York City.

But there were some hard feelings on Dr. Thorpe's part. When he learned his wife and Kaufman were having an affair he sued for divorce and was awarded not only $60,000 in securities but also custody of their daughter, Marylyn. That was in 1935.

Early in 1936, Mary Astor filed suit to set aside the custody and property awards. Dr. Thorpe immediately filed suit in Los Angeles Superior Court to counter her action by claiming she was an unfit mother. And to back up his allegations he disclosed the existence of a diary, written in her hand, in which he claimed she wrote in great detail of her many amorous adventures, including naming names, keeping a rating system of all her lovers' performances in bed, and referring to her latest Romeo as "G."

Thorpe tried to have the diary entered as evidence, and when Judge Goodwin Knight (later governor of California) rejected the motion, the irate doctor leaked portions of the diary to the press. The resultant publicity kept the newspaper-reading public spellbound for months.

The trial went to court in July and August of 1936, which just about coincided with the shooting schedule of *Dodsworth*. Since Mary Astor was a key player in both dramas, Judge Knight, in an unprecedented move, allowed the actress to make her courtroom appearances at night, so as not to hold up Sam's production.

But the testimony—with its accusations and counter-accusations linking Mary Astor to just about every man in Hollywood—was the spiciest ever to come out in a California courtroom. As a result, the press had a field day with it, and major stories, like Hitler's Berlin Olympics and the Spanish Civil War, were knocked right off the front pages. Even the dignified *New York Times* couldn't resist playing up the trial (perhaps because George S. Kaufman had once been their drama critic). On August 11, the *Times* carried two headlines of equal size: "CORN CROP WORST SINCE 81" and "WARRANT OUT FOR KAUFMAN."

Time magazine alluded to things allegedly in the diary but never proven—things such as Kaufman's virility, enabling him to have intercourse twenty times daily. Other weeklies published Mary Astor's top ten list of lovers, with Kaufman in *numero uno* position.

A shy man, except in the bedroom, Kaufman had no wish to be humiliated in court by his former girlfriend's husband's lawyers, and when the case began to focus on him, he hid out from reporters and process servers all over Los Angeles, Beverly Hills, and Culver City.

When Kaufman was needed in court but couldn't be served, Judge Knight finally had to issue a bench warrant for his arrest, and sent sheriff's deputies to stake out the various places where he might be found—the Goldwyn studios, the Goldwyn residence, MGM, Irving Thalberg's house, and Moss Hart's house.

Actually he was at none of those places. Unbeknownst to all but a few friends, he was holed up in Frances Marion's house in Hollywood. She was out of town but had given him a key. He was afraid to leave the premises, so friends, including Harpo and Zeppo Marx and Zeppo's wife, Marion, had to smuggle food and drink in to him.

Finally the cops caught on by following Kaufman's friends and eventually traced him to his hideaway. And there one night, while Harpo and Zeppo Marx distracted the gendarmes at the front door by pretending to be insane, Kaufman fled through the bushes in the rear of the house and ran down to Hollywood Boulevard, where he found a cab to take him to MGM in Culver City.

At MGM, the costume department dressed Kaufman in some English naval officer's clothes left over from their production of *Mutiny on the Bounty*, smuggled him out of the back gate in a studio limousine, and drove him to a yacht club at Wilmington. There he was put aboard Irving's Thalberg's seventy-foot yacht and smuggled across the channel to Catalina Island.

Learning of this deception, Judge Knight sent deputies to Catalina, and a chase ensued on the high seas worthy of a "Hawaii Five-O" episode. Kaufman was never apprehended. But Mary Astor was anxious to squelch the newspaper innuendoes inspired by the diary, and she made a motion in court to have the diary produced as evidence to show it contained no salacious material or proof of any extramarital affairs.

While the judge was weighing the advisability of this, a high-level meeting of the town's leading picture moguls was taking place at Goldwyn Studios late one night. Present were Sam Goldwyn, Jack Warner, Harry Cohn, Irving Thalberg, Louis B. Mayer, and also Mary Astor.

The purpose of the meeting, which had been called not by Sam but by the others, was to persuade Mary Astor not to allow her diary to be brought into court as evidence. All the studio bosses were convinced that this kind of publicity would be the absolute ruination of the movie business, which had for many years been trying to make the public forget past Hollywood scandals—namely, the Thomas Ince death aboard the Hearst yacht; the Fatty Arbuckle affair; and the William Desmond Taylor mystery killing, which had never been solved.

Mary Astor refused to capitulate, for she was fighting for her personal reputation, and the only way she knew how to save it was to prove that all the so-called salacious material in the diary was a sham and a figment of someone's pornographic imagination.

Sam sat quietly through the entire meeting, not voicing any opinion one way or the other until Mary Astor left the room. At this point, the other executives ganged up on Sam and demanded that he invoke the "morals clause" and fire Mary Astor from the picture instantly.

It was then that Sam showed the kind of class that made him Sam Goldwyn and not Harry Cohn. Instead of yielding to the hypocritical demands of the other executives, not more than one of whom could have passed the test of the "morals clause" if put to it, Sam finessed the situation with a simple declaration. "A mother fighting for her child," he mused in a tone calculated to give a heart-tug to even the most calloused. "That's good."

Showman that he was, Sam just might have had his eye on the box office when he refused to fire Mary Astor. After all, *Dodsworth*, with the extremely competent but colorless Walter Huston in the title role, couldn't help benefiting some from the reams of newspaper stories that had been written about one of its stars. And if Sam read the public mood right, chances were good that they'd side with the underdog in the custody battle and that no great harm would come to his production or to Hollywood either.

Which is about what happened.

The trial petered out, with George Kaufman riding off into the sunset and disappearing into the canyons of Manhattan without ever having to testify at the trial, and Mary Astor being awarded custody of her daughter nine months a year and getting back some of her money.

But for Sam his days of trial were just beginning.

For a good part of 1936 he had been suffering from an enlarged prostate gland. Surgery had been recommended but because of a busy production schedule—he had two pictures in the works simultaneously, *Dodsworth* and *Come and Get It*—he had procrastinated about going into a hospital. But finally the condition became too uncomfortable to ignore, besides the possibility that the enlarged gland might be malignant, and on September 12, Sam entered the hospital for surgery. The operation was a success, with no malignancy being found.

But two days later, while he was still stretched out in a hospital room, Sam received another blow. His good friend Irving Thalberg, already suffering from a rheumatic heart, caught pneumonia while attending a Jewish charity affair at the Hollywood Bowl one night, and died suddenly—only three months after his thirty-seventh birthday.

Sam and Thalberg had never been bosom buddies—Sam had only a couple of those: Abe Lehr and Edgar Selwyn. But Sam had played bridge with him regularly, and he had respected his producing genius and what he had done to build motion pictures into a respectable business, and according to his nurse, he wept genuine tears upon hearing the news.

Thalberg's funeral, which took place at the B'nai B'rith Synagogue, was one of the biggest since Rudolph Valentino's, with every important personality and executive attending the services, and people like Clark Gable, Douglas Fairbanks, Walt Disney, Charlie Chaplin, and the Marx Brothers acting as ushers and honorary pallbearers.

Sam, languishing in his hospital bed, was about the only important personage not to attend. But he was so broken up that, in a strange turnaround, Thalberg's widow, Norma Shearer, visited Sam and brought him flowers while he was still in the hospital.

Returning home twelve days later, Sam insisted on seeing the rough cuts of his two newest pictures. *Come and Get It* was based on Edna Ferber's best-selling novel about lumberjacking in the great woodlands of Wisconsin. Though a potboiler in many respects, it was way ahead of its time in another. It had a strong ecology theme and it exposed what the lumbermen were doing to the forests and how the sawmills were polluting the streams.

Sam had high hopes for *Come and Get It*, for in addition to its having a good script, it starred Edward Arnold, Joel McCrea, and Frances Farmer. Featured in a supporting role was an unknown character actor named Walter Brennan. For director, he had hired one of the best in the action field, Howard Hawks, who shot a good deal of it on the stage next to the one where Willy Wyler had been filming *Dodsworth.*

Finishing touches on both films had been completed, while Sam was still in the hospital, by his associate producer, Merritt Hulburd.

After running both films in his projection room at home, Sam flew into a rage. He liked *Dodsworth,* but felt that the last half of *Come and Get It* had been ruined by some rewriting that he had not approved or even seen. Sending for Hawks, Sam demanded an explanation.

"Well, the scenes needed rewriting," said Hawks, "so I rewrote them."

"Directors are supposed to direct, not WRITE!" sputtered Sam, and he ordered Hawks to reshoot the last half of the film.

But Hawks was no longer available. He was already committed to start shooting another picture, *Bringing Up Baby,* for RKO the following morning.

"That's the trouble with directors," roared Sam. "Always biting the hand that lays the golden egg."

He fired Hawks (even though he was already off the job), then summoned Willy Wyler to his bedside and ordered him to reshoot the last half of *Come and Get It.*

"I don't do that—shoot another man's picture," said Wyler. "Why don't you get Hawks to do it?"

"No, no," said Sam. "He and I had a fight. I want you to do it."

Again Wyler refused, throwing Sam into a fit of near-apoplexy.

"Well, we had a scene I'll never forget," recalls Wyler with a grin. "Sam was in bed, but he raised such hell that Frances ran in with a fly swatter and started beating him over the legs with the swatter while he was screaming at me. He said he was going to ruin me—fix it so I'd never be able to get another job in Hollywood as long as I lived if I didn't do as I was told."

To escape Sam's abuse, Wyler ran out of the house and rode off on his motorcycle to confer with his agent. There he discovered that the fine print in his contract didn't permit him the luxury of turning down any assignments. "I had a straight three-year contract, with no rights at all," says Wyler. "I got paid a good salary, but I had no choice about anything Sam wanted to throw at me."

So in the end Wyler acquiesced and reshot the last half of *Come and Get It,* at an additional cost to Sam of $900,000, according to *Variety.*

"I don't know if I improved the picture," admits Wyler. "If I remember, the best parts, the first half hour, were done by Hawks and the magnificent logger operations footage by second-unit director Richard Rosson. When I finished, Goldwyn still was sore at Hawks and wanted to take his name off the picture altogether and give me credit alone. I said, 'Absolutely not' and we had another blowup. The Directors Guild was just being formed but was not yet recognized by the studios and there was no way of appealing or bringing to arbitration such a decision.

"Goldwyn finally agreed to a half measure—putting both our names on the screen and I insisted that Hawk's name come first and that's how it appears—directed by Howard Hawks and Willy Wyler. Needless to say, I don't count *Come and Get It* as one of my pictures whenever somebody asks me for a list of my credits."

Wyler doesn't take that stance through any sense of false modesty, or because he doesn't wish to be connected with one of Sam's "worst failures." Far from being a failure, *Come and Get It*, released two months after *Dodsworth*, received excellent reviews from all the major publications. The *New York Times*'s Frank Nugent wrote: "It's as fine in its way as those other Goldwyn successes of this year, *These Three* and *Dodsworth*. It has the same richness of production, the same excellence of performance, the same shrewdness of direction. There is nothing static about this one, thanks to Howard Hawks and William Wyler."

It was a big commercial success, too, and for an additional bonus, one of its actors, Walter Brennan, picked up his first Oscar for best performance in a supporting role at Academy Award time the following spring.

Dodsworth fared well at the hands of the nation's critics, too, with most of the kudos going to Walter Huston's brilliant performance. "It would have been an inexcusable accident had Walter Huston's *Dodsworth* not been fine, but there hasn't been any accident and the Huston Dodsworth should please people who saw the play and people who didn't," wrote the *New Yorker*. And Archer Winsten said, "Walter Huston gives a performance that makes you forget acting."

The members of the motion picture academy liked *Dodsworth*, too, and gave it seven nominations—best picture, director, actor, supporting actress, sound recording, art direction, and screenplay. But only the art director, Richard Day, collected an Oscar.

Even more disappointing to Sam, *Dodsworth* only did mediocre business, despite its welter of good reviews and its many academy nominations. This seems like something of an injustice inasmuch as it is the only one of Sam's early pictures that holds up under serious scrutiny today. Anyone wishing to verify this can do so by simply turning on the television set. *Dodsworth* seems to be all over the tube these days and nights, and it is still eminently good entertainment.

18

Diamond Jim Goldwyn

UNTIL 1937, WHEN HE RELEASED *Dead End*, Sam had deliberately shied away from making gangster films. He was willing to leave that kind of fare to the studio that specialized in exploitation-action pictures, Warner Brothers. Warners was riding the crest of the gangster wave and making a fortune turning out films like *The Public Enemy*, *Little Caesar*, and *The Petrified Forest*. These films starred some of the toughest guys in Hollywood's underworld—Humphrey Bogart, Edward G. Robinson, James Cagney, and George Raft—and the public loved them.

Sam no longer made pictures just to make money. He didn't go out of his way to lose money, but in order to please him, a picture had to have some substance to it, something that would make people recognize it as a Goldwyn picture.

Which is why, until *Dead End* came along, he refused to capitalize on the gangster craze. And in the strict sense of the word, *Dead End* was not actually a gangster film, either. A gangster, whose character name was Baby Face Martin, figured importantly in the plot, but it was more the story of East River slum children in Manhattan and how they were corrupted by their environment—the rich who lived in elegant new apartments next door in what is now Sutton Place, and their own tenement area, which bred crime. In that light, *Dead End* had an important statement to make about poverty and social injustice.

Dead End had the additional prestige of being based on Sidney Kingsley's hit play, which had opened on October 28, 1935, at the Belasco Theater and ran for several standing-room-only seasons. That, of course, appealed to Sam, who made up his mind to see it when he and Frances were passing through New York on their way to Europe shortly after the play opened. With them was Sam junior, who was then nine years old and about to be treated by his father to his first trip to Europe aboard a luxury liner.

Willy Wyler happened to be in New York at the same time, conferring with Sidney Howard about some directorial touches for *Dodsworth*, which would go into production the following spring. So Sam invited Wyler to come along and see *Dead End* with him and Frances—probably because he didn't quite trust his own judgment.

"How do you like it?" asked Sam after the first curtain call.

"I like it," said Wyler.

"I can get Lillian [Hellman] to do the script," said Sam.

"Then buy it," said Wyler.

"Okay, I buy it," said Sam.

And he was on the phone that same night with James Mulvey, instructing him to contact Kingsley's agent first thing in the morning and make a deal for *Dead End*, no matter what the asking price.

Mulvey ran Sam's New York office and held the lofty title of president of Goldwyn Productions, but he made no policy decisions, and in actuality was just a glorified bookkeeper. But he was one of Sam's most trusted lieutenants, having been with him since 1923. Before then he had been an accountant for Price-Waterhouse, where he had done some bookkeeping work for Sam. Impressed with the young man's ability, Sam offered him the post of treasurer in his new company, Potash and Perlmutter Productions, which he was forming to make the first of his independent films, *Potash and Perlmutter*. Later Sam made him president of Goldwyn Productions, Inc., and Mulvey remained with the Goldwyn organization until Sam stopped producing pictures in 1960.

The following day Sam and Mulvey wrapped up a deal to purchase *Dead End* for $165,000—the largest price paid up until then for a hit play. "That was the great thing about Goldwyn," declares Wyler today. "When he made up his mind to buy something, he bought it just like that. No hesitating, no quibbling."

Before leaving for Europe, Sam secured the agreement with a $25,000 cash down payment, with the remaining $140,000 to be paid on a specified date upon his return to the States.

With his mind finally free of business worries, and a "prestige" property to be announced for future production, Sam could now look forward to showing his son the sights of Europe with a great deal of fatherly anticipation. Sam junior was wild with anticipation, too—so much so that when Sam senior suffered a gallbladder attack the day before sailing, he refused to disappoint the boy and brushed off Frances's suggestion that they postpone the trip by saying, "It's just a little stomach upset. A glass of bismuth will fix it."

And it did help, temporarily, and the trip went off as planned, with Sam acting as tour guide for the three Goldwyns. Which is not as funny as it seems. Sam may have got lost trying to show Frances the lot for their new home, but he knew his way around Europe better than most professional guides. Not only had he been born in Poland and raised in England, but by now he had distribution offices in most of the major European cities and had been making annual trips to Europe for both business and pleasure ever since he had banked his first million.

As always, Sam did a little business on this trip, too. But most of his time was devoted to showing Sam junior all the major tourist attractions, from the Tower of London and Buckingham Palace to the Eiffel Tower and the Roman Colosseum. When they weren't sightseeing, the Goldwyns were eating their way through every Michelin guide "Three Star–Four Fork" restaurant between London and the French Riviera.

Rich French cooking was not exactly the proper diet for a man with gallbladder trouble, however. And on the day before their ship was due to dock in New York on the return trip, Sam staggered into the cabin where Frances was packing, and said, "Frances, all of a sudden I'm awfully sick."

Whereupon he collapsed on the bed, moaning and holding his stomach, and Frances had to send for the ship's doctor. After a hasty examination, the doctor wasn't sure whether the stomach pain and nausea were caused by Sam's gallbladder or whether he was having an attack of appendicitis.

Whichever, he didn't recommend operating on board the ship. All he could do was alleviate Sam's discomfort with sedatives and ice packs on his tender appendix.

Somehow Sam got through the rest of the afternoon and night, and the next day after they docked, Frances phoned Sam's doctor, who recommended that she take him straight from the pier to Doctors Hospital, at East End Avenue and Eighty-seventh Street. He'd meet them there.

An hour later, Sam, who never did anything in a small way, even getting sick, underwent an operation to remove both his gallbladder and appendix. He was on the operating table three hours, but fortunately his general physical condition was excellent for a man of fifty-two, and he survived the lengthy ordeal with no complications and little pain except the usual soreness in the area of the foot-long incision which bisected the front of his torso.

A week later Sam was sitting up in bed and feeling strong enough to complain to Frances and the doctor, "A hospital is no place to be sick. I am dying of boredom in this place."

Against his better judgment, but falling victim, as did many people before him, to Sam's persuasive salesmanship, the doctor reluctantly acquiesced and gave Sam permission to have some visitors—Jay O'Brien, Irving Berlin, and Bill Paley—for a few minutes that afternoon.

The "few minutes" lengthened into a couple of hours as O'Brien and

Paley regaled Sam with amusing anecdotes and Irving Berlin serenaded him with his latest song. Sam had a wonderful time, listening and laughing.

Early the next morning, the doctor summoned Frances to Sam's bedside and informed her that Sam was in very grave condition. It seems that Sam's stitches had burst from all that laughing the previous day, and he was bleeding internally. The doctor said Sam would have to be opened up and sewn back together again. But the prognosis wasn't good. He might live for an hour or two, but beyond that, he could make no promises.

And then the attendants put Sam's motionless body on a cart and wheeled him out of the room and down the corridor.

As Frances, alone in the corridor, watched Sam go with an aching heart, a harried-looking James Mulvey emerged from one of the elevators.

"Frances," he said, "I have to talk to you."

"What about?"

"Well, when Mr. Goldwyn made that deal for *Dead End* he secured it with a down payment of twenty-five thousand dollars."

"I know that," snapped Frances, "but for heaven's sakes, don't bother me with such talk now."

"I have to," said Mulvey. "I can't wait any longer."

"Why?"

"Because we have to pay the other $140,000 by noon today or forfeit the property." It was then eleven-thirty. "They have to have a decision."

"Can't you tell them Sam's deathly ill in the hospital? Won't they wait?"

"I tried that, but they say they've got other offers. And I know Sam'll be disappointed if he doesn't get to make this picture. Of course if he doesn't pull"—evidently he thought better of saying anything so gloomy and cut his sentence off abruptly. "Well, you know—I guess you'll have to make the decision."

Frances's mind was suddenly filled with a vision of Sam's lifeless face as he was wheeled away from her on the cart. It didn't seem possible that he'd ever produce another picture again. Still, he wanted that property desperately.

Suddenly Frances's face was filled with determination. "Pay the money, Mulvey," she said. "Sam's going to get well and make the picture. And it'll be good. I've got that faith in God and Sam Goldwyn."

And, of course, he did recover, and he made *Dead End*, and it was one of the finest, most successful pictures of his career.

But before that could come to pass, there would be many months of convalescence ahead of him back in Beverly Hills, in his luxurious new home on Laurel Lane.

A few weeks of lying around, with little to do except think about what a close brush with death he had had, depressed Sam terribly. Finally, Marion

Davies, a close friend of the Goldwyns', heard about Sam's low state of mind and invited him and Frances up to the Hearst ranch at San Simeon for a few days of fun and relaxation. The Hearst ranch was always peopled with interesting guests who would be able to take Sam's mind off himself. But for several days after he and Frances got there, Sam remained cloistered in his bungalow and refused to mingle with the others.

Finally, on about the fourth day he emerged and appeared at the main house.

"What have you been doing over there all this time?" asked Marion Davies.

"I've been thinking," replied Sam.

"About what?"

"About life and death."

"What about life and death?" she persisted.

"Well," said Sam pontifically, "you just don't realize what life is all about until you have found yourself lying on the brink of a great abscess."

Back home in southern California again, there were many more weeks of convalescence before the doctors allowed Sam to return actively to work at the studio.

It was during this period that Frances, now that Sam junior was old enough to fend for himself in the asphalt jungle of Beverly Hills, made the full transition from housewife to Sam Goldwyn's associate producer without portfolio.

At home she acted as his secretary and assistant, reading scripts, intercepting phone calls, talking to columnists, and making suggestions. When he was well enough to return to the studio, Frances went with him and took an office adjacent to his. There she was always available to give advice when Sam asked for it (and sometimes when he didn't), on subjects ranging from story material to casting, from costume and scenic designing to what Sam was going to have for lunch.

Prior to Sam's illness, her main chores were to supervise the commissary and act as studio housekeeper and perhaps hostess at official luncheons, but now Frances sat in on most story conferences and meetings where major studio decisions were being made.

Furthermore, Frances *always* made it a point to be around when Sam was interviewing beautiful actresses. Whether she sat through these interviews with some of the town's loveliest creatures because she wanted Sam to cast the best woman in the part, or because tales of Sam's office peccadillos had gotten back to her and she was interested in discouraging more of the same, has never been ascertained. Perhaps it was a little of both. At any rate, most people who worked with Sam from that time on seem to remember Frances always hovering around in the background or sitting mouselike in the corner, listening, observing, sometimes commenting, and occasionally acting as mediator when Sam lost his temper, as he was frequently doing.

In the thirties, Sam had a financial interest in a picture Alexander Korda was producing in England. But the production ran into trouble, costs ran over, and Sam refused to accept the picture for American distribution. Their arguments finally culminated with Sam suing Korda. While the matter was still waiting to go before the courts, Korda came to Hollywood, and Sam invited him to dinner at his house.

"How can we have dinner together when you're suing me?" asked Korda.

"What's one thing got to do with the other?" asked Sam.

Korda accepted the invitation, and all talk of the suit was avoided through dinner and during the several hours of conversation afterward. Finally, at two in the morning, Frances took the matter into her own hands and said, "Sam, Alex—don't you think it's time you started patching up that lawsuit?"

The matter was settled before Korda left for his hotel.

As a diplomat Frances had to be on the same level as Henry Kissinger, because as Sam grew older, his short temper became shorter and his unreasonableness more unreasonable.

"He was the only man in Hollywood I've ever been afraid of," recalls Eddie Chodorov. "They used to say Louis B. Mayer and Harry Cohn were tough. Well, they were like babes compared with Goldwyn. I used to shake when I had to face him in a story conference."

On the same theme, Sam's secretary of five years, Goldie Arthur, says, "Most of the people who worked on the lot were scared to death of him. When I was working for him, he treated me very nicely, but I always tried to ease things up with everybody else and keep tensions down. For example, whenever it was Sam's birthday, I'd tip everybody on the lot off, so they could wish him a happy birthday if they ran into him on the lot. That always made Mr. Goldwyn very happy—for a short time, anyway."

One morning before going into a story conference with two of his writers, Sam confided in Goldie, "My doctor doesn't want me to get angry anymore. He says it is very bad for my health. So if you hear me hollering, write me a note reminding me of this and bring it in."

Goldie promised and returned to her typing as the story conference began behind the closed doors of Sam's well-appointed office. At first Goldie heard nothing coming from within but the muffled tones of normal conversation, punctuated occasionally by a few staccato shouts of ordinary give-and-take argument, which she ignored. But then suddenly she heard her boss unleash a fusillade of the most explosive language and uncomplimentary epithets she'd ever known him or anyone else to use.

Goldie quickly dashed off a note, ran into Sam's office with it, laid it on the huge desk in front of Sam, who seemed to be in such an agitated state that a less hardy man would have had a heart attack on the spot. "When Mr. Goldwyn got angry," recalls Goldie, "his eyes seemed to bulge and you could almost see the sparks coming out at you. But after glancing at my note, he turned to the writers and said, 'All right, boys, my doctor doesn't want me to get excited, so I guess you win. Write it your way.' "

Three days later, Sam was having another conference with the same writers. Halfway through the meeting his temper again exploded, and Goldie rushed in with another note. He took one look at it, crumpled it, threw it in the wastebasket, and shouted, "God damn it, Goldie, mind your own business! How can I not get mad at these two schmucks?"

Frances hadn't been present at either of those two meetings, but if she had been, Sam would have lost his temper just the same. Just because Frances was around was no automatic guarantee that he would act like a reasonable man or take her advice.

Jerry Chodorov recalls one story conference in which he was faced with the unnerving task of having to read an entire screenplay of his aloud to Sam and Frances. It was based on *Billion Dollar Baby*, a Broadway musical by Betty Comden and Adolph Green.

It had been a flop on Broadway, but when Sam acquired the rights he went around town boasting, "I got a great bargain today. I bought *Billion Dollar Baby* for only a hundred thousand dollars."

Billion Dollar Baby was the story of a young girl who married a rich older man and the problem their age difference caused in their relationship.

"When I finished reading my screenplay to them," relates Chodorov, "Frances threw her arms around me and kissed me. 'Oh, Jerry, it's wonderful,' she said. 'Don't you think so, Sam?' "

"I wouldn't make it in a million years," snapped Sam irritably.

And that was the end of *Billion Dollar Baby* as a film. "Sam shelved it, and Frances was absolutely shocked," says Chodorov today. "And I'm sure I know the reason, outside of the fact that it may have been a bad screenplay, which Sam wouldn't have known. Sam didn't like the theme of a young girl latching on to a rich older man. It was too close to his own life."

Sam was fifty-two at the time, and Frances was about thirty. But Sam shouldn't have felt touchy about the age gap. In their case, a twenty-two-year difference seemed to be the prescription for an ideal marriage.

On the surface Frances may have seemed like nothing more than just a rich dilettante who liked to dabble in her husband's movies for want of something better to do. But peel away the Christian Dior trappings and one would find a warm, self-effacing, level-headed wife and mother who was not afraid to pitch in and help with the housework, if that was necessary. "I do about the same things any other housewife does," Frances often boasted, "with the exception of the actual cooking. But I do plan all our meals and do all the marketing."

Unlike many a Beverly Hills matron, Frances never took the easy way out and phoned Jurgensen's or the Premier Market to have her groceries delivered. At least once every two weeks she would go to the local supermarket and lay in a heavy supply of staples and other nonperishable items, and every Friday, promptly at nine A.M., she would be at the Farmer's Market buying her fresh vegetables, meats, and other specialties which the ordinary supermarket didn't carry. Also on her list would be a five-gallon can of Sam's favorite ice cream from Humphrey's, which is world famous for its ice cream.

Frances became such a familiar sight to the proprietors who ran the fruit and vegetable stalls that the tradesmen who worked there used to greet her by her first name as she wheeled her little wooden shopping cart through the marketplace.

It was no savings, of course, to shop at the Farmer's Market, where the produce and steaks are displayed like jewels in a Tiffany showcase, with prices equally out of reach of the average working stiff.

But the Goldwyns entertained important people in their home, and it would be a form of reverse snobbery not to give their guests the very best. The Goldwyns were never guilty of reverse snobbery; they enjoyed their money.

Sam and Frances usually saved Friday and Saturday nights to do their serious entertaining—very likely a formal sit-down dinner party for about twenty people.

To keep a party of that size running smoothly required a cook, plus one person in the kitchen to help her; another person in the pantry; two butlers to serve the meat; and a couple more people to help pass the vegetables and gravy. Shades of Buckingham Palace, to be sure, but actually, Frances and Sam preferred smaller, more intimate get-togethers. "Four or six at the table, but served very elegantly, is the way we like to entertain best," Frances used to say.

Usually the guests would be given some warning beforehand as to what size soiree to expect, but once in a while even the efficient Frances slipped up on this. When that happened, the evening could be disastrous—like the time the Goldwyns invited Brian Aherne and his wife, Joan Fontaine, to dinner.

The Ahernes had never been to the Goldwyns before and had been invited this time only because Joan Fontaine had suddenly shot up into major stardom as a result of her performance in *Rebecca*, and Sam wanted to look her over at close range.

Joan and her husband were told to be at the Goldwyns' at eight on a certain Thursday, or so they thought. Believing it to be a large affair, and in keeping with the time-honored social custom of not being first, the handsome couple didn't arrive at the Goldwyns' hilltop residence until around eight ten.

When they saw no other cars in the driveway, Joan told her husband, "Well, we can't be first. Let's take a spin."

When they returned twenty minutes later, there were still no other cars in the driveway. Again they killed some time driving their Rolls through the hilltop streets, not returning until about a quarter to nine. Still the courtyard was empty.

"Let's go back home and check our calendar," suggested Aherne. "Perhaps we made a mistake in the date."

They did this, confirmed they had the right date and the right hour, and sped back up the mountainside to the Goldwyns'. There were still no other cars around, but they rang the doorbell anyway.

They were met at the door by a stern-faced butler, who took their wraps and escorted them into the dining room, where Sam and Frances were eating alone at a table set for four.

"We thought you weren't coming," said the embarrassed Frances. "Sam couldn't wait any longer."

Too late the Ahernes realized that in their eagerness to do the right thing, they had pulled the social *faux pas* of all social *faux pas*—not being on time to dine alone with the Goldwyns, a privilege not many outside the family were extended.

Like most Hollywood moguls, Sam frequently showed movies to his guests after dinner at his smaller, informal get-togethers. Not necessarily his own movies—in fact, more than likely it would be the opposition's latest product—and usually before it was released. Most studio heads had arrangements whereby they exchanged one another's latest films for home viewing. That way everybody in the industry could keep abreast of the latest trends, imitate each other's successes, and know who was doing the best acting, writing, and directing—in case they wanted to borrow them for their own pictures.

If the showings began early enough, Sam junior would most likely be privileged to watch the movies, too. But until he was a teenager, he was rarely allowed to eat with the company. He'd dine earlier by himself in the breakfast room and would remain discreetly out of sight, except for a brief appearance to say hello and shake hands with his mother's and father's illustrious guests, or longer if it happened to be one of those nights when he was being allowed to watch the movies. Otherwise he didn't dare intrude. But like most kids, he resented not being a part of the festivities and would often spend a good deal of the evening leaning over the second-floor banister in his pajamas, eavesdropping on the conversation floating upward from the candle-lit dining room, which was just off the front entrance hall. According to his mother, Sam junior got a liberal education in Hollywood social mores leaning over that banister. And some of the gossip he heard could have gotten an "X" rating.

But the Goldwyns were strict and sensible parents, and not just by Hollywood's permissive standards. Having witnessed many of the progeny of the movie mighty going astray from overindulgence, Sam and Frances took great care when Sam junior was growing up to see that he avoided similar pitfalls.

"I raised Sammy with an iron hand," Frances once said in recalling his childhood. "I made him earn his way. He used to mow the lawn and get paid by the hour. And when I caught him spending too much of his time on the telephone, I'd make him hang up and tell him to spend it there on his own time, when he was paying the phone bills, and not on mine.

"Taking care of the swimming pool was his job, too. I used to tell him that using the pool was a privilege, and he had to learn you pay for your privileges in life."

Like most rich parents bent on raising their children with the common touch, the Goldwyns sometimes carried their "earn-your-own-way" policy to ludicrous lengths.

After the Lindbergh baby kidnaping in 1932, everyone in Hollywood was afraid of being kidnaped. And with good reason, for the children of many Hollywood celebrities, including the Goldwyns', received extortion threats during that period. As a precaution, many film families yanked their offspring out of public schools and sent them to the comparatively safe surroundings of private halls of learning.

A popular place to send boys was Black-Foxe Military Institute, founded by silent movie star Earl Foxe and a retired army major named Black. Being on Melrose Avenue and Wilcox, Black-Foxe was far off the beaten path for Beverly Hills children, and since it provided no bus service for those students not boarding on the premises, private transportation was necessary. Cadet Goldwyn rode to school every morning in the family limousine and was picked up again at the end of the school day.

But the chauffeur didn't drive Sam junior straight home. Instead he would drop him off at the corner of Beverly Drive and Wilshire Boulevard. There Sam junior would set up a stand and sell newspapers. As for kidnappers, Sam junior didn't have to worry about them. One of the several day and night watchmen the Goldwyns employed to keep an eye on their home—and their son—was discreetly parked in a car across the street with a gun across his lap. Oh, to be lucky enough to learn the value of money while growing up in Beverly Hills!

But Sam's and Frances's intentions were right, and the results were good. Not only didn't Sam junior ever get kidnaped, but he grew into a strapping young man who never got into trouble, who served on General Eisenhower's staff during World War II, and who took over the running of his father's studio after the latter became ill and had to retire.

Between running a movie mogul's establishment, keeping her son from becoming another spoiled Beverly Hills brat, and fulfilling her duties at the studio, Frances found herself rolling out of bed at seven o'clock most mornings. Sam was an early riser also, and the two would generally eat breakfast together, served to them in their sunlit breakfast room or on the terrace overlooking Coldwater Canyon and the rest of Beverly Hills. Following breakfast, Sam would read the trade papers and leave for the studio in his chauffeured limousine, arriving there around ten, while Frances would remain behind, busying herself with household duties—among them seeing to it that all Sam's clothes were cleaned and pressed and had no buttons missing, discussing the state of the house and garden with the maids and gardener, and planning that night's dinner menu.

After dispensing with her household chores, Frances would drive herself to the studio in her small convertible. She liked having her own car at hand in case she wanted to make a side excursion to the Farmer's Market or do other errands during the day if things were slow around the studio.

At the studio, Frances would spend the rest of the morning in her own office, reading scripts; attending story conferences; looking after the thousand and one details of making a picture that Sam couldn't be bothered with (as long as he had Frances to do it for him), like supervising the costumes and the women's clothes; and planning Sam's lunch. Sam had a private kitchen adjacent to his office for the times he didn't care to go downstairs and mingle with the rest of his staff in the executive dining room.

After lunch Sam would, without exception, retire to a dressing room converted to a bedroom near his office and nap for at least an hour. Sam was convinced that a daily nap after lunch was the secret of good health and longevity and was always recommending it to his friends.

One afternoon following his daily nap, Sam, looking awfully fit, dropped into the office of two of his writers, Bob Pirosh and Don Hartman (who later became the head of Paramount), to inquire how their work was progressing. At the time they were writing the script for *Up in Arms*, Danny Kaye's first movie.

After they assured Sam that their labors were going well, Hartman happened to comment to Sam that he was looking unusually well.

"That's because I take an hour's nap every day after lunch," said Sam. "You boys ought to try it, too." Then realizing he might be costing Goldwyn Studios money if they napped on his time, he quickly added, "But in your cases, eat a half hour, sleep a half hour."

Finishing his work day around five P.M., unless there was a studio crisis, in which case he'd remain until it had passed, Sam would be driven home by his chauffeur, but not all the way home. Depending on how much time he had, what the weather was like, and the state of his health, Sam would instruct the chauffeur to stop the car on Santa Monica Boulevard somewhere between the studio and his home (but never less than three miles from Laurel Lane) and walk the remaining distance. The chauffeur would follow in the limousine about a hundred yards to the rear.

Because at fifty-two Sam still refused to carry anything in his pockets that would spoil the line of his suits or sport jackets, Sam got into trouble one afternoon. While walking home he stopped at a fruit stand on Santa Monica Boulevard, picked out a delicious-looking plum, and started to gnaw on it. When the proprietor demanded payment, Sam signaled the chauffeur to bring him his wallet. It was then that he remembered that he had let the chauffeur go home early because it was such a lovely afternoon he wanted to walk the whole distance.

Sam introduced himself as Sam Goldwyn.

"Then you should have a dime to pay for a plum," said the grocer. Sam explained that he never carried any money on his person. The grocer couldn't buy that story and threatened to call a policeman.

"Look, you've heard of Sam Goldwyn, haven't you?" asked Sam. "Sam Goldwyn makes great pictures."

"Yes, but Sam Goldwyn doesn't sell them for nothing," said the grocer.

"Look," said Sam, "you don't think Sam Goldwyn would cheat you, do you? I'll pay you tomorrow on my way to work."

"But how do I know you're Sam Goldwyn?"

Since Sam didn't have a wallet, he couldn't even identify himself, and he couldn't call anyone at the studio to identify him because the grocer wouldn't loan him a nickel to use the pay phone. Finally Sam freed himself by giving the grocer his gold wrist watch to keep as collateral until he could drop by the next day and give him a dime. The watch was obviously worth a good deal more than a plum.

But Sam never dismissed the chauffeur early again.

It may even explain why he never learned to drive a car himself, although there are a couple of old-timers around the studio who say it's not true that he *never* drove a car, and they can cite an incident to prove it.

It seems that way back in the days when it wasn't necessary to be able to read or write or know how to drive a car in order to apply for a California driver's license, Sam took a couple of driving lessons from his chauffeur, learned the fundamentals of shifting and braking, and then soloed for the first time one morning when he drove his car to the studio, without telling Frances. Sam actually managed to get there without having an accident. But when he was leaving the lot later that day he shot his car out of the studio gate without troubling to notice that a streetcar was bearing down on him.

The motorman saw Sam's car, however, and slammed on his brakes just in time to avoid a collision. But the sudden application of the air brakes caused the streetcar to jump its tracks. This infuriated the motorman, who leaped from the streetcar and ran down the street shaking his fists at Sam, who was making a Keystone Kops getaway as he wove in and out of traffic in his own vehicle.

Frances didn't learn of Sam's near-miss until the next morning, when the studio policeman at the gate, who'd witnessed the whole thing, tipped her off. Frances quickly found Sam, confiscated his temporary license, and made him promise never to get behind the wheel of an automobile again. "He just had too many other things on his mind to be a safe driver," sighed Frances when asked by a friend why she never allowed him to drive. It was back to walking for Sam, if he wished independent transportation.

The only times after that when Sam didn't walk at least part of the way home were the summers that he, Frances, and Sam junior spent living at the beach.

Until Sam junior grew up, married, and moved away from home, the Goldwyns also maintained a luxurious beach house at the foot of Wilshire Boulevard in Santa Monica, a strip of high-priced ocean frontage where most of Hollywood's studio heads cooled off in the summer months. Among the Goldwyns' neighbors were Louis B. Mayer, Jack Warner, Darryl F. Zanuck, William Goetz, Jesse Lasky, Harry Cohn, and Marion Davies and William Randolph Hearst, who maintained an establishment just a few doors away from the Goldwyns' that was as large as a hotel. It was so large, in fact, that after they died it was turned into a beach club.

The Goldwyn beach house was too far from the studio for Sam to entertain any notions of walking home after work. But he made up for this by getting his daily constitutional in other ways. Sam's swimming hadn't improved any since he had nearly drowned in Long Island Sound in the summer of 1923, so he avoided going in the turbulent Santa Monica surf except during heat waves. But he did take an occasional dip in their private swimming pool, and every morning before leaving for work he would religiously walk five miles along the shore. Jogging was not yet in style, but at the pace Sam walked, there was very little difference.

"I'll never forget the night Sam took Howard and me to the opening of his picture *Guys and Dolls*, which Howard did the publicity for," recalls Lucinda Dietz, wife of Howard Dietz. "It was a formal affair, and we all had to go to a party afterward at the Waldorf. I had on a long dress and high-heeled satin shoes. Frances Goldwyn got in the limousine first. Howard hopped in after her. But Sam took my arm and said, 'They're so lazy. Come on, Lucinda, let's you and I walk.' The Waldorf was about twenty blocks away, but I figured Sam would give up after a block or two and want to take a cab. After all, he was about seventy at the time. But no such thing happened. Sam walked so fast I had to run to keep up with him. By the time we reached the Waldorf, I was a wreck and my shoes were in shreds. Sam was hardly breathing."

Sam's daily walkathon—whether it took place on city streets or along state beach—was part of an almost ritualistic fetish to keep fit. Since his two major operations, Sam was more conscious of man's mortality than ever. He never discussed death very much, but at fifty-two, and while lying in a hospital room, it must have crossed his mind once or twice. Sam's physical-fitness program paid good dividends, however.

At fifty-two, he was in better shape than many a man half his years. His figure was trim, with no sign of a middle-aged pouch, he stood erect, he walked with springy steps, and he was imbued with the kind of boundless energy and enthusiasm for new projects that made physical wrecks of many of his associates. For example, Merritt Hulburd, his associate producer for several years, and at least ten years Sam's junior, finally had to quit the Goldwyn organization on his doctor's advice and return to the relative peace and quiet of editing a magazine. His symptoms were uncontrolled hypertension and headaches that couldn't be turned off with aspirin or even stronger drugs. According to Hulburd's physician, both these ailments were indirectly the result of trying to keep up with Sam's frenzied work pace, not to mention coping with his temper.

As a result of Sam's tremendous drive and explosive temper the turnover of employees at the Goldwyn plant was tremendous. Over the years he must have employed at least fifteen different publicity chiefs, all able men who went on to score huge successes on their own after Sam had let them go. Two years as Goldwyn's story editor was about as long as any sane person could last. His only associate producers, Merritt Hulburd and George Haight, finally were forced to resign because Sam blamed all his "worst failures" on them (after Hulburd left, Sam never had another associate producer). And on most scripts he changed writers as regularly as he did razor blades.

Only a few writers were able to maintain more than a one-picture relationship with him—Frances Marion, Sidney Howard, and Lillian Hellman—while Willy Wyler was the only director to last for eight pictures. Sam knew he could rely on these people and always sent for them first. When they weren't available, he'd feel crushed but, of course, would have to hire someone else to get the job done.

At one point in the thirties, Sam wanted Sidney Howard for a certain picture, couldn't get him because he was tied up elsewhere, and hired Adela Rogers St. Johns instead. Two weeks after she had gone to work for Sam, Sidney Howard became available. Sam was desperate to get rid of St. Johns and replace her with Howard. But because St. Johns had an iron-clad contract and no intention of quitting, Sam had to resort to more round-about methods to terminate their relationship.

He started by telling her he didn't like the work she'd already done on the script. When she asked for specifics, he said he didn't know, but hinted she was possibly "written out" and suggested that she go home to her house at the beach, relax, and have a swim in the ocean. No sooner had she arrived at her beach house and stretched out on the sand than Sam, who lived a few doors away, appeared and said she was fired.

When she demanded to know why, Sam replied that he was not paying her all that money to spend her days swimming in the ocean.

"You can't fire me. I have a contract," protested St. Johns.

"That doesn't matter. You can't do anything about it if I fire you," said Sam.

"Of course I can. I'll take you to court."

"But you won't," he replied, "because you can't afford to let people know Sam Goldwyn fired you."

St. Johns remembered all the prominent writers Sam had fired in the past. "Oh, yes, I can," she said. "What I can't afford is for people to say I worked for Sam Goldwyn and he didn't fire me."

Sam honored the contract.

Don Hartman, one of a long string of production assistants, had been working for Sam only about six months when he had trouble with him over some alleged breach of contract. Hartman was finally forced to sue. But so he wouldn't be guilty of breach of contract himself, Hartman remained on the job. However, the two remained outwardly friendly. Sam rarely let the fact that a person was suing him destroy a relationship. One afternoon when his chauffeur wasn't around he asked Hartman if he'd drive him home.

Hartman said he would, but regretted it as soon as he stepped in the car with Sam. During the entire ride to the Goldwyn house, Sam berated him for not seeing the disputed clause in their contract *his* way. To Hartman's relief, he finally pulled his car into the courtyard in front of the Goldwyn manor. Sam thanked him profusely for the ride and stepped out, disappearing from Hartman's view.

Thinking Sam had gone into the house, Hartman suddenly backed his car up to turn it around. From behind he heard an enraged yell from Sam. "Watch out!" he screamed. But Hartman couldn't put on his brakes in time and his car knocked Sam flat on his back into a flower bed.

Rushing from the car, Hartman ran over to Goldwyn and pulled him to his feet, saying, "Are you all right, Mr. Goldwyn?"

"Yes, I'm all right."

"Well, I'm certainly sorry," stammered Hartman, nervously brushing the dirt off the back of Sam's three-hundred-dollar suit.

"That's all right, young man," said Sam with a grim smile. "You didn't do it on purpose."

"Yeah," said Hartman morosely, "but who would believe it?"

Aside from taking daily walks and chasing pretty starlets around his office when Frances was at the Farmer's Market, Sam's only other physical activity was playing croquet. Sam had quit handball after breaking his ankle on the court and had given up golf because he was much too high-strung for it, though he retained his membership at Hillcrest Country Club to the end of his life because of the eating privileges. But he loved croquet with a passion because it gave him the chance to do the two things he liked best besides producing movies—being out in the fresh air and sunshine and gambling for high stakes.

Gambling was Sam's one real vice outside of imbibing chocolate sodas, and it was not unusual for him to have a thousand dollars riding on the outcome of a single game of croquet, which was a serious sport the way Sam and his cronies played it and not just some backyard pastime for children and little old ladies.

Sam had originally been introduced to croquet by two renowned exponents of the sport, Harpo Marx and George S. Kaufman, back in the twenties when he was living among the rich on Long Island. Seeing its potential for gambling—Harpo and Kaufman liked to play for high stakes, too—Sam quickly became one of the game's most ardent enthusiasts, and he'd been knocking wooden balls through little metal wickets ever since.

As befitting a man of Sam's wealth, prestige, and reputation for doing things in a big way, the croquet setup at his home was no jerrybuilt, do-it-yourself affair that the ordinary citizen would put together rather haphazardly after purchasing a croquet game at the local sporting goods or toy store.

Sam's croquet court cost thousands of dollars and had been given to him by Frances on his fiftieth birthday. (What to give the man who has everything.) It was about the size of a tennis court and took up the whole lot next door, which the Goldwyns also owned. The playing field had a grassy surface as smooth and well manicured as one of Hillcrest's putting greens, and the wickets and posts had been symmetrically laid out by a professional croquet-court builder.

There was also a "scorekeeper's shack," wherein players could rest and refresh themselves with soft drinks from the refrigerator between games and kibitz other matches and talk about the movie business.

To this croquet Valhalla flocked most of America's best mallet swingers, plus a goodly assortment of grifters. Among the notables who hung out there, in addition to Harpo and Kaufman, were Moss Hart, Alexander Woollcott, Mike Romanoff, Ben Hecht, Charles MacArthur, Louis Jourdan, Gig Young, and Charles Lederer.

It was considered such a privilege to play on Sam's croquet field that many people showed up there without invitations and, on days when the host wasn't around, helped themselves to his facilities. A few, in fact, made it a point to show up only when they were fairly certain Sam was still at the studio or in Europe, or at least somewhere other than on his croquet field.

The reasons for this were threefold: To begin with, Sam wasn't much of a player. In games with the experts, he was automatically given the handicap of not having to shoot through the center wicket at all. Nevertheless, to get stuck with him for a partner meant almost certain defeat, coupled with the loss of considerable money. Secondly, Sam's temper displays were frightening to behold when he was losing. And thirdly, Sam wasn't averse to kicking his ball through a wicket when he thought his opponents weren't watching, or resorting to other forms of cheating. Like the time he tried to kick Charlie MacArthur's ball over the edge of the mountainside one day when he was losing to him.

Catching him in the act, MacArthur shouted, "Hey, Sam, that's cheating!"

"What's that between us?" asked Sam with childlike candor.

That was one of the disconcerting things about playing a game of anything with Sam: he seemed to think he had a divine right to take advantage of his opponent, and even when caught he did not feel any particular guilt about it. He was so guileless about it, in fact, that his opponents usually wound up laughing at him rather than becoming angered by his attempts to be dishonest.

It was a strange dichotomy in the Goldwyn character that Sam, who was basically conservative in his business dealings, should take to gambling with such enthusiasm. If one wanted to split hairs, one could say that the movie business was a gamble, but not in Sam's estimation. He was sure every picture produced by Sam Goldwyn was going to be a winner, so where was the gamble?

Perhaps it gave him an additional feeling of importance to be able to throw his money around recklessly at croquet, bridge, poker, faro, backgammon, and, in fact, just about all games of chance. A psychiatrist would probably put it another way—that Sam was fulfilling some long-repressed desire to be like the big-time gamblers he'd seen and envied when he was a young man living in Gloversville. Sam had been bitten by the gambling bug that long ago.

Gloversville was only a few miles by streetcar from Saratoga Springs— the home of the world-famous resort hotel, the race track, and a number of gambling casinos, the most famous of which was the Canfield Club, which was patronized by such turn-of-the-century personalities as Diamond Jim Brady, Harvey Firestone, and Lillian Russell.

On Sundays, his one day off from the glove factory, Sam would, often in the company of his best friend, Abe Lehr, take the streetcar to the race track at Saratoga. When he first used to frequent the place, he'd never bet, for he had no money to spare. He'd just stand along the rail and watch the ponies run. Later, he would drop in at the Canfield Club and watch Diamond Jim Brady go for broke and wish he could be just like him.

But after he became the world's greatest glove salesman, Sam stopped being a voyeur and became an active participant. Not on Diamond Jim's scale, but he lost enough money every week at his favorite game, faro, to cause him considerable anguish.

One night as Sam and Abe Lehr were on their way into the gambling casino, Sam pulled out his whole bankroll of one hundred and twenty dollars, kept a twenty-dollar bill himself, and gave the rest to Lehr for safekeeping.

"No matter what I say, don't give this back till tomorrow," Sam instructed his friend.

Sam quickly lost the twenty dollars and then demanded another twenty from Lehr. When Lehr refused to give it to him, Sam fell back on his persuasive genius, which was already in full flower, to make him change his mind. At first he tried cajolery and when that didn't work, he started screaming, and when threats didn't work, he broke down and cried real tears. At that point Lehr was so unnerved that he abjectly handed Sam twenty more dollars. Sam lost the second twenty as quickly as the first and came after Lehr for more. Again Lehr refused, and again Sam played on his human weaknesses until he surrendered another twenty, and then another twenty until finally there was no more left.

Learning his funds had run out, Sam turned on Lehr in a white rage and, in a voice loud enough to be heard clear over in Gloversville, denounced him for being treasonous, undependable, completely without courage or moral rectitude, and in addition a lousy friend. Sam refused to talk to Lehr for a week. It was good training for Lehr in his later career as Sam's chief whipping boy at the studio.

After Sam started traveling in the more sophisticated circles of Broadway and Hollywood, he took up contract bridge, backgammon, and poker for very high stakes. Sam liked bridge the best of all card games, but because of his inability to get along with partners, he was probably the least suited to play it. As a result, he lost regularly and was always getting into fights at the bridge table.

One day Sam attended a bridge party aboard Joe Schenck's yacht, which was anchored somewhere in Long Island Sound. The bridge table where Sam was playing was set up on the stern. Frances, who never played, was socializing with the other wives at the other end of the yacht.

When an uproar broke out at the bridge table, Schenck, who was kibitzing, walked nervously to where the wives were seated and said, "They're having a fight."

"Sam and who?" asked Frances.

On another occasion Sam scolded his partner, actress Constance Bennett, for overbidding her hand.

"How did I know you had nothing?" she asked.

"Didn't you hear me keeping still?" asked Sam.

While playing in a bridge game at Hillcrest County Club with Hollywood lawyer Edwin Loeb, Sam went down with eight hundred points in one play, according to the scorekeeper. But by Sam's calculations it should have been only seven hundred points. An argument ensued, with Sam offering to bet Loeb one hundred dollars that seven hundred points was correct.

"I won't bet," said Loeb. "It would be betting on a sure thing."

Sam derided him for being too cheap to bet and finally forced the man to make the wager.

The group then consulted Culbertson's book, which said Sam was wrong. Sam paid off but complained he shouldn't have to, because he was the victim of a swindler.

"Why do you say that?" asked Loeb.

"Because you were betting on a sure thing," replied Sam.

Sam liked to play bridge for much higher stakes than most people felt they could afford. To him, twenty-five cents a point was a modest game, and anything below that was like playing for matchsticks. For that reason, plus the fact that he was a lousy bridge player, plus the fact that no partner could take his abuse, those who could avoid being Sam's partner without being too blunt in their refusals usually did.

Sam's former publicity chief Howard Dietz is an excellent bridge player; so is his wife, Lucinda. And socially they were very fond of the Goldwyns, and vice versa. The two couples went on trips together, and the Dietzes were always welcome as houseguests at Sam's and Frances's home when they were in Los Angeles, even if the Goldwyns weren't in town.

"But if Sam ever asked us to play bridge," says Lucinda, "I would always tell him, 'I'll play but only if I can have Howard as a partner. I'm no good otherwise.' It was the only way I could get out of being Sam's partner tactfully."

A major drawback to having Sam as a partner, besides the fact that he was a poor bridge player, was that, as much as he complained when he was losing, he really didn't mind how much money he had to pay out at the end of the game. "That's because he never actually did the paying," says Howard Dietz. "Frances acted as his exchequer. She wrote out the check."

Since Sam didn't actually see the balance in his checkbook getting lower, there was no reality to his losing. Consequently he'd be more reckless in his bidding than he had any right to be, which drove his bridge partners right up the wall.

Fortunately for the health of the Goldwyn marriage, Frances never learned to play bridge and therefore didn't have to suffer the agony of having Sam for a partner. Moreover, she didn't mind if Sam played. Unlike most wives, who resent being left out of things while their husbands are enjoying themselves, Frances would be perfectly content to sit nearby in a chair, reading a book or magazine and occasionally kibitzing. As long as Sam was happy, she was happy. And Sam was happy when he was playing bridge.

By the same token he was most unhappy when he couldn't get a fourth, which became more and more of a problem as Sam's reputation for being the Attila the Hun of the Culbertson set became more widely known.

Often Sam would have to dredge the bottom of the barrel in order to find a fourth willing to be his partner. During a trip to New York, the Goldwyns invited the Dietzes over to their suite in the Hotel Pierre to have dinner and afterward, Sam hoped, a game of bridge, provided Sam could find a partner. "Sam hadn't found a fourth by the time we arrived," recalls Dietz. "But all through dinner he kept getting up from the table to phone people, but he kept getting turndowns. By the time we were finished eating, Sam was so desperate that he went down to the lobby and picked up some drunk who was there for a convention and brought him back to his suite. Between Sam, who couldn't play very well, and a conventioneer who'd been drunk for three days, he lost a fortune to Lucinda and me."

But Sam had the philosophy of the true gambler. It was the only game in town, and if he had his choice beforehand of not playing and hanging on to his money or playing and losing a small fortune, he'd take the latter every time. It was his love of battle that motivated him. The winning of money was secondary.

It was the nuisance of trying to recruit bridge partners that in the end drove Sam to more singular games. For example, backgammon, in which you only needed an opponent and it was far easier to cheat. Some Hollywood wit once said that backgammon, as Sam Goldwyn played it, was as honest as wrestling. And Chico Marx, another renowned gambler, paid Sam the supreme tribute when he said, "Sam is the only man in the world who can throw a seven with one die."

In backgammon games where Sam was hopelessly trapped and about to be doubled, strange things happened. Sam would suddenly be playing with five less men than his opponent. Or Sam would accidentally overturn the board, spilling men all over the floor, while getting out of his chair to fetch a drink from the bar or to go to the bathroom.

"How clumsy of me!" Sam would exclaim. "Well, I guess we'll have to start over."

When opponents became suspicious of this gambit, Sam would enlist the aid of his son, who on a given signal would rush into the room to greet his father, trip on the braid rug, and fall against the backgammon board, knocking everything onto the floor including drinks. Or it might just happen while Sam junior was sitting in a chair by the table, learning the fine points of the game by watching his father lose to an opponent. At the proper moment he'd knock a drink into Sam's opponent's lap, causing the opponent to jump up and overturn the board.

There were so many variations on the same theme that serious backgammon players often refused to sit down at the board in the Goldwyn den until Sam had banished his son to another part of the house. But Sam junior, high spirited, headstrong, and precocious, enjoyed hanging around with his father and his illustrious friends, and a few minutes after he'd been banished he would return on some pretext or another.

Once during a backgammon encounter between Goldwyn and Chico Marx, who was by far the better player, Sam junior knocked over the board three times, causing the games to have to be started over. Chico told Sam to get rid of his son. Goldwyn did on three occasions, but Sammy kept coming back like a boomerang.

Fed up, Chico took the boy out of the room and returned five minutes later without him. The game commenced, and this time Sam junior didn't return. Even Sam was amazed at Chico's child-handling ability, and he finally asked, "How'd you do it?"

"I taught him to masturbate," replied Chico proudly.

During the thirties and forties, when everyone in the picture business was prospering, no-limit poker, in which it was possible to lose $50,000 in an evening, was very much in vogue among Sam's card-playing cronies—a group whose regulars included David Selznick, Norman Krasna, Ben Hecht, Harry Kurnitz, Orson Welles, Harpo Marx, and David May, the department store heir.

Because the big losers never wanted the big winners to go home without giving them a chance to get even, these games, which alternated from home to home each week, frequently didn't break up until four and five in the morning.

One night when the game was to be played at the Goldwyn house, David May, who was recuperating from a serious operation and didn't have his strength back yet, agreed to play only if there could be a time limit on the game. Because May was their "pigeon" and nobody wanted to lose him, it was agreed that no matter who was winning, the game would break up at the stroke of midnight.

When midnight rolled around, May was the big winner, with Sam personally owing him $30,000.

As May rose to leave, Sam said, "Hey, where are you going? I want a chance to get even."

"Don't you remember, Sam?" said May. "We all agreed to quit at twelve o'clock, win, lose, or draw."

"Sure, I remember," said Sam, "but I'm a sport. I'll play you one more hand, double or nothing."

Double or nothing was one of Sam's favorite ways of getting even, though he rarely did. In his golfing days, Sam once lost eight dollars to Zeppo Marx during an eighteen-hole encounter on the links at Hillcrest Country Club. While eight dollars wasn't a great deal to a man who played in no-limit poker games where fifty thousand dollars could pass hands in an evening, he was nevertheless still steaming by the time the two of them reached the locker room. Before paying off, Sam said, "Let's cut the cards—double or nothing." A sport, Zeppo agreed. They sent for a deck of cards, the two of them cut, and Zeppo won. Now Sam owed him sixteen dollars.

"One more time," offered Sam.

Again they cut, and again Zeppo won—a process that repeated itself six more times, or until Sam owed the comedian the staggering sum of $2048."

Sam wanted to continue, but Zeppo said, "No, Sam, I have to go."

"But you have to give me a chance to get even," cried Sam.

"I'll tell you what I'll do," said Zeppo. "Just give me the original eight dollars and I'll call it even."

"You really mean that?" said Sam gratefully.

"Yeah. Just give me eight dollars."

Sam started to hand him the money, then pulled it back and said, "Let's cut one more time for double or nothing!"

19

Willy Wyler: The Man Who Didn't Come to Dinner

ASIDE FROM THE AGONY Frances Goldwyn and James Mulvey had gone through in order to keep Sam from losing *Dead End* when he was on death's doorstep, the Kingsley play made the transition from stage to film with a minimum of complications and off-scene histrionics.

To play the romantic leads, Sam turned to his old reliables, Sylvia Sidney and Joel McCrea, both of whom he had under contract, and borrowed Humphrey Bogart from Warner Brothers to perform the pivotal part of the gangster Baby Face Martin. Bogart had just finished playing another gangster role, Duke Mantee, opposite Bette Davis in *The Petrified Forest*, and was on the verge of permanent stardom and immortality as a film tough guy, but in *Dead End* he had to settle for third billing.

Also in the cast were Marjorie Main (Baby Face's mother); Claire Trevor (his girlfriend); and the Dead End Kids (Leo Gorcey, Huntz Hall, Bobby Jordan, and Billy Halop), making their movie bow in the roles they had created on the stage—that of the wise-cracking guttersnipes.

Lillian Hellman had written a very good screenplay, and Willy Wyler was, of course, in charge of the direction.

Sam felt Willy Wyler could do no wrong now that he had directed two previous hits for him, *Dodsworth* and *These Three*, and had helped him salvage *Come and Get It*, and he gave him pretty much his own head in most matters during the production of *Dead End*.

"There was one thing, however, I couldn't swing," relates Wyler. "I wanted to do the picture in New York, on the streets where the picture would be made if it were done today. I wanted to juxtapose a block in the East Fifties with the Sutton Place elegance. But Goldwyn wouldn't let me shoot back East. He was afraid I'd get away from him."

Sam had to have his hands on the reins, even though he was letting the horse have his own head. As consolation, however, for not allowing Wyler to shoot in New York, Sam overextended his budget by some $300,000 to have a set built that was almost as good as the real thing. It wound up being the talk of Hollywood.

Designed by Richard Day, who'd won an Oscar for his work on *Dodsworth*, the *Dead End* set was a realistic complex of slums, seedy shops, Sutton Place terraces, and an East River pier, in front of which was real polluted water for the Dead End Kids to jump into and cool their dirty hides during the searing August heat.

However, Sam rebelled against having too much realism in *Dead End*, just as he did in all his pictures. It was one of his quirks, perhaps a hangover from the squalor of his youth, that made him believe that picture audiences demanded a certain amount of beauty and glamour even though the story might call for the characters to dress in rags and look dirty and the backgrounds to be ugly and decrepit. This was one of the things that Sam was always taking Wyler to task about during the shooting of *Dead End*.

According to Wyler, Sam was continually dropping in on the tenement-street set, surveying the filth as if it were repugnant to his sense of aesthetics, and shouting in his high-pitched voice, "Why is everything so dirty here?"

"Because it's supposed to be a slum area, Sam."

"Well, this slum cost a lot of money. It should look better than an ordinary slum."

While Wyler was shooting *Wuthering Heights*, Sam wandered onto the set one day and noticed that Laurence Olivier's face was smudged with soot.

"Why is that?" he asked Wyler.

"Because he's a stable boy in this part of the story," explained Wyler. "But just wait. In the last part of the picture, when Heathcliff comes back a rich man, he'll look marvelous."

During another part of the filming, Olivier sprained his ankle while jumping off a horse and had a bad limp for several days. But in the best show-must-go-on tradition, he refused to take any time off. He limped and made the best of it. One day when Sam was visiting the set, Olivier limped over to him to say hello and possibly get a compliment for being such a good sport about working despite his aching leg. But all Sam noticed was the soot on his face. "That's the ugliest man I've ever seen," said Sam turning to Wyler. "If he continues to look dirty like that, I'm going to close the picture."

Despite Sam's quirk about everything having to look beautiful, Wyler managed to bring enough realism to *Dead End* to please both critics and audiences. The *New York Times* said of it when it opened in New York on August 25, 1937: "Sam Goldwyn's screen translation of *Dead End* as it came to the Rivoli last night deserves a place among the important motion pictures of 1937." And the *New York Post* devoted an editorial to it, the main thrust of which was: "The best thing that could have been done at the last session of Congress would have been to show the film *Dead End* to the committee which crippled the Wagner Housing Act."

The picture did big business both in America and abroad, and by the following spring most people in Hollywood were predicting it would win an Academy Award. And, indeed, it received four nominations: best picture, best actress in a supporting role, best direction, and best art direction.

Sam didn't argue with the fact that *Dead End* was the kind of picture he was proud to have his name on. And according to Frances, he was secretly hoping to get an Oscar when he showed up at the awards ceremony in 1938. But he wasn't counting on it. Sam was enough of a realist to know from past experience that it was difficult for an independent producer like himself to come out a winner when faced with the bloc voting of the major studios.

Major studios in the thirties and forties had a great many academy members on their permanent payrolls and also the power to coerce them into voting for the home team's picture, even though it might not be their favorite. That kind of electioneering is strictly against academy rules. But Academy Awards are big business, and big business often disregards the rules of the game. Which is why the major studios usually walk off with the lion's share of the awards and why Sam was not terribly surprised when *Dead End* failed to win in any category—not even best art direction for its magnificent river-front set. When the votes were tallied, Warner Brothers won the best picture Oscar for *The Life of Emile Zola*, which starred Paul Muni. Though not a surprise, it was a disappointment to Sam. But he was much too proud a man ever to voice it to anyone but Frances.

Sam wasn't the kind, however, to worry about past disappointments or lost opportunities for very long. His head was either in the "now" or on future projects. Of the latter there was never any shortage. Between *Dead End*'s release in 1937 and America's entry into World War II, Sam produced thirteen more films at his usual three- or four-a-year clip. Two of these, *Wuthering Heights* and *The Little Foxes*, were serious contenders for best picture Oscars. And the majority were good, solid pieces of entertainment and moneymakers: *The Westerner*, with Gary Cooper and Walter Brennan; *Stella Dallas*, a remake of the original, with Barbara Stanwyck and John Boles; *Hurricane*, starring Dorothy Lamour and Jon Hall and directed by John Ford; *They Shall Have Music*, a bit of schmaltz about a music school with Jascha Heifetz; *The Real Glory*, another "oater" with Gary Cooper; *Raffles*, a remake of the original, with David Niven in the Ronald Colman role; and *Ball of Fire*, by Billy Wilder and Charles Brackett, and starring Barbara Stanwyck and Gary Cooper.

Mixed in with the jewels, however, were a few films so egregious that they have become famous for that reason alone: *Woman Chases Man*, *The Adventures of Marco Polo*, *The Cowboy and the Lady*, and *The Goldwyn Follies*, otherwise known as "Goldwyn's Folly."

At the time Sam was active, there was never any accounting for his taste in story material, or why he stubbornly clung to what seemed to be pet projects and went ahead and sunk a couple of million dollars of his own money in them against the advice of some of the best minds in the business. But in retrospect, a definite pattern seems to emerge. Except for *The Best Years of Our Lives*, which was totally original from concept to completed film, Sam's major successes were based on successful plays and novels, and most of his "worst failures" were made from originals. Sam was obviously aware of that pattern, too—he as much as admitted it when he refused to buy *Dodsworth* in novel form. Still, it didn't stop him from occasionally trying to start from scratch. In so doing, perhaps he was trying to prove to his doubters that Sam Goldwyn could make a successful picture without having to base it on an already proven property.

There are no available records on the original properties Sam started and shelved, but of the ones he refused to drop, no one was less subtle about telling him that he ought to than his favorite director and verbal sparring partner of the period, Willy Wyler.

As previously pointed out, Wyler had no rights in his Goldwyn contract. He was being paid $2,500 a week for forty weeks a year to direct what Sam told him to. But Wyler did have excellent taste and extremely good hunches as to which of Sam's proposed gems would be bombs and therefore were to be avoided. When Wyler voiced his objections and refused to direct, Sam would use the one weapon at his command: he'd put him on suspension, which would automatically extend his contract for the same length of time he refused to direct.

But Wyler could be as stubborn and independent as Sam. No bully-boy, big-stick tactics frightened him, and neither did the loss of salary. The moment Sam put him on suspension, Wyler would take off for the ski slopes of Saint-Moritz or the fishing waters along the coast of Mexico. Wyler was a man who liked to live well—and dangerously. He was a good all-round athlete, and motorcycling was his favorite form of transportation way back before it became popular among the *Easy Rider* set. And long before anyone had ever heard of Evel Knievel, Wyler, in a moment of drunken abandon at a party at the Beverly Hills Tennis Club, actually rode his motorcycle off the diving board and into the deep end of the swimming pool.

Obviously the threat of suspension wasn't going to intimidate a man with that kind of nerve and *joie de vivre*.

"As a result," recounts Wyler, "I had a three-year contract with Sam that ran for almost five years."

The one thing Sam could have done but which he never did when Wyler turned him down was to sue him for breach of contract. But Sam wouldn't risk a permanent break. Wyler was too valuable to let go completely. Better just to suspend him and take him off salary until he found a picture he would direct. Or loan him out to other studios. Wyler was in big demand all over town, and Sam could always get five hundred or a thousand more per week for him than he was paying him, thereby turning a handsome profit.

Dead End hadn't even been released when Wyler had his first suspension-go-round with Goldwyn over *Woman Chases Man*. *Woman Chases Man* was an original by Lynn Root and Frank Fenton. Sam had assigned a number of writers to the screenplay since Eddie Chodorov had originally turned down the chance to fashion the wacky farce into a movie for Miriam Hopkins and Joel McCrea. Credit for the final draft Sam handed Wyler to direct went to the celebrated wit Dorothy Parker; her husband, Alan Campbell; and Joe Bigelow.

Despite all that talent on it, *Woman Chases Man* remained a silly story about a millionaire's son (Joel McCrea), his ne'er-do-well father (Charles Winninger), and a scheming architect (Miriam Hopkins) who fell in love with Joel McCrea and chased him until she cornered him on the limb of a tree, from which there was no escaping. Those are the high points.

Wyler read the script and promptly rejected it.

"Why?" asked Sam.

"I don't like it," said Wyler.

"Well, do me a favor. Just work on it for a few weeks with the writers," pleaded Sam. "Maybe you can improve it."

Since Sam couched it so nicely, how could Wyler refuse? He agreed to put two weeks, at the most three, into helping out his boss.

Wyler struggled bravely but after three weeks found he could do nothing with the material. It was hopeless, without one redeeming feature, and he told Sam he was quitting the project.

"But you've been drawing a salary all this time," Sam cried out in paranoiac anguish.

"Would you like me to give it back to you?" asked Wyler facetiously, never dreaming for a minute that Sam would take him up on it.

"Yeah," said Sam, never dreaming for a minute that Wyler wasn't really offering it to him.

What Wyler had intended as a joke wound up costing him $7,500.

Seventy-five hundred dollars was a drop in the bucket compared with what the picture eventually cost Sam. After putting Wyler on suspension, he approached John Blystone, who specialized in Westerns and cheap comedies, to direct *Woman Chases Man*. Blystone did, and he's never been heard of since, though, in all fairness, it wasn't his fault that the picture was no good.

Sam took Wyler off suspension long enough to offer him *The Cowboy and the Lady*—the first of two originals he was preparing for Gary Cooper. The other was *The Adventures of Marco Polo*, a kind of tongue-in-cheek account of the famous traveler's life in the Orient. Sam had acquired this treatment from Doug Fairbanks, who had decided not to produce it and appear in it himself, one of the shrewdest moves, it turned out, Fairbanks had ever made.

The Cowboy and the Lady was another Goldwyn project that had a very sick script. In fact, it had been terminally ill since its conception, despite the contributions of many talented writers during its gestation period. Among the group who worked on it in 1937 were Anita Loos, John Emerson, Garson Kanin, Sonya Levien, and S. N. Behrman.

The Cowboy and the Lady was the story of a shy cowpoke (Gary Cooper) who gets involved with a lady (Merle Oberon) who is the daughter of a presidential candidate. When the cowpoke falls in love with her and marries her, she exposes him to sophisticated city life. There he's laughed at by her friends, and he becomes embittered and returns to cowpoke country. After he's gone, she realizes she loves him and follows him out West for a happy riding-into-the-sunset ending.

That's the story *after* all those writers worked on it. But the original idea was even thinner than that. It had originally been conceived by director Leo (*Going My Way*) McCarey, who told it to Sam and a group of his contract writers one day while he, McCarey, was lying on a couch in Sam's office. McCarey had little more to sell than the title, *The Cowboy and the Lady*, and one comedy sequence in which Cooper shows Oberon through a house he's planning to build for her, but which at the time is still in the planning stage. In fact, it's just a few pegs in the ground connected by some pieces of string, but he leads her through it room by room. McCarey had nothing on paper, but he was a clever enough storyteller to con Sam into paying $50,000 for his idea.

According to Garson Kanin, who was under contract to Goldwyn at that time and who was one of the writers in Sam's office the day McCarey told it, Sam realized the story needed lots of work, but liked the title. And so he bought it, mainly for the title, and assigned writers to make it into a story, which was a common practice in studios in those days. Not so common was the fact that McCarey didn't have the right to sell him the title. *That* was owned by Paramount, and Sam wound up having to buy that as well.

Eventually Sonya Levien and S. N. Behrman licked the story, as the saying goes, and Sam, deciding he liked it enough to make, phoned Leo McCarey and offered him the opportunity to direct his brainchild.

"You think I want to spend my valuable time on a worthless piece of shit like that!" exclaimed McCarey, and he hung up.

Wyler didn't want to direct it, either, but since he was just coming off a two-month suspension, he needed the cash. Reluctantly he accepted the assignment. But it was a struggle to bring life to a contrived story and lines that didn't seem to want to play once the actors were on their feet. As a result, Wyler fell behind schedule, and Sam yanked him off the picture because he was "too slow" and replaced him with H. C. Potter, who the previous year had directed Merle Oberon in a picture at MGM, *Beloved Enemy*.

The Cowboy and the Lady opened on November 25, 1938, at New York's Radio City Music Hall, on a twin bill with Walt Disney's *Ferdinand the Bull*. After devoting the opening paragraph to noting that "Disney's bull" was more interesting than Goldwyn's cows, the *New York Times* reviewer went on to write:

> It has been freely admitted by his own press agents that Mr. Goldwyn, Hollywood's most passionate revisionist, was up to his knees in authors and abandoned scripts before *The Cowboy and the Lady* was completed. But this time the legend is hard to believe as the picture still seems to be in need of a final revision to bring it either more clearly into conformity or more ludicrously into non-conformity with life as it is lived outside of movie studios.
>
> Of course there is always Gary Cooper, but even Mr. Cooper, the picture's greatest asset, has his moments of diminishing returns, when he seems to be imitating himself, or when ultimately forsaken by the authors or director, he looks about helplessly, like a ghost who wonders if he isn't haunting the wrong house.

Reactions like that should have given Sam some food for thought the next time he offered Willy Wyler a picture and he turned it down. The next time was *The Adventures of Marco Polo*, which had a script by Robert Sherwood, whose reputation as a playwright had been so enhanced by a couple of Broadway hits and a Pulitzer Prize that when he hired him Sam had been willing to overlook the unpleasantness on *Roman Scandals* stemming from the fact that Sherwood and Kaufman had been unwilling to write any more "jokes" for him.

Ostensibly *The Adventures of Marco Polo* was based on historical fact, but about the only thing factual about it was its leading character's name. As biography, it was as biographical as Sam's account of his own life in *Behind the Screen*. In fairness to Sherwood, he had conceived it as travesty and not serious biography, and so felt he had the license to do anything he pleased with his famous character.

Because Wyler had been on loan-out to RKO when Sherwood finished the script, Sam gave the job to another director, John Cromwell, who'd just completed *The Prisoner of Zenda* for David Selznick, and cast Gary Cooper as Marco Polo and a Norwegian discovery of his casting department's, Sigrid Gurie, as Polo's Oriental enamorata.

Sam didn't like the first week's rushes, bounced Cromwell, sent for Wyler, who was just then available, and offered *Marco Polo* to him. Wyler read the script, ran the footage already shot, and announced he wouldn't touch it with a ten-foot Marco Polo. Sam wheedled, cajoled, pleaded, and even cried a little, but when he still couldn't persuade Wyler to change his mind he hired Archie Mayo, who had directed several films at Warner Brothers, including *The Petrified Forest*. Sam was so grateful that Mayo didn't turn him down that he even gave him a three-year contract.

After signing him, Sam said to Wyler, "See, Willy, there's a fellow who helps you when you're down."

"I'm not here to help you," replied Wyler. "I'm here to make good pictures. I have to believe in them."

If there's one thing Sam respected, it was artistic integrity. He promptly put Wyler back on suspension.

Marco Polo turned out to be Sam's worst financial disaster since he had gone down for the third time with Anna Sten. Curiously—and like the Sten pictures—*The Adventures of Marco Polo* did not get the kind of maltreatment from the critics that it deserved when it opened at Radio City Music Hall for an Easter holiday run in the spring of 1938. *Film Daily* called it "diverting" and "colorful" and "a pleasant romp while taking great liberties with historical fact." and even the *New York Times* hatchet man wasn't too unkind when he wrote:

> On Mr. Goldwyn's magic carpet Mr. Cooper travels exclusively without ever seeming to get very far from home.
>
> Possibly one of the limiting factors has been the remarkable range of accents Mr. Goldwyn culled to fill the court of Kublai Khan. The Khan speaks with George Barbier's nasal Philadelphian, the Viennese Marco with Mr. Cooper's Montana drawl, the Saracen with Basil Rathbone's clipped Londonese, the Princess Kukachin with Sigrid Gurie's Norwegian, the servant Binguccio with Ernest Truex's bifurcated Kansas-Broadway. And we're not counting Binnie Barnes' cockney, Stanley Fields' growling Pennsylvanian, and Frederick Gottschalk's whatever-it-is.

One of Sam's less endearing characteristics was his eagerness to blame others for pictures he wasn't willing to take the blame for himself. After

Marco Polo failed to attract customers in the numbers sufficient to earn back its investment of $3 million, Sam decided that it had to be the director's fault and started a vigorous campaign to get Archie Mayo to break his three-year contract with him.

Sam was none too subtle in his methods. He'd make unkind remarks about Mayo's directing in front of others, embarrassing him. He'd order him around like an office boy, giving him menial tasks to perform, such as asking him to run over to another studio and pick up a script for him (the Goldwyn studio had no messenger service of its own). And he'd order him to an early morning conference with him and then not show up for several hours, if at all.

Mayo, an amiable fellow with a build like Fatty Arbuckle, had never run up against a man like Goldwyn before. The treatment he was receiving confused him, and he asked Willy Wyler what to do.

"Quit," Wyler advised him, "before he breaks your spirit. It's the only way to handle him."

But Mayo said he couldn't afford to. He'd just built an $85,000 home in Beverly Hills, and he needed the money and the security of a three-year contract. So he stubbornly hung in there. But two could play at that game. The stubborn Sam just let him languish on the lot, without giving him an assignment.

Sam got rid of George Haight in a similar fashion, presumably for being associate producer on *Woman Chases Man*. In addition to heaping verbal abuse on Haight, Sam stripped him of his large producer's office and consigned him to a cubbyhole about the size of a toilet booth. Then he sent him stories to read and synopsize, as if he were no better than a sixty-dollar-a-week reader—a reader being about the lowest person on the Hollywood totem pole. Having been a playwright of some reputation before migrating west to dig for Hollywood gold, Haight couldn't stomach this kind of humiliation and eventually quit.

Mayo, however, couldn't afford to. So he swallowed his pride and settled for collecting his $2,000-a-week salary for forty weeks a year. That Mayo was being paid all that money without doing anything for it seemed to annoy Sam more than his lack of talent, and eventually he gave in and assigned him to direct a second picture for him—*They Shall Have Music*. The only excuse for this picture's existence was that it featured the artistry of Jascha Heifetz, whom Sam decided ought to be introduced to picture audiences, even though he had no property in which to put him.

A number of writers, however, strived valiantly for over a year and a half to devise a suitable vehicle in which to showcase Heifetz's talents, but the best they could come up with was a trivial pastiche about an underprivileged boy who discovers classical music, attends a music school run by an old maestro (played by Walter Brennan), learns the school is on the verge of bankruptcy, and talks Heifetz into performing for nothing in order to raise funds to save the school.

While the script was being prepared, Sam nearly lost Heifetz, who grew tired of waiting and decided to invoke a "pay or play" clause in his contract. If Sam lost Heifetz, of course, there wouldn't have been any reason to make the picture, so while the script was still being written, Sam ordered Wyler to shoot the concert sequence, Mayo having not yet been assigned to the project.

The critics liked the concert sequence. The *New York Times* said Heifetz's screen debut was "the source of considerable delight" and went on to comment enthusiastically about "the crystal purity of Mr. Heifetz's playing, the eloquent flow of melody from his violin, and the closeups of his graceful fingers upon the strings." And *Variety* said, "Mr. Heifetz makes no pretense about being an actor, but when he faces the camera his confidence is easily discernible. And his solos are tops."

Because of Heifetz and the excellent filming of the musical numbers by Wyler the picture was a modest success. But Archie Mayo never worked for Goldwyn again and swiftly disappeared into obscurity after Sam let his contract run out.

Both Archie Mayo and George Haight had committed the one sin Sam couldn't forgive—being connected with his "worst failures." Instinctively Willy Wyler knew this about Sam, which was why he always took suspension rather than have anything to do with Sam's two-ton bombs.

Another of Sam's mistakes that Wyler elected to go on suspension for turning down was *The Goldwyn Follies*. Sam hadn't made a musical since the early Cantor films, but the other studios were turning them out regularly and apparently making fortunes with them. MGM had its Judy Garland and Eleanor Powell; RKO, its Astaire and Rogers; Warners, its Ruby Keeler and Dick Powell; Universal, its Deanna Durbin; and Twentieth Century–Fox, its Alice Faye and Don Ameche. So it was no surprise to Sam's associates when he announced that he was going to get back into the musical-comedy act.

Besides, for a good many years now, in fact since he had joined with Florenz Ziegfeld to produce *Whoopee*, Sam had been nurturing a dream—a dream to emulate Ziegfeld by releasing one large, girl-filled musical extravaganza every year under the title *The Goldwyn Follies*. (After all, didn't the *New York Times* already refer to him as "the Ziegfeld of the Pacific"?) Not only would an annual *Goldwyn Follies* perpetuate Sam's favorite name, but how could a movie filled with levity, comedians, beautiful girls, dancing, hit songs, filmed in color, and produced by Sam Goldwyn, fail to attract a large audience—especially in those worrisome times when Hitler was starting his saber-rattling across the Atlantic?

There was only one difficulty—getting a script together that would embody all those elements. It was acknowledged among show people that a review was just about the hardest kind of entertainment to bring off.

Sam was not daunted by the past failures of others. As usual, he went for the best talent money could buy, including George and Ira Gershwin to write the songs, George Balanchine, the master of American modern ballet, to stage the dance sequences, and a dozen or so scriptwriters, including Garson Kanin, Dorothy Parker, Alan Campbell, Ben Hecht, Charlie MacArthur, and Sonya Levien.

But this was to be another "trouble" picture for Sam. He just couldn't get a script to satisfy him. In a period of about a year and a half more than a dozen versions must have crossed his desk. Writers were put on and off the project with the regularity of substitutions during a pro football game, and in about those numbers. Sam wasn't the first Hollywood producer to use the "platoon" system. It was a common practice in those days, especially when preparing comedies featuring a number of comics with different styles and comedy demands.

But the more drafts there were, the more confused Sam became. "Sam really didn't understand that kind of script," recalls one of the gag men who put in time on *The Goldwyn Follies*, "because it was a review format, with no real continuity."

During this period Sam was continually calling story conferences, sometimes at odd hours, and occasionally at his house on Laurel Lane. Ira Gershwin remembers a time when he and George were summoned there one Saturday at noon, for a light lunch down on the patio, to be followed by a conference upstairs in Sam's den.

The lunch was pleasant enough, with few references to the sick script. But immediately after they'd eaten, Sam wiped his mouth with his napkin, shoved his chair back, and said in businesslike tones as he stood up, "Okay, boys, now let's go upstairs and have a little cuddle." Ira Gershwin swears to this day that he heard it with his own ears.

That was one of the lighter moments. *The Goldwyn Follies* was also touched with tragedy before it was finished. All during the writing of the score, George Gershwin kept complaining that the headaches he'd been troubled with for years were becoming increasingly severe. Everybody thought he was just being his usual hypochondriacal self—until he went to the doctor one day and it was discovered that he had a brain tumor. The doctor diagnosed it as operable, and Gershwin entered Cedars of Lebanon Hospital that afternoon. To the shock of the whole world, he died on the operating table that night.

Sam seemed completely out of his element producing that kind of musical mélange, and the dance numbers, in particular, threw him completely.

In one meeting with his associates to discuss who he should hire to do the choreography, somebody suggested Martha Graham.

"What kind of dancing does she do?" asked Sam.

"Modern dancing."

"No, no. I don't want her then," said Sam.

"Why not?"

"Because modern dancing is so old-fashioned." Another Goldwynism, but under close scrutiny it made a point clearly. Modern dance was currently being done in so many movies that, to Sam, it was already old hat.

Finally Sam hired George Balanchine, because he'd been told he was the absolute tops. But Sam didn't understand his work at all.

When Balanchine dreamed up a dance sequence based on Gershwin's *An American in Paris*, Sam threw it out, saying it wasn't for motion picture audiences. Later that same ballet became the basis of the Academy Award winner *An American in Paris*, starring Gene Kelly and Leslie Caron, which MGM produced.

Ben Hecht finally wound up with a solo writing credit on the first and only *Goldwyn Follies*, but it was no great victory for him to have to take the blame himself.

One hit song came out of the picture, "Love Walked In," which George Gershwin dashed off a few hours before he entered the hospital for his fatal brain operation, but other than that, it was undistinguished.

A number of good musical-comedy names filled out the all-star cast— Vera Zorina, Adolphe Menjou, Andrea Leeds, Phil Baker, Kenny Baker, Ella Logan, and the Ritz Brothers, but the only real hit of the picture was Edgar Bergen, with his adopted child, Charlie McCarthy.

When Sam signed Bergen for the *Follies*, the ventriloquist was virtually unknown. But during the year and a half that it took to complete the film, Bergen had been appearing weekly on *The Chase and Sanborn Hour* on coast-to-coast radio. By the time the *Follies* was previewed, Bergen was a nationwide hit, which everyone in America was aware of except Sam, who never listened to the radio.

He was pleased to see the preview audience rolling in the aisles at Bergen's and McCarthy's sure-fire routines, however, and immediately after the preview, Sam called a group of his lieutenants together on the sidewalk in front of the theater and whispered to them: "This ventriloquist fellow . . . this fellow with the dummy. I have only signed him for one picture. But I would like to make a deal with him for more. So please, don't anybody tell him how good he is!"

Sam didn't sign Bergen, nor did he ever make another *Goldwyn Follies* after seeing the notices and the box-office returns.

Reviewing *The Goldwyn Follies* in the *New York Times*, first-string reviewer

Frank Nugent wrote: "Sam Goldwyn has been dreaming of a *Goldwyn Follies* for so many years it was inevitable that its realization, on the Rivoli's screen, should have a certain nightmarish quality. . . . I stayed awake, sometimes with an effort, and found his Follies a hodgepodge."

Recalling that period in the late thirties when he was either on or off suspension, or Sam's fair-haired boy or pariah, Wyler says with a grin today, "Somehow all the scripts I turned down were enormous failures. I guess I was just lucky."

A picture Wyler says he would have liked to direct had he not been on loan-out at the time was *Hurricane,* based on the Nordhoff and Hall bestselling novel. This film, which starred Dorothy Lamour and Jon Hall, was an excellent example of a romantic action picture and was a big moneymaker. It even collected a couple of Oscars (best sound, best special effects, for its hurricane sequences).

John Ford, the explosive Irishman, directed the film and did a magnificent job, but he got along so badly with Sam that he regretted ever taking the assignment. First of all, Sam went behind Ford's back and looked at the dailies without him. Ford didn't approve of producers looking over his shoulder or playing Monday-morning quarterback. He preferred that Sam didn't see any of the footage until he had made his first cut. Or if he couldn't wait for that, at least look at the dailies with Ford, so he could explain things to him he didn't understand. Sam, however, was much too curious, or "nosy," as Ford termed it.

One day Sam looked at the dailies with his story editor, Sam Marx, and came to the conclusion that Ford wasn't shooting enough close-ups— especially of Dorothy Lamour in her sarong. Commanding Marx to accompany him, Sam set out for the sound stage where Ford was shooting. All during the walk, Sam kept reiterating what he was going to tell Ford. "Either he shoots more close-ups of Dotty, or he gets the hell off the picture."

Striding onto the sound stage, Sam saw that Ford was in the middle of a take and waited quietly on the sidelines for it to be finished. The moment Ford called, "Cut," Sam approached him timidly and said, "I'd like to talk to you."

"What about?" snarled Ford.

"I think you should take more close-ups of Lamour," said Sam.

"Is that all?" demanded Ford.

"Yes," said Sam nervously.

"Well, let me tell you something," roared the bellicose Irishman, grabbing Sam by the lapels. "Only I am going to determine what close-ups to get—and *when* I need them. If I want them this size, I'll shoot them from here." To illustrate, he slapped Goldwyn in the belly. "Now I may want bigger ones, so I'll frame them from here," he raged, tapping Sam on the chest a little more forcefully. As Sam winced, Ford clenched his fist right in his face, as if he were going to punch him, and screamed, "Or I may want even bigger ones." He punctuated his sentence by putting his clenched fist right up against Sam's long nose.

Sam looked apprehensively down his nose at the fist, then wheeled abruptly, grabbed Marx by the arm, and marched quickly off the sound stage with him. Out on the sunlit studio street, Sam continued along in angry silence for about fifty yards, or until he was sure he was out of Ford's earshot, and then turned to his companion and exclaimed, "Well, anyway, I put it in his mind." If Sam couldn't win, he at least had to have the last word.

While Sam was having his troubles with Ford, Wyler was on loan-out to Warner Brothers, where he directed Bette Davis in *Jezebel*.

Although Sam wasn't crazy about giving Warner his best director, the *Jezebel* loan-out turned out to be a most fortunate contact for Sam, because if Bette Davis hadn't liked being directed by Wyler, Sam might never have been able to persuade her to work for him when he needed her later for the Tallulah Bankhead role in *The Little Foxes*. Even more important, the Bette Davis–Willy Wyler contact led, in a strangely convoluted way, to Sam's decision to make a film of *Wuthering Heights*.

Later in life, Sam would call *Wuthering Heights* his favorite of all the films he produced, including *The Best Years of Our Lives*. But in 1937, Sam viewed the whole prospect of making a film of the Emily Brontë novel with the brooding cynicism of Heathcliff himself.

It was through a remarkable series of events that the script first found its way into Sam's hands, because the one thing he had warned all his story editors about was not to bother him with any stories where the characters appeared in "period costumes and wrote with quill pens." And Emily Brontë's novel was all of that—a dark, romantic story played against the gloomy background of the Yorkshire moors in the late eighteenth century. Moreover, its leading character, Heathcliff, a stable boy who falls in love with Catherine, his benefactor's beautiful daughter, is a sullen, brooding type whom literary critics in Brontë's day termed unpleasant and unsympathetic—hardly Sam's idea of a romantic hero. But then it had never been Sam's idea to make a film of the Brontë classic at all.

It had actually been the idea of the men who'd written the screenplay— Ben Hecht and Charlie MacArthur. One summer while vacationing in Alexander Woollcott's cottage in Vermont, they had invested a couple of months of their own time toward knocking out a screenplay, purely on speculation. These two highly literate gentlemen knew enough about Hollywood and the men who ran it to realize that none of the reigning heads had the vision or literacy to see a picture in the Brontë story just from the novel, which was long, difficult to read, and filled out with a confusing subplot plus some censorable material (implications of incest).

As they subsequently discovered during a year of making submissions, none of the majors were interested in *Wuthering Heights* in screenplay form either, in spite of the workmanlike job they'd done in simplifying the story and heightening the romanticism so it would be palatable to picture audiences.

Finally their script got into the hands of Walter Wanger, who was renting office and stage space on the United Artists–Goldwyn lot and looking for properties to release under his new United Artists releasing deal. He liked their script and bought it for around $50,000—short money for Hecht and MacArthur, but by then they were glad to unload it at any price.

But a couple of turndowns from directors and actors he had hoped to attract to the project caused even Wanger to cool toward the script after a few weeks. Desperate, Wanger handed the script to Sam for an opinion.

"Maybe you can tell me how to lighten it up," said Wanger.

Sam's reaction was surprising. "It's the best damn script I've read in years," he said. "You'd be crazy to change it."

"Then perhaps you'd like to buy it from me," suggested Wanger.

"I wouldn't think of it," said Sam. "That Heathcliff is too damn nasty."

"But you just told me not to change it," said Wanger.

"Look," said Sam. "If you're going to make *Wuthering Heights*, make *Wuthering Heights*—not *Potash and Perlmutter*."

On those pearls of wisdom, Wanger left Sam's office, shaking his head. But he hadn't given up on unloading the property. Next he showed the script to Willy Wyler, who loved it and brought it back to Sam with the suggestion that he buy it and let him direct.

"Buy it?" exclaimed Sam. "Hell, no."

"Why not?" asked Wyler.

"It's too gloomy," said Sam.

"But it's a great love story," insisted Wyler.

"I don't like stories with people dying in the end," said Sam. "It's a tragedy."

Several months passed, and Wyler was at Warner Brothers, making *Jezebel* with Bette Davis. The two got along so well that even before they had finished *Jezebel* they were discussing future projects together.

"Anything in mind?" asked Davis between takes on the ballroom set.

Wyler told her about the *Wuthering Heights* script. She asked to read it, and after she did, she took it into Jack Warner's office and told the studio head, "Buy this for me."

While Warner was reading it, Wyler phoned Sam and said, "You'd better act fast. J. L.'s very hot to buy *Wuthering Heights* for Bette Davis."

Wyler was pulling a trick as old as the movie business itself, but Sam fell for it.

"Thanks for tipping me off," he said. "Can Merle play it?"

"Why not?" said Wyler. "She's English, isn't she?"

So Sam, who had Merle Oberon under contract, and was desperate for a vehicle for her, finally bought the script from Walter Wanger and promptly had his publicity department sound the clarion call to the rest of the world that he was going to film *Wuthering Heights*.

To the English press, it practically bordered on heresy that a man of Sam Goldwyn's unlettered capabilities would attempt to make a film of Emily Brontë's novel. "Mr. Goldwyn is a legendary figure who has a fine autocratic way with the English language and chronology and things like that," wrote the London *Times* in one of its editorial columns. "Still the title is not everything and its retention does not—witness among others the conspicuous case of *Bengal Lancer*—at all imply that the film will be even remotely identifiable with the book."

Sam had no intention of tampering with the basic story as it was interpreted by Hecht and MacArthur. But he still wasn't crazy about an ending that saw both hero and heroine lying in graves, and he did his utmost to persuade Wyler and John Huston, who'd been put on the script for additional polish because Hecht and MacArthur weren't available, to write something more satisfying.

As in any story conference in which Sam participated, there was a good deal of screaming from him when he did not get his way. Huston and Wyler were pretty good screamers too, with the result that sometimes the verbal combat reached such a crescendo that no work was accomplished. Finally, before one of the conferences, Huston suggested a fifty-dollar forfeit from the first one of them to raise his voice.

When everybody agreed, Wyler and Huston each put up fifty dollars and laid the money on Sam's desk.

"I'm good for it," announced Sam, who never soiled his pants pockets with filthy lucre.

The conference proceeded with all three behaving themselves like overpolite schoolboys. "It was the quietest story conference in my memory," recalls Wyler.

As the meeting broke up, Sam said, "Well, I win," and he started to pocket the hundred dollars.

"What do you mean, you win?" asked Wyler.

"Well, I didn't yell, did I?" said Sam, deadly serious. It took Wyler and Huston about an hour to explain to Sam why he wasn't entitled to the money.

To bring the Brontë story off, Wyler insisted on an all-British cast. Sam had no argument with that. He already had two Britishers under contract—Merle Oberon and David Niven, who would play Edgar, the cuckolded husband. But Heathcliff presented a bit of a problem. There didn't seem to be any actors among Hollywood's British colony with the qualities to play Heathcliff—at least who were prominent enough to suit Sam.

How Sam happened to give the part to Laurence Olivier was about as fortuitous as how he acquired the script, says Helen Hayes, who was married to Charlie MacArthur at the time and remembers the whole series of events—mainly because she and her husband played a part in bringing Olivier to Sam's attention.

At the time, Sam had never heard of Olivier. In fact, many people in this country hadn't, although he frequently trod the boards in London's West End and was a member of the Old Vic Theatre Company. But he was anything but a star when Noel Coward brought him to America to play the role of the dumb husband in *Private Lives* in 1933.

Finishing his stint with Coward, Olivier served some more time in the London theater, then returned to Broadway in *No Time for Comedy* opposite Katharine Cornell. There he attracted the attention of Greta Garbo, who asked her bosses at MGM to let her have him for her leading man in *Queen Christina*. Louis B. Mayer then signed the Englishman and brought him to Hollywood. After testing him, Rouben Mamoulian, the film's director, decided *he* didn't like Olivier and took the part away from him.

"So," says Helen Hayes, "Larry was left to gather dust on the shelf after he got to Hollywood, and he was very unhappy."

While he was waiting for MGM to find another part for him, Olivier used to hang around the Beverly Hills Tennis Club, where Charlie MacArthur and Willy Wyler like to bat tennis balls back and forth when they weren't working.

"One afternoon," recalls Helen Hayes, "Charlie came home and said to me, 'There's this fellow . . . a surly-looking guy I see at the tennis club every day, leaning against the fence and glaring at everybody, like he's got a large chip on his shoulder. He'd be perfect for Heathcliff. I understand he's an actor, but I don't know if he's any good. His name is Laurence something or other.' When I told Charlie that this 'Laurence something or other' had been on the stage with Noel and Katharine Cornell, he was delighted. And the next day he told Goldwyn about him."

Sam was as interested as he could be in hiring a "no-name," but in order to humor MacArthur, he paid him the courtesy of calling Olivier in for an interview.

Surprisingly, Sam thought Olivier perfect too and was seriously considering hiring him, when the actor informed him that he wouldn't take the part unless Sam gave the female lead to his girlfriend, Vivien Leigh. At the time, Vivien Leigh was married to Leigh Holman and Olivier to Jill Esmond, but they were living together, nevertheless, in a townhouse on Christchurch Street in London while they were waiting for divorces.

But Sam was not interested in playing Cupid and told Olivier that two unknowns in the same picture would be too dangerous for him to take a chance on. His nose bent, and fed up with Hollywood anyway because of the way MGM had treated him, Olivier told Sam what he could do with Heathcliff and returned to London.

Two months later Wyler was convinced that Olivier was the only man for the part and made a special trip to London to see if he could persuade him to change his mind. He had dinner with Olivier and Leigh in their town house, but when Olivier kept repeating that he was through with "bloody Hollywood," Wyler decided it was hopeless and made a screen test of Robert Newton instead.

Meanwhile, Olivier was still angling to throw the part of Catherine to his girlfriend, and one night took Wyler to see a film Leigh had just made with Charles Laughton. Wyler liked her in it, and the next time the three were dining together, he offered her the part of Isabella in *Wuthering Heights*.

"I want to play Cathy," insisted Leigh.

Wyler explained that that was out, because the only reason Sam was making *Wuthering Heights* at all was because he needed a vehicle for Merle Oberon.

"Then I don't want any part," she pouted.

Back in his hotel room, Wyler phoned Sam by transatlantic cable and told him Olivier's and Leigh's latest ultimatum.

"You tell her," said Sam, "that she'll never get a better part than Isabella until she has made a name for herself."

"I already did," said Wyler.

Six months later David Selznick cast Vivien Leigh as Scarlett O'Hara in *Gone with the Wind*, proving Sam and Wyler not very good prophets.

Despite his bravado about not taking the part unless Leigh got to play Catherine, Olivier eventually succumbed to Sam's and Wyler's persuasions, proving there is no love quite so large as what an actor "hath for himself."

Again Wyler recommended that the film be shot in its authentic background—the Yorkshire moors—and again Sam refused to let the company get that far out of his reach. However, he lavished money on the production with his customary expansiveness. He sent a camera crew to England to film the Yorkshire moors so they could be matched with what was shot locally; and he literally left no stone unturned in order to transform a piece of desert in Chatsworth in the San Fernando Valley into a perfect simulation of the English countryside, complete with stone walls, crags, and real heather.

It would have been cheaper to go to England. Sam had to import a thousand heather plants from the British Isles, then had trouble with the United States Agriculture Department over whether or not they could be brought in. A little money under the table helped convince Uncle Sam's guardians of vegetable health that Sam's heather would not spread disease among Chatsworth's flora. Sam also paid handsomely to import one thousand panes of hand-blown stained glass to make the interiors authentic for the period.

One concession to Sam's idiosyncrasies was that the period of the story was changed from the late eighteenth century to 1841. This was because Sam didn't like Merle Oberon in the dresses of the earlier period. He wanted to be able to see her beautiful shoulders and the cleavage of her bosom.

In addition to the trouble with the Agriculture Department, Sam had to go up against the animal lovers of the world. The script called for a lot of farmyard livestock. Most of the larger animals, horses, cows, and pigs, were leased from local ranchers, but the ducks and geese were rented from a Hollywood animal trainer, because he was the only one who would guarantee that they wouldn't quack and honk during the barnyard scenes and interfere with dialogue, necessitating costly retakes. The trainer was able to promise this because he had cut the vocal cords of the ducks and geese before reporting to work with them. The ducks and geese were not in any pain and apparently quite happy though unable to quack and honk. But then Sam's publicity department got into the act. It thought it would be cute to release a story saying what a tough time Willy Wyler had keeping the ducks and geese quiet on the set and how he finally had been forced to insist that their vocal cords be snipped.

When this story went out over the wire services, Sam, Wyler, and in fact everybody connected with the production were suddenly inundated with letters from animal fanciers and antivivisection groups, calling them fiends, sadists, and butchers. The SPCA even tried to stop the production. But by then the duck and goose sequences were in the can.

The only other problems during the shooting had to do with the *homo sapiens*. David Niven did not like working under Wyler, because he was too exacting and, in Niven's words, "a sonofabitch to work with." And Merle Oberon was not terribly fond of being made love to by Olivier, because she claimed he spat in her face when he was emoting.

After she complained of this to him in front of the crew several times, Olivier blew up and said a number of uncomplimentary things about her, including references to her pockmarked face—a disfiguration left over from a case of smallpox she'd contracted when she was being raised in India by her British general father when she was a child.

Their bitter exchanges led to both walking off the set and threatening never to return. Wyler persuaded them to return, but they continued to rage at each other inwardly as they made love before the cameras. Strangely enough, these love scenes came off more passionately than many that had been filmed in Hollywood until then.

Olivier continued to overact, however, which Sam became increasingly aware of each time he saw the previous day's rushes. Sam felt not only that he wasn't portraying Heathcliff correctly, but that he was "hamming it up" terribly. Hints to Wyler and the cast that he did not like what he was seeing seemed to go over all their heads. Sam asked for one scene to be reshot three times. When he still didn't like the results he called the cast together and said, "I'm calling the picture off. I don't like the acting."

"Mr. Goldwyn," said Olivier, "I think you're referring to me. May I speak to you in private?"

Sam granted him a private audience in his upstairs office. There he explained to the talented young actor that it wasn't necessary to act like Theda Bara or even Mary Garden in order to emphasize a point. Sincerity and credibility, he pointed out, were more important than flailing his arms, spitting, and thrashing around. "For example," said Sam, "I'm telling you this just like people talk. You understand me without my going through all those histrionics." But as he was explaining this to the actor, Sam kept knocking his head against the wall behind his desk chair, like a battering ram against a stone wall. Olivier got the message, however, and from that day on turned in a first-rate, Academy Award–contending performance.

A romanticist to the end, Sam still wished that the two lovers could be alive instead of dead at the final fade-out, and kept telling everyone so.

After viewing a rough cut, Sam was satisfied with everything, except, you guessed it, the ending, and ranted to Wyler, "I don't want to look at a corpse at the fade-out."

"What can I do?" asked Wyler. "They're dead."

Sam had the perfect solution, he thought. He told Wyler to shoot a new ending showing the dead lovers reunited in heaven.

"That's too hokey," said Wyler, and he went back on suspension.

Perhaps it was for that reason that Sam didn't invite Wyler and his wife, Talli, to the dinner party at his home immediately preceding the première showing of *Wuthering Heights* at the Pantages Theater on April 13, 1939. It was one of Frances's "small but elegant" affairs. Among the guests were Irving Berlin and his wife, Ellen, Norma Shearer, Merle Oberon and her boyfriend, and the first lady of the nation—Eleanor Roosevelt. The Goldwyns had become friendly with Eleanor through her son Jimmy, whom Sam had hired and elevated to the position of vice president of his organization in January 1939. That Sam would rather have a Democrat at the table than Wyler is some indication of Sam's current opinion of his favorite director.

After dinner, Sam put the first lady and Merle Oberon in his limousine and rode with them to the Pantages Theater, while Frances and the rest of the party followed in a second limousine.

There was the usual Hollywood opening pandemonium at the theater when Sam and his distinguished guests pulled up in their limousine and alighted. In front of the theater searchlight beams made geometric patterns in the southern California sky, and mobs of screaming fans had to be held back by policemen. The area under the marquee abounded with newspaper photographers, publicists, other personalities, the major Hollywood columnists—Louella, Hedda, and Sidney Skolsky—and a large army of Secret Service men as Sam strode up to the red-carpeted walk into the theater with Merle Oberon on one arm and the first lady on the other.

It was a wonderful evening for everyone but Wyler. Not only had he not been invited to have dinner and attend the première with the Goldwyns, but when he saw the film that night for the first time since he had made his final cut, he realized that Sam had got his happy ending after all. For there suddenly appeared on the screen, just before the final fade-out, a double exposure shot of Heathcliff and Catherine seen from behind, walking on some billowy white clouds—Sam's idea of heaven.

"It's still there," grins Wyler thirty-five years later. "It's a horrible shot, but nobody seemed to mind very much."

Despite the "horrible shot," *Wuthering Heights* was a resounding success that night, and the following spring it was nominated by the academy in seven categories: best picture, direction, cinematography, supporting Actress, art direction, screenplay, and music. Gregg Toland picked up the Oscar for best cinematography, but *Wuthering Heights* was an also-ran in the other six races.

But even to be nominated was something of a victory when one considers the competition in the 1939 Oscar race—*Gone with the Wind; Goodbye, Mr. Chips; Dark Victory; Ninotchka; Love Affair; Stagecoach;* and *Mr. Smith Goes to Washington.*

Sam's vice president's father, Franklin D. Roosevelt, delivered the keynote address at the awards dinner, and Bob Hope was the emcee. When *Gone with the Wind* walked off with all the major awards, Hope told the gathering, "This year's event has turned into a benefit for David Selznick."

Sam had some consolation, however. *Wuthering Heights* won the New York Film Critics Circle Award for best picture of 1939—which many people consider more of an honor than an Oscar.

20

At Long Last—
His Very Own Studio

A GOLDWYNISM THAT SEEMS to make everybody's list of top ten has one of Sam's associates at the studio coming to him and warning him off a certain property because "it's too caustic for films." To which Sam was supposed to have replied, "To hell with the cost. If it's a good story, I'll make it."

Whether the story is true or a piece of apocrypha coined by a gag man or press agent, the property under discussion could very well have been Lillian Hellman's second hit play, *The Little Foxes*, which opened on Broadway in February 1939 and ran for a full year.

The Little Foxes, the story of a greedy family of southerners who coldly devour the earth, scheming, twisting, and driving their way to material success, was an example of Lillian Hellman's writing at her caustic best. It wasn't a very optimistic glimpse of the human character but Sam didn't care. It was a hit, and he had to have it, and he outbid the rest of Hollywood for the film rights. Moreover he acquired them over the objections of the Hays Office, which didn't care for the subject matter nor the manner in which it ended.

As was his wont, Sam brought Lillian Hellman west to write the screenplay, and a very good one it turned out to be. Sam thought it was an improvement on the original work, and was about to put it into production, when unhappily he was sidetracked for a year and a half by a recurring affliction—partner trouble.

For a number of years—in fact, almost from the day he had become a member-owner of United Artists—Sam had been chafing under what he considered an unfair distribution of the profits of the company. He claimed that Mary Pickford and Doug Fairbanks were not as active as he was, and that Charlie Chaplin had made only one picture, *Modern Times*, in five years.

Sam believed that of all his partners, only Alexander Korda was contributing enough product to justify an equal split of the profits.

As a result, Sam and Korda attempted in 1937 to buy the three-fifths of United Artists owned by Pickford, Fairbanks, and Chaplin for $6 million. But when their effort became bogged down by what seemed like insurmountable legal obstacles raised by Chaplin's lawyers, Sam and Korda gave up the fight.

Over Sam' objections—he was constantly being outvoted at meetings of the board of directors—the other member-owners, under the leadership of United Artists' new president, Maurice Silverstone, voted to form new producing alliances which would allow other independent filmmakers to release through United Artists. Sam believed that United Artists, which had been formed by Chaplin, Fairbanks, Pickford, and D. W. Griffith to distribute their own pictures, was defeating its purpose in accepting less distinguished products. Sam also felt that their actions were jeopardizing his own interests. But no one seemed to care what Sam, the most productive member of the company thought. So in the spring of 1939 he filed a lawsuit against the other member-owners in the New York State Supreme Court, seeking to break his releasing contract with United Artists.

Those close to him at the time believe that Sam, through his legal action, was not trying to get out of his United Artists deal so much as he was hoping to force some concessions from his fellow board members on the matters to which he was objecting so strenuously. But none of the others was willing to compromise on any of the points. In fact the group, headed by Silverstone, fought him tooth and nail, every inch of the way.

Acting for the corporation, Silverstone answered the filing of Sam's suit with a statement disputing all of Goldwyn's claims. "At the last meeting of our stockholders," stated Silverstone, "Mr. Goldwyn demanded a voting trust of which he or his designee would be the sole trustee, thereby giving him control of the company. The remaining stockholders of the company considered this demand ridiculous and they unanimously and promptly turned down Mr. Goldwyn's proposal.

"The stockholders thereupon offered to cancel Mr. Goldwyn's contract and to release him from all further obligations thereunder, if he would turn back to the company his stock interest therein for which he had made no monetary payment. This proposal Mr. Goldwyn turned down.

"In the opinion of this company the suit has no merit whatsoever, and will be vigorously resisted."

Silverstone went on to say that the suit wouldn't have the slightest effect on the company or its operations or on the "important program" of pictures it was releasing or would release in the 1939–40 season. Specifically, he was referring to *Wuthering Heights, The Real Glory,* and *The Westerner*—all Sam's product. Sam couldn't hold those back because he'd already approved contracts with the United Artists exhibitors for their release by the time he filed suit. He had no intention, however, of risking fattening the earnings of the other inactive member-owners by producing any more films that United Artists might legally lay claim to.

So once he filed suit, and United Artists decided to fight it rather than compromise, Sam immediately called off his plans to put *The Little Foxes* before the cameras and literally quit producing films for a year and a half. He didn't stop preparing future productions, however. He had a number of these in the works and at least half a dozen high-priced writers scribbling madly away in their cubbyholes on the lot.

It was during this fallow period that Frances talked Sam into taking her on a trip to Honolulu aboard the *Lurline.* Except for his illnesses, Sam hadn't had a real vacation from work since he was between studios in 1923, and he was all a-bubble with anticipation as he called his staff together in his office one day in the spring of 1939 to inform them of his imminent departure and to exhort them all to continue working hard while he was away.

"There were about ten of us," recalls Sam Marx, "all standing in a semicircle in front of his desk. First he made a little speech about not letting up on our duties while he was away, and then he stood and made his way around the semicircle, saying goodby individually to each one of us. And as he shook each person's hand, he'd say to him or her, 'Bon voyage . . . bon voyage.' "

On board the *Lurline,* which only plied the waters between California and the Hawaiian Islands, Sam and Frances ran into Howard Dietz and his wife in the ship's dining room one night. Delighted to see his former publicity chief on board the same ship, Sam pumped Dietz's hand enthusiastically and said, "Howard, where are *you* going?"

"Sam," Frances reminded him, "the same place you are."

Following his sojourn in the islands, throughout which, according to the Dietzes, he did nothing but play bridge with them "and never once went near the water or even looked at it," Sam returned to the studio and faced the future with new vigor. His legal embroilment with United Artists had not yet been straightened out and wouldn't be settled until February 1941, but in the meantime Sam had a couple of interesting projects still in the drawing-board stage, in addition to *The Little Foxes,* to keep him occupied.

One of these was *Ball of Fire,* a comedy for Gary Cooper and Barbara Stanwyck, which was being written for him by Billy Wilder and Charles Brackett. Brackett and Wilder were probably the hottest new writing team in Hollywood after having written the highly successful travesty on Russian communism, *Ninotchka*, for Greta Garbo at MGM the year before.

For that, their first collaborative effort since Wilder, a German refugee, had come to this country—the talented writing combination had been honored with a nomination for best screenplay in the 1939 Oscar derby. They didn't win—*Gone with the Wind* did—but they got recognition of another kind. Paramount signed them to a long-term contract and their services were suddenly very much in demand by every producer in Hollywood, including Sam.

How Sam happened to get them for a picture was due, in part, to his negligence—or was it stupidity?—in letting *For Whom the Bell Tolls* slip away from him. When Sam didn't buy the Hemingway best seller because it wasn't completed yet, Paramount did and decided to star Gary Cooper in it. But Cooper was under contract to Goldwyn, so Paramount had to come to Sam for a loan-out.

Sam was very cooperative. He said he'd be glad to loan Gary Cooper to them. But in exchange he wanted Bob Hope, who was under contract to Paramount, to appear in a picture for him, plus Brackett and Wilder to write a script.

Paramount agreed and Brackett and Wilder went over to Goldwyn's. There Sam welcomed the team to the lot and ordered them to write a comedy for Gary Cooper that he could do when he returned from his loan-out.

"At the time," says Billy Wilder, "Sam had a lot of scripts already in the works for Mr. Cooper. In fact, there must have been eleven scripts of every story he had bought: *Ashenden*, some other stuff by Somerset Maugham, stuff by whoever you could think of. He always had the same eleven writers who would be working on scripts for Cooper, because Sam always felt that the more cooks the better. Anyway, he gave us all the scripts to see if there was anything we could salvage. Brackett and I studied and studied them, but we didn't like anything. And then I remembered a story I had written in Berlin before I ever came to America, which was the basis for *Ball of Fire*. Of course it didn't quite fit Mr. Gary Cooper yet, but it could be tailored to fit him. So I said to Sam, 'I have an original story. Would you be interested in that?' He said, 'Let me see it.' "

Roughly it was the story of a very dignified college professor, who becomes involved with a stripteaser who disrupts his scholarly calm, nearly gets him fired from the university, and in the end winds up marrying him.

Sam took the story home to study overnight and the next morning called in Wilder and said to him, "I like it . . . Frances likes it. How much do you want for it?"

"Ten thousand dollars," replied Wilder.

"Ten thousand dollars? You're crazy!" exclaimed the same man who had paid $50,000 for *The Cowboy and the Lady*.

"I'm sure you've paid much more than that for material," said Wilder, not at all nonplused by Goldwyn's uncharacteristic niggardliness.

"I'll tell you what I'll do," bargained Sam. "I'll give you seventy-five hundred now, and when it's a hit, I'll give you another twenty-five hundred."

Wilder agreed and he and Brackett went to work on the screenplay.

In February 1941, Sam' long court battle with United Artists came to an end, but it cost him $300,000 to win his release. At that time Sam's one-fifth share of United Artists had a reported book value of around $600,000 exclusive of the real estate on which the studio stood. But to obtain cancellation of his contract Sam had to sell his interest back to the other member-owners for only $300,000.

Because of his litigious nature, Sam probably wouldn't have let them off so cheaply had it not been for a recent Supreme Court ruling which outlawed block booking. This was a practice employed by the major studios whereby they sold their product to exhibitors in large lots rather than on a picture-by-picture basis. Under that setup, the majors could force exhibitors to buy pictures they didn't want by threatening to hold back their good product. As a result of this monopolistic practice, independent producers not aligned with a major distributing outfit such as United Artists were hard pressed to find theaters to show their films.

But now that the Supreme Court had outlawed block booking as a monopolistic practice and was about to start considering cases that would cut the umbilical cord tying theaters to major studios, Sam realized he no longer was dependent on United Artists to get him good rentals on his pictures. If anything, he would probably be able to improve his distribution deal by releasing through Warner Brothers or Fox or RKO.

So feeling that under the new order other releases offered as much, if not more, potential revenue, Sam gave up the fight, sold out to Chaplin, Pickford, Fairbanks, and Korda at their asking price, and made a deal in 1941 to start distributing his forthcoming films through RKO.

That settlement, however, did not bring lasting peace between Sam and his former good friends and partners. Still to be settled was the matter of actual ownership of the eighteen acres of sound stages, office buildings, and other studio equipment situated at the corner of Formosa Avenue and Santa Monica Boulevard and known to the film industry as Goldwyn Studios.

When Sam originally became a member-owner of United Artists, a proportionate or one-fifth share of the land was deeded to him. Since all the partners were active in the beginning, all had the use of the United Artists facilities. But when the others ceased serious production and Sam expanded his operations, he gradually took over the whole lot as his own, erecting new buildings and sound stages as he saw fit, and in general contributing a great deal to the improvement of the property.

For this privilege, Sam had been paying, since 1933, $2,000-a-month rent to the other member-owners for the four-fifths of the property that did not belong to him. This arrangement continued until 1949, and considering he was getting an entire motion picture studio for $2,000 a month, it was actually quite a bargain. But Sam wanted to own the property himself and so, over the years, gradually started buying up the land holdings of whoever was willing to sell to him—namely, Alexander Korda and Joe Schenck. In the beginning, for some strange reason, the property had been divided into eightieths—probably because it was easier to divide up that way. In the interim some of these eightieths had been sold off or given away to children, divorced wives, heirs, and so on. Acquiring the property by bits and pieces was no simple matter, for there were always holdouts. But in January 1949, Sam, according to *Variety*, was finally able to purchase the interest in the studio held by the next-to-last holdout, Lady Sylvia Ashley, Fairbanks's widow. This acquisition made Sam a sole co-owner of the property with Mary Pickford, Sam's bitterest enemy at the United Artists board meetings. Unfortunately it didn't make his holdings quite equal to hers. Over years the wily Miss Pickford had also been picking up fractions of the land holdings of the other member-owners. So by 1949, when Sam concluded his deal with Lady Ashley, Miss Pickford owned 41/80 to Goldwyn Productions' 39/80. This wasn't very much difference, but it was enough to give Mary Pickford a controlling interest and Sam a sour stomach, for he now had to pay *her* $2,000-a-month rent.

Mary Pickford was more than fair about it, however. She offered to sell her share to Sam for $3 million. When he balked at the price, she raised the rent to $30,000 a year for her half. Outraged, Sam went to court to get permission to take down some of the improvements he had made on parts of the studio lot owned by Mary Pickford—namely Stage 8 and the writers' building. Fighting mad herself, Mary Pickford went to court to force Sam to desist from "malicious and wanton destruction of studio property."

Deciding he could win more favors from America's erstwhile sweetheart with honey than he could with subpoenas, Sam devised a plan, inspiration for which was derived from the huge 70,000-cubic-foot natural gas storage tank which stood on Formosa Avenue directly across from the building in which Mary Pickford maintained an office.

Grabbing the phone on his desk, Sam placed a call to his favorite antagonist. "Mary, this is Sam," he began in his most conciliatory tone. "I'm worried about your health."

"I feel fine, Sam."

"But you don't know what could happen to you."

"Are you threatening me, Sam?"

"No, no, it's that gas tank across the street from your building. I'm worried about it."

"What are you worried about?"

"Well, it's full of gas, you know. They tell me it could explode at any minute and you could get hurt. Maybe even killed. I wouldn't want that to happen."

"Why should it, Sam? It's been there for years."

"Mary don't be funny; just sell out to me—and at a reasonable price—before it's too late."

"You know something, Sam, I'm just as worried about you. You could get killed in the explosion, too."

"But I'm older. It doesn't matter what happens to me."

"I don't want to see an old man get killed. Forget it, Sam."

It was a Polish-American stand-off for about six months, but with Sam reminding her at every opportunity of the grave danger she was in. If he read about a great fire or explosion in the newspaper, for instance, he would cut the story out and mail it to her, or if the cost of studio fire insurance was on the rise, he'd remind her of that. But she was just as stubborn as he, and finally the entire question of ownership had to be adjudicated. On February 2, 1949, Sam petitioned the Superior Court of Los Angeles to have the Formosa lot legally partitioned.

However, because of the way the property had been chopped up into fractional parcels over the years, there didn't seem to be any way to divide it equitably—especially when several of Sam's buildings were on Mary Pickford's property, and some of the sound stages he had constructed stood on the dividing lines, and vice versa.

Listening to the two protagonists bickering in court, Judge Paul Nourse immediately recognized that it would take a mediator of King Solomon's talents to please both Mary Pickford and Sam Goldwyn, and he did the only thing possible: he ordered the property be put up for sale at public auction, with the money realized being split between the two parties in accordance with their percentage of ownership.

As a result, the historic studio lot was put up for public auction in the fall of 1949. A large throng of real estate men, fans, and the merely curious attended the auction, but the only ones to submit bids were Sam Goldwyn and Mary Pickford.

"Everyone else," recalls Gordon Sawyer, who had been a witness for Sam's side at the trial, "was afraid to bid."

Sam's side was represented by James Mulvey, the president of the Goldwyn Company, and George Slaff, Goldwyn Studio's attorney, who submitted a closed bid of $1,920,000. This was $20,000 more than what was bid by America's sweetheart. She was in court and cried when the bids were opened and it turned out Sam was the winner.

Forty-one–eightieths of the $1,900,000 went to Mary Pickford and Sam kept the rest and also the studio.

It had been a long, rigorous battle between the two friendly enemies, and it had cost him a fortune in legal bills. But to Sam the fruit of victory was worth all the *tsuris* Mary Pickford and the other member-owners had given him, for at long last the Goldwyn studios belonged to Sam Goldwyn and nobody else. Well, maybe Frances. But no one other than her.

21

If I Promise,
I Promise on Paper

WITH HIS PARTNER PROBLEMS out of the way by the spring of 1941 (except, of course, for his personal real estate hassle with Mary Pickford), and a new distribution deal with RKO about to be finalized, Sam started the wheels rolling to put *The Little Foxes* and *Ball of Fire* into production simultaneously.

Sam wanted to get them both out before the year was over, because he'd released only two films in 1940—*The Westerner*, with Gary Cooper and Walter Brennan, who played Judge Roy Bean, and a remake of *Raffles*, with David Niven and Olivia de Havilland. Both were only mildly successful, with the *New York Times*'s Bosley Crowther calling *The Westerner* "a disappointment." Walter Brennan won an Oscar, however, for best supporting actor—his third since *Come and Get It*, and his second under Willy Wyler's direction.

Because of Wyler's rapport with Lillian Hellman's material, Sam assigned him to direct *The Little Foxes*, and he gave Brackett's and Wilder's superb script of *Ball of Fire* to Howard Hawks. Sam had managed to patch up his differences with Hawks after seeing the grosses of *Come and Get It*. Sam never allowed friendship to interfere with money.

On Broadway Tallulah Bankhead had played the role of Regina Giddens, the scheming, rapacious villain in *The Little Foxes*, and she'd done it superbly. But she wasn't a picture name, and besides, Wyler liked working with Bette Davis, so the role eventually went to her.

How Davis, who was under contract to Warner Brothers, wound up playing Regina again revolves around Gary Cooper, who was turning out to be as valuable to Sam for trading purposes as he was for his acting.

In 1940 Jesse Lasky was at Warner Brothers about to make *Sergeant York*, the story of the Okie who became a Medal of Honor winner in the First World War because of his sharpshooting ability and other heroic qualities.

Lasky, who hadn't been doing too well of late, had purchased the story of Sergeant York with his own funds in kind of do-or-die effort to make a comeback after having been extirpated from Paramount. A number of studios had turned down the property, but Lasky had faith in it and had somehow been able to talk the hard-boiled Jack Warner into financing the production. To be a hit, however, both felt it needed ideal casting in the title role, and who could be more ideal to play a tall, handsome, shy country fellow than Gary Cooper?

Unfortunately Goldwyn had Cooper, and Lasky, knowing how much Sam still hated him, was afraid to approach his ex-brother-in-law for a loanout and procrastinated for days. However, when Warner threatened to call off the production if he couldn't get Cooper, Lasky, a shy man as picture moguls go, had no choice but to beard the fearsome Goldwyn lion. So determined was Lasky to get Cooper that he decided he would even play upon Sam's emotions if he had to and remind him that it was he who was responsible for getting him started in the movie business. Ordinarily Sam didn't fall for sentimentality, but it was worth a gamble. But to Lasky's surprise, this gambit wasn't necessary.

"Sure, you can have Mr. Cooper," said Sam to Lasky's timidly stated request. "I'll be glad to loan him to you, Jesse."

Lasky couldn't get over this wonderful spirit of cooperation that had come over Sam. Little did he know that Sam was actually desperate to loan out Cooper, for this was when he was suing United Artists and not making any pictures anyway. It was costing him a hundred and fifty grand a year to have Cooper on the payroll when he wasn't even using him. But thinking Sam was doing it out of the goodness of his heart, Lasky hurried over to Jack Warner's office to tell him of his windfall. Warner didn't believe Sam would loan him Cooper, and he immediately phoned him back to verify it.

"Jesse just told me you're loaning us Coop," said Warner in tentative tones.

"That's right."

"Well, Sam, I just don't know how to express my appreciation," said Warner.

"Don't express it," shot back Sam. "Just loan me Bette Davis for *The Little Foxes.*"

But Warner didn't loan Bette Davis to anybody, especially not to Sam Goldwyn. Davis was Warner Brothers' biggest star, and he wasn't going to risk having Sam steal her from him, the way he had lured Cooper away from Paramount. The deal was off—until Hal Wallis, who was production head of Warner Brothers at the time, realized there wasn't anybody else in town who could play Sergeant York. Eventually he persuaded Warner to change his mind about loaning out Davis, or else there'd be no Sergeant York.

But Bette Davis herself would first have something to say about the exchange. For she had her own little ax to grind with Sam—dating clear back to 1929, when he was looking for an actress to play opposite Ronald Colman in his original version of *Raffles*. At the time, Bette Davis was a complete unknown. But she'd made a screen test, which Sam's casting director ran for him one afternoon at the behest of her agent. After seeing it, Sam jumped out of his chair and angrily shouted, "What are you guys trying to do to me?" He'd hated her pop-eyed looks, as well as her clipped way of speaking.

Sam's words had somehow got back to the struggling actress, who had vowed that if she ever had the opportunity, she really would *do* something to Sam. There couldn't be a better time than this. She asked what in 1941 was an unheard-of price for her services—$385,000. What's more, to get back at Warner for loaning her to Goldwyn, she insisted on keeping the entire sum herself. In those days the standard practice was if the studio holding the contract could get more for the loan-out than it was paying the employee, it was perfectly all right to pocket the difference—a form of slavery not unlike baseball's reserve clause.

Again Sam hollered, "What are they trying to do to me?" but in the end he paid the full $385,000.

But can an actress be really happy making only $40,000 a week for eight or nine weeks' work? Some can; Bette Davis could not. From the first day of shooting until she was back at Warner Brothers, Bette Davis was angry with Willy Wyler.

"She thought I was making her play the part like Tallulah Bankhead," recalls Willy Wyler. "I was not. It was the story of this woman who was greedy and high handed, but a woman of great poise, great charm, great wit. And that's the way Tallulah had played it on the stage. But Bette Davis was playing it all like a villain because she had been playing bitches and parts like that—this is what made her at Warner Brothers—*Jezebel* and things like that, but she was playing Regina with no shading . . . all the villainy and greediness of the part but not enough of the charm and wit and humor and sexiness of this woman. So, anyway, she thought when I tried to correct her that I was trying to make her imitate Tallulah Bankhead, which I was not. And she was also trying to make herself look older because she had a daughter of nineteen in the story who was played by Teresa Wright. And it's true . . . perhaps she wasn't quite old enough but it wasn't necessary to play a character part either. I wanted her to be more attractive, more sexy. This is often the case with actors and actresses. They don't like to play their age. They don't mind playing ten years older or younger but not their exact age."

As the picture progressed, the fighting between Wyler and Davis over their differing interpretations of the part intensified. "I don't expect actors to be simply obedient . . . like robots," states Wyler. "I can help them, but I can't give the performance. They've got to give it. But I do expect my general direction of how a scene should be played to be followed. And while Bette and I had gotten along marvelously in two previous pictures that we had made—*Jezebel* and *The Letter*—we had terrible disagreements over the way we saw Regina, so things were kind of cool between us. Goldwyn stuck up for me, which is the smart thing for a producer to do . . . because actors and actresses only look at their own part. They don't look at the overall picture. So somebody has to equalize things—either the director or the producer or both, if it takes two to get a performer to come around."

But even with Wyler and Sam both ganging up on her, Bette Davis would not bow to their demands. The quarrels about the part and her looks were endless. As the shooting continued into the uncomfortably warm days of summer, nerves became raw and normally placid tempers flared.

The real fireworks started when Los Angeles was suddenly hit by a week of ninety- and one-hundred-degree temperatures brought on by Santa Ana desert winds. With no warning Bette Davis appeared on the set one morning with calcimine smeared all over her face.

"What's that for?" asked Wyler.

"It's to make me look older," said Davis.

"You look like a clown," said Wyler. "Take it off."

She not only took it off, she ran away from the studio and disappeared for three days. When they found her, she was hiding out in her beach house at Laguna Beach, and she said she was not coming back.

With Bette Davis a pronouncement like that could be more than an idle threat made by an actress who'd simply had her feelings hurt. Hollywood rumor mills were saying that *The Little Foxes* would be another one of those pictures that Sam Goldwyn was going to have to start over.

But Sam wound up having the last word. In his contract with the actress was a little clause she hadn't noticed. The clause simply said that if Bette Davis failed to complete the picture for any reason other than ill health, that she was liable for the entire cost of the production. After Sam's lawyers pointed this out to her, Bette Davis was back on the set the next day, and without the calcimine on her face. But she continued to fight Wyler on the interpretation of the part and even boasted about it in her autobiography when she wrote, "It took courage to play her the way I did, in the face of such opposition."

Although the picture was a success when it opened at Radio City Music Hall on August 21, 1941, most of the critics tended to agree with Wyler that her performance was "much too black and white." Commenting upon it in the *New York Times*, Bosley Crowther wrote of Bette Davis's acting in *The Little Foxes:*

> She performs queer contortions, like a nautch dancer in a Hindu temple, and generally comports herself as though she were balancing an Academy "Oscar" on her high coiffed head. But the role calls for heavy theatrics, being just a cut above "ten-twent-thirt" melodrama . . . Miss Davis is all right as Regina, but *The Little Foxes* will not increase your admiration for mankind. It is cold and cynical. But it is a very exciting picture to watch in a comfortably objective way, especially if you enjoy expert stabbing in the back.

Despite Wyler's troubles with Bette Davis and vice versa, *The Little Foxes* was a smashing box-office success and wound up receiving nine Oscar nominations: best picture, best direction, best actress, best art direction, best film editing, best dramatic score, best screenplay, and two for best supporting actress (Teresa Wright, in her first movie role, and Patricia Collinge). Very few films have ever received more than nine nominations—certainly an indication of the overall high quality of *The Little Foxes*—yet in the final balloting it failed to come up with a single Oscar.

The filming of *Ball of Fire* was marked by no such histrionics as anyone walking off the set or production being delayed while producer, director, and lawyers tried to placate a temperamental star. However, it was the picture responsible for beginning Billy Wilder's legendary career as a director. He didn't direct *Ball of Fire*, but when he expressed an interest in becoming a director, Sam, out of gratitude for the good script he and Brackett had written, gave him permission to sit on the set beside Howard Hawks throughout the entire filming and learn the business through personal observation and by asking the old pro all the questions he wanted.

Hawks must have been as good a teacher as Wilder was a pupil. From there, Wilder went on to write and direct such classics as *The Lost Weekend*, *The Apartment*, *Some Like It Hot*, *Sunset Boulevard*, *The Seven Year Itch*, and many others. And at last count he had a total of six Oscars tucked away in a closet in his apartment. It's such an impressive array of gold statuary, in fact, that the modest Mr. Wilder refuses to put them on display in his home for fear his guests will think he's a showoff. (Modesty like that is unusual in Hollywood. Most Academy Award winners keep their Oscars either in glass display cases or on their mantels. And one comedian of note keeps his Oscar on the night stand next to his bed, along with a large framed photograph of himself.)

Around the time that *Ball of Fire* was being released, a girl named Betty Rowland, who billed herself as "The Ball of Fire," was the star attraction at the Burbank Theater, Los Angeles's leading burlesque house. Sam's ever-alert publicity department, headed at the time by Irving Fein, saw a natural tie-in for news breaks. Fein hired a half dozen of the most beautiful extras in town, clad them as scantily as the times would allow, and had them picket the Goldwyn lot. Posing as stripteasers, they walked up and down Formosa Avenue and Santa Monica Boulevard carrying signs which read, "Goldwyn Unfair to Stripteasers," "Why Don't You Use Real Strip-teasers?" and so on.

In addition, Irving Fein got the further inspiration to cook up a phony lawsuit with Betty Rowland, who would bring action against Sam for usurping her trade name, Ball of Fire.

"It'll get us a million dollars' worth of headlines," Fein explained to Sam. "All we'll have to pay is for the lawyers and her court expenses."

Sam, of course, was ecstatic over the idea and ordered him to get the legal machinery rolling immediately. Fein, who was friendly with Betty Rowland's press agent, first checked out the idea with his friend and after getting his approval and a promise of cooperation, he phoned the bump-and-grind girl and explained the plot to her, including giving her assurances that Goldwyn would foot all the legal bills.

"Are you kidding, buddy?" snapped Rowland. "You're too late."

"What do you mean?"

"My lawyers already filed suit this morning. I mean for real, honey."

Sam never believed it wasn't Irving Fein's fault that he actually got sued by Betty Rowland for half a million dollars in damages. Of course, Sam settled for a great deal less than that, but Fein was never really in his boss's favor again.

As it turned out, *Ball of Fire* didn't need the help of such press-agent gim-mickry to be a success. The reviews were excellent when it was released in the fall of 1941 (the *New York Times* called it "a delight"), business boomed, and Sam had himself another hit. The picture was also nominated for three Academy Awards: best original story (Billy Wilder), best actress (Barbara Stanwyck), and best musical score (Al Newman). Those three, plus nine for *The Little Foxes*, gave the Goldwyn camp a total of twelve nominations at that year's ceremonies. Certainly the law of averages should have been on Sam's side, but once again he didn't have enough clout to beat the voting bloc of the majors. Darryl Zanuck's *How Green Was My Valley* took most of the honors. But Sam had reason to be proud, anyway. *Ball of Fire* proved he could make a successful picture not based on a proven hit in another me-dium.

For that reason alone, Billy Wilder felt he was entitled to receive the $2,500 bonus Sam had promised him when he made the deal for his origi-nal story. So one morning after the picture was in release, Wilder phoned

Sam, congratulated him on the smash reviews and the business *Ball of Fire* was doing, and said, "What about the money?"

"What money?" asked Sam, totally surprised.

"Don't you remember?" said Wilder. "You promised to give me an extra twenty-five hundred if it was a hit."

"I don't remember any such thing," said Sam.

"You promised," said Wilder. "Twenty-five hundred."

"If I promise, I promise on paper," exclaimed Sam indignantly.

"All right, Mr. Goldwyn, let's forget about it," said Wilder angrily, and he hung up.

A few minutes later the phone in Wilder's office rang, and it was Sam on the wire again. "Listen," said Sam, "I just talked to Frances. She doesn't remember either."

"Forget about it . . . forget about it!" said Wilder. "Let's just pretend we never met." And he again hung up on the Great Goldwyn.

An hour went by, and Sam phoned Wilder a third time. "This is Goldwyn," he said. "I don't want anybody to think I'm a sonofabitch. I don't remember it, but if you say so, come on over and pick up the two thousand!"

22

I Love the Ground I Walk On

PERHAPS BECAUSE THE REST of the world was in turmoil and America's entry into the war seemed imminent and the future uncertain, Sam had only one picture in production when the bombs fell on Pearl Harbor on that infamous Sunday in December 1941. The picture turned out to be one of Sam's best—*The Pride of the Yankees,* based on a story by Paul Gallico about Lou Gehrig, the Yankees' great first baseman.

It was a strange time for anyone to be making a picture about such a frivolous pursuit as baseball. Even without a war just over the horizon, baseball pictures were supposed to be "poison" at the box office, because the women of America, who constituted more than half the audience, didn't understand the sport, didn't like pictures about it, and usually wouldn't walk around the corner to see one. They were also known to wield considerable influence over their husbands' and boyfriends' choices of movies. Besides that, the entire overseas market was lost because few people over there— man or woman—knew anything about baseball or its idols.

But to Sam, *The Pride of the Yankees* was more than just a baseball picture. It was the story of a very courageous American battling heroically, and silently, against a crippling, death-dealing disease. And because Babe Ruth also figured importantly in the story, *The Pride of the Yankees* was a great piece of Americana and a plug for the American character and way of life. The latter, more than anything, was what prevented Sam from abandoning the picture after a number of good writers had worked on it in 1940 and 1941 and had come up with one unshootable script after another.

Despite Sam's seeming obsession with money and making movies, he also had a great interest in America and its opportunities and was extremely appreciative of what it had done for him. Over and over Sam had said, "I resent anyone who attacks the ideology we live under—democracy. Believe me, I love the ground I walk on. Just look what it has done for me." A

Goldwynism in its purest form, but who could quarrel with the thought? Sam loved America and was willing to go to any lengths to plug it. For that reason it was important to Sam that the rest of the world see America in the right light. Moreover, he deeply resented any story that would give America or its people a bad image. And although he wasn't a religious man, or particularly chauvinistic about Zionism or his Jewish heritage, he was extremely sensitive about what people said, thought, and wrote about American Jewry.

For example, before *What Makes Sammy Run* was published in 1941, galleys of it circulated through all the studios, as do most books from important publishers. Most Jews in Hollywood who read it were shocked because of Budd Schulberg's vicious portrayal of Sammy Glick—a pushy Jewish boy from Manhattan who double-crosses his way from the ghetto to the top of the motion picture business. Despite the usual disclaimer that Sammy Glick wasn't based on any real person, living or dead, it was a composite of several well-known people in Hollywood—with Schulberg taking the worst characteristics of each and lumping them together to form one repellent Jewish monster.

But whether the character was real or fictional, *What Makes Sammy Run* was not a pretty picture of either the Jews or the motion picture business, and everybody thought that by publishing it, Schulberg was doing a disservice to the Jews. Particularly upsetting to them was that the book was coming out at a time when Hitler was persecuting Jews and doing his best to convince the world that he was justified in killing them by the millions.

In addition to the Jews being outraged, Hollywood Gentiles weren't too happy about the book either. They felt that it was an unfair picture of the industry and that Schulberg was merely trying to get back at Hollywood for what he felt Hollywood had done to his father, B. P. Schulberg, a former head of Paramount who was kicked out in a change of ownership and died broke and brokenhearted.

As a result, most people in Hollywood felt and wished that Budd Schulberg hadn't written the book at all. But Sam Goldwyn didn't just "feel" it or complain about it on the Hollywood cocktail party circuit. After he read the galleys, he phoned Schulberg and actually offered him $200,000 not to publish the book.

"Why?" asked Schulberg.

"Because you are double-crossing the Jews," said Sam, going on to explain how by publishing *What Makes Sammy Run* he would be supplying additional fuel to the fires of anti-Semitism burning all over Germany and eastern Europe.

As any writer would, Schulberg defended his position by saying his book mirrored Hollywood life as it actually was, that he knew many "Sammys," and that people like that ought to be exposed, whether they be Jew or

Gentile. He further pointed out that to suppress his book would constitute censorship, which was not good in a free society.

"I'll give you three hundred thousand not to publish it," offered Sam. "Come on over now and I'll write you a check for it."

Schulberg refused to be bought off, and the book became an international best seller. A few months after it made all the top-ten lists, Edward R. Murrow, while interviewing Adolf Hitler in his office, asked him if he didn't think his persecution of the Jews was unfair.

Hitler smiled and said, "You think I'm the only one who doesn't like them. Here's a Jewish writer who feels the same way about his people." And he took a copy of *What Makes Sammy Run* from his desk and held it up for Murrow to see.

Sam Goldwyn was never in favor of censorship per se. All his life he spoke out against it. But if somebody showed him—as he tried to show Schulberg—that a particular story or subject matter could be damaging to a group or a good cause, he would abandon it.

Shortly before the Schulberg incident, Sam had been planning to make a picture called *Thirteen Go Flying*, which was based on an Atlantic Ocean crash in 1939 of a British Imperial Airways flying boat on its way from Bermuda to New York City. A few passengers survived to tell a heroic tale of twelve days on a raft in the stormy Atlantic with all the attendant hardships—hunger, thirst, and having to fight off hungry sharks with paddles and bare fists.

Sam was very excited about the possibilities of filming such a real-life saga, purchased the rights, and had writers already at work on the screenplay when he received a call one day from George Messersmith of the United States State Department. Messersmith told Sam that he was calling at the request of Pan American Airways, which was about to inaugurate transatlantic clipper service between the United States and Great Britain. Pan Am felt that because people were scared enough already of flying across water, a motion picture exploiting a crash such as the one that Imperial Airways suffered on their Bermuda run would be harmful to the transatlantic service they were about to institute.

Sam mulled it over for a couple of days, came to the same conclusion, and issued a statement to the "trades" announcing the cancellation of the picture.

"I don't want to place any hindrance in the path of American aviation's fine progress," he explained.

The story of Lou Gehrig—with Gary Cooper in the lead—could not possibly hurt anybody, and in addition it had a great statement to make about the character of the American sportsman while at the same time being full of that substance that usually could be counted upon to pull people into the box office—heart with a capital *H*.

One thing for sure: Sam's decision to film the life of Lou Gehrig had nothing to do with his being a baseball fan. Sam had been to only a couple of baseball games in his lifetime and barely knew the difference between a catcher's mask and a fielder's glove. What's more, his reading of the final draft screenplay by Herman Mankiewicz and Jo Swerling did nothing to further Sam's understanding of the great American pastime, judging by the following anecdote.

As part of the ballyhoo for the picture, Irving Fein suggested to Sam that he use Gehrig's actual teammates in the baseball sequences. Babe Ruth and Bill Dickey, the Yankees' great catcher, had already been set to play themselves in the film. Sam agreed and sent out wires to the rest of the Yankees, offering them $500, plus travel and hotel expenses for themselves and their wives for a week's stay in Hollywood.

All the players, including Babe Dahlgren, who took over at first base after Gehrig retired, wired Sam their acceptances, except the third baseman, Red Rolfe.

Rolfe, who had a good job with an automobile agency in Miami in the off-season, wired back that he wanted $1,500 to come west. He said it wouldn't pay him to leave his work for anything less than that.

Sam hit the ceiling. "Highway robbery," he yelled. "A third baseman wanting fifteen hundred dollars! Doesn't he know I got a *first* baseman for only five hundred?"

While he was reading the script, Sam came across the word *dugout* and had to have its meaning explained to him. Several weeks later, Sam, playing host to the visiting baseball greats at a studio luncheon, found himself sitting between Bill Dickey and his wife.

"How do you like the script?" asked Sam.

"I haven't read it yet," confessed the catcher. Whereupon Sam started to fill him in on the story, especially his part. "We fade in on you for the first time in the dugout," began Sam.

Unfamiliar with movie lingo, Dickey seemed puzzled. Sam misinterpreted his confusion. "I'll tell you what a dugout is," explained Sam. And while everybody at the table listened in amazement, Sam launched into a detailed description of a baseball dugout to a fellow who had probably spent more time in one than Sam spent screaming at his writers.

From the beginning, there had never been any doubt that Gary Cooper would play the role of Lou Gehrig. That role had been sent down from heaven for the shy man from Montana. There was only one thing wrong. God apparently didn't know that Gehrig was a southpaw and that Cooper was right-handed. When Cooper tried to swing a bat left-handed, he looked more like Teresa Wright, who was playing Mrs. Gehrig, than he did her husband. The director, Sam Wood, realized they could get away with using a southpaw double in the longer shots, but in the close-ups, Cooper had to bat for himself.

For a moment it looked as if the picture would either have to be called off, or Cooper would have to bat right-handed and risk incurring the jibes and perhaps the wrath of true baseball fans. But at the height of their quandary William Cameron Menzies, Goldwyn's art director, came up with a very simple solution: let Cooper swing the bat right-handed and print the film backward.

Which is what they ended up doing, and nobody who wasn't at the filming of the baseball sequences knew the difference. With the possible exception of the *New York Times*'s Bosley Crowther, who said of Cooper's baseball playing, "he resembles Gehrig around the eyes, but he doesn't look too good slamming or scooping them up. And when he's in there snagging the hot ones, he isn't likely to be mistaken for the real thing." However, he liked the picture in general, writing:

> *The Pride of the Yankees* is the life of a shy and earnest young fellow who loved his mother, worked hard to get ahead and then at the height of his glory was touched by the finger of death.
> As a baseball picture—in which for some reason Veloz and Yolanda dance—it is not anything to raise the blood pressure. But as a simple moving story, with an ironic heart tug at the end, it is a fitting memorial to the real Lou.

Sam had been right in making *The Pride of the Yankees* more the story of Lou Gehrig the man than of Lou Gehrig the baseball player. For when it was released in July 1942, it was an unqualified success throughout the nation, thereby disproving the long-standing Hollywood maxim that all baseball pictures are box-office "poison," even if Bosley Crowther didn't believe it was a genuine picture about baseball.

In general the movie business boomed during the war years. In fact, it was the last period of genuine prosperity, with all the majors going full blast, that Hollywood (in terms of what it once was in its halcyon days) would ever know. Perhaps the people on the home front were simply trying to forget the loss of Corregidor and the Philippine Islands and the horrible bloodshed that was taking place on Guadalcanal. Despite the wartime shortages, the dim-out, gasoline rationing, and the draft, great pictures were being made and people were flocking to them. Among the outstanding ones were *Casablanca*, *Going My Way*, and *Mrs. Miniver*, which Willy Wyler directed on loan-out to MGM and which was his last Hollywood assignment until the war ended.

Wyler won his first Oscar for *Mrs. Miniver,* which opened at the Radio City Music Hall in June 1942, and in a ten-week stand broke a house record by playing to 1,499,891 people. The critics didn't spare their adjectives either, with Bosley Crowther writing, "Perhaps it's too soon to call this one of the greatest motion pictures ever made. But certainly it is the finest film yet made about the present war and a most exalting tribute to the British."

As a rule, Sam avoided topical pictures, but the figures on *Mrs. Miniver*— not to mention Wyler's Oscar—must have impressed him. Otherwise he might never have let Lillian Hellman talk him into making *The North Star,* one of his more spectacular catastrophes.

The North Star was an original Hellman had written about a group of Russian villagers as they held off the German armies invading their land in the winter of 1941. Like most of the pre–World War II liberals, Lillian Hellman had been an enthusiastic supporter of the Soviet Union. She'd been forced to curb her enthusiasm somewhat when Stalin and Hitler formed their unholy alliance. But once Hitler double-crossed Stalin, putting the Russians more or less back on the side of the Allies, Hellman again became their firm booster. She even wangled an assignment in Moscow for herself as a war correspondent for one of the newspaper wire services. It was during her brief stay in Russia that she got the inspiration for *The North Star,* and upon her return to New York in the summer of 1942 she imparted her enthusiasm for doing a picture based on her idea to Willy Wyler, who was in New York for the opening of *Mrs. Miniver.* The idea appealed to Wyler, and the two of them took on Sam Goldwyn by long-distance phone to try to persuade him to make a picture about the Russians—not one of his favorite peoples in view of his treatment at their hands when he was a youngster.

Their enthusiasm was so contagious that Sam found himself saying yes to the project—and also the idea of filming it in Russia—before he'd even seen a story line.

The next day Hellman and Wyler flew to Washington to persuade the Soviet ambassador, Maxim Litvinov, to grant Goldwyn permission to shoot the picture in Russia. To Hellman, this was not so unfeasible a request as it might seem on first examination. She had previously met Litvinov and "knew and liked him," she wrote in her memoirs. "But Litvinov said our plan was impossible, wouldn't work without full cooperation from the Russian government, and that they were too hard pressed to give it."

However, Litvinov promised to take it up with Vyacheslav Molotov, Stalin's foreign secretary, when he arrived in Washington for consultations with President Roosevelt at the end of the week. To everyone's great surprise, Molotov, when apprised of the Goldwyn project, liked the idea of *The North Star* and said his government would guarantee a Russian bomber, a camera crew, and anything else that was needed.

While Lillian Hellman was writing the screenplay, the United States Signal Corps was working on some of Hollywood's most talented filmmakers to get them to join the armed forces. With eight million draftees being called up, there was a desperate need for training and indoctrination films—and obviously the men who could make them best were those whose livelihood was films.

Commissions were being handed out to almost anyone who had two good eyes, was between the ages of twenty-one and death, and who'd worked in the studios. But the most sought after were the filmmakers with proven reputations and big names. By the end of 1942, a veritable *Who's Who* of Hollywood had impressive titles in front of their names: Colonel Darryl Zanuck, Major Frank Capra, Lieutenant James Stewart, Captain John Huston, Captain Robert Riskin, Lieutenant Norman Krasna, Lieutenant Jerry Chodorov, Colonel Sy Bartlett, Private Clark Gable, Private Mickey Rooney, and Chief Petty Officer Rudy Vallee, among a great many others.

Being in his early forties at the time, Wyler was over the draft age, but like a great many others wanted to do his bit for the war effort, and he joined the army air force with the rank of major. Soon after that he was sent to England, where his first assignment was to make a documentary about the Eighth Army Air Force. By early 1943 he was in charge of a combat air force camera crew, flying regular missions over Germany and central Europe in Flying Fortresses. Under his last contract, Wyler still owed Sam another picture, but that obligation would have to wait until he returned from the war, if he returned.

Meanwhile, back on Formosa Avenue Sam was coping with a problem many bosses were having during the war—that of losing his best personnel to the armed forces. In addition to Wyler, the army drafted Sam's publicity chief, Irving Fein, and the navy grabbed his right-hand man, Collier Young.

Under the draft act all employers were required by law to take back their former employees when they returned from the service, but according to both Irving Fein and Collier Young, Sam was always a wee bit reluctant to commit himself to this beforehand.

On the day Collier Young was going into the navy as a lieutenant (j.g.), Sam threw a farewell luncheon for him in his private dining room on the Goldwyn lot. Among others present was Lillian Hellman, who was in Hollywood polishing her script of *The North Star*.

At the finish of the meal, Sam stood up and made a very warm, touching speech about how much he would miss working with Young, how he would worry about his safety, and he capped it off by thanking him for a job well done.

Young, in turn, rose to his feet and said a few of the usual clichés in reply. He then paused while he tried to think of a fitting way to get off.

Suddenly Lillian Hellman's voice broke the silence. "Why don't you cut out the bullshit, Collier, and ask him if he's going to give you your job back after the war?" All eyes turned expectantly to Sam, who sat staring straight ahead in stony silence. After the laughter died down, Sam mumbled something about it being "time for my nap" and left the room.

Irving Fein reports that Sam gave him the same kind of reassurances on the day he left for the army. It wasn't that Sam didn't like these men, or appreciate what they were doing for him and the rest of the country. But he was a realist and well aware that he would have to fill the void left by them with somebody else. And supposing he liked that somebody better?

There was no likelihood, however, that he wouldn't want Willy Wyler back—not after his experience with Lewis Milestone, the director he chose to replace him with on *The North Star*.

In addition to the fact that Milestone had a good track record in Hollywood (*All Quiet on the Western Front, The Front Page, Rain*), Sam picked him because he was a Russian and therefore would have a great feel for the story and its characters. Milestone agreed but was hesitant about working for Sam because he knew that one of Sam's idiosyncrasies was that he liked writers to write and directors to direct, and the less contact between the two the better. Milestone didn't feel he could do his best work that way, because he was the kind of director who liked to sit down with the writer and work on the script with him or her in its final preparatory stages. But because he was a great admirer of Lillian Hellman's talent, he accepted the assignment, in spite of his reservations. When he was alone with Hellman, however, he confided in her that he expected to have much to contribute to the script that would be helpful.

Hellman wasn't crazy about collaborators, even ones as talented as Milestone, and she finessed his move with a little artful white lying. "The only way to work with Sam," she said, "and I know after these many times out, is to discuss your ideas for changes on the phone with me. Sam doesn't have to know. I'll get the idea to Sam. If *you* do it, there'll just be bedlam."

Milestone found much to complain about in the script, which oversentimentalized the Russians and had Russian guerrillas performing such heroic feats as destroying Nazis with their bare hands. After he finished reading it and jotting down his suggestions in the margin of the script, which he had delivered to her by messenger, he phoned Hellman and went over the points with her. She listened politely, and after he hung up, Milestone had the feeling that she would incorporate his proposed changes in the script. A couple of days later Sam phoned Milestone in a rage.

"Lillian has called up," he screamed. "She was in tears. She says you want to change her whole script."

Milestone explained that (a) he didn't want to change her *whole* script, just the unbelievable portions, and (b) he and Lillian had formulated this working agreement beforehand.

"Why did you make an agreement like that?" raged Sam.

"To keep you the hell out of things," said Milestone, who felt he had been double-crossed by Hellman, and by now didn't care who he hurt.

Despite this jab, Sam kept Milestone on the picture—after all, there was a manpower shortage and directors of Milestone's talent weren't easy to get—but after that the relations between the three of them—Hellman, Milestone, and Goldwyn—went steadily downhill. Feelings were especially rancorous between Hellman and Milestone, who refused to have any further contact with her at all. There came a time, however, when necessity required a meeting between the three of them to discuss "story." Sam invited the two of them to dinner at his house, with a meeting scheduled afterward. But, upon learning Hellman would be there, Milestone refused to accept.

"You have a contract," said Sam.

"There's nothing in it that says I have to have dinner with you," said Milestone.

"You're right," agreed Sam. "Come *after* dinner for the discussion."

Milestone arrived in time for coffee, and the moment he did, Lillian Hellman pulled out the script he'd marked up and started defending her story point by point. To Milestone's astonishment, Sam sided with the director on the changes he wanted. This led to an argument so violent between Sam and his favorite writer that Milestone couldn't stomach any more of it and quickly departed, leaving the two of them to fight it out. And fight they did. "It was a horrifying fight," recalls Hellman, who refused to do any more work on the script and returned to New York.

It was a permanent estrangement. Hellman bought back her contract with Goldwyn and never worked for him again. She even went so far as to sell her next hit play, *Watch on the Rhine*, to Warner Brothers.

Sam replaced her with Eddie Chodorov, who labored in vain to make something worthwhile of *The North Star*. But it remained an incurably sick script, although when Sam finally gave the green light to shoot it, he was convinced it would make a great picture and would do much to help the war effort.

Because of the exigencies of the war, *The North Star* finally ended up having to be filmed at the corner of Santa Monica Boulevard and Formosa Avenue instead of on the Russian steppes. However, before that decision was made, Sam had sent a copy of the script to the Russian ambassador in Washington to get his general approval.

A day or two later Goldie Arthur answered the phone in the Goldwyn office and found herself talking with a gentleman with a very thick Russian accent who identified himself as Maxim Litvinov, the Russian ambassador.

Running into Sam's office, Goldie said, "Mr. Goldwyn, it's Mr. Litvinov on the phone and he sounds very angry."

Afraid there was going to be trouble over the script, Sam grabbed the receiver with a trembling hand and put it to his ear. "Hello, Mr. Litvinov," said Sam timidly. "Did you read the script?"

"I have read it, Mr. Goldwyn," said Litvinov, "and I have a request to make of you. I have a brother who is an actor, and I would like you should give him a job in your picture." Evidently even Russian dignitaries pull that sort of thing.

Fortunately, because of the decision not to shoot the picture in Russia, Sam never had to say either yes or no to the ambassador's request. But perhaps a few real Russians in the cast might have added to the credibility of the final product. The leading roles were played by Anne Baxter, Dana Andrews, Walter Huston, Walter Brennan, Farley Granger, and Ann Harding—all good actors but not exactly Russian prototypes. What the cast could have used were a few Akim Tamiroffs and Gregory Ratoffs.

When the picture was shot and assembled, Sam called his staff together for a running in his projection room and invited Goldie Arthur to see it too.

Afterward, he polled each one individually for his or her opinion. Although no one liked it very much, there wasn't a person there courageous enough to say no for fear of losing his or her job. Each was properly deferential in his or her reply, finding some point, usually minor, to rave about. Goldie at first was going to tell her boss the truth, but she, too, chickened out when it came her turn, and she ended up saying, "Mr. Goldwyn, it's a very powerful picture."

Later, when she was alone with Sam, he said to her, "Tell me, Goldie, what did you really think of it? Don't try to spare my feelings."

"All right, then, Mr. Goldwyn. I didn't like it at all."

"What didn't you like about it?" asked Sam.

"I didn't feel I knew any of the people," explained Goldie. "And when you don't know the people, it's hard to care about them."

"What about when the little girl got killed?" asked Sam. "Weren't you moved?"

"Yes, that was the only time."

"What about when the truck overturned and the whole truckload of little girls was killed?" persisted Sam.

"That didn't touch me at all," said Goldie, "because I didn't know any of them."

Sam thought it over, then said, "If I wanted your opinion, I would have asked for it."

Because it was a "Goldwyn picture," written by Lillian Hellman, *The*

North Star created quite a lot of interest in its preparation stages, and a number of Hollywoodites attended the preview to see if it lived up to its advance publicity. It did not. In fact, the audience was quite indifferent to the plight of the beleaguered Russians and even laughed in a few places. Sam rationalized it as "nervous laughter" brought on by the tenseness of the war sequences, and at the studio the next morning he raved about it to one of the writers working on the Bob Hope picture he was preparing.

"It's the greatest picture I ever made," he said. "The story's great, the directing's great, the acting's great."

"I saw it, Mr. Goldwyn," said the writer. "I went to the preview."

"It can be fixed," snapped Sam.

Sam re-edited the picture and shortened it. By then he was convinced it was one of his best creations—not only from an entertainment viewpoint but because of its anti-Nazi propaganda—and he called his publicity staff together for a pep talk.

"I don't care anything about box office on this picture," he said. "I don't care how much money it makes. I just want every man, woman, and child in America to see it."

Perhaps out of respect for Lillian Hellman and the good intentions of Sam Goldwyn, Bosley Crowther in the *New York Times* did not attack *The North Star* when it was released in November 1943 with as much venom as he probably would have had the story been about pearl diving in Samoa. He wrote:

> The story of Russia's recent ordeal has been variously reported in many mediums. And now comes a picture which images that conflict in a way intended to state its human meanings without any political probing at all. . . . *The North Star* has so much in it that is moving and triumphant that its sometime departures from reality may be generally overlooked.

It was not overlooked by audiences, however. And, unfortunately for Sam, every man, woman, and child in America did not see *The North Star*.

About a year after its release, Sam was sitting at his desk going over the latest figures on *The North Star* when Goldie Arthur entered to fill his water pitcher.

"You know something, Goldie?" said Sam, looking up at her sheepishly. "I think you were right. *North Star* is a lousy picture."

Possibly because there was a war on and a need for humor to take the home front's mind off the grimness of the casualty lists, Sam's latest Goldwynisms—"I love the ground I walk on" and "I don't care how much money this picture makes, I just want every man, woman, and child in

America to see it"—were getting exceptionally wide circulation throughout the nation's press.

For some reason, his father's Goldwynisms were a source of extreme embarrassment to the serious-minded Samuel Goldwyn, Jr., who by 1943 was seventeen years old and a freshman at the University of Virginia. Shortly after his enrollment there, Sam junior wrote his father complaining that all the students were kidding him about his old man's unorthodox use of the English language, and he signed off by asking, "Can't you please do something about it, Pop?"

Coincidentally, Sam was beginning to feel the same way about Goldwynisms and would forever after. Prior to Sam junior's complaint, Sam *père* had been willing to look on the birth of each new Goldwynism with a certain amount of forbearance—almost like a man who's fathered a child he really didn't want, but now that the kid turned out to be a genius and he can bathe in his reflected glory, he's almost glad his wife forgot to take the pill. Or to borrow a Goldwynism to describe his feeling about them, "I can take them with a dose of salts."

But with the dignity that accompanies success and mature years—Sam celebrated his sixtieth birthday in 1942—he'd begun to lose whatever sense of humor he'd once had about them back in the days when he actually encouraged his press agents to get them into print. Now he could no longer swallow them, even with a dose of salts. He craved a more dignified image, and Sam junior's letter was just what he needed to make him do something about it.

Realizing it would take more than just an ordinary press agent to change him from a clown into an industry elder statesman, Sam asked his good friend Albert Lasker to suggest somebody. Lasker recommended Benjamin Sonnenberg, who headed his own public relations firm in New York City. Sonnenberg was no ordinary show business hack. He catered only to the elite, the rich, and the powerful, and handled the accounts of firms like J. S. Bache and Company, the Wall Street brokerage house, Beech-Nut Gum, and Remington Rand. He charged exorbitant fees, but according to a profile on him in *Harper's*, he had a past record of miraculous accomplishments. Quoting the columnist Leonard Lyons, the article said: "For fifty-two thousand a year, Sonnenberg could provide his clients with honorary degrees, the French Legion of Honor, and their picture on the cover of *Time* magazine."

So anxious was Sam to meet Sonnenberg that he had Lasker bring him out to Doris Warner's* beach house, where he and Frances were having dinner one August evening. Sam would never hire anybody without first

* Harry Warner's daughter, who was married at various times to Billy Rose, Mervyn LeRoy, and director Charles Vidor.

meeting him, and Sonnenberg was leaving for New York the following day.

After spending an evening with the plump little man with the bald head and brown walrus mustache, Sam was impressed "and gave me," recalls Sonnenberg "a two-year contract for fifty thousand a year to transform him from Mr. Malaprop into an English don."

Sonnenberg wasn't that much of a Merlin. An English don Sam would never be, "although he dressed like it," remembers Sonnenberg. "Whenever I'd meet him in his suite at the Sherry-Netherland he'd be in a very expensive lounging robe, with a gray silk ascot and very expensive made-to-order slippers or shoes. And if he wanted, he could charm the pants off you."

The first thing Sonnenberg did was undertake a very special campaign to get the cooperation of such prominent columnists as Walter Winchell, Hedda Hopper, Louella Parsons, and Leonard Lyons, who rarely let a week go by without printing a half dozen choice Goldwynisms, real or spurious. Somehow Sonnenberg persuaded them to lay off, and for a couple of years the publication of Goldwynisms almost entirely ceased in the important columns.

Simultaneously, Sonnenberg ghosted—or had ghosted—a series of magazine and newspaper articles bearing Samuel Goldwyn's by-line which were printed in all the important publications—the *Reader's Digest*, *Life*, the *American Weekly*, *Variety*, *Look*, and even the *New York Times Magazine*. The *New York Times Magazine*, in fact, carried several of Sam Goldwyn's by-lined pieces in which he pontificated on the state of the movie business or what it took to be a success in Hollywood, and in such elegant syntax that people who knew him began to wonder if there could possibly be *two* Sam Goldwyns in the world. His articles bore such titles as "The Story Makes the Movies," "The Best Advice I Ever Had," "Good Movies: A Cure for an Ailing Industry," and "What America Means to Me."

Just because he wanted his image changed, however, was no guarantee that Sam would stop spewing Goldwynisms in the company of people who were likely to quote him.

Sonnenberg remembers attending a party during the war at the Goldwyns' Laurel Lane residence to which a number of Hollywood personalities of the stature of Merle Oberon, David Niven, and Orson Welles had been invited. Sam was a great admirer of Welles's multitudinous talents and was after him to make a picture under the Goldwyn banner, which was the real reason he'd been invited to this particular soiree. But being a triple-threat man who wrote, directed, produced, and acted in his own movies, Welles didn't really need Sam and had consistently resisted his overtures (while at the same time never turning down an invitation to partake of the Goldwyns' excellent cuisine). Sam kept after Welles with his usual doggedness over the years, however, and on this occasion had backed Welles into a corner by midnight and had talked him into a state of near insensibility as he tried to tell him how much making a picture for Goldwyn would help his career. When finally Welles's armor seemed to have a small crack in it, Sam blurted out, "Look, Orson, if you'll just say yes to doing a picture with me, I'll give you a blank check right now."

When this exchange of Hollywood party talk was reported by one of the gossip columnists, "blank check" somehow became "blanket check." That made Sam furious enough. But when it subsequently turned up in the *Reader's Digest's* Picturesque Patter of Speech department and Sam received a twenty-five-dollar check in the mail for it, he was absolutely livid.

Which just possibly had a lot to do with the fact that Sam told Sonnenberg after the first year of their two-year deal was up that he didn't need him anymore.

"We have a two-year contract, Mr. Goldwyn," Sonnenberg reminded him.

"I'll give you six months' salary if you'll just leave now," bargained Sam, and he got his wish.

"When Goldwyn was through with you, he couldn't wait to get rid of you," states Sonnenberg, echoing what a number of others who also fell out of Sam's favor have reported.

If Sam hadn't been so busy worrying about his image, perhaps the other pictures he produced during the war would have been more memorable. In 1943 and 1944 he produced two mediocre comedies with Bob Hope: *They Got Me Covered*, a spoof on wartime espionage which had the comedian being chased by a Nazi (Otto Preminger) for seven reels; and *The Princess and the Pirate*, a satire on the swashbuckling pirate era.

Sam was somewhat out of his element producing broad comedies, and, amazingly, he was the first to admit it. Once, after he unsuccessfully tried to sign up the Marx Brothers following their release from Paramount and they went with Irving Thalberg instead, Sam ran into his close friend Harpo at a party.

"Sorry it turned out that way," apologized Harpo.

"You fellows made the right move," said Sam. "Thalberg knows more about comedy than I do."

Sam recognized, however, that the public liked comedies, and that furthermore there was a particular need for them during the war, and so he had signed Hope for two pictures. But getting a good comedy script together was a struggle for Sam, and as a result he went through more writers in the making of a comedy than he normally did. All the comedy teams in the business who hadn't been drafted were called on to help Sam out with *The Princess and the Pirate:* Sheekman and Perrin, Panama and

Frank, Shavelson and Rose, Buloigne and Morrow, Hartman and Pirosh, Boretz and Kenyon, Spiegelglass and Kurnitz, in fact, so many teams were used that Sam, whose forte wasn't names, anyway, couldn't remember who had worked for him and who hadn't.

One of the last to be put on the script was Bert Granet, later an RKO producer. While Sam was giving Granet his indoctrination speech about *The Princess and the Pirate*, he got hung up on a point, summoned his new story editor, Pat Duggan, and said, "Bring me those pages those two writers wrote."

"What two writers?" asked Duggan.

"The two writers who worked on this picture two writers ago," said Sam impatiently.

About *They Got Me Covered*, for which Harry Kurnitz received writing credit, Bosley Crowther wrote: "Maybe the switch in producers—Sam Goldwyn instead of Paramount—wasn't best. Maybe, or rather, most likely, the story is rather flat. Anyhow, *They Got Me Covered* doesn't quite measure up to Hope's previous excursions into melodramatic farce."

Don Hartman, Mel Shavelson, Everett Freeman, Allen Boretz, and Curtis Kenyon received final credit for putting *The Princess and the Pirate* together, but the *New York Times* cared for that one even less, saying: "Hope proves he can literally keep a film alive when his writers rather obviously and languidly despair. For there come moments in this highly colored burlesque when it seems that all the authors have run out, leaving Mr. Hope and plot to fumble and bluff as best they can."

Sam's other two wartime releases starred Danny Kaye in his first movie appearances—*Up in Arms* and *Wonder Man*—and they were somewhat more successful, but not necessarily because Sam had learned anything about making broad comedies. It was probably due more to Kaye's being a fresh face to movie audiences.

Sam discovered Danny Kaye long after New Yorkers had discovered him at the Copacabana and La Martinique, where he scored initially in the big time. Before that Kaye had served a long comedy apprenticeship in the borscht-belt summer hotels.

Sam wasn't a habitué of nightclubs, but when reports of how funny the tall, angular, dark-haired and long-nosed comedian was in the hit Broadway show *Lady in the Dark* started drifting back to Hollywood, Sam and Collier Young (before he joined the navy) entrained to New York to see him.

"Sam and I sat in the second row of the theater," recalls Young, "and I can't remember ever hearing him laugh so loud or have such a good time as he did when Kaye was performing." The only thing Sam didn't like was Kaye's face, which featured a Pinocchio-type nose.

Following the performance, Sam and Young called on Kaye backstage in his dressing room. With him was Sylvia Fine, his wife, mentor, and writer of most of the tongue-twisting scat songs and comedy routines he was killing New York audiences with.

"You're a very funny man," said Sam. "But if I sign you, you're going to have to have your nose fixed. It's too long."

"No," said Kaye.

"He's doing all right with it the way it is," said his wife.

"It's not photogenic," said Sam.

"I'll make a deal with you," said Kaye with an impish smile. "I'll have mine fixed if you'll have yours fixed."

After watching Danny Kaye perform a couple more times, Sam became convinced that a comedian didn't have to have Robert Taylor's looks in order to be appealing to audiences, and he signed him, long nose and all, and without giving him a screen test.

He then went back to the Coast and assigned his usual army of writers to the job of fashioning a screen vehicle for the brash young comedian. After discarding many drafts of many different stories by many different screenwriters, Sam finally decided to go with *Up in Arms*, which was the story of a hypochondriac from Brooklyn (Kaye) who gets drafted into the army and, when hospitalized, falls in love with an army nurse (Dinah Shore). This concoction was written by Don Hartman, Bob Pirosh, and Allen Boretz, with "special material" by Sylvia Fine, and was loosely based on the Owen Davis play *The Nervous Wreck*, the rights to which Sam already owned, having had to acquire them when he made *Whoopee*, which was also based on the Nervous Wreck character.

It wasn't until after the script was completed and sets were being built that Sam brought Danny Kaye to the Coast and gave him a screen test.

Sam and Frances viewed the results together in the projection room, and what they saw made them rue the day Sam hadn't insisted on a nose bob. Kaye's face was all angles and his nose was even less photogenic than Sam had originally thought it was. But in addition there was something else Sam didn't like about Kaye's appearance that he couldn't quite pinpoint. His face under those shaggy black locks seemed more menacing than comic. But why? Three more tests were made, with Kaye being photographed from every conceivable angle to see if he didn't have a good side. But there didn't seem to be one, and all of Sam's advisers and directors were urging him to buy off Kaye's contract and take the loss rather than try to make this ugly Brooklyn duckling into a film personality.

Sam kept insisting that there had to be a way to make Danny Kaye more photogenic. Then one morning, when he was sitting despondently in the projection room with Frances, after having just seen another unsatisfactory test, he suddenly let out a yelp, picked up the phone, and called the studio hairdresser.

"I've got it," he yelled. "I've got it. Expect Kaye in ten minutes. He's having his hair dyed blond!"

For some reason, a bottle of peroxide was able to transform Kaye from a Fagin into a *mensch*, whom audiences adored and the nation's major film critics took to their hearts. Bosley Crowther wished there could have been "more of a story," but conceded that between Kaye's sure-fire comedy routines, which he'd been doing for the past two years around New York, and Dinah Shore's singing, "what more could a person need to be entertained?"

In the case of *Up in Arms* what was needed most were theaters in which to run the film.

For years Sam had been waging virtually a one-man war against the motion picture exhibitors of America. His complaint—aired in some of his by-lined *New York Times* and *Variety* pieces—was that independent moviemakers, such as himself, were throttled by the monopolistic major producing companies (which controlled theaters grossing 70 percent of United States movie receipts) and theater chains (which controlled a substantial part of the rest). Independents, declared Sam, were forced to sell their movies on a take-it-or-leave-it basis.

The only things that had kept the Goldwyn company in the black were superior product and Sam's super salesmanship. But by 1944, the exhibitors, egged on by the knowledge that they could get all the product they needed from the major studios, started to show far too much muscle to suit the maverick Sam. His wrath finally boiled over when he was dickering with San Francisco's powerful McNeil-Naify Company, which owned one hundred theaters in California and Nevada. Sam insisted on a percentage of the gross deal for *Up in Arms*, but McNeil-Naify would buy it only on a flat rental basis, which would automatically give them a tremendous profit while Sam, who had risked a couple of million dollars of his own money to bring Danny Kaye to the screen, would have to settle for peanuts. Negotiations between the two broke down in February 1944.

In a move to dramatize the plight of the independent producer, while at the same time getting some nationwide publicity for *Up in Arms*, Sam decided to carry the battle into the enemy's home territory of Reno, where McNeil-Naify controlled five large theaters. Sam sent some of his agents to Reno to try to get an option on the State Auditorium. He'd show McNeil-Naify; he'd exhibit the picture himself. But McNeil-Naify outmaneuvered him by getting to the state officials ahead of Sam's men. When Sam's men showed up to rent the auditorium, they were turned down on the grounds that it was a public building and could not be rented to private enterprise for profit. Undaunted, Sam's men leased the El Patio ballroom, alongside the Southern Pacific railroad tracks. Then Reno's fire chief, George M. Twaddle, got into the act. He regretfully informed them that their portable projection booth did not conform to Reno's fire laws.

Next Sam's men tried to rent a parking lot, planning to surround it with a ten-foot canvas fence and show the movie outdoors. The building laws stopped them.

Still not ready to run up the white flag, Sam's forces finally built a platform outside the El Patio ballroom, on the sidewalk. They hoped to get around the fire laws by pointing the lens of the projector through one of the ballroom's rear windows in order to project the image on the screen inside. The fire department couldn't complain about this, but the police then took over and said they couldn't have the platform where they'd built it because it was blocking the sidewalk. In addition McNeil-Naify started running large ads in the newspapers pointing out to Reno moviegoers some of the hardships they would have to endure if they paid to see the Danny Kaye movie in the El Patio ballroom—"uncarpeted floors . . . the whistle of freight trains as they rumbled past, shaking the building . . . and static in the sound system."

But it would take more than the police and fire departments and building code inspectors to discourage a man who had (1) run away from Poland at the age of twelve, (2) outwitted the Customs Department at the age of eighteen, (3) bested the feared movie Trust in 1913, (4) made a million by the time he was twenty-five, (5) stolen Gary Cooper from Paramount, and (6) told Willie Bioff, one of the toughest labor leaders in the land, to "include me out."

Remembering that there was a "shooting war" going on overseas, Sam decided to make use of it in his present battle. Calling the Reno press together, he announced that he was donating all of the opening night's receipts of *Up in Arms* to the local Camp and Hospital Service Committee. The moment this hit the newspapers, all official Reno opposition vanished. In fact, the local townspeople helped him build a false wooden floor in the dance hall so that the 400 borrowed chairs could be nailed down to conform to the building laws. After that, all Sam had to do to have his week's showing was to guarantee that he would use nonflammable film.

Artistically *Up in Arms* was a triumph opening night, and in addition the Camp and Hospital Service Committee walked off with a lot of much-needed loot.

Personally Sam didn't do very well financially that week. It cost him $25,000 to run *Up in Arms* in his own theater against a week's gross of only $2,000. But that wasn't the main point. By his dazzling maneuver, Sam had brought worldwide attention to the plight of the independent picture producers, and it was no coincidence that only three months later the United States Department of Justice filed a court application aimed at forcing the big distributors to sell their theaters within three years. Although the majors fought the action through all the courts over the next several years, the Justice Department's suit eventually ended in victory for the independents, thereby assuring them a future in the industry.

Danny Kaye's future was assured, too. When his second picture for Goldwyn, *Wonder Man*, released in 1945, was also a hit, Danny Kaye was given a permanent stall in the Goldwyn acting stable.

That's the way it was with Sam. If you came through for him professionally and didn't double-cross him, if he liked you and the public liked you, he'd use you in every picture that he possibly could.

Dana Andrews was one who'd recently come into Sam's favor. First he was in *The Westerner*, making his screen debut. Then he was in the highly successful *Ball of Fire*, then *The North Star* (which didn't fit him at all, but Sam liked him), and after that *The Best Years of Our Lives*. Another of Sam's "crushes" in the early forties was the comely young actress Teresa Wright. She was married to the novelist Niven Busch, whom Sam had once fired. Following her role as Alexandra in *The Little Foxes*, which won Teresa Wright an Academy Award nomination, Sam cast her as Lou Gehrig's wife, and now, as the war was winding down in the early summer of 1945, he was preparing a script in which she would have the starring role.

The picture was *Those Endearing Young Charms*, which Jerry Chodorov, just recently back from a three-year hitch in the army air force, was adapting from his brother's play. Sam was very enthusiastic about the project and about making Teresa a star on her own until one morning Chodorov got an urgent summons to Sam's office. As Chodorov entered, Sam was sitting at his desk, crestfallen.

"What's the matter, Mr. Goldwyn?" asked Chodorov.

"Niven Busch fucked me," he cried out in his high-pitched Polish-accented voice.

"What are you talking about?"

"He got Teresa pregnant," said Sam, "and he did it deliberately because I fired him so I won't be able to make the picture with his wife. He fucked me."

"You've got it wrong," explained Chodorov. "You're not the one he fucked."

Sam's peculiar kind of paranoia would not allow him to believe that even a pregnancy could be anything but an act of revenge.

Sam called off *Those Endearing Young Charms* as a result of what Niven Busch had done to him and sold the property to RKO, but not before he had one final story conference on it with Jerry Chodorov. In the meeting, Sam was extremely insistent on retaining a scene that Chodorov felt ought to be thrown out because it was in bad taste.

"What's bad taste?" asked Sam.

"For one thing, we're still at war," explained Chodorov. "We can't have our lead girl lying around the house complaining about doing nothing and buying black market meat stamps so she can serve her company steaks while people are out getting killed overseas. And there's no telling how long the war will last."

"Aw, don't worry about that," said Sam. "The war's all over but the shooting."

23

The Best Year of His Life

IT TOOK A WORLD WAR to win an Oscar, in fact a whole slew of them, for Sam, plus the vision and perspicacity of his number-one reader, Frances. The two of them were sitting in their den one evening in August 1944, when Frances became intrigued by an article and photograph she saw in the latest issue of *Time*. The photograph showed a group of homecoming Marines leaning out of windows of a railway car on which had been painted in white lettering, "Home Again!" The accompanying story suggested that many servicemen probably weren't as happy about returning home as one would imagine, because of the problems they would have readjusting to civilian life. Many would have to live with physical disabilities incurred in the war; others were apprehensive about returning to their dull nine-to-five jobs, which many of them had hated before leaving them; and still others would have to make an emotional readjustment with their wives and girlfriends, from whom they had been separated for a number of years.

Frances showed the article to Sam, who agreed with her that the subject could make a very important picture, if it was written right. But what writer whom he could trust was qualified to handle such an important and serious subject? He was no longer speaking to Lillian Hellman. Sidney Howard had been killed in a tractor accident on his farm in 1939. And Robert Sherwood was working for Roosevelt as the head of the Office of War Information, overseas division.

On a hunch Sam picked up the phone and called MacKinlay Kantor at his home in Palm Beach, Florida. Kantor was a mildly successful novelist who specialized in writing historical fiction about the American Civil War. Later he would write *Andersonville*, a major best seller about a prison camp during the Civil War. But in the mid-forties his books, *Arouse and Beware* and *Gentle Annie*, had not been widely read. They had been sold to the movies, however, which is how Sam was aware of him. Kantor's agent had once offered Kantor to Sam for a picture assignment, and Sam had promised to use him someday if something came along that fit his particular talents.

A story of returning servicemen could be right up MacKinlay Kantor's alley, thought Sam, and so he phoned him. Luckily, Kantor was not in the service, as Sam discovered when he reached him that night. Sam told him the idea, and when Kantor responded favorably to it, he offered him $10,000 to fashion a screen treatment from it.

Six months later, in January 1945, Kantor delivered a manuscript to Sam called *Glory for Me*. It was more than a screen treatment. It was a short novel about the trials and tribulations of three men coming back to face civilian life, but written in, of all things, blank verse. Sam thought Kantor had done a lousy job, mainly because he couldn't understand anything in blank verse, and promptly consigned *Glory for Me* to his graveyard of discarded manuscripts in the back room.

For $10,000 he could afford to swallow the loss, and he went back to his other projects: First on his future slate of postwar films was another Danny Kaye vehicle, *The Kid from Brooklyn*, based on the old hit play *The Milky Way*, about a schnook who makes it from milkman to middleweight champion. Sam turned this into a big splashy musical starring, in addition to Kaye, Eve Arden, Lionel Stander, Virginia Mayo, Vera-Ellen, and the Goldwyn Girls. It also had songs by Jule Styne and Sammy Cahn.

At the same time Sam was preparing *The Bishop's Wife*, based on the Robert Nathan best-selling novel about an angel (Cary Grant) sent down from heaven to save the marriage of an Anglican bishop (David Niven) and his wife (Loretta Young), and James Thurber's "The Secret Life of Walter Mitty," which he had bought as a future vehicle for Danny Kaye, provided his writing staff could lick its inherent story problems. Ken Englund and Everett Freeman eventually got screen credit for the concoction, but whether they licked it is a matter of opinion.

In the meantime the war had ended in the Pacific, and most of Hollywood's important names who had gone off to battle were now returning to the studios and resuming their careers. Among those to survive was Lieutenant Colonel Willy Wyler, who resigned his commission after distinguishing himself in the army air force and reported back to Sam for a directing assignment early in 1946. Not because he was so crazy about working for Sam again, but "because I still owed him one picture on my last contract," says Wyler.

Sam welcomed his favorite director back warmly and promptly handed him the script of *The Bishop's Wife* to direct. To Sam's disappointment, Wyler turned the assignment down, saying it "was no good." He also rejected another story "which was quite good—I can't remember the name of it—but it just didn't interest me," says Wyler.

The Willy Wyler who came home from the war was a different fellow from the happy-go-lucky Hollywood film director who used to go on suspension every other minute and rode his motorcycle into swimming pools. He felt everything had changed. "The war," he said, "had been an escape into reality. In the war it didn't matter how much money you earned. The only thing that mattered were human relationships; not money, not position, not even family. Only relationships with people who might be dead tomorrow were important."

Wyler had seen men close to him killed and maimed. He'd permanently lost the hearing of his own left ear when a cannon went off too close to his head. And he'd also seen and heard the reactions of other servicemen to typical Hollywood screen heroics when they watched movies in the mess hall between flying missions. According to Wyler, they used to let out howls of derisive laughter when Errol Flynn mowed down a whole platoon almost single-handedly, or Tyrone Power bested a German ace in a dogfight in the wild blue yonder, even with a jammed machine gun.

Wyler's outlook on life and the kinds of movies he wanted to direct in the future had also been changed by the reception given to the forty-five-minute army air force film he had made called *The Memphis Belle*. This documentary was a personalized account of the twenty-fifth and final mission of the Flying Fortress *Memphis Belle*, told through the eyes of the bomber's crew.

Along with John Ford's *The Battle of Midway* and John Huston's *The Battle of San Pietro*, *The Memphis Belle* was considered one of the three finest examples of on-the-spot reporting documentaries to emerge from the war. Wyler had risked his life to get the footage, sometimes perched in the open catwalk of the bomb bay five miles above Germany, and sometimes sitting in the tail gunner's bubble. As a result, the commander of the Eighth Air Force recommended him for the Distinguished Service Medal. Wyler did not get it, but he had the satisfaction of sitting through a special running of the film in a chair beside Franklin Delano Roosevelt in the White House and hearing the president tell one of his aides, "This has to be shown everywhere, right away."

Now that he was out of the service with an entirely different perspective of life, Wyler told Sam that he was no longer interested in making the conventional brand of entertainment. "I want to do something about the war," said Wyler, immediately having visions of going back on suspension again.

"Well, I also own this," said Sam, and he held up a thin book called *Glory for Me* by MacKinlay Kantor, which had just been published. "Tell me what you think of it."

Wyler read *Glory for Me*, liked it, and informed Sam that he would like to do it. Although it was in blank verse, it was essentially a very solid story about three servicemen returning to the same town and trying to pick up their lives from where they had been interrupted when they had gone into the service. "It was basically the same story we went with in *The Best Years of Our Lives*," says Wyler, "the only difference being that the Harold Russell character was a spastic in MacKinlay Kantor's version and not an amputee."

Sam was disappointed that Wyler liked *Glory for Me* and "tried to talk me out of it," remembers Wyler. "He thought it was nothing—ten thousand wasted."

To divert Wyler, Sam mentioned that he had still another project—also about the war—that might interest him. This was the story of General Dwight Eisenhower, which Sam had commissioned Robert Sherwood to write a screen treatment on.

Wyler, indeed, was interested in directing a full-length biographical film of the supreme commander of Allied forces in the European theater, and Sam put him and Sherwood together for conferences. Their collaboration seemed to be going well, and the two were even considering making a trip to Germany together to spend some time talking with Ike, when Wyler happened to mention to Sherwood one day that Goldwyn owned a property called *Glory for Me*, which he thought would make a better film than the life of Dwight Eisenhower, because it was about the ordinary GI—not a general.

This piqued Sherwood's interest. He read *Glory for Me* that night and immediately decided to abandon the Eisenhower project and do the story of returning servicemen instead. Together he and Wyler tackled Goldwyn, and this time Sam said, "Well, if you both like it so much, let's make it."

Sam gave Sherwood and Wyler pretty much their own heads during the preparation stages of the script. He had only one piece of advice. "Don't be too radical."

Sherwood explained that he had no intention of being radical, but he and Wyler did want to show the world of peacetime America to which the GI's were returning as less than perfect.

"That's okay," said Sam. "Just don't knock America." And he promptly scotched an idea Sherwood had for a sequence showing a group of angry GI's staging a riot over inadequate housing. It never did get in the picture. Despite Sam's reluctance, there was plenty of social comment and good healthy criticism in the film before Sherwood was finished. Sherwood wasn't a Pulitzer Prize winner for nothing.

Before Sherwood did any writing, however, he and Wyler explored very thoroughly the general postwar scene. "Luckily," recalls Wyler, "I didn't have to ask a lot of questions of GI's on how it felt to be back. After four years in the service, I knew damn well what it felt like. It was easy for me to put myself in their places."

Using Kantor's novel as a general guide, Sherwood set about constructing a screenplay. He didn't alter two of the three main characters very noticeably: Captain Fred Derry, the Eighth Air Force bombardier, who was only a soda jerk before the war, and who is too proud to return to that kind of work now; and Al Stephenson, a middle-aged family man who was an infantry sergeant, and who in civilian life prior to that had held a minor executive position in the local bank.

But Wyler strongly felt that the character of Homer, the disabled veteran, had to be altered for picture purposes. In the Kantor version, Homer had been the victim of spastic paralysis, brought on by shell shock. But Wyler believed that spastic paralysis was something that had to be "acted." When shown on the screen, a character afflicted with that was liable to come off funny—like something Jerry Lewis might do.

"Even if it were perfectly acted," says Wyler, "it was going to look funny. So we decided to substitute some real injury. But what exactly, we didn't know."

In their search for the right disability, Wyler and Sherwood ran an instruction short made by the army, showing amputees how to use hooks in place of hands and false limbs instead of real legs. That decided them on changing Homer to an amputee. If they could find the right person, they would even use a real amputee in the picture instead of a professional actor.

To learn how real amputees felt and looked, Wyler and Sherwood visited the Veterans Hospital in Pasadena.

"They took us into one little house," says Wyler. "Three fellows were in there, and not a hand among them. Not even hooks, and they were very resentful when they found out what we planned to do."

"So you're going to make a picture about guys like us?" said one of them. "Going to make money, huh?"

Sherwood explained that they weren't trying to exploit the war amputees. They were just after "total honesty" in their picture, which, if it were handled correctly, might even help other amputees become adjusted to a life without hands.

The three men were bitter and doubted the possibility of anyone becoming adjusted to living without hands.

"What about this fellow Harold Russell?" pointed out Wyler.

Russell was the handless army sergeant they had just seen in the medical short demonstrating how to get along with hooks. Russell had lost his hands when a dynamite charge exploded prematurely during training maneuvers in North Carolina.

"Ah, Harold, we know him," one of the amputees said. "He's a lucky guy."

"Lucky?" exclaimed Wyler.

"Yeah. He's got his elbows. When you've got your elbows, they can put claws on you."

Because Russell had already been in front of a camera and seemed totally adjusted to getting along with hooks in place of hands, it was eventually decided to use him to play the part of Homer, the navy veteran who resented anyone feeling sorry for him. This characterization wasn't too far removed from the real-life Russell.

"He really did resent anyone feeling sorry for him," recalls Wyler. "Of course we had to teach him acting, such as it was. And that was a bit difficult. But I didn't have to explain to him how it feels to lose your hands. He knew that."

Although Wyler claims in retrospect that *"The Best Years* is the easiest picture I ever made," there were times when Sam Goldwyn was ready to abandon it before it ever went before the cameras. There were moments when even Sherwood was ready to chuck the whole thing and return to New York City and writing plays. One problem Sherwood couldn't lick and which had Sam deeply concerned too was the Fred Derry story. In the Kantor version and in Sherwood's first draft, Fred came home from the war to find his wife, Marie, in the arms of another man, an ex-marine. Fred immediately gives her the money for a divorce and his marriage is over, leaving no barrier to his romance with Al Stephenson's daughter, which started soon after he returned from the war. No one could figure out how to strengthen that part of the story until Sherwood, Sam, and Frances were having a story conference in the Goldwyn living room one evening in the spring of 1946. In the midst of a discussion in which Sam was seriously talking about calling off the picture, the solution of the Fred Derry story suddenly came to Sherwood. "What would be wrong," he asked, "with *not* having Fred discover his wife in this guy's arms his first night home, and not know right away she's having this affair with the Marine? That way he'll stay married to her—unhappily, of course—and he'll have to wrestle with this moral dilemma of whether to divorce her when he falls in love with Stephenson's daughter. That's good drama." Sam and Frances agreed with him, and Sherwood returned to New York, where he rewrote over a third of the script to conform to the new idea.

Completing the rewrite, Sherwood shipped the new pages to Sam, who took them home and stayed up until after midnight reading them. He liked them, and Frances liked them, and so he immediately snatched up the phone and called Sherwood, forgetting in his eagerness that it was nearly four A.M. in New York.

"Hello, Bob," said Sam excitedly after a sleepy-sounding Sherwood answered. "This is Goldwyn. I like the script generally, but I want to talk about a few changes. I think the character of—"

"For Christ's sakes, Sam," interrupted Sherwood groggily, "do you know what time it is?" Whereupon Sam turned to Frances and said, "Dear, do you know what time it is? Bob wants to know."

The script was finally completed around the first of March, and Sam sent it down to the production department to have a budget run on it. When it came back budgeted at $2 million—and this was a conservative estimate yet—Sam again began to get cold feet on the project.

"One reason for this," says Wyler, "was that everybody started telling him and me, 'Listen, fellows, the war is over. Forget about it. Make something funny . . . make a musical . . . make something glamorous.' And then when they found out about the Harold Russell character, they told us, 'You're going to have a fellow without hands—using hooks! Christ, do you want people to come into the theater or are you trying to drive 'em away?' "

But Sam respected Robert Sherwood's and Willy Wyler's opinions that there would be interest in the subject of returning servicemen. He didn't take their word for it completely. He also consulted the Audience Research Institute—an organization which was supposed to have its finger on the pulse of the American audience and which, for a fee, would give a studio or individual producer a reading on the theatergoer's interest in any subject. To Sam's surprise, the institute reported back that there was a great deal of interest in the problems of the average war veteran. That was the clincher as far as Sam was concerned, and he told Wyler and his casting department to start recommending actors.

By this time, of course, Harold Russell was set for the part of Homer, and he turned out to be the only real World War II veteran in the cast. Neither Fredric March, who played the part of the sergeant, nor Dana Andrews, who was given the role of the disillusioned air force captain, had gotten any nearer to the war zone than the armed forces radio station at Hollywood and Vine. March, in fact, wasn't particularly enthralled with the part at all and wouldn't have taken it if he hadn't been on the rebound from a part he had highly coveted but didn't get—the role of Father in *Life with Father* for Warner Brothers.

Sam very much wanted Myrna Loy for the role of Millie Stephenson, Fredric March's wife in the film, but when she expressed some reluctance, he immediately assumed it was because she didn't want to play the part of an older woman—Teresa Wright's mother. In an effort to persuade her otherwise, he and Frances invited Miss Loy to dinner at their Beverly Hills home one evening.

Sam was exceptionally articulate that evening and spoke very convincingly about the mistake most actors made in only looking at their own individual roles, the sizes of them, and the age brackets they were supposed to play.

"What's important," he told Myrna Loy, "is to look at the picture as a whole, and not just the fact that you have less lines than someone else . . . or have to play older."

"But, Sam, that's not what's bothering me," said Miss Loy. "It's the director. I hear Willy Wyler is practically a sadist on the set."

"That isn't true," Sam assured her. "He's just a very mean fellow."

In the end Myrna Loy accepted the part and joined the superb cast, along with Fredric March, Dana Andrews, Harold Russell, Virginia Mayo (as the two-timing wife), Teresa Wright, Gladys George, and Hoagy Carmichael, the popular song composer ("Stardust"), who was playing the role of Butch Engle.

Filming began on April 15 and ended August 9—almost four months. It was an exceptionally long shooting schedule, but then it was an exceptionally long script (190 pages), and Wyler paid meticulous attention to every detail.

Although the trend was to shoot most films in color, Wyler felt black and white would give the picture more of the stark realism he and cameraman Gregg Toland were striving for. Wyler carried his quest for realism to still another extreme. He had the costume designer, Irene Sharaff, buy the clothes for the characters in a department store rather than have them made, and after they were distributed to the actors, he insisted that they wear them for a few weeks before the picture began shooting so that the clothes wouldn't look brand new.

Because it was obviously going to be a costly picture, Sam insisted that Wyler change his usual method of working with actors and rehearse them fully, around a table, just like with a Broadway play, before shooting the major sequences. This accounted for remarkably smooth performances and kept them from going over schedule by too many days.

Although *The Best Years of Our Lives* was engrossing from start to finish, it contained two sequences that packed such emotional wallop that they no doubt contributed much to the picture's overall greatness. Both were the result of the exceptionally good rapport that had developed between Wyler and Sherwood. One was the airplane graveyard scene, in which Dana Andrews, who won the Distinguished Flying Cross but who has now failed in civilian life, is seen sitting in the cockpit of a dusty Flying Fortress that has been junked, mentally reliving his days of glory as a Flying Fortress bombardier. The symbolism being that his own days of usefulness are over, too—just like the Flying Fortress's. Strong stuff for a nation just coming out of a four-year war.

And the second was the sequence in which Harold Russell tells his girl, Wilma, that the reason he's been avoiding her is not that he doesn't love her, but that he doesn't feel it fair to her to marry her. "You don't know,

Wilma," he tells her, "what it would be like to live with me, to have to face this"—indicating his hooks—"every day, every night." She replies, "I can only find out by trying, and if it turns out I haven't got courage enough, well, we'll soon know."

This led into a scene in the bedroom in which Homer demonstrates his helplessness without his hooks. "This scene," says Wyler, "affords a good example of how writer and director can function together, for I had to decide whether or not I could do such a scene on the screen. There were delicate problems in bringing a boy and a girl to a bedroom at night with the boy getting into his pajamas, revealing his leather harness which enables him to work his hooks, and finally, taking the harness off. After discussions with Bob, we solved the problems and felt we could play the scene without the slightest suggestion of indelicacy and without presenting Homer's hooks in a shocking or horrifying manner. As a matter of fact, we felt we could do quite the opposite and make it into a moving and tender love scene."

Which is how it turned out. Wilma meets the test squarely and makes Homer see that she doesn't mind the hooks, that what she feels for him is not pity, but love.

In the four months of filming, Wyler shot over 400,000 feet of film. This was edited down to 16,000 feet. At this point, a decision had to be made, and only Sam could make it. The final-cut length of the average picture in those days was between six and eight thousand feet, and ran no longer than an hour and twenty minutes. Sixteen thousand feet would run nearly three hours, and who knew whether an audience would sit still that long— especially for a picture that didn't figure to be a barrel of laughs anyway?

Aside from the artistic standpoint, there was a financial matter to consider. A three-hour picture cost more to distribute, and therefore Sam would have to charge road-show prices. *Gone with the Wind* had run three hours, but it had been broken halfway through with an intermission, and Sam considered Selznick lucky to have gotten away with such a long picture. Sam felt that *Best Years* ought to be cut down to normal size, but when Wyler and he ran it together, he realized it was very "tight" as it was, with no dead wood that either of them could spot. At least before the picture was previewed. And so in the end, Sam decided to do nothing about cutting it until he saw what the reactions were like at the preview.

The Best Years of Our Lives was previewed with a "temp" music track in October 1946, and the audience reaction, both during the running and on the preview cards, was so fantastic that Sam decided that cutting it down to normal length wasn't necessary. In fact, Sam was so delighted with what he saw on the screen that night that when he bumped into David Selznick as they emerged from the theater he didn't ask, "How did you like my picture?" He asked, "How did you *love* my picture?"

Best Years, with a stunning musical score by San Francisco–born Hugo Friedhofer, was ready for release November 1. Sam was high on it, but he wasn't really thinking of Academy Awards when he told Wyler he had booked it into Hollywood's Pantages Theater the first week in January.

"My God, Sam, aren't you going to get it out in time to qualify?" asked Wyler. He was talking about the academy rule that stipulates that to qualify a film must play two weeks to paying audiences in greater Los Angeles before the end of a calendar year.

"Do you really think it has a chance to win anything?" asked Sam. His hopes had been raised falsely so many times in the past that now, with this blockbuster of a film about to be released, he was pushing the possibility to the back of his mind.

"Maybe," said Wyler. "At least, let's try."

Although he liked the January booking at the Pantages, Sam changed it to mid-December to satisfy Wyler. But Sam's thoughts were actually on the New York opening.

In New York Sam wasn't willing to settle for just any theater. He desperately wanted it to be showcased in the Astor, where Laurence Olivier's film production of *Henry V* was nearing the end of its run. Not only was the Astor a large house with a reputation for running "class" entertainment, but it was right on Times Square, where all the action was.

The Astor wasn't an easy house to get, however, for it was in great demand. In addition, it was owned by a fellow named Robert Dowling, who was president of the City Investing Company, a multimillion-dollar corporation. Dowling wouldn't play just any picture in his theater. Besides that, he was notorious for driving a hard bargain when it came to making a deal for the producer's product, because he knew *everybody* wanted the Astor.

From previous experience, Sam was aware that only one thing impressed a man like that—a display of wealth and power by the person he was dealing with. Consequently Sam felt he ought to talk "deal" with him in opulent surroundings, and not in some schleppy hotel room. Ideally, someone's plush townhouse—and one with a 35-mm projection room.

The only place Sam knew like that belonged to Ben Sonnenberg and his wife, and they were living in it. But this didn't stop Sam. Sam rented the house, complete with butler and servants, from the Sonnenbergs for a week and paid for them to go on a vacation to the Bahamas.

That's class.

Then he and Frances moved in and invited the Dowlings to dinner and to see *The Best Years of Our Lives* in the luxury of their own projection room. Dowling didn't know what he was impressed with the most—the Goldwyns' high standard of living or *The Best Years of Our Lives.* At any rate, Sam not only got the Astor Theater for an open-end booking, but Dowling liked the film so well that he agreed to pay Sam an unheard-of rental of 40 percent of the gross. Thirty percent was considered exceptionally high in those days.

The Best Years was set to open at New York's Astor Theater on November 22. For one of the few times in the history of the movie business, tickets would be sold on a reserved-seat basis, with admission on the weekends going up to $2.40 per person. Sam was not altogether certain that the public would go for such a high tab just to see an ordinary black-and-white motion picture—you could get into a legitimate play for not much more than that.

But having made a great picture was not enough. Sam also saw to it that there was plenty of advance publicity, including a personal appearance for himself on the Bob Hope radio show.

A few days before he was to go on the air, Sam buttonholed Harry Tugend, one of his writers, in the executive dining room and said, "Harry, I'm going on the Bob Hope Show. You're a clever writer. What should I say about the picture?"

Tugend thought it over, then came up with a bit. "You have Hope say to you, 'Well, Mr. Goldwyn, how have things been going since I left your studio?' And you reply, 'I'll tell you, Bob—since you left, we've had the Best Years of Our Lives.'"

That appealed to Sam, and he told Hope's radio writers to insert it in the script. Then came the big night when Sam was standing before the microphone in one of NBC's broadcasting studios.

"Well, Mr. Goldwyn," said Hope, "how have things been going since I left your studio?"

"I'll tell you, Bob," replied Sam without bothering to look at the script, "since you left, things are better than ever." Which totally confused the audience but had Hope doubled over with laughter.

A few days before the New York opening, Sam called a press conference in his suite in the Sherry-Netherland and held forth for an hour or so on the state of the movie business. The theme he hit the hardest was that "Hollywood isn't producing enough *significant* pictures."

After reading this in the newspapers, Darryl Zanuck couldn't help paying Sam a tribute. "The man's a genius when it comes to getting attention for his product," he said. "If he doesn't have any significant pictures to release, if he's putting out some little musical comedy or other, he will issue a statement that it's Hollywood's job to brighten the lives of the people and not worry them about serious issues. And then, when he has a significant picture to release and he knows it is going to be praised for its significance—something like *The Best Years of Our Lives*—he will wait until just a day before it comes out and issue a statement saying that Hollywood isn't producing enough significant pictures!

"My God! It's so obvious! Nobody else would have the nerve to do it! But it doesn't faze Sam. He never bats an eye!"

In this case, Sam's audacity really wasn't necessary. The raves of the critics were all that was necessary to bring a line of customers to the box office that extended clear around the block, and for many weeks to come.

On November 23, Bosley Crowther wrote:

> It is seldom that there comes a motion picture which can be wholly and enthusiastically endorsed not only as superlative entertainment but as food for quiet and humanizing thought. Having to do with a subject of large moment—the veterans home from war—and cut, as it were, from the heart-wood of contemporary American life, this film from the Samuel Goldwyn studio does a great deal more, even, than the above. It gives off a warm glow of affection for everyday, down-to-earth folks.

In its editorial column, the *Los Angeles Times* said:

> *The Best Years of Our Lives* represents the better American spirit. It deserves to be seen by people throughout today's chaotic world. It typifies the kind of life most people know and understand in this country. It is not linked with the gangsters and racketeering so often exploited in the homegrown cinemas, and which give such a false idea of America.

Financially the picture was a phenomenal success. During its first two years of release it earned $11 million in the United States and Canada. In Great Britain it outgrossed *Gone with the Wind*. It ran sixty weeks in London, seventeen in Stockholm, nineteen in Rio de Janeiro, twenty-nine in Sydney, Australia, and seventeen in Buenos Aires.

In December the New York film critics gave *The Best Years* the award for best movie of the year; and in its preliminary balloting soon after the first of the new year, the motion picture academy nominated it in eight categories: best picture, best direction, best screenplay, best actor, best supporting actor, best film editing, best musical score, and best achievement in sound.

Eight nominations was an encouraging sign, and Sam was grateful to Willy Wyler for talking him into releasing the picture in Los Angeles prematurely in order to qualify for the awards. But he didn't allow himself to become too optimistic. He'd been there before, only to be disappointed when the envelopes were opened.

But this time the gods rewarded Sam Goldwyn for his patience. *The Best Years of Our Lives* won in seven of the eight categories in which it was nominated, failing only to pick up an Oscar for best sound achievement. But

Harold Russell, handless and without any professional acting experience, surprised everyone in the banquet hall by winning for best supporting actor. It was a notable achievement for both himself and Willy Wyler, who had taught him to act.

When the envelope for best picture was opened, and *The Best Years* was announced as the winner, Sam wept tears of unabashed joy as he strode down the aisle in his elegant tuxedo and climbed the stairs to the stage to accept his gold statuette. That wasn't his only award. Besides awarding him the Oscar for best producer, the academy also bestowed on Sam the additional honor of the Irving Thalberg Memorial Award—"for that producer whose creativity over the years reflects consistently high quality of motion picture production."

In his acceptance speech Sam was most gracious and thanked all the talents who were responsible for the picture's great success, naming each one individually—Bob Sherwood, Fredric March, Willy Wyler, Harold Russell, Danny Mandell, and Gordon Sawyer.

Miraculously, he didn't make a boo-boo until he reached the final name. "And last but not least," said Sam, "I'd like to thank Hugo Carmichael." At least it got him off the stage with a laugh—and kept his image intact.

With the phenomenal success of *The Best Years of Our Lives*, Sam was anxious to reward his two-time Oscar winner, Willy Wyler, with a new three-year contract. But Wyler had more ambitious plans. Financially Wyler had done all right—or rather, would do all right—with *The Best Years*. In addition to his salary, he'd been on a percentage of the profits deal since Sam had renewed his last contract in 1939. And he was getting 20 percent of the profits of *Best Years*, which eventually netted him over a million dollars.

Although money was important, it wasn't the root of Wyler's discontent. He wanted to be his own producer as well as director, and as a result decided to join Frank Capra, George Stevens, and Sam Briskin in a new independent company they were forming called Liberty Films. Under this setup, Wyler wouldn't be an employee; he'd be a partner.

Sam, naturally, was shocked when he learned Wyler was defecting. "What do you want with all that headache?" he asked.

"For one thing, I can make more money," replied Wyler.

"More money?" exclaimed Sam. "You're getting twenty percent of *Best Years*. That's more money than I'll make on it."

"What are you talking about?" asked Wyler.

"Well, I gave Bob Sherwood five percent," said Sam.

"That still leaves you seventy-five," pointed out Wyler.

"I don't own anything," cried Sam. "I gave it all away. I swear. You're making more on it than I am."

"I don't believe you," said Wyler. "Who'd you give it to?"

"To Frances and Sam junior," confessed Sam, unabashed.

24

As Good as Your Last Oscar

THE MORNING AFTER Sam hit the jackpot at the 1947 Academy Awards ceremony, his office was inundated with wires of congratulation from the other reigning studio heads—Zanuck, Schary, Selznick, Cohn, and Jack Warner—plus hundreds more from friends, agents, well-wishers, and people who had worked for him over the years.

According to Frances, "Sam was like a kid with a new toy." And like a kid with a new toy, he soon tired of the adulation and of staring at the Oscars on his desk, and started thinking of something new to play with—like the script of his next picture.

"It's not good enough to win an Oscar," he told Roger Butterfield, who was interviewing him for *Life*. "Suppose next time I make a stinker? I'm worrying about that now."

This was another way of stating the usual Hollywood fear—"You're only as good as your last scripture," as someone once cracked to Cecil De Mille.

It was indeed something to worry about. For although Sam couldn't know it at the time, the best years of his producing life were over after *The Best Years* won the Academy Award. He continued to be productive: he made twelve more pictures before he retired in 1960, the most notable being *The Secret Life of Walter Mitty*, *The Bishop's Wife*, *Hans Christian Andersen*, *Guys and Dolls*, and *Porgy and Bess*, but nothing comparable in quality or emotional impact to the string of pictures he produced starting with *These Three* and ending with *The Best Years of Our Lives*.

Of course, he was sixty-five years old by the time he won his first, and only, Oscar—an age when most people usually retire. But physically Sam was still healthy and vigorous. Wealth and success had done nothing to dull his enthusiasm for filmmaking; it was still his all-consuming passion from the moment he climbed out of bed at six A.M. until he retired around midnight.

Not only did Sam have his own full slate of future productions to keep his mind occupied, but he was also running a studio that rented stage and office space to other independent producers—Walter Wanger, Eddie Small, William Goetz, Leo Spitz, the Mirisch brothers, and anyone else who could afford his facilities. This alone made large demands on his time and required almost daily meetings—often around the lunch table—with the men charged with keeping the lot running smoothly and profitably: Gordon Sawyer, the head of the sound department, and Jack Foreman, the studio's general manager. (Frances rarely participated in these luncheon staff meetings, preferring to bring a sandwich from home and eat it in her office.)

If all this was a burden to him, Sam didn't know it. In fact, he seemed to be thriving on it. His only concession to advancing years—and this was an admission more than a concession—was that he was carefully grooming Sam junior to take over the studio someday—but not soon.

Sam junior—a tall, athletic young man who, with his glasses on, bore a startling resemblance to Franklin Roosevelt when he was twenty-one—had worked for his father only once. And that was during a three-month period between his leaving the University of Virginia and a two-year hitch he served in the army, as a lieutenant on General Eisenhower's staff in Paris, during the war.

Working for his father had been "a disastrous experience," recalls Sam junior. "I was looking over the story properties we owned one day and recommended the sale of one that another studio was interested in." Sam senior hit the ceiling, for the story was *Hans Christian Andersen*, one of his favorites.

After that contretemps, the two realized it would be better for both if they didn't work together. So following Sam junior's discharge from the army in 1946, his father got him a job with the J. Arthur Rank Organisation, in London, not primarily to keep him away from Goldwyn Studios, but more because he wanted him to learn about the foreign market.

With the typical foresight—or instinct—that had guided most of his moves all his life, Sam recognized that the foreign market was soon to be extremely important to any filmmaker anxious to get a return on his money, because the bottom had dropped out of the domestic market by the spring of 1947. In the ensuing panic, people who'd been employed by the studios for years were being laid off, and everyone was forecasting doom.

The boom years of the war, when any film, no matter how lousy, could make money, were suddenly at an end—partly because audiences were becoming more discriminating, partly because there wasn't that terrible need to forget and lose themselves in fantasy, partly because the government had stopped a practice called block booking, and partly because of a new medium called television that was keeping those who could afford sets home.

And those who couldn't afford their own TV sets were watching at the homes of their friends who could.

Sam didn't see television as a serious threat to good movies such as the ones he made. In fact, he felt it might be a blessing in disguise, for it would weed out the bad filmmakers, who were really the ones keeping audiences away from theaters anyhow.

At sixty-five, Sam was confident that he could still deliver the quality that brought out long lines to see *The Best Years of Our Lives*. But he never quite hit that peak again. Something seemed to be missing, and many people believed it was Willy Wyler.

But whatever it was—age, the loss of Willy Wyler, or just a general inability to adjust to a swiftly changing world of entertainment—most of Sam's pictures following *Best Years* were flawed, some seriously, some only from a critical point of view, but all could have been better in one way or another.

Examples of this were the two films he released immediately in the wake of *Best Years*—*The Secret Life of Walter Mitty*, based on the James Thurber classic *New Yorker* story about a Caspar Milquetoast who is a "man" only in his fantasy world, and *The Bishop's Wife*, from the Robert Nathan novel.

Neither of these, of course, was intended to be a really significant picture—just good entertainment. In fact Sam decided to make a picture of "Walter Mitty" primarily because he was looking for another vehicle in which to star Danny Kaye, whose last film for him, *The Kid from Brooklyn*, had been a major success in 1946.

Sam never actually read the *New Yorker* story, a confession he made later in a script conference with the picture's two writers—Ken Englund and Everett Freeman. Sam had bought "Mitty" from a synopsis, and in that form it was impossible to tell exactly what Thurber's intent was in writing the story in the first place. It just looked to Sam like a good peg on which to hang a lot of songs and comedy routines. Sam generally wound up in script trouble when he embarked on a picture from that premise, and "Walter Mitty" was no exception to the rule.

The big bone of contention, claims Ken Englund in looking back on the experience, was that Sam could never quite make up his mind whether the dream sequences in which Walter Mitty fantasized the manly side of his self were necessary in the picture. It would seem that they were, since that was what the story was about, and in the beginning Sam favored retaining them, as did Thurber, Norman McLeod, who directed the film, the scriptwriters, and his story editor.

But as "Walter Mitty" was being turned into a movie script, a number of other people started filling Sam's ears with all sorts of doubts to the effect that dream sequences were "too literary," "too smart," "too subtle," and "too *New Yorker*ish."

In other words, the average moviegoer in the Middle West would never understand the nuances of Thurber's gentle humor. Besides that, there was a school of thought that claimed the inhibited Mitty character as conceived by Thurber would not afford Danny Kaye the scope he needed for his wild kind of comedy. Consequently the real Kaye would be sacrificed in order to please a handful of Thurber buffs.

This last frightened Danny Kaye and his wife, Sylvia Fine, who were, understandably, more interested in promoting Kaye than Thurber. Once Kaye and his wife, friends, and agents started articulating their doubts around the studio, Sam tended to side with them. Yes, he was making a Danny Kaye picture, he agreed, and not something to please a few *New Yorker* readers.

Englund and Freeman tried to stick to their own artistic integrity, which told them to go with Thurber's conception. But finally Sam called Englund into his office and said, with a weary sigh, "Ken, I can't keep listening to you on this point. Frankly, let me tell you something for your own good as a writer in Hollywood. Outside of a few thousand people in Manhattan, you are the only one in the rest of America that ever reads that *New Yorker* magazine."

When Englund retorted, and cleverly, he thought, that "Walter Mitty" had also been reprinted in full in the *Reader's Digest*, which had a circulation of millions, Sam silenced him with: "Look, Ken, to break even on a big 'A' picture in color, you have to appeal to more people than the combined readership of the *Reader's Digest* and the *New Yorker*."

Sam finally decided on a middle-of-the-road posture: keep the Walter Mitty character but do everything possible to provide a platform for the varied talents of Danny Kaye. That, of course, meant doing a face-lift on "Walter Mitty."

When the script was finished, Sam and Frances met with Thurber and his wife, Helen, in the Goldwyns' suite in Manhattan's Waldorf Towers to get the author's opinion. Since Thurber was virtually blind, Helen had to read the script aloud to him. Thurber didn't like it at all.

"It's too melodramatic," was his verdict.

Returning to the Coast, Sam decided to junk the project, and he let the writers go. Thirteen days later, Sam called Ken Englund back and said he'd decided to try again, but added that he felt the script needed a lot of work.

"Can't you be more specific?" asked Englund.

"I'll be specific," exploded Sam. "I hate the last sixty pages."

Eventually Sam sent Englund to New York to work with Thurber, who did his best to instill in the script some of the spirit of the original Walter Mitty. But although the picture was financially successful when it was released in 1947, it suffered from being a Danny Kaye vehicle and it never lived up to Sam's earlier expectations. Nor the critics'. Reviewing it in

August 1947, Bosley Crowther wrote: "Much of the Thurber character is lost because of the lack of contrast between Walter Mitty's dream world and actual experience. After an appropriate hum-drum start as a timid proof reader, he is suddenly thrust into a melodramatic adventure involving a pretty girl, stolen art treasures and murder, which rivals the boldest of his fancies."

James Thurber wasn't too pleased with the final results either. He felt that the disputed dream sequences contained far too much violence and gore for a gentle comedy.

An often-told story around Hollywood has it that when Sam heard of Thurber's displeasure, he was very upset and wrote him, "I am very sorry that you felt it was too blood and thirsty." To which Thurber was alleged to have wired back, "Not only did I think so, but I was horror and struck."

As amusing as that exchange may be, it obviously has no basis in truth, because all of Sam's secretaries were paid to know their job and were extremely scrupulous about seeing to it that their boss's letters—no matter how garbled the language and thoughts when they came flying out of his mouth—were grammatically correct in their final form.

"The first time I took a letter from him," recalls Goldie Arthur, "I couldn't believe it. He called me on the intercom and said 'Bring in your book.' I'd barely got through the door when he started talking—very fast . . . never completing a sentence . . . jumping back and forth . . . making absolutely no sense. Then he said, 'Read that back to me.' Now there was no way I could read it back to him, because there were no sentences—just garbled thoughts that the CIA would have difficulty deciphering. So I said, 'Let me go out and make a rough draft of it.' And I did, and I rewrote the letter, making it grammatical and just keeping what he wanted to say. And that's how we worked from that point on."

So no matter what the jokesters say, trying to discredit Sam, there's little chance that "blood and thirsty" ever passed through his secretary's typewriter.

To attempt to turn a gentle story like "Walter Mitty" into a boisterous Danny Kaye comedy was a risky proposition from the beginning. But Sam couldn't have played the movie game safer with *The Bishop's Wife*. After buying the best-selling novel from Robert (*Portrait of Jenny*) Nathan, he commissioned Robert Sherwood to write the screenplay—his first movie-writing assignment since winning the Oscar for *Best Years*. However, the kind of fantasy in which an angel in Cary Grant's clothing comes down from heaven to save Loretta Young's and David Niven's shaky marriage was not exactly up Sherwood's alley. A realist, he didn't have the lightness of touch required, nor the ability to plug some of the holes Sam, Frances, and his story chief, Pat Duggan, saw in the script.

All during the script-preparation stages, however, Sam had been cognizant of one fact—the role of the angel required a special kind of casting, otherwise the whole thing would fall apart. From the beginning, Sam knew that Cary Grant was right for it—in fact, in his opinion, no other person would do. And so even before Sherwood was off the script Sam had contacted Jules Styne of MCA about getting his client Cary Grant for *The Bishop's Wife*.

"Absolutely not," Styne had told him. "He had four commitments right now that'll keep him busy for the next four years."

"I'll give him anything he wants," offered Sam.

"It's not money," said Styne. "He just doesn't have the time unless you want to postpone production until 1955."

Nevertheless, Sam hounded Styne every day for the next six months. "Only a crazy person would take that kind of rejection," says Goldie Arthur. "But Mr. Goldwyn felt that only Cary Grant could play the angel, and he kept calling him right up until the day he had to make a decision about who to cast in the role if he couldn't get Grant. And then he phoned Styne one last time, and would you believe it? The picture Cary Grant was supposed to go into next had just been called off—and Grant had a six-month hole in his schedule beginning immediately. Naturally, Styne said he could have him."

Judging from the way the picture started off under William Seiter's direction, Sam had some cause to regret his perseverance. For some reason, Grant was playing the angel a little too fey. Sam wanted him to be more manly and put some "sex appeal" in the character, and he insisted Grant do it *his* way.

"I won't be happy playing it that way," pouted Grant. "You want me to be happy, don't you, Mr. Goldwyn?"

"I don't give a damn if you're happy or not," replied Sam. "You're going to be here only a few weeks, and this picture will be out for a long time. I would rather you should be unhappy here, and then we can all be happy later." Sam had a theory that when people were happy making a picture, it was usually a stinker.

After seeing the first week's rushes, Sam fired Bill Seiter, giving him his full fee, and threw out everything that had been shot. Before he was through, that move wound up costing him $900,000.

"The angel stuff just isn't believable," said Sam. He next brought in Henry Koster, who'd directed *Three Smart Girls* and a number of schmaltzy Pasternak pictures for MGM, to start all over and try to make an angel acceptable to war-weary, cynical audiences.

There were no crises until the first preview, which took place on a Thursday night. "On Friday morning, the phone in my bedroom rang at seven o'clock," recalls Billy Wilder, who had nothing to do with *The Bishop's*

Wife, and who, at the time, was preparing to shoot a picture of his own at Paramount two weeks later. However, he had been a friend of Goldwyn's and a frequent guest at his and Frances's dinner table ever since *Ball of Fire*.

"This is Goldwyn," blurted out a pathetic-sounding voice on the other end of the line. "We're in terrible trouble. I previewed *The Bishop's Wife* last night, and it doesn't make sense." Sam sounded practically in tears.

"Sam, *you're* in trouble," Wilder corrected him. "I had nothing to do with the picture. I don't even know what it's about."

"You're a friend of mine!" cried out Sam. "Come over. I'll run it for you. And bring Brackett. We'll discuss this."

After seeing it, Wilder and Brackett agreed that *The Bishop's Wife* needed "clarification." In fact, in their opinion, it needed "three major scenes."

"You'll fix it for me!" said Sam eagerly. "I have to have it by Monday morning, so Henry Koster can start shooting."

Having a picture of their own they were preparing, the two writers hesitated.

"I'll make it worth your while for you," said Sam. "If you'll just fix it. I'll give you twenty-five thousand dollars!"

To complete the repair job by Monday morning at eight o'clock, Wilder and Brackett worked all night Friday, all day and night Saturday, and all day Sunday. They handed the new scenes in to Goldwyn late Sunday afternoon. Sam read the pages over, thanked them for helping him out in an emergency, and they left.

The new scenes were shot and inserted in the picture, and *The Bishop's Wife* was previewed a second time. The next morning Wilder received another phone call from Sam. "We previewed the picture," he said enthusiastically. "There's a difference like night and day. I couldn't believe it."

"I believe it," said Wilder wryly.

"I want you and Brackett to come over and have lunch with me today, and we'll discuss what I'm going to do for you," said Sam.

On their way to meet Goldwyn, Brackett said to Wilder, "Why don't we make a gesture? Who the hell needs twenty-five thousand dollars? With taxes the way they are, we won't be able to keep much of it anyway. So let's be generous."

"I'm with you," said Wilder.

During the lunch in Goldwyn's private dining room, Sam raved about what a great picture *The Bishop's Wife* had turned out to be, thanks to their efforts, and then said, "Now about the money I told you I was going to give you—"

"Mr. Goldwyn," Brackett interrupted him, "Billy and I have discussed it, and we have decided we don't really want it."

"That's funny," said Sam. "I've come to the same conclusion."

When *The Bishop's Wife* finally reached the screen of the Astor Theater during the Christmas holiday season, Bosley Crowther gave it a surprisingly warm greeting:

> Emissaries from Heaven are not conspicuously exceptional on the screen. And certainly communion with Angels is traditional at Christmastime, which is the season most of us mortals need reassurance, anyhow. So there is nothing surprising about the miracle that occurs in Samuel Goldwyn's *Bishop's Wife* . . . except that it is superb. We cannot recommend to you a more delightful and appropriate Christmas show.

Sam had proven once again that perseverance plus money, not to mention a little help from two angels named Brackett and Wilder, could produce the vaunted Goldwyn Touch or something resembling it.

Sam and Wilder had very little in common besides a mutual desire to make good movies, Wilder being an intellectual with a sharp wit, which he used to puncture the pomposity of men exactly like Sam, who took themselves very seriously. But because Wilder was tops in his field and a handy man to know in an emergency, Sam remained on extremely close terms with him until the end of his days. They dined and played bridge together, and Sam and Frances made it almost a yearly habit to go with the Wilders to the famous European spa of Badgastein.

That's the way it was with Sam; he had to be friendly with whomever he felt could do him the most good. Or as Ben Sonnenberg put it, "Sam couldn't help gravitating toward the seat of power—whether it was in the entertainment world, government, big business, or even soldiering."

During World War II, for example, Sam was close to the entire Roosevelt family—so much so that he even voted the Democratic ticket for the first and only time in his life. He was on intimate terms with General Eisenhower—even after he became president—and often used to call him on the telephone, or have him and Mamie as houseguests when they came to Hollywood. And when he was in London, Sam used to call on Winston Churchill at 10 Downing Street, where he was always welcome. It was there, in fact, that Sam met and became friendly with Field Marshal Montgomery, the commander at the battle of El Alamein.

Later, when General Montgomery came to Hollywood to give Darryl Zanuck some technical advice on a film he was making about Rommel, *The Desert Fox*, Sam could hardly wait to get him up to the house so he could show him off to a small circle of select guests. He got him, and his introduction of him has never been forgotten.

"And now," said Sam, introducing the medal-bedecked British general to his guests, "I'd like you to meet my good friend—Marshall Field Montgomery."

Although it was evident that Sam hadn't lost any of his ability to coin a phrase or confuse a name, he wasn't much of a formal speechmaker. In fact, the very thought of standing up before a gathering of strangers and giving a talk was enough to have his stomach turning flip-flops and his hands breaking out into a clammy sweat. But no public appearance ever frightened him more than the talk he had to give to the glove manufacturers of Gloversville, when he and Frances were visiting Saratoga Springs one fall in the late forties. Sam had gone there for a rest, which was an impossibility after it got around to the people of Gloversville that one of their most famous alumni was in the neighboring health spa.

Shortly after they checked in, the phone in the Goldwyns' suite rang, and it was Sam's old boss, Albert Aaron, calling to invite him and Frances to dinner at the Kingsborough Hotel. Afterward, asked Aaron, would Sam make a short speech to a gathering of local businessmen—mostly glove manufacturers at the Businessmen's Club?

Sam was not enthusiastic over the prospect, but being somewhat sentimental about the town where it had all started for him—and also curious to see it again before he died—he accepted Aaron's invitation to be at the Kingsborough the following evening at seven.

As the hour of the ordeal approached, Sam grew more nervous than a thoroughbred colt entering the starting gate for the first time. When he was dressing for the occasion, according to Frances, he couldn't make up his mind what suit to wear. After she helped him choose one, he couldn't decide on a tie to go with it.

Finally she got him ready. Then he wasn't satisfied with Frances's appearance, especially when she put on her mink coat.

"Take if off," he ordered her. "It's too showy."

Frances obediently changed it for an old nutria coat.

"That's *too* old," said Sam, studying her. "Put back the mink, but take off your jewelry."

Frances wasn't wearing any jewelry except a wrist watch, but in order to calm Sam down, she removed that and slipped it in her pocket instead.

Sam had hired a limousine and chauffeur to drive them the twenty miles to Gloversville in style. But three times during the short ride Sam's nerves played such havoc with his bladder that he had to have the car stopped while he got out and relieved himself behind a bush.

Finally they arrived at the stately Kingsborough Hotel, which was not quite so grand as Sam remembered it when he was reminiscing about his childhood to Frances. Still, it did have real marble floors, mahogany walls, leather chairs, and polished brass spittoons, and it was easy to see that it had once had class—at least enough to impress a fourteen-year-old immigrant from Poland and give him the incentive to make something better of his life.

Once inside the lobby, Sam and Frances were converged upon by Albert Aaron—now a very successful glovemaker who owned his own plant—and about twelve of his glove-manufacturing friends. Aaron was older than Sam, but fit and prosperous-looking as he beamed at the boy who made good in Hollywood and pumped his hand vigorously.

As Aaron started to lead Sam and Frances toward the dining room, where a large table was set up with floral decorations in the center, a man touched Sam's arm and said that there was someone in the other end of the lobby who wanted to know if he remembered Hamburg.

Looking back over his shoulder, Sam appeared startled, then taking those brisk, long strides he was noted for, headed across the lobby to where a white-haired old man was seated in a worn leather chair. Sam studied his wrinkled face hard for a few moments, then threw his arms around him and exclaimed, "Of course . . . of course."

It was Jacob Libglid, the glovemaker's apprentice, who'd rescued Sam from starvation on the streets of Hamburg on a bleak day in 1894, and raised the money to send him across the Channel to his relatives in England.

"My God, my God," exclaimed Sam. "What are you doing in Gloversville?"

"Hitler," answered Libglid with a sardonic smile.

"Well, what are you doing?" asked Sam. "Do you need anything? How do you make a living?"

"No, I'm getting along fine," said Libglid. "I'm a pretty good glovemaker."

"Pretty good?" said Aaron, coming over to witness the reunion. "He's the best in my plant, the best in America."

Sam invited Libglid to join him and the others at dinner, and afterward he took him to the Businessmen's Club, where about a hundred people were gathered in the small auditorium to hear Sam speak. Sam's nervousness had returned by the time he addressed the group—so much so that he forgot to put his hat down and kept fiddling with it in his hands as he made a short but poignant speech. In conclusion, he said: "Gentlemen, I'm no speechmaker, and no businessman either. But I'm glad you asked me to be here tonight. Because, well—I got my start here in Gloversville. And the people were good to me—and—well, I've always tried not to do anything to make Gloversville ashamed of me. And before I sit down, I'd like to thank the fellow who made it all possible—Jacob Libglid." And he made his old benefactor get to his feet and take a bow.

Sam's words would never go down in the archives alongside Patrick Henry's "Give me liberty or give me death," and Nathan Hale's "I only regret that I have but one life to lose for my country." But they did make a lonely old man happy for a few brief moments that night.

Jacob Libglid lived only a couple of years more. He died in March 1950, at the age of eighty-five. But, thanks to Sam's speech, he did not die a nonentity. All the major newspapers carried a wire-service story of his passing which made note of the fact that Jacob Libglid was the man responsible for getting Sam Goldwyn to America.

25

Sam Takes on the Majors

THE FIFTIES WERE NOT the healthiest years the movie business had ever known. They were marked by an enormous drop in theater grosses, uncertainty and fear about the future, and the ascendancy of television as the entertainment medium, or opiate, of the masses.

"There is not a single film company of any importance which has not been in the red since the last quarter of 1947," stated Eric Johnston, president of the Motion Picture Association of America, in February 1948. "Salaries are far too high in every field of film production."

Even the normally optimistic Sam was running a little scared, and shortly after Johnston's statement, he issued one of his own in which he announced that he was not only slashing the salaries of all the executives at his studio by 50 percent, but was taking the same cut himself (whatever that meant, since he was paying his own salary). "I practice what I preach," proclaimed Sam to the trade papers. "The stars and artistic creators who have the foresight to cooperate in making fine pictures on a sound economic basis will find their careers in this industry more secure."

Sam had never had the same overhead problem as the majors, who amortized the cost of running the entire studio by charging expenses against each production that had nothing to do with the actual making of the picture. Moreover, many of their "B" pictures were made just to have something to charge studio overhead to. The "B" pictures weren't supposed to be good, and most of them weren't, but who cared, because the exhibitors were forced to take them—until the government handed down its "consent decree" that put an end to block booking. With no sure place to sell their "B" pictures, the majors had to stop making them, with the result that hundreds of studio employees had to be laid off. And when they stopped making "B" pictures, the "A" pictures had to assume all studio overhead costs that heretofore had been divided up between the "A" pictures and the "B" pic-

tures. That, in turn, made the "A" pictures more costly and meant they
had to gross more in order to break even. Because of television, they were
grossing less and, as a result, most were losing money. So in a strange way
the "consent decree," healthy as it was in the long run for the movie industry, was one of the causes of the 1947 movie depression.

Since Sam had never made "B" pictures, he didn't have as much fat to
cut from his studio's payroll. Each of Sam's pictures was produced under a
separate corporate title (Potash and Perlmutter Productions, for example).
Only expenses incurred in the actual making of a particular film would be
charged against it. Sam's various corporations were so separate, in fact, that
each of his productions paid rent for stage space and other studio facilities,
just as the outside producers on the lot did.

Until the depression hit Hollywood, the majors—MGM, Fox, Warner
Brothers, and Columbia—kept under contract dozens of high-priced producers, writers, directors, and actors who sat around collecting four-figure
weekly salaries even when they weren't assigned to any particular project.
It wasn't that way with Sam's operation. Except for his small personal staff
and the people charged with running the physical end of the studio, like
Jack Foreman and Gordon Sawyer, nobody worked for Sam who wasn't assigned to a picture. And when their jobs were over, they immediately went
off salary.

As a result, Sam Goldwyn wasn't in the same kind of money trouble as
the major studios—as long as he could turn out high-quality pictures and
sell them to exhibitors at profitable rental rates. There, unfortunately, was
the rub, for with the sudden drop in American movie attendance, theater
owners resisted paying the high rentals that the very successful independent
producers, such as Selznick and Goldwyn, had demanded for their product, and got, in the past. The theater owners claimed they had to do some
belt tightening, too, if they expected to survive, and that therefore the film
producers would have to settle for less profit on their product.

Sam didn't believe the theaters weren't making good profits. He believed
this was just a ploy on the part of the large, monopolistic theater chains—
many of which, like Fox West Coast Theaters, were still under control of
the majors—to squeeze the independent producers out of business.

When Sam voiced his opinion to the powerful Association of Motion Picture Producers, to which all the majors belonged, but couldn't get them to
do anything about it, he withdrew from that organization in 1949 and announced his intention to give his "undivided support" to the newly formed
Society of Independent Motion Picture Producers. On the same day he also
resigned from the Motion Picture Association of America.

In a formal statement accompanying his resignation from the MPAA,
Sam said, "I find myself unable to agree conscientiously with many of the

policies formulated by the Association and feel that they do not represent the interest of the independent producers. The fight of the independent producer for an open market is a fight for survival, not only for themselves and their employees but also for the continuance of the independent creative efforts which contributed so much to the vitality and progress of the screen. There must be a return to real free enterprise in our industry—an opportunity for all producers to show their pictures to the public in every community on a fair and nondiscriminatory basis.

"The future of good motion pictures is completely bound up with the efforts of the Society of Independent Motion Picture Producers to bring this about. From now on, I intend to concentrate my energies on the efforts of the Society to bring about a fair deal for independent producers."

Upon hearing the news of Sam's resignation, Eric Johnston, president of MPAA, stated to the press: "Our members are relieved by Mr. Goldwyn's withdrawal. During his association with us he has demonstrated a unique and singular flare for saying one thing and doing exactly the opposite."

Sam was undeterred by Eric Johnston's verbal slap on the wrist, and in May 1950 he demonstrated his determination to break the theater monopolies by filing suit against them.

"GOLDWYN IN FILM WAR," screamed a headline in the *Los Angeles Times* on the morning of May 17, 1950. The story said:

> Trebled damages amounting to $6,750,000 and dissolution of an alleged booking monopoly of 445 moving picture theaters were asked today by Samuel Goldwyn, film producer, in a suit filed in San Francisco in a U.S. Court against Charles P. Skouras, President of Fox West Coast Agency Corporation, and ten other defendants. The suit charged the defendants, since 1925, have violated the Sherman Anti-Trust Act by unlawfully contracting, combining and conspiring to monopolize for restraint of trade in commerce for licensing and exhibition of motion pictures. Also named as defendants besides Skouras were: Fox West Coast Theaters, Fox West Coast Agency Corporation, National Theaters, Inc., Golden State Theaters, and United California Theaters.

One of Sam's attorneys in the case was Joseph Alioto, who would later be mayor of San Francisco and a big wheel in the California Democratic organization.

In a statement to the San Francisco press, Sam declared himself as being for "open bidding" on pictures, with the highest bidders getting the film. "We independents in Hollywood are making the best pictures in years, but we can't market them, because we're up against a barrier of monopoly, conspiracy, and collusion, which, if not broken, will inevitably destroy our incentive," he said. "We owe it to them, the young producers, who are coming along. I am the first producer to fight the asserted exhibition monopoly, and I have a little money left, and I'm going to use it all up if I have to."

He took a final parting shot at the Skouras brothers by saying to the reporters, "They are completely greedy and ought to be sent back to Russia, where they came from." As usual, Sam's best Goldwynisms popped out when he was under tension. The Skouras brothers, of course, were Greek immigrants.

As the trial proceeded, the testimony presented by both the plaintiff and the defendants centered around the extremely complicated details of film distribution, mostly involving comparison of percentages paid for film rental of movies made by independents as opposed to what films made by the majors were receiving.

Many so-called expert witnesses were produced by both sides to back up their respective claims. For months they submitted statistical studies on film rentals, profits and losses of theaters, theater operations, along with accompanying charts, ledgers, and so forth. To detail the reams of testimony would fill a thick book. In fact, the court testimony became so convoluted and wearisome to listen to that at one point Judge Edward Murphy, who'd been trying the case for over six months (with only a break for the Christmas holidays) snapped, "I am fed up with all this expertise. This case is going to be decided on principles of law and not economics."

The case dragged on for eleven years, which must have established some kind of record in jurisprudence. It went on so long, in fact, that the original judge on the case died in the middle of it—in 1958. This, in turn, caused further delays while his replacement, Judge George B. Harris, familiarized himself with the past proceedings.

Three years later, on May 5, 1961, the trial came to a conclusion. Reported the *Los Angeles Times:* "GOLDWYN WINS SUIT AGAINST FILM GROUP." Three days later Judge Harris awarded Sam $300,000 in actual damages. The defendants, of course, immediately appealed, but, happily for our tenacious hero, the verdict was upheld by the United States Court of Appeals in March of the following year.

Sam's court expenses undoubtedly ate up more than the $300,000 he won, but it was a moral victory in that he must be given credit for—almost single-handedly—breaking the backs of the monopolistic theater chains. Twentieth Century–Fox was forced to divest itself of all its theater holdings, with all the other major studios soon following suit. Today, thanks largely to Sam Goldwyn, the independent producers are the backbone of the business.

While Sam was fighting the theater Goliaths, he was also turning out movies—but not at the rate he once had. As Sam said earlier, "I practice what I preach." And what he was preaching most often in the fifties was that studios should concentrate on quality, not quantity, and that the sooner everybody cut down on production, the healthier the film industry would be as a whole.

By that yardstick, the film industry should have been in the midst of a boom, because Hollywood's total output had dropped from around 600 films in its peak years to something less than 300 by the mid-fifties. Less quantity, however, wasn't the complete answer to an ailing box office, which saw attendance figures drop from 85 million people a week to 35 million a week in a decade. But quality, at least as it related to size, seemed to contain a few of the answers.

The wide-screen revolution, which began in 1952, was an outgrowth of the thinking that posed the question: What could theater exhibition give the customers that they couldn't get at home? Quality alone wasn't the answer, because they were beginning to get some of that on their TV screens. But something the public couldn't get at home was size. And so theater screens were made wider and taller by using a new projection lens that did just that. Then ordinary wide screen was quickly improved upon with new filming and projecting processes such as Cinerama, 3-D, Twentieth Century–Fox's CinemaScope, Paramount's VistaVision, and Mike Todd's 65-mm Todd-AO.

All were variations on the same wide-screen theme, which lent more scope to films, spectacle pictures in particular, and thereby gave the filmgoer something he or she could not see on the tiny TV screen, which, when one thinks about it, has never grown much larger than its early models.

Fox's *The Robe* was one of the earliest spectacles made in CinemaScope, and it was a spectacular success. It cost $5 million to make, but it grossed $18 million in the United States and Canada alone. Mike Todd's *Around the World in 80 Days*, made in Todd-AO, was also a box-office bonanza. With those two successes, the wide-screen rush was on, with every theater in America that wasn't out of business switching to one of the new processes.

In the interim, Sam had produced a few modest moneymakers: *A Song Is Born* with Danny Kaye, Tommy Dorsey, and Louis Armstrong; *Enchantment*, in which he vainly attempted to make a major star of Farley Granger; *Our Very Own*, a soap opera about an adopted child, starring Ann Blyth; *Roseanna McCoy*, an updated version of the Hatfield-McCoy feud; *My Foolish Heart*, with Susan Hayward; and *Edge of Doom*.

The latter was a starkly realistic drama about a young man in violent revolt against poverty and the moral precepts of the Catholic Church. Like *Dead End* it had an honest statement to make on the subject, and many critics regard it as one of Sam Goldwyn's better films. But it was neither a spectacle, being in black and white on ordinary wide screen, nor escapist entertainment, and audiences would not buy it. Smelling a flop, Sam yanked it out of the theater during its initial New York engagement and reshot some of it, but to no avail. The public still did not buy it.

When *I Want You*, a story of army induction during the Korean war, starring Dorothy McGuire, also failed to live up to the Goldwyn label, Sam decided to resurrect one of his pet projects—*The Story of Hans Christian Andersen*, which for lack of a good script had been lying dormant in his desk drawer since he had acquired it from its author, Myles Connally, fourteen years before. In *Andersen* Sam saw one of those rare opportunities to make a musical film that would have universal appeal. But when script after script, by some of Hollywood's brightest writers, had failed to bring any life to the story of Denmark's great spinner of fairy tales, Sam was advised by Frances and Pat Duggan, his story editor, to sell the property in 1950 to another studio which was showing an interest in buying it from Goldwyn at a price that would give him a healthy profit.

Looking anguished, Sam said, "No one understands—not my wife, not my son, not my story editor—nobody understands that I can't possibly sell *Andersen*. Its possibilities are too good."

"But you'll never make it," scoffed Duggan. "You can't even get a writer."

"That's where you're wrong," smiled Sam. "I just signed Moss Hart."

If anyone had the qualifications to write the story of Hans Christian Andersen, it should have been Moss Hart, coauthor with George S. Kaufman of many successful Broadway plays, including the Pulitzer Prize winner *You Can't Take It with You*. He was also sole author of *Lady in the Dark*.

But *Hans Christian Andersen*, at least under Sam Goldwyn's aegis, was not destined to be a great picture, or even a good one, in spite of a script by Moss Hart, hit songs by America's hottest popular song composer, Frank Loesser, and a cast including Danny Kaye in the title role and the great ballerina Renée Jeanmaire as his costar, plus the entire Paris Ballet Company.

Because Jeanmaire tore a tendon during one of the ballet sequences, the production had to be postponed for several months and didn't open at New York's Criterion Theater until November 22, 1952. Sam and Frances attended the première, which Frances remembers as being a success.

The critics weren't quite so sanguine. They raved about Jeanmaire's ballet sequences and Frank Loesser's score, but felt that Danny Kaye was terribly miscast as the most famous Dane since Hamlet, and that Moss Hart's script had little or nothing to do with the life of Hans Christian Andersen.

In addition, an AP dispatch from Copenhagen reported that the Danish foreign office was considering making a strong formal protest against the picture, "because it was insulting to the memory of the beloved fairy tale writer."

Sam saw his hopes of a world première in Copenhagen's Tivoli Gardens shattered, and lost no time in counterattacking. He invited the Danish consul to dinner, and he inundated the Danish foreign office with clippings of the picture's best reviews plus stories of how well it was doing at the box office.

Nothing dented Denmark's armor until Frank Loesser's song "Wonderful Copenhagen" suddenly caught on and became a worldwide hit. Miraculously this started a tourist boom in Copenhagen, which pleased the Danish government so that they forgave Sam his trespasses on Andersen's character and invited him to hold the world première there, after all.

This gave the picture a boost, and it wound up making money on both sides of the Atlantic.

Sam was nearly seventy when the musical play *Guys and Dolls*, with a libretto by Jo Swerling and Abe Burrows and a score by Frank Loesser, opened in New York City on November 24, 1950. It drew raves from Broadway's "Murderer's Row" and was an immediate and sensational hit.

Naturally Sam coveted it for Goldwyn Studios, but when MGM bid $850,000 for it, his dreams of making a movie of the great musical were shattered. No studio had ever paid that much for a single property before, and Sam didn't think it prudent for him to make a higher bid, either.

However, after several sleepless nights worrying about it, Sam astounded all of Hollywood by buying *Guys and Dolls* for $1 million cash, plus 10 percent of the worldwide gross over $10 million. Most people thought he was insane to spend that in 1953—a time when most movies were failing. How in the world was he going to get his money back, much less make a profit? everybody was asking.

But Sam knew how: by making a good picture and buying the biggest names available to star in it.

At the time, the two hottest male names at the box office were Frank Sinatra and Marlon Brando. One did not have to stretch one's imagination too much to envision Frank Sinatra in the role of Nathan Detroit, the New York sharpie. He wasn't quite Sam Levine, but at least he could sing. Brando, on the other hand, could neither sing nor dance. Moreover, his "method school" of acting didn't quite generate the lightness expected of Sky Masterson, the gambler who falls in love with the Salvation Army lass (Jean Simmons). Brando didn't think so, either, and had to be talked into accepting the role by Sam over dinner one night at the Goldwyn residence.

"Before I realized what was happening," Brando recalled later, "I was drifting off on a cloud saying to myself, 'You're only a bathtub singer, boy, but if the man insists you can sing and dance, why not take the chance? After all, it's *his* money.' "

Michael Kidd, who was doing the choreography, was given the job of transforming Brando into a musical-comedy star, and after a couple of weeks in the studio dance rehearsal hall he had him high kicking and two-stepping like he'd never heard of Lee Strasberg or Tennessee Williams.

In the rushes Sam was pleased with the performance all his stars were giving under the direction of Joe Mankiewicz, and before the picture was half finished shooting he was convinced he had another hit. However, with what it was going to cost him—$5.5 million before it was in the can—he realized it would take some exceptional promoting to make it all worthwhile financially. Luckily Howard Dietz, who'd just retired from MGM after thirty years on the job, was available and willing to do a final chore for his first movie boss.

Being no fool, Dietz wanted Sinatra and Brando to make personal appearances in conjunction with the film's various openings. But both Sinatra and Brando had publicly avowed their dislike of participating in any promotional gimmickry, no matter whom they were working for. Sam decided to handle them in his usual subtle way.

One day Sam dropped down on the set, and between takes asked Brando to step out into the street with him while Mankiewicz was preparing his next setup. Brando did, and found parked by the entrance to the sound stage a brand-new white Thunderbird.

"That's for you," beamed Sam.

"What for?" asked Brando.

"Just a bonus because you're doing such a good job."

Brando accepted the automobile, though not quite certain why Sam had given it to him—until the picture was about to be released and Sam asked him to make personal appearances at both the New York and Chicago openings. Ordinarily Brando would have refused, "but how could I—after he gave me a brand-new Thunderbird?" he bleated later to a friend.

Sinatra received a Thunderbird, too, but when Sam asked him to go on "The Ed Sullivan Show," the singer replied, "Why should I? I can get a helluva lot more doing my own special."

As it turned out, Sam didn't need to much press agent wizardry, because the New York reviews were sensational. On the morning of November 5, 1955, the *Daily News*, the *Herald Tribune*, and the *Times* were all raves, with the *Tribune* saying, "It retains the purity of the Broadway original," and the *Times* writing: "Sam Goldwyn was playing an odds on favorite when he plunked down to make a film of *Guys and Dolls*, and as any smart player will tell you, an odds on favorite is a more than somewhat tricky thing. But the gamble this time has paid off richly. *Guys and Dolls* romped across the finish line in its première last night at the Capital well in front where it belongs." There was, however, some minor quibbling about Sinatra's Nathan Detroit ("Too bland," wrote Bosley Crowther) and Brando's Sky Masterson ("He doesn't seem to understand the part").

Brisk business, plus four Academy Award nominations, cheered Sam sufficiently to plan a world première in Tokyo the following spring, which Sam and Frances attended. Concurrently with the Tokyo première, Brando was in Japan shooting *Teahouse of the August Moon*. When Sam heard about it, he asked Brando to attend the opening, promising the actor that the rest of the cast would be there, too. Brando said he would, but when Sinatra refused to go, Brando changed his mind. "I've done enough for that white Thunderbird," he told Sam.

As Sam learned from Brando and Sinatra, directors aren't the only ones who bite the hand that lays the golden egg.

26

Doctor's Orders

ALTHOUGH EVERY MOVE of Sam Goldwyn's as a producer seemed to be crassly calculated to draw attention to himself and his pictures, he actually was a very private man. He tried to live apart from the normal Hollywood glitter—there were no drunken orgies or swimming pool incidents ever reported at his house—and he drew a curtain of secrecy around the many generous things he did for the community, for charitable organizations, for the movie industry, and for individuals who needed help or encouragement.

Because of Sam's reluctance to publicize such matters, most of his donations remain known only to the family and the Goldwyn Foundation—a group set up to distribute Sam's generous outflow. Over the years, however, there have been enough leaks to the press to convince anyone who doubts it that Sam was an extremely charitable fellow.

In 1947 Sam was elected president of the United Jewish Appeal, succeeding Joe Schenck, and through his tireless efforts he helped to raise $8,750,000 for war relief, resettlement in Israel of the homeless, and maintenance of the many Jewish charities in the United States. From then until his death, he personally donated $100,000 annually to United Jewish Welfare, a total of about $2.5 million.

In addition to that he organized the Permanent Charities Committee of the Motion Picture Industry and donated $75,000 so that the organization could have a headquarters building. He also contributed $250,000 to the Motion Picture Country Home and Hospital, which takes care of Hollywood's old, infirm, and homeless, of which there are many.

The world would never have known about the latter two contributions had not Y. Frank Freeman, who was head of Paramount Studios at the time, come to Sam and specifically requested that he *not* keep his generosity a secret.

"What business is it of anybody else?" asked Sam.

"We need it as an inducement to the others who can afford to give but who so far haven't," pleaded Freeman.

So grudgingly Sam let the two charities make public his donations.

Down through the years, the film industry has held a number of fund-raising luncheons and dinner banquets at which the guests were asked to make sizable pledges. Sam and Frances could always be counted upon to be in the vanguard of the biggest contributors.

At one luncheon for the City of Hope, at the Beverly Wilshire Hotel, Sam and Frances found themselves seated next to Irving Brecher, a well-known Hollywood comedy writer and director. Brecher remembered that the food consisted of the customary hotel-style creamed chicken in a patty shell. Sam took one look at the dish in front of him, then told Frances he could not possibly eat anything so rich and asked her to get something simpler for him while he went out to the lobby to make a phone call to the studio.

While Sam was gone the actor who was emceeing the affair started asking for pledges. Since Sam wasn't back yet, Frances pledged $200,000 in both of their names. As his pledge was being announced, Sam returned to the table and started to dig into a pair of broiled lamb chops that the waiter had just set before him.

Never at a loss for a funny quip, Brecher leaned over to Sam and whispered to him, "Mr. Goldwyn, if I'm not mistaken, those lamb chops just cost you $100,000 apiece."

"Can't help it," shrugged Sam. "Doctor's orders."

Politically Sam was an enigma. He voted for Franklin Roosevelt during the war years. But except for that period, he had voted the straight Republican ticket since Woodrow Wilson ruined the glove business for him in 1912. But when the J. Parnell Thomas House Committee on Un-American Activities started investigating the movie business in the late forties, Sam came out strongly in defense of the Hollywood Ten, the writers accused of infiltrating Communist propaganda into films, while others, like Louis B. Mayer, were too cowardly to disagree with the committee.

In a meeting called by studio heads at Hillcrest Country Club to discuss the "Communist" problem, Louis B. Mayer mentioned the name of a young writer who was suspected of being the ringleader of the Hollywood radicals and suggested that he be blackballed.

Upon hearing the name mentioned, Sam stood up and said, "If that snot-nosed baby is the Red boss in Hollywood, then, gentlemen, we've got nothing to fear. Let's go home."

Later, when the committee announced it was planning to summon before them Sam's close friend Robert Sherwood, in order to examine certain aspects of *The Best Years of Our Lives* (which couldn't have been more pro-American if it had been written by the Daughters of the American Revolution), Sam challenged the committee to come up with "facts" or he would sue them for damages.

Sam's stand in refusing to jump on the anti-Communist bandwagon was given credit for causing the committee to suddenly drop its entire investigation of Hollywood.

Because Sam never lost his belief that the writer is the keystone of every successful movie production, he established scholarships at the UCLA film school. He also sponsored an annual Goldwyn Creative Writing Award, with $2,000 going to the winner, and $500 to the student who takes second prize. Nearly 100 percent of the winners have gone on to professional careers in TV and films, but Francis Ford Coppola, writer and producer of *The Godfather* and *Godfather II*, is perhaps the most notable, not to mention the richest.

Sam's faith in the young had always been unshakable, but because he was such a busy man, it wasn't always easy for the young to get an audience with Sam. One neophyte writer, after six months of trying, was finally granted a fifteen-minute interview with Sam to tell him a story he had written.

While the young author was enthusiastically spinning his yarn, Sam fell sound asleep in his chair. Incensed, the writer ran around the desk and shook Sam awake. "Mr. Goldwyn," he exclaimed, "it has taken me six months' time, expense, and energy to get this fifteen-minute interview with you to tell you my idea for a sensational movie. All I'm asking for is your opinion, and you fall asleep!"

Sam shrugged and said calmly, "Isn't sleeping an opinion?"

27

Exhausted from Not Talking

ALVA JOHNSTON WROTE of Sam in 1937, "He has boundless courage, and is always at his best in disaster." If ever a project was designed to test those words, it was his last film, *Porgy and Bess*, which he decided to make when he was seventy-five years old—an age when he was surely entitled to retire in luxury, play a little croquet, and perhaps write another book of memoirs in which he would reveal nothing. But Sam was still too restless and his health too robust for him to stop doing what he loved to do best.

The thirty minutes of setting-up exercises which he performed daily before coming to the studio kept him, as always, perfectly trim. He still strode through the streets of his studio with his shoulders squared and the brisk, arm-swinging gait of a man who gets things done. He was becoming slightly deaf in one ear (which was really no inconvenience to a man who doesn't like to listen, anyway), but he wasn't much balder than he'd been as a young man—just a lot grayer. His sharp nose and jutting jaw seemed pinched together over his thin lips more than they once did—like one of those rubber faces kids used to play with and squeeze into many different weird expressions. Occasionally he wore tortoise-framed glasses—mostly for reading and croquet—but his blue eyes still sparkled penetratingly and gave someone looking at him the impression of alert impatience.

The only thing that possibly dated Sam was his suits and sport jackets, which were always razor-pressed and impeccably clean, but looked in their wide-lapelled and double-breasted splendor as if he had bought them around World War I. If he were alive today, of course, he'd be right in style, but in 1957, the narrow look was in. Sam was a big spender at the studio, but he saw no reason to dispose of perfectly good $300 custom-made suits just because some Seventh Avenue clothes designer was trying to hypo sales. However, he did make a slight concession to the new look by having some of his lapels made narrower—as if he couldn't afford to buy a whole new suit.

All things considered, he probably could have passed for a man of fifty-five, and certainly felt like one. But even if he'd felt like a man of seventy, nothing would have stopped him from making *Porgy and Bess*.

Sam loved Gershwin's and DuBose Heyward's American folk opera with the same passion as Porgy loved Bess, and he'd felt that way about it ever since he'd seen it on the boards in New York in 1935.

Sam felt that George Gershwin was the greatest American composer who ever lived, and he had an autographed portrait of him hanging in his office, which he prized highly. He also felt that the DuBose Heyward libretto was the best he'd ever seen in the musical theater.

Add to that the fact that he could afford to do things in a movie of *Porgy and Bess* that couldn't possibly be done on the stage, and he saw an opportunity to make the best picture of his long career.

Just acquiring the rights to *Porgy* had taken eleven years and a great deal of patience and tenaciousness, not to mention money. To begin with, because both Gershwin and Heyward were dead, there were legal problems involved with the two estates that seemed reluctant to become untangled. And secondly, just about every major studio or producer in the United States had been interested in buying it at one time or another.

As a result, the bidding was fiercely competitive, and many producers dropped out of the race early. As usual, Sam hung in there the longest. As an agent for one of the losers remarked about Sam, "Goldwyn has a Chinese viewpoint toward time." Of course, only a man who'd sweated out as many deals as he had and who expected to live as long as he did could afford to have a Chinese viewpoint.

Even when another studio came up with an offer of $1 million for the property, Sam did not lose heart. Uncharacteristically, he did not bid $2 million. Instead, he offered only $650,000 cash, but that was against 10 percent of the gross receipts.

Rarely did a producer offer a percentage of the *gross*, for that allowed little leeway for book manipulating. In a percentage of the *profits* deal it was easier for a producer to cheat, for he could charge so many costs to the production that, on paper at least, there'd be no profits. (Willy Wyler, in fact, wound up having to sue Sam to get what he thought was his rightful percentage of the profits of *The Best Years*. The disagreement in that case grew out of the fact that Sam tried to charge what Wyler had earned in percentages against the production cost, while Wyler claimed it should have been excluded. Wyler was right. In an out-of-court settlement, Sam reluctantly came up with an extra $500,000 for Wyler.)

But money wasn't Sam's primary interest in making *Porgy and Bess*. In fact, upon acquiring it, he had pledged 100 percent of the profits to charity. What he was striving to give the world was a masterpiece—something of a film memorial to George Gershwin.

Considering his noble ambitions, it's difficult to conceive why the gods would conspire to put so many obstacles in Sam's path. But they did and before the picture was finished, Sam was heard to mutter, "The only thing left that hasn't happened is for me to go to jail."

For a change, the script, written by N. Richard Nash, was no problem, for Sam had decided to take very few liberties with the original. It was just a question of putting the words into screen form and getting the right director, who, in the beginning, he believed to be Rouben Mamoulian.

Sam's real trouble started with the casting—nobody wanted to play in it, because they felt that it would not show the world the image the black race wanted to popularize. The story, which took place in the early part of the century in Catfish Row, an impoverished Negro quarter in the wharf district of Charleston, South Carolina, certainly painted anything but a pretty picture of black culture. It told of the love of Porgy, a crippled beggar, for Bess, a beautiful girl struggling to break away from a tarnished past. Beyond that, it was a story of violence and passion, involving not only Porgy's pure love for Bess, but also illicit cohabitation, drug addiction, and murder.

Porgy never had been intended as an exposé of Negro life. It was merely "telling it like it was" in Catfish Row at the turn of the century. But the NAACP didn't see it that way. Neither did the Council for the Improvement of Negro Theater Arts. The latter organization was so incensed over the forthcoming production of *Porgy* that it took out a double-page center ad in the *Hollywood Reporter* condemning Sam and any Negro performers who cooperated with his efforts to film *Porgy and Bess*.

The ad, written by Almena Lomax, doubted that *Porgy* could be made with "taste" and "dignity," as the producer had promised.

> Dorothy and DuBose Heyward used the race situation in the South to write a lot of allegories in which Negroes were violent or gentle, humble or conniving, and given to erupting with all sorts of goings-on after their day's work in the white folks' kitchen or the white folks' yard was over, like sniffing happy dust, careless love, crapshooting, drinking, topping it all off with knife play.
>
> But it never occurred to them that the Negro was not innately any of this, and that he was just like anybody else and that this was a human being's way of reacting to the dehumanizing pressure of a master race.

The ad even took Sam to task for running what the ad referred to as "a lily-white lot out there on North Formosa. The only Negroes we saw were a couple of guys trundling large containers of trash."

With such malice being spewed from the mouths of Hollywood's black acting community, it was no surprise that Sam had a difficult time, at least in the beginning, attracting top Negro performers to the film. One of the loudest to come out against the movie was Harry Belafonte, who, according to his agent at the time, turned down the part of Porgy "because I don't want to play a role on my knees." But his voice was just one in a large chorus of protesting voices.

Among the top names under consideration, Sammy Davis, Jr., was the first one not to consider the making of *Porgy and Bess* a blot on the Negro escutcheon. He not only was agreeable to playing the part of Sportin' Life, the joyously evil character who sings "It Ain't Necessarily So" and leads Bess astray, but he actively campaigned to get it. On the other hand, Pearl Bailey and Dorothy Dandridge, who eventually accepted the role of Bess, were borderline holdouts—wanting the roles but not quite willing to make up their minds one way or the other until they saw which way the racial winds were blowing.

Sam, of course, was stunned that any performer in his right mind would even dream of turning down a part in his beloved *Porgy and Bess*. His public stance, and it was a valid one, maintained that *Porgy and Bess* was a distinguished American folk opera, that a *Porgy* company touring the world in 1955 and 1956 had enjoyed a tremendous success, and that Negro performers in the past had found nothing distasteful in the story.

To demonstrate that he was not anti-Negro, Sam even gave $1,000 to the local NAACP drive. This promptly drew another blast from Lomax, who accused him of trying to "buy" his way into the black community's good graces.

Then Sam hired Russell Birdwell, one of the top publicity men in the business, to see what he could do to stem the tide of bad publicity. Birdwell promptly called a series of press conferences and invited some black character actors who had agreed to appear in the picture to be at them to espouse the Goldwyn viewpoint. In retaliation, Lomax publicly accused them—plus Pearl Bailey and Sammy Davis, Jr.—of being Uncle Toms, who would do anything to go on "working and eating."

Sam's propaganda brought results. Just when it seemed as if he'd never find a Porgy, Sidney Poitier sent word through his agent that he was considering the part, but before making a decision he requested a meeting with Goldwyn at the producer's home. He wanted to hear Goldwyn's concept of the movie, from Goldwyn's own lips. This was a little like a fly inviting himself up to dine with a spider. More stubborn actors than Poitier had been caught in Sam's oratorical web, Marlon Brando, for one.

At the meeting, to which Rouben Mamoulian was also invited, Sam promised that *Porgy* would be a great movie, that Poitier would never have a greater opportunity, that *he* would emerge from it a superstar and his black brothers would be beloved and respected for their courage and dignity in standing up against racial injustice and its consequent poverty.

Suddenly Poitier's resistance crumbled. Jumping to his feet and sounding more like a Baptist minister than a Hollywood actor, he said, "I will come to you completely pure, virginal, and unprejudiced."

Then, to charges from the Negro press corps that he was another Uncle Tom, Poitier replied, "I am happy to say that my reservations were washed away by Mr. Goldwyn in his plan for *Porgy and Bess*. I am very happy that I met with Mr. Goldwyn. I found him almost as sensitive as I am."

Pearl Bailey's and Dorothy Dandridge's resistance was also washed away by Poitier's acceptance of Sam's intentions, and they, too, signed to do the picture.

With the signing of Dandridge, Bailey, Poitier, Sammy Davis, Jr., and several other competent but little-known black actors, the NAACP retracted its disapproval of the project.

Only the Council for the Improvement of Negro Theater Arts continued to take pot shots at Sam in the press, but now that he had his cast—and a great one, at that—this no longer bothered him the way it once had.

In March 1958 Sam called a meeting of his production heads and announced that he wanted to start filming in early summer. No amount of money was to be spared to make this the greatest Goldwyn production ever. Irene Sharaff would do the costumes, Andre Previn the music, and all of Stage 8—the second largest sound stage in Hollywood—would be used to house the set of Charleston's Catfish Row. Goldwyn's Catfish Row would be better than the original—and no doubt cleaner.

The first dress rehearsal for *Porgy and Bess* was called for nine on the morning of July 3. At six, the phone rang at the Goldwyn house, and Frances, always up earlier than Sam, intercepted it in her bedroom. The caller was Jack Foreman. Shortly before dawn, Stage 8 had burned completely to the ground, taking with it in the conflagration all of the Irene Sharaff costumes for the picture, her sketches, and the camera and lighting equipment. All that was left of Sam's $2 million Catfish Row, he said, was a pile of rubble.

After assuring Foreman that she would break the news to Sam gently, Frances waited until she heard Sam stirring upstairs in his bedroom, then put his usual breakfast of orange juice, warm milk, and coffee on a tray, and carried it up to him.

As she oversolicitously got him comfortably settled in bed with the tray on his lap, Sam fixed his beady eyes on Frances's concerned face and said, "What happened?"

"Something dreadful," said Frances, wondering how she could possibly tell him of the disaster. But somehow she blurted the whole story out.

In past times, news like that coming on an empty stomach would have caused Sam to cast a baleful glance at the sky and scream out in anguish, "God, why are you doing this to me?"

But this time Sam did not bat an eye. He simply reached for his orange juice and asked, "Was anybody hurt?"

"No, thank God," said Frances. "Nobody's been hurt."

"Good," smiled Sam. Following that, he calmly finished his breakfast, shaved, bathed, and dressed in a dark brown, wide-lapelled jacket, knife-sharp creased gabardine trousers, and pointed brown-and-white shoes. As someone remarked who saw him at the studio later, he looked more like the owner of a race horse than the landlord of a smoking ruin.

At nine o'clock, he kissed Frances good-by at the front door, told her not to worry, and stepped into his gray, chauffeur-driven limousine for his ride to the studio. The only part of his normal routine that he had eliminated that morning was his thirty minutes of setting-up exercises.

As Sam's limousine drove onto the studio lot, it was evident that morale was awash on the flooded company street. Irene Sharaff was in tears and near hysteria. There were gloomy clusters of cast members and technicians, all talking and wondering what the future held for them. And from the direction of the still-smoldering ruins came the sounds of sirens and fire bells, intermingled with the voice of the fire chief shouting orders to men carrying dripping hoses.

Alighting briskly from his car in front of his office building, Sam found himself facing a retinue of department heads waiting to brief him on the holocaust. Sam nodded a curt "Good morning" and started to climb the outdoor staircase to the back door of his second-floor office.

"Mr. Goldwyn?" one of his associates called up. "Don't you want to see the fire?"

"Hell, no, I don't want to see the fire," responded Sam as he continued his climb. "What for?"

It was too much to ask of even a man as iron-willed as Sam Goldwyn to survey the damage personally. But once he was in his office, he took full charge of the crisis. And crisis it was. From preliminary reports, it would cost $2.5 million and at least two months' time to reconstruct another Catfish Row. Of course he was insured, but there's no insurance for wear and tear on the insides of an excitable seventy-five-year-old man.

Meanwhile messages of condolence were pouring in from just about everybody except the Council for the Improvement of Negro Theater Arts. But the one that touched Sam's heart the most was from one of the original triumvirate who helped make *The Squaw Man*.

"THE PHOENIX AROSE FROM THE ASHES OF A GREAT FIRE AND SO WILL YOU WITH YOUR GREAT STRENGTH. . . . WITH LOVE, CECIL."

As the day progressed, the cause of the fire was investigated. Some said it was faulty wiring, but there was a strong undercurrent of feeling that it might have been caused by arson—an angry black, perhaps, trying to sabotage Sam's effort to make the picture. Sam took issue with that, saying he felt the fire was completely accidental. And the NAACP issued a statement charging that "the implications were ridiculous."

Nevertheless, the fire chief sided with the arson school of thought and said he would investigate further. But nothing further was ever revealed, and the fire was officially attributed to faulty wiring.

Later in the day, after the sounds of fire trucks and sirens had faded away and some of the excitement had subsided, Sam called an emergency meeting in his office. Present were Mamoulian, the principals of the cast, and the heads of his various departments, including Irene Sharaff, who was still sniffling.

Most had come with the notion that they were about to hear Sam burying *Porgy* for good. Instead they heard Washington at Valley Forge, MacArthur at Corregidor, and John Wayne at the Alamo. After declaring that the fire was terrible, the damage dreadful, and his whole day so far a catastrophe, Sam announced that he was not giving up the fight. He'd already ordered a whole new set to be built. New costumes would be made, "fireproof" this time. Production would have to be postponed—two months at the least. The cost to him in time and money would be appalling, but he didn't care. He was firm in his resolve that *Porgy and Bess* would be made— perhaps even in time to be released in the summer of 1959.

When it hit the trades that Sam Goldwyn's initial reaction to the fire was, "Was anybody hurt?" it evoked a rash of cynical comments. Some said his generous calm probably stemmed from the fact that he was overinsured and would somehow make a profit on the fire—perhaps he'd even set it himself. While others remarked, a trifle sadly, that it was a sure sign of old age; at seventy-five he was getting mellower. Poor Sam, they said. He was so slowed up that he couldn't even lose his temper anymore.

Sam himself was somewhat amused by their reactions. And when asked by a reporter to explain how he could face disaster so calmly, he thought about it a moment, then said, with a thin smile, "Well, there's *always* a crisis. If it's not me, it's Israel."

In addition to the lost time and money that could never be fully recovered, and the hundreds of people thrown temporarily out of jobs, the fire had a dangerous side effect: it gave Sam time to worry. Hours he would otherwise have devoted to the multitudinous details of day-to-day production were now spent fretting about what was wrong with the entire project up until the fire. What worried him most of all was Rouben Mamoulian. What did a Russian know about life on Catfish Row? And did he really have the right rapport with the all-black cast? From reports he'd heard, several important members of the cast weren't too happy with his imperious ways of handling them.

But beyond that, there was a vast difference of opinion between Sam and Mamoulian about where and how the picture should be shot. From the moment he had signed to do the picture, Mamoulian had wanted to take the company to the real Catfish Row in Charleston and shoot all the exteriors there. But Sam insisted that everything be shot on Stage 8, where he could keep tight control of the company. His feelings about location shooting had changed not a whit since the days when he refused to let Willy Wyler go east to shoot *Dead End* or to Europe to shoot *Dodsworth*.

Now that the simulated Catfish Row had gone up in flames, Mamoulian dared make the suggestion that Sam reconsider going to Charleston. That way, some of the shooting could be done while the set was being rebuilt.

That enraged Sam, for he felt Mamoulian was simply using the fire as an excuse to get his own way. And if there was one thing Sam couldn't stand, it was disloyalty. As he had said more than once in his long career to personnel who questioned his authority and wisdom, "I'll take fifty percent efficiency to get one hundred percent loyalty."

So several mornings after the fire Sam sent Mamoulian's agent to his house to inform him that he was being discharged and to pay him his full salary of $75,000, as his contract called for. He then phoned Otto Preminger, who was in New York, and hired him to direct *Porgy and Bess* for $150,000.

When Preminger had last worked for Sam, it was as an actor—playing the bald-headed Nazi who chased Bob Hope in *They Got Me Covered*. But in the fifteen-year interim he had progressed to being one of Hollywood's highest-priced directors. He had also just finished directing an all-black picture, *Carmen Jones*, which led Sam to believe he was the right man for *Porgy*.

As was his style, Sam didn't believe in publicly divulging his real reason for ever firing anyone, and this time his announcement to the press simply said that he had "the greatest respect for Mamoulian as a director, but basic differences of opinion had forced him to relieve him and replace him with Otto Preminger."

Mamoulian was furious and took his complaint to the Screen Directors Guild, to which all working directors and assistant directors must belong. The guild promptly condemned Sam for dismissing a director for "frivolous, spiteful, or dictatorial reasons" and ordered its members not to work for Goldwyn. There were even reports that some of the actors would refuse to work for Preminger and that the other guilds would picket the Goldwyn lot.

Sam refused to dignify Mamoulian's accusations by even commenting on them and maintained a regal silence through the entire verbal donnybrook. He also refused to appear before the directors guild to answer their charges of unfairness to one of its members, but he did offer to meet with their representatives in his office or on some neutral ground. *They* turned this down, and Sam continued to maintain his silence. Meanwhile, Mamoulian's publicity man continued to plant anti-Goldwyn items in the newspapers and trades.

It seemed as if Mamoulian had sentiment on his side—until the last trick he pulled. He called a press conference and produced one of the black bit players in the cast, who made a statement clearly implying that Otto Preminger was anti-Negro.

This backfired on Mamoulian. Everyone in Hollywood who knew Preminger was aware that this was not so—and particularly the black performers who'd been directed by him in *Carmen Jones*. Suddenly the most rabid Goldwyn haters in Hollywood were on Sam's side. And the Directors Guild backed down and removed its ban. Sam had triumphed, but when a newspaper reporter asked him how it felt to be the victor, he shrugged wearily and said simply, "I'm exhausted from *not* talking."

Three months later the new Catfish Row had risen out of the ashes, just as Cecil De Mille had predicted it would. As production started over again, the movie lot bubbled with all the excitement typical of every Goldwyn epic. Costumed extras mobbed the crowded studio streets, the small commissary was difficult to get into at lunchtime, still photographers and reporters were in constant evidence, and the red warning lights flashed outside the sound stage where Otto Preminger was filming scenes on Catfish Row.

The one person who didn't seem to be around as much as usual was Sam Goldwyn. Normally he'd be bustling back and forth between his office and the set, barking orders, arranging pretty girls' hairdos, and telling the director he wanted more close-ups.

But during most of this production, Sam remained mysteriously locked in his office. If he communicated with anyone on the set, it was by squawk box and telephone, or perhaps a written message delivered by hand. It was most unlike him. What was going on? everybody asked.

What was going on—and which has never come to light before—is that Sam wasn't speaking to Otto Preminger, either, after the first few days he was on the picture.

At an early morning breakfast meeting at Goldwyn's house, Preminger complained to Sam, "I'm just killing myself on this picture. I get up at five in the morning, rehearse the cast, shoot all day, look at the rushes, study the next day's shooting in the script all night. I'm just killing myself."

"Listen," snapped Sam, "I'm not paying you a hundred and fifty thousand dollars for nothing."

Soon after that, they had a major disagreement over the way Preminger was actually shooting the picture.

"He was shooting nothing but boom shots," recalls an associate of Goldwyn's. "He was riding the boom like he was getting ready for the Ontario Racetrack. He was shooting everything from up high, and rarely stopped the camera until an entire scene was over. He'd even use the boom to dolly in for a close-up."

What infuriated Sam about that technique was that it made it almost impossible for him to cut the picture the way he wanted it. In his sly way, Preminger was cutting the picture as he shot it—right in the camera. "And there was no footage left over for Sam to play with," recalls the same associate.

When Sam complained, Preminger threatened to walk off the picture if he didn't keep his nose out of the director's business. Furthermore, he didn't want him hanging around the set, either.

Sam was at a point of no return by that time. From both a financial and public relations viewpoint, he couldn't afford to get rid of a second director on *Porgy*. His reputation as a fair employer really would be in ruins if Preminger walked off. And so Sam swallowed his pride and remained holed up in his office, barely speaking to Preminger when he bumped into him on the lot.

Despite the embittered feelings, the racial strife, and all-around hard luck that had been visited upon the production, *Porgy and Bess* opened in New York City in June 1959, just as Sam had promised it would when his beautiful set lay in ashes.

Bosley Crowther's review in the *Times* augured well for *Porgy and Bess*'s financial well-being and did much to cheer Sam after all the troubles of the past year. Wrote Crowther on June 25:

> The mills of the gods have ground slowly, but they have ground exceedingly well in delivering at last a fine film version of the famous folk opera *Porgy and Bess*.
>
> For this we can thank Samuel Goldwyn, who was finally able to convince the solemn guardians of this sacred theater treasure that he was the man most competent to bring it to the screen. . . .
>
> To be sure, there are some flaws, but for the most part this is a stunning, exciting and moving film, packed with human emotions and cheerful and mournful melodies. It bids fair to be as much a classic on the screen as it is on the stage.

Although most critics were equally enthusiastic, *Porgy and Bess* was an extreme disappointment to Sam at the box office. And those average moviegoers who were enticed into the theater by the good reviews felt it was slow, stagy, and outmoded in both story matter and in the way it was executed on the screen.

Insiders in Hollywood felt that perhaps Sam had made a mistake by firing Mamoulian and hiring Preminger, because the only things they liked about the picture were the Gershwins' music and the way Andre Previn had orchestrated it.

The members of the motion picture academy confirmed how the general public felt when they voted *Porgy and Bess* only one Oscar—for best scoring for a musical picture, which went to thirty-one-year-old Andre Previn.

Sam didn't need to see Previn's Oscar to be excited about the job he had done for him. He had felt that way months before, when he heard the score for the first time on the soundtrack in his projection room, along with Previn and Ira Gershwin. For forty-five minutes Sam sat enthralled as he listened to Previn's arrangements of "Summertime," Bess, You Is My Woman Now," "It Ain't Necessarily So," and "I Got Plenty of Nuttin' " soar through the room. When it was over, Sam sat almost stupefied with emotion for an entire minute without saying anything. Then, with a tearful glint in his eyes, he walked over to where Previn was sitting, placed a fatherly hand on his head, tousled his long black hair, and then exclaimed, "You should be goddamned proud, kid—you should never do another thing in your life!"

28

The Beginning of the End

WHAT SAM MEANT as a compliment turned out to be another Goldwynism—and oddly enough, one that applied more to *his* future career than to Andre Previn's. Sam never produced another picture after *Porgy and Bess*. He had fully intended to. In fact, in answer to a reporter's query shortly before his eightieth birthday as to whether he had any plans of retirement, Sam had shot back, "Making films is my life. It keeps me going. When the time comes that I stop working, then you will know that I am dead."

He added, however, that he had still not decided on another project, which in itself was some kind of admission that he was slowing up, or perhaps only fed up with the direction in which Hollywood seemed to be going.

In his entire career, Sam told friends, he had never worked quite so hard to get a picture off the ground as he had with *Porgy and Bess*. Nor had he ever invested quite so much of his own capital—$7 million—before he was through. But for all that, public reaction to *Porgy* was lukewarm, which evoked criticism in some quarters that perhaps Sam Goldwyn's style of film producing was just a trifle passé.

Sam, himself, didn't believe he was passé. He just wasn't enthusiastic about producing the kind of films that seemed to be attracting large audiences in the sixties—ones that traded heavily on sex.

"Some people," he expostulated, "apparently are simply interested in making a fast buck with pictures that have as much exposed anatomy as exposed film. I myself am disgusted with pictures today—American and foreign. I have never made a picture that the whole family could not go to see together. As long as pictures are well made, with fine stories and in good taste, we will always have a large audience. It's a lot of baloney that a good picture won't attract."

That's what he stated publicly—but for the first time in his movie career, Sam Goldwyn wasn't putting his money where his mouth was.

And so he slipped quietly into a well-deserved retirement. There was no big announcement. He just stopped making films and going to the studio, except perhaps to oversee his rental business, which still was thriving—not only from feature production but also TV.

But after eighty pictures, thirty-four Academy Award nominations, twenty-seven Oscars, and some $19 million in assets to prove that most of them were moneymakers and of high quality, Sam had nothing to feel ashamed about when he stepped down from active producing.

In fact, of all the film pioneers, Sam was the only one to finish out his days in full ownership of his own studio. Jesse Lasky died in 1957, broke and almost forgotten by all but his family and a few friends. Louis B. Mayer died in 1957, after losing control of MGM to Doré Schary and getting kicked out in a stockholders' battle. And Cecil B. De Mille passed away in 1959, just a few months after sending Sam his flowery telegram about the Phoenix rising out of the ashes.

Only Adolph Zukor is still alive. He's 104 years old, and when last heard from was still smoking big cigars and kibitzing the card games at Hillcrest Country Club—but it's been nearly fifty years since he had anything to do with running a studio.

Moreover, though he had stopped making movies, Sam was still in full command of a studio that was bringing him, even in retirement, an income estimated to be in the neighborhood of $600,000 a year.

With retirement came not just relaxing days in the sun at the edge of his hibiscus-bordered pool, but elder statesman status and the customary tributes to his wisdom and knowledge by his younger peers. Studio heads who formerly feared him as a rival, or perhaps hated him, now revered him and were consulting him on their own problems or asking him to use his influence with important people he knew in government or business to help them overcome obstacles or legislation harmful to the film industry.

With elder statesman status also came the customary public accolades and testimonial banquets. In 1959 Sam was honored by the Hollywood Foreign Press Association's Golden Globe Awards dinner at the Coconut Grove. Some of the biggest names in show business were there to pay Sam tribute—Maurice Chevalier, Sophie Tucker, Susan Hayward, David Niven, Rosalind Russell, Danny Kaye, Burl Ives, Ann Sothern, Loretta Young, Red Skelton, and Ed Sullivan. The following January the Producers Guild honored Sam at a banquet at the Beverly Hilton one night and bestowed on him their highest tribute—the Milestone Award—"for quality in production over the years and service rendered to a grateful industry." And in 1962 the movie industry gave Sam a testimonial dinner to celebrate his

eightieth birthday. It was held on a Sunday night at the Beverly Hilton
Hotel in a banquet hall packed with 1500 celebrities, including Bob Hope,
Frank Sinatra, Jack Benny, Jimmy Stewart, Milton Berle, Loretta Young,
Harpo Marx, George Jessel, and that year's Republican gubernatorial can-
didate for California—Richard Nixon.

With such an abundance of talent on the dais, some of the humor was
sparkling, and no Goldwynisms were needed to enliven the proceedings.
For a change, Sam simply sat and listened—and laughed heartily at the
barbs aimed at him and some of the visiting notables.

Bob Hope emceed the affair and as usual was not lacking for good one-
liners. "Eighty years old," led off Hope. "Isn't that a little late to be having
a bar mitzvah? . . . It's wonderful how times have changed in Hollywood.
I was just remarking about this to my waiter, Spyros Skouras. . . . And
it's a thrill to see Mr. Nixon here. He's a great fellow, and he's come a long
ways for a Protestant."

In his remarks, Milton Berle couldn't resist kidding the gubernatorial
candidate, either. "Well, this week President Kennedy is in Hyannis Port,
and Jackie is in Italy. Dick, here's your chance—the White House is
empty."

But banquets and large affairs were actually alien to the way Sam and
Frances wanted to live—and did live during the remaining years left to him.
They traveled some—to New York or London occasionally, but mostly
back and forth to their home in Palm Springs. They rarely ventured out in
the evenings, preferring to stay home with close friends or family.

By Sam's eighty-fifth year, the family circle had expanded considerably,
thanks to Sam Goldwyn, Jr. In 1950, while in Paris producing a film, Sam
junior had run into his former childhood sweetheart, Jennifer Howard,
daughter of Sidney Howard. Because of the close ties between the Goldwyns and the Howards, Sam junior and Jennifer had seen a great deal of
each other when they were growing up, meeting originally on Sidney Howard's farm in Connecticut one summer. They continued seeing each other
all during their college days, when Sam junior was east attending the University of Virginia and Jennifer was a student at New York's Hunter College. It looked like love for a time, but when Sammy went into the service
during the war, Jennifer married someone else. That marriage didn't work
out, however, and Jennifer was once again single and available when Sam
junior met her in Paris in 1950 and started taking her out. A whirlwind
romance followed their first date, and that summer the couple returned to
the States and were married on August 16 at the home of Jennifer's aunt
and uncle in Berkeley, California. Sam and Frances flew there to attend the
wedding, as did Sidney Howard's widow. Following the ceremony, the
bride and groom returned to Paris.

In the ensuing years, Jennifer bore Sam junior four children—a daughter and three sons. Their first, a girl nicknamed Cricket, was born in the American Hospital in Paris on July 12, 1951. According to Frances, Sam Senior cried tears of joy when they received the cable from Sam junior informing him that he was a grandfather.

Soon after Cricket's birth, the young Goldwyns moved back to southern California, where they took up residence in a modest house on Tigertail Road in West Los Angeles and continued to proliferate.

Since Tigertail Road was just a ten-minute drive from Laurel Lane, the grandchildren were easily accessible to Frances and Sam, who, now that he was in retirement, had plenty of time to get to know them—probably better than he did his own son, with whom, according to Collier Young, he was never terribly close. "They tried," maintains Young, "but they were worlds apart."

Another member of the family whom Sam was finally getting to know was his daughter, Ruth, by his first marriage. Ruth, by then around fifty, was married to McClure Capps, a Hollywood art director. Thanks to Frances, who somehow had managed to thaw the frost that had existed between father and daughter since Sam's and Blanche's divorce in 1915, Sam and Ruth were once again on friendly terms and frequently saw each other at family get-togethers.

A born fence mender, Frances never stopped trying to patch things up between Sam and the friends he'd had differences with over the years. Hearing Lillian Hellman was in town one day in the late sixties, Frances phoned the writer at her hotel and said, "It's a shame you don't see Sam anymore. Everybody's getting older. He wants to make up with you. But he's just stubborn. So why don't you come to dinner, Lillian? We'll have just the people you like— your friends."

More for Frances's sake than Sam's, Hellman accepted, and arrived at the appointed hour. As Frances had promised, it was just a small group consisting of the Goldwyns, Willy Wyler and his wife, Talli, and Arthur Kober, Hellman's former husband but still a good friend.

The atmosphere was strained, but everybody was terribly polite as they drank their cocktails and proceeded into the candle-lit dining room, where Frances seated Hellman next to Sam.

As the conversation turned from small talk to what was happening in the movie industry, the name of Bette Davis was somehow mentioned.

"Yes," said Sam, "I had her in a very good picture I once made called *The Three Little Foxes*."

"Did you?" snapped Hellman, bristling slightly that after all these years he should still be referring to her play as *The* Three *Little Foxes*. "Well, I wrote the play and I wrote the movie."

"Of course. Who said you didn't?" replied Sam testily. "Who said you didn't write the play and the picture? Who said it?"

After a moment of uncomfortable silence, Sam turned to Wyler and said, "Did you ever see it? It was a great picture, wasn't it?"

"Yes, it was," replied Wyler. "I directed it."

"Who said you didn't?" screamed Sam. "Who said it?"

There was no doubt of it. Senility was making Sam even more querulous and difficult to be around than he had been as a young man.

As a result, Sam was even beginning to have trouble inveigling friends to come up to the house to play croquet with him in his later years. Most of his bridge and croquet cronies who understood his foibles were dead— Harpo Marx, George Kaufman, Ben Hecht, Charlie MacArthur, Moss Hart, Mike Romanoff—or else extremely ill, like Howard Dietz and Charlie Lederer. And the younger players, such as actors Louis Jourdan and Gig Young, who still frequented his lush croquet grounds, deplored Sam's temper tantrums and now would run or fictionalize some excuse not to play with him whenever they saw the old man approaching with a mallet.

One afternoon, out of loneliness and desperation for a game of croquet, Sam phoned a young accountant he knew at the Goldwyn studio and asked him to come up and play with him.

"Gee, I'd like to, Mr. Goldwyn," apologized the youth, "but I'm right in the middle of figuring out a budget sheet."

"You're absolutely right," said Sam. "Your work and the studio comes first."

A half hour later, Sam called the young man back, and this time more or less ordered him to put down his pencil and come up to the house on Laurel Lane and play croquet with the boss.

Having no choice, the accountant got in his car and headed for the Goldwyn croquet grounds. There he picked up a mallet and proceeded to give the old man a royal shellacking. Not satisfied, Sam insisted on a return match, and again the upstart displayed his mastery over Sam, despite some cheating on the latter's part.

By now Sam was in a vile mood and he threw down his mallet angrily. As the young accountant watched, somewhat frightened, Sam glared at him and shouted, "What the hell are you doing here, anyway, this time of day? You're supposed to be at the studio, working!"

Whether from lack of opponents, or just plain inertia brought on by old age, Sam hung up his croquet mallet for good by the fall of 1968. However, he still kept his interest in the latest trends of the movie business, and whenever he and Frances were tipped off in advance about a sneak preview at one of the neighborhood theaters, they would attend. On one of Sam's last nights on the town, in the fall of 1968, he and Frances attended a preview of a movie made by one of the industry's young producers. Eddie Chodorov and his wife, Rosemary, were also at the preview, but mostly the crowd consisted of Hollywood's new wave of filmmakers and their friends, many of whom had long hair and were dressed in wide-bottomed trousers and lots of leather. Some even wore love beads.

As the Chodorovs walked out into the lobby after the preview, they noticed Sam and Frances standing rather forlornly off in a corner by themselves, silently being ignored by the studio personnel who were bustling importantly about.

Sam was his usual well-groomed, distinguished-looking self, tanned from a week at his desert home, and still appearing amazingly fit for his years. But he appeared lost and somewhat forgotten, and possibly even a little hurt, for no one in this younger crowd seemed to know that he was the Great Sam Goldwyn. For all these youngsters knew, Sam could have been a retired cloak and suiter from Seventh Avenue.

Feeling the least they could do was pay their respects to this once mighty and feared producer, Chodorov and Rosemary strolled over to the other side of the lobby and said, "Hi, Sam. Hi, Frances. How are things?"

"Just wonderful," replied the vivacious Frances.

"You look marvelous—tan and lean," Chodorov said to Sam. "You must be in great health."

"Yeah," replied Sam, glancing wistfully around at the new generation of filmmakers in the lobby, "but what good is it?"

Epilogue

IN 1969 SAM WAS FELLED by a severe stroke, which partially paralyzed him and took away some of his powers of speech (an indignity that must have been unbearable to the once-bombastic Sam). Until the end of his life, Sam was to be either bedridden or confined to a wheelchair, under the vigilant care of round-the-clock nurses and his devoted and loving wife.

Because of Goldwyn's weakened physical condition in his final years, in 1969 the court appointed Frances "conservator" of her husband's $20-million estate, while Sam junior took over the job of running Goldwyn Studios.

As time went on and Sam sank even deeper into the quagmire of geriatric problems, he saw fewer and fewer of his friends, until finally, on the occasion of his ninetieth birthday, in August 1972, Frances admitted to an inquiring press that her husband was "too out of things" for her to have a birthday party for him, even for "just family."

Perhaps the only bright spot of Sam's final years was a visit to the Goldwyn estate in 1971 by the president of the United States, Richard Nixon, who pinned on the ailing producer the Medal of Freedom—the nation's highest civilian award—as he sat up rather rigidly in his wheelchair and forced a weak smile.

Though he had won many awards for his acievements in filmmaking, this last had to be the climactic moment in the career of the Polish immigrant who at the age of twelve had run away from a crowded slum in a city under the leaden skies of eastern Europe to seek his fame and fortune in a distant land called America.

Although few people—even among his remaining close friends—were aware of it, it was the beginning of the end when Sam Goldwyn, early in

358

January 1974, was quietly checked in to St. John's Hospital in Santa Monica, California, "for treatment of a kidney ailment," according to the hospital press release. Apparently the malfunctioning kidney responded to treatment, for three weeks later Sam was released to his home on Laurel Lane. But on January 31, at two in the morning, his ninety-one-year-old heart suddenly stopped beating, and he slipped quietly into eternity.

Sam's burial at Forest Lawn was simple and private, in accordance with his wishes. Sam junior delivered a short eulogy in which he apologized for the lack of pomp to those excluded from the services. "My father," explained Sam junior, "attended enough Hollywood funerals to know he didn't want one himself."

Bibliography

Brandt, Carl. "Samuel Goldwyn." *The New Yorker*, April 25, 1925.

Butterfield, Roger. "Sam Goldwyn." *Life*, October 27, 1947.

De Mille, Cecil B. *Autobiography*. Edited by Donald Hayne. Englewood Cliffs, N.J.: Prentice-Hall, 1959.

Farrar, Geraldine. *The Autobiography of Geraldine Farrar: Such Sweet Compulsion*. New York: Greystone Press, 1938.

Furnas, J. C. *The Americans: A Social History of the United States, 1587–1914*. New York: G. P. Putnam's Sons, 1969.

Goldwyn, Frances. "Dear Sam: Do You Remember?" *Woman's Home Companion*, December 1950.

Goldwyn, Samuel. *Behind the Screen*. New York: George H. Doran, 1923.

———. "The Best Advice I Ever Had." *Reader's Digest*, June 1956.

Hellman, Lillian. *Pentimento: A Book of Portraits*. Boston: Little, Brown, 1973.

Johnston, Alva. *The Great Goldwyn*. New York: Random House, 1937.

Kanin, Garson. *Hollywood*. New York: Viking Press, 1974.

Lasky, Jesse L., with Weldon, Don. *I Blow My Own Horn*. Garden City, N.Y.: Doubleday, 1957.

Luft, Herb. "Samuel Goldwyn." *Films in Review*, December 1969.

Meredith, Scott. *George S. Kaufman and His Friends*. Garden City, N.Y.: Doubleday, 1974.

Niven, David. *The Moon's a Balloon*. New York: G. P. Putnam's Sons, 1972.

Oppenheimer, George. *The View from the Sixties: Memories of a Spent Life*. New York: David McKay, 1966.

Rivkin, Allen, and Kerr, Laura. *Hello, Hollywood*. Garden City, N.Y.: Doubleday, 1962.

Selznick, David O. *Memo from David O. Selznick*. Edited by Rudy Behlmer. New York: Viking Press, 1972.

Stine, Whitney, with Davis, Bette. *Mother Goddam: The Story of the Career of Bette Davis*. New York: Hawthorn Books, 1974.

Wilk, Max. *The Wit and Wisdom of Hollywood*. New York: Atheneum, 1971.

Wyler, William, and Madsen, Axel. *William Wyler*. New York: Thomas Y. Crowell, 1973.

Zierold, Norman. *The Moguls*. New York: Coward, McCann & Geoghegan, 1969.

Index